To remember wh[...] your
initials in a squ[...]

1558

DATE DUE 2/18

3/20/18

MURDER AT THE
BOOK GROUP

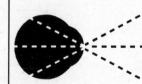

This Large Print Book carries the
Seal of Approval of N.A.V.H.

MURDER AT THE BOOK GROUP

MAGGIE KING

THORNDIKE PRESS

A part of Gale, Cengage Learning

GALE
CENGAGE Learning·

Farmington Hills, Mich • San Francisco • New York • Waterville, Maine
Meriden, Conn • Mason, Ohio • Chicago

GALE
CENGAGE Learning·

LIBRARY OF CONGRESS CATALOGING-IN-PUBLICATION DATA

King, Maggie, 1950–
    Murder at the book group / by Maggie King. — Large print edition.
        pages ; cm. — (Thorndike Press large print mystery)
        ISBN 978-1-4104-7439-1 (hardcover) — ISBN 1-4104-7439-9 (hardcover)
        1. Book clubs (Discussion groups) —Fiction. 2. Murder—Investigation—
Fiction. 3. Large type books. I. Title.
PS3611.I58336M87 2015
813'.6—dc23   2014045901

Published in 2015 by arrangement with Pocket Books, a division of Simon & Schuster, Inc.

Printed in Mexico
1 2 3 4 5 6 7 19 18 17 16 15

CHAPTER 1

Yea, though I walk through the valley of the shadow of death, I will fear no evil . . .

I tuned out the Twenty-third Psalm and focused on my mission: ferreting out who poisoned the current wife of my first ex-husband, sending her on a premature stroll through the valley of the shadow of death.

Scanning the assembled crowd, I looked for signs of guilt, hoping to divine something, anything, that screamed "killer!"

No divination came, but I figured that such insights took more than the time allotted the standard memorial service.

If only someone would pinch me and tell me this was all a bad dream. Given Dorothy Gale's options I could tap my ruby slippers together three times, saying to myself, "There's no place like home, there's no place like home, there's no place like home . . ."

Alas, I had no ruby slippers. Maybe I

could find a pair on eBay.

In the meantime, like I'd done countless times during the four days since Carlene Arness became known as the "dearly departed," I replayed every moment of that evening that had started with a meeting of our nice little book group and ended in tragedy.

And that had convinced me that our nice little book group harbored someone who wasn't so nice . . . and that in this earthly valley there was evil aplenty to fear.

"This book sucks. There should be a law protecting the reading public from such trash!" And with that Carlene Arness hurled *Murder in the Keys* into her fireplace, the drama of the action diminished by the lack of a fire.

"What is it you didn't like about it, Carlene?" Helen Adams's mild tone contrasted with Carlene's strident one.

"Where do I begin? There was no mystery, no plot, and, get this, no ending! I finally got to the last page and expected the numerous loose threads to be tied up — but no, just blank paper. I couldn't believe it! It just *ends.* I guess the author got bored with her own writing — completely understandable — and *quit.*"

Carlene paused, but not for long before continuing with her thumbs-way-down review, bracelets jingling as she waved her arms around. "And it was riddled with editing errors, continuity problems, and — and just plain bad writing. I want to read books that are well written," she pronounced, giving her expensively cut auburn hair a toss. "And another thing — I don't think the author ever set foot in Key West, but that didn't stop her from setting this piece of trash there."

"Did it at least have good sex?" Kat Berenger, Carlene's stepsister, looked hopeful.

"It had *no* sex. The author effectively neutered the characters."

Our group had its share of critical readers. Sarah Rubottom, a retired English teacher, often lambasted authors for poor writing. She'd issue her judgment with pursed lips and crossed arms, spelling curtains for that author.

But that night Sarah exchanged questioning looks with me. What was going on with Carlene? Her tirade was quite a departure for someone normally so soft-spoken and composed. Maybe her recent publishing success explained her more exacting standards with her fellow writers. Carlene's debut mystery, *Murder à la Isabel,* a contemporary mystery set in Richmond, Virginia, was quite good.

Or, more likely, her uncharacteristic angst stemmed from her separation from Evan Arness, her husband and, incidentally, my ex-husband. I didn't know if any of the group's members knew about the split. I only found out recently when I ran into Evan at Target and he'd said they were taking a "break."

As an aspiring romance writer, I felt more than a little sensitive to book trashing. I wanted to tell Carlene to get a grip and give the author some respect — poorly written or not, she had made a creative effort. I held my tongue as I rescued the book from the fireplace, where it had landed in a pages-splayed position next to a brass vase brimming with dried flowers. Returning to my chair, I picked up my jacket, which had fallen on the floor, and draped it over my purse before glancing at the paperback. The six-toed cat, icon of the Florida Keys, graced the front cover. I turned it over and skimmed the back cover — it looked like another cute cozy filled with eccentric characters. The author's first name was Annette and her last name contained a long string of mostly consonants. I passed the book around.

Carlene carried on — and on. Aiming for a light tone, I said, "Did you ever hear of the fifty-page rule, Carlene? If you don't like a book after fifty pages, give it the heave-ho."

Carlene ignored my advice. "And the author uses that old standby cyanide, putting it in the victim's tea. Isn't cyanide supposed to smell like bitter almonds? So wouldn't you think the idiot would get suspicious when her tea smelled like almonds?"

"Not everyone can detect the bitter almond smell. It's genetically determined," Sarah explained. "You either have the gift, or you don't." Several of us nodded and said, "That's right," indicating this was common knowledge. Apparently not to Carlene, judging by her blank look. Sarah continued, "And I'm not sure it would smell like almonds in the tea . . . Seems I heard that it can be smelled on the breath of the person who ingests it, but not before."

Carlene regarded Sarah thoughtfully. "Still, it must smell like *something* in the tea . . . something off."

I looked around and wondered if there were any gifted noses in this group. Did size count? At any rate, if anyone knew of a bitter almond–smelling talent, she or he wasn't telling. "If you do have the gift you could offer your services at autopsies," Art Woods, Helen Adams's son and our sole male member, quipped. He ran a hand through his mass of dark curls.

I gave Art what I imagined was a knitted-brow look, but without a mirror it was hard to tell. The mere thought of observing an autopsy gave me chills. But if faced with a cash-flow problem an autopsy gig might be a welcome option. I asked the group, "What do bitter almonds smell like anyway? Is it a smell you'd instantly recognize, like something similar to the nonbitter variety?" No one responded.

"Maybe the tea, no matter what flavor, would mask the smell of the cyanide," Helen mused.

"And where do you even get cyanide? The killers in these mysteries always manage to have it on hand, ready to dump in some hapless victim's tea." Carlene remained nettled by the author's lack of writing skill. "It can't be that easy to get. Wouldn't you have to sign for it, like you do for medications?"

Art laughed and said, "Carlene, you need to use cyanide in your next book. Show everyone the right way to do the evil deed."

Carlene frowned at her nails, but her

French manicure looked fine to me. "That's my plan, Art. I'm researching cyanide and similar poisons. In fact that's why I read this one, to see how the poisoning was handled." She added the unnecessary "*Not a good example.*"

Sarah, fiddling with her long gray braid, asked, "Remember those Tylenol killings in Chicago — when was that — back in the eighties?" We digressed into a discussion about the unsolved case involving a number of Chicago-area victims who died after ingesting cyanide-spiked Tylenol capsules. We all started talking at once. "Wasn't there some Tylenol thing in Seattle as well?" "What about Jonestown — didn't nine hundred people — ?" The sound of the doorbell put off segues into the Jonestown mass suicides as well as the Seattle killings, the details of which eluded me.

Kat jumped up to answer the door. Her long platinum hair curled in all directions, creating an Einstein effect. Her black leather vest displayed well-toned biceps, good advertising for her job as a personal trainer. Leopard tattoos decorated each bicep, and leopard-print cuffs topped stiletto-heeled chartreuse boots. The chartreuse also streaked across both eyelids.

"Hey, everyone, this is Linda Thomas,"

Kat announced as she shepherded the newcomer into the living room. Annabel Mitchell, a longtime member, followed. "Linda came to Carlene's signing at Creatures 'n Crooks," Kat explained. "Being a mystery fan, she jumped at the chance to visit our group. And, small world, she and Carlene know each other from their L.A. days." Two weeks before, Creatures 'n Crooks Bookshoppe, a local independent bookstore specializing in mysteries, had hosted a signing for *Murder à la Isabel.*

I remembered Linda from the signing. Highlights like hers were hard to forget: a series of contrasting shades produced a tigerlike effect. Next to Kat with her leopard paraphernalia, I felt like I was viewing a surrealistic safari. Linda favored heavy makeup, eyes rimmed in thick black, shadow in a slightly paler black shade covering her lids. Aquiline nose. From the neck down, she was less dramatic; she wore a plain white turtleneck and tight jeans that she likely purchased in the plus-size department. I guessed her age to be anywhere between fifty and sixty, which meant she was around forty-five. Age estimation wasn't my strong suit.

Carlene smiled, welcoming Linda in a gracious but restrained manner, a greeting usually given to a stranger, not an old friend. But, I realized, no one said they were old friends, just that they knew each other. And, although I doubted it, their reunion at the signing may well have been warm and heartfelt. Carlene started to get up, saying, "We need more chairs . . ." At that moment Annabel carried two chairs in from the dining room and set them next to Kat.

Annabel was dressed for success in a black pantsuit, pale strawberry blond hair framing her face in soft waves with an artful tousled look, silver jewelry discreet. Annabel was the first of our group's three writers to publish her work, having written her first mystery during the midnineties. Her works fell into the hard-boiled genre, dark, gritty, and violent. Annabel lived in a duplex in the Fan, one of Richmond, Virginia's many historic areas. Before Carlene's marriage, she and Annabel had shared the common wall in the two-family house.

Kat introduced Linda to each member in turn. A few people expressed surprise at discovering that Carlene had lived in L.A. Others said they knew, but had forgotten. Carlene said that L.A. was, after all, years before.

Kat asked, looking first at Linda, then at Carlene, "How long since you two last saw each other?"

After a pause, Carlene said, "Well, I moved here in ninety-six."

Linda looked amused as she said with an airy tone, "Sounds about right. It's 2005 now, so that makes 1996 . . ." She closed her eyes to do the calculation. "Ten, twelve years ago?" No one commented on her inexact math.

Carlene returned to her earlier appraisal of her nails. Her anxiety level had ratcheted up a few notches since Linda's arrival. Was Linda a possible agitator? Unless it was Annabel . . . although I couldn't imagine why.

Linda fielded questions about her reading habits — who are your favorite authors, do you like cozies, thrillers, courtroom dramas, and so on. "Oh!" She looked stricken with a sudden worry. "I hope I didn't forget my book for tonight." She rummaged through her purse, pulling out a wallet, a makeup bag, a VHS cassette, a phone, and a tattered paperback with a title from Elaine Viets's Dead End Job series, set in Florida. "Aha!" She stuffed everything but the book back into the purse. "I knew it was in here some-where."

Sarah said, "Well, Linda, it's nice to have you with us. Before you arrived, we were having this fascinating discussion about cyanide, and —"

But Carlene interrupted with a nervous laugh. "Oh, let's move on. We can continue the poison talk another time." Turning to Art, she smiled. "Tell us about your book, Art."

When Carlene and I started the Murder on Tour book group three years before, we wanted to stray from the practice of the numerous other book groups that met monthly and discussed the same book. Each member of the group read a different mystery based on a geographical setting, and we met every other Monday to "booktalk" our selections — a fancy way of saying we gave oral book reports, reminiscent of grade school. We met our needs to be both armchair detectives and travelers without having to suffer through someone's vacation slides of Disney World. Our current literary tour of murder and mayhem took us through the American South, and tonight's stop was Florida. With its intoxicating blend of steaminess, exoticism, and often strange goings-on, Florida provided a fertile setting for mystery aficionados.

Art returned Carlene's smile, then gave us an account of *The Paperboy,* by Pete Dexter, a disquieting and riveting story of a newspaper family in Northern Florida during the late sixties. I made a note on the back of an envelope to add it to my to-read list. Art usually chose historical mysteries, but he claimed that Florida offered little in that subgenre and that, besides, he'd been wanting to read *The Paperboy* for a while. "Besides," he added with a shrug of his bony shoulders, "the sixties are historical."

I watched the interplay between Linda and Carlene. Linda's steady smile telegraphing wry amusement contrasted with Carlene's worrying a beaded necklace like a rosary. What was the history between these two? Anyone who could discompose the normally self-possessed and poker-faced Carlene was a force to be reckoned with. Intrigued, I continued to keep an eye on them.

Despite Carlene's preoccupation, part of her remained engaged in the discussion. The rest of us shared our selections sans drama, tension, and author maligning. We "traveled" the state of Florida, from the panhandle to the Key Largo of Raymond Chandler's classic of the same name. Helen raved about John MacDonald's *The Deep Blue Good-by,* the first in his Travis McGee color-coded series. She assured us that she intended to read every last one of the prolific author's works. I added the title to my envelope list.

Eventually we wound down and addressed the next meeting's theme of Appalachia. Helen reminded us that she had posted a list of Appalachian authors on the group's website. She also agreed to host the group at her apartment.

"And I have a request to make — that you turn off your cell phones during book group. They're very distracting."

Sarah looked puzzled. "I didn't hear a cell phone tonight."

"No, not tonight. But often folks are getting calls. Some more than others." Kat and Annabel were likely the "some" that Helen cited. Both appeared unfazed.

"Not me. My phone sits in the bottom of my purse, turned off. I check for messages once a week." I laughed, adding, "That is, if I think of it."

We agreed to put our phones on vibrate mode and Helen expressed her thanks. Then she took advantage of having the floor and launched into a blow-by-blow description of the pro-life conference she'd recently attended. Kat had warned me about it when I'd first arrived.

"Her big thing now is the whole stem cell thing." Kat had sighed. "The woman just wears me out. And I'm sure Sarah will put in her two cents on the subject."

Nodding in agreement, I had said, "We'll all be giving Helen a wide berth tonight. Maybe Sarah as well." Often I enjoyed hearing people's viewpoints, especially if they differed from mine. But I avoided Helen's endless soapbox speeches whenever I could, otherwise I endured them. Sarah was the only one who bothered to challenge Helen. Even though Sarah held conservative views, they sat far to the left of Helen's on the Republican political spectrum.

Helen used her hands to emphasize her points. Her long fingers and a dangling thread from the ruffled sleeve of her periwinkle blouse distracted me from her earnest account. But loose threads and dancing fingers didn't capture my attention for long, so I looked around the room, wondering if Carlene had added anything new to the decor since the last time I was here. Being a minimalist, she had more likely subtracted. Touches of burgundy and forest green accented the soft yellows and peaches of the conversational grouping of sofa, love seat, and oversized chairs. No knickknacks interrupted the smooth table surfaces, but a couple of large modern paintings and a sculpture filled up the wall space.

Just as Sarah started with, "Helen, don't you realize the potential benefits of stem cell research ..." I felt a tap on my shoulder. Carlene whispered, "Hazel, I need to ask you something. Let's go to my den." Then, flashing a smile at the others, she said, "Please excuse us — business," and we moved off, leaving the others to suffer through the debate.

Carlene detoured into the kitchen to switch on the coffeemaker before we walked up a short flight of steps to her den. "I figured we could forgo the conference recap," she grinned. "It could go on forever. And they'll probably get into the childbirth tales."

I rolled my eyes and smiled. Childbirth stories were a frequent staple of this group. They usually started with someone announcing the birth of a grandchild and included complete details of the pregnancy, labor, and birth. Conception as well, if they were privy to those details. Being childless, Carlene and I had missed out on a lifetime ticket to female bonding. In my fifty-something years I'd acquired husbands and cats, but children, not a one.

Carlene said, "We don't have to worry about Art. He can busy himself with everyone's books."

Carlene's minimalist leanings extended to her den. A Persian rug in a black and teal pattern covered the gleaming hardwood floor. Only a lamp, laptop, printer, and cordless phone disturbed the polished wood surface of the desk. Not a plant in sight, no pictures on the walls. An ergonomically correct chair and a bookcase provided the only other furniture. I wondered about the correlation between uncluttered surroundings and an uncluttered mind. Would it enhance my own writing to establish order out of the chaos in my den? Would I try it? Probably not.

"Hazel, I'm sorry I created such a fuss over that silly book. I get so irritated when people go on and on about hating a book." Her voice, now reverted back to its usual near whisper, was so soft that I risked violating the standard conversational distance between us by moving closer. It was either that or take a shot at lip reading.

"Don't worry about it." By now I was more interested in broaching the subject of Linda. "So — are you excited about your friend Linda showing up?"

Carlene gave a brief laugh and said, "Well, no. To be honest, I don't even remember the woman. It's embarrassing since she seems to remember me so well."

"Oh. So she wasn't a friend in L.A.?"

"Oh, no. She says I worked with her husband. Maybe I met her at a work party. I simply don't remember." She spread her hands as if asking how she could possibly remember everyone she met.

"Looks like hers would be hard to forget."

"I guess." She waved a dismissive hand, setting off those dissonant bracelets. "I just finished an Agatha Christie. I keep reading them over and over." Pulling a book out of her bookcase she offered it to me. "This one's a Miss Marple. *The Mirror Crack'd.* Want to borrow it?"

Okay, Linda was off limits. I wondered why. "Oh, no thanks. I have a copy." Carlene reshelved the paperback.

"Hazel, the real reason I wanted to talk to you, aside from getting away from Helen, was to share my big news. I booked a trip to Costa Rica for December. Georgia and I are going to stay with a friend of hers."

"Oh, Carlene, that's great. You'll love it. So will Georgia." Georgia Dmytryk was Carlene's lifelong friend and the executive director of the Richmond Women's Resource Center.

"I know you went there a while back. Maybe you can give us suggestions. Do you have time for coffee this week? Our treat.

Maybe early one morning before Georgia goes to the center?" I wasn't hot on early-morning activities, but I *was* hot on free coffee, so I agreed to meet Carlene and Georgia at Panera at Stony Point on Wednesday morning.

Then my eye was drawn to a couple of photographs on the shelf over her laptop. How had I missed them in this monkish room? I pointed to one and said, "I don't think I've seen these before." Neither picture included Evan, but I didn't comment on my observation.

A smiling foursome posed next to a Christmas tree. Kat dominated the group with her abundance of everything: hair, makeup, cleavage, jewelry. Her twenty-something daughter, Stephie, took her mother's flamboyant fashion statements several steps further with her riotous assortment of piercings and tattoos. Dean Berenger, Kat's father and Carlene's step-father, wore a crewneck sweater and sported a buzz cut.

Carlene's elegant style was apparent even with her tacky Christmas sweater and jeans. Her eyes stared impassively into, maybe through, the camera. I never tire of her mesmerizing eyes, which happen to be the same color and shade as mine, "money green." My thoughts digressed along a path from green eyes to husbands, recalling one of my exes declaring an exact match when he held a dollar bill up to my eyes. While he was puzzled that they weren't hazel, suiting my name, they failed to mesmerize him.

Besides our eyes, Carlene and I shared a number of physical attributes. We both stood at five feet four inches without shoes. We'd remained slim, but the pounds were creeping up in that insidious way that pounds crept. Our hair color belonged to the red family, hers a vibrant auburn and mine an autumn chestnut. No doubt her salon tab far exceeded mine.

"That was taken last Christmas," Carlene explained, but didn't elaborate.

"And what about this one?" I pointed to an eight-by-eleven image in a brushed metal frame. "This has to be your mother." Despite the beehive and thick black eyeliner, the woman could only be Carlene's mother, so striking was the resemblance.

"It is."

"Father?" I asked, pointing at the handsome, smiling man holding a pipe, who didn't look remotely like Dean Berenger. Carlene nodded.

A perhaps ten-year-old Carlene towered over an unhappy-looking boy. "I guess that's your brother."

"Yes, that's Hal. I hate to cut this short, Hazel, but I've got to get the food ready. They'll be winding down their stories soon and will want to eat." True to my prediction, a loud and intense childbirth discussion was in full swing downstairs.

The rebuff didn't surprise me as Carlene didn't allow many personal questions. In no time the inevitable "it's none of your business" messages would start, nonverbal but clear all the same. As a result, I knew little about her. That didn't stop me from wondering if Hal served as the family's black sheep, making him off-limits for discussion.

"Okay, I'll give you a hand," I offered with reluctance. I wanted to stay in the den and look at photos and ask nosy questions. But even if Carlene was willing to satisfy my curiosity, there were only the two photos anyway.

Carlene stopped at the door and turned to me. "Hazel," she started, looking uncertain. "I have a, um, hypothetical question for you."

"Yes?"

She continued to look indecisive before finally taking the proverbial nosedive. "Have you ever made a huge mistake?"

"Mistake?" I laughed. "Of *course.*" My

26

mistakes were too numerous for a quick mental scan. There were the failed marriages, Evan being the first of them. And more than one wrong turn on the career path. But huge? "What do you mean by huge?"

"The kind that comes back later to haunt you."

CHAPTER 2

I looked at Carlene, trying to get a bead on her meaning. Did her question have to do with Evan, with their separation? But the haunting bit threw me — haunting implied a past mistake. That thought took me to the not-remembered Linda. Carlene's eagerness to leave the subject of Linda shed doubts on her claims of not remembering her. Who could forget hair like that? Of course, the hair may have been different at the time — for all I knew, Linda had been a nondescript type until a midlife crisis led to her falling in with a creative hairdresser.

Perhaps Carlene was about to confess to a crime. Or she'd been an accomplice, a mobster's moll. "Carlene, does this have anything to do with Linda?"

The rebuff didn't surprise me. "Linda again? I *said* I didn't remember her." Then, smiling, she offered, "Sorry, I guess I'm be- ing . . . fanciful." Fanciful. A writer's word.

Anyone else would say "silly." "You see, it's for this book I started . . ." Carlene went on to describe the book, how the main character meets up with her past — a past she had hoped was, well, in the past. Carlene had talked about her upcoming book at the signing so I guessed that this was her third book. "I'm just collecting experiences, that's all." And with that, she left the den and proceeded down the short flight of steps to the kitchen, apparently forgetting her question about my own mistakes. I thought about Carlene's conveniently falling back on her writing to explain her provocative question. I held to my suspicion that Linda had triggered this haunting business.

Carlene's kitchen, with its barn-red walls, white cabinets, black-and-white-checkered floor, and black appliances was a study in elegance and simplicity, simplicity being the operative word. My own kitchen abounded with plants, refrigerator magnets attaching shopping lists and emergency numbers, cat dishes, cats themselves, and often pleasant cooking aromas. Carlene's kitchen gave off a model house feeling. A round wooden table held a tray of refreshment paraphernalia and a Tupperware container of what looked like brownies. The notion that less is more can be inaccurate, and sometimes less is just less.

Curious about what was going on in Carlene and Evan's private world I asked, "Carlene, how's Evan these days?" The fact that it was their private world didn't temper my nosiness. I waited to see if she'd mention the separation.

Not a chance. She only stiffened and said "fine" in a tone that brooked no further questions. I felt a twinge of guilt for asking. Terse or not, the woman could well be suffering — her behavior throughout the evening indicated that. Now, using more concentration than necessary, she filled a kettle with water, set it on the stovetop, and turned on the electric burner. No doubt she was preparing one of those odious teas she favored — tonics, she called them — claiming they promoted longevity and well-being. I'm all for longevity, well-being, and the whole shebang, but if it took downing one of her lethal concoctions to have it, I'd seriously reconsider. She took a white mug with a gold "C" identifying it as hers off the tray on the table and set it on the counter. Then she removed the cellophane wrap from a box covered with Chinese characters.

"Is that a new tea?" I asked. Not that I cared, but I thought it was a question she'd answer.

And she did. "Yes, I've never tried it, but someone suggested it." She opened a drawer, produced a scoop, and measured loose tea into a strainer. Then she opened the refrigerator, grabbed a plate of apple slices and what looked to be goat cheese, used her hip to push the door shut, and headed for the dining room. "Do you mind pouring the decaf? The carafe's right there." Using her chin, she pointed toward the table before disappearing through the doorway.

Normally, I didn't bother with such niceties as carafes and served guests from the coffeepot itself, but that was me. As I poured, I thought back to when Evan was *my* husband. Very much in love, or perhaps lust, we couldn't wait until graduation from Rochester Institute of Technology and married while still in college. Then the "open marriage" craze of the early seventies appealed to him, but not to me. Since I had, even in that permissive era, eschewed premarital sex and pushed for marriage, I failed to understand why he thought I would embrace such a radical concept as open marriage. While I shed my prudish ways during our marriage, my commitment to monogamy, in or out of marriage, lasts to this day. After two years of grappling with the open marriage issue, in addition to others, I hightailed it to a divorce lawyer.

Once safely unmarried, I acted on a spirit of adventure and moved to Los Angeles, where I remarried not once but three times. Evan remained on the East Coast, taking a vow to abstain from marriage, open or not. We remained friends, keeping in touch over the years and miles. In between my own marriages, I entertained fantasies of remarrying him and living happily ever after, managing to forget why I'd divorced him in the first place. But his enduring commitment to the single life kept me from acting on my fantasies.

In 1999 I found myself a widow. Dispirited, I considered my options, one of which was another uprooting. My cousin Lucy Hooper, a recent widow as well, offered temporary living quarters in her home in Richmond. The fact that Evan had retired from his management job in Rochester after winning the New York lottery and taken a position as an adjunct business professor in Richmond provided added incentive to reverse the cross-country move I'd made a quarter of a century before. Perhaps we were meant to be together after all, his chronic marriage phobia be damned.

Evan responded to the news of my impending move with enthusiasm, saying it would be great to see each other often. I kept mum on my special plans for the two of us. One month after that conversation, on a bright and sunny day in April 2000, I landed in Richmond with my calico cat, Shammy, in tow. But my hopes were dashed. In the space of that one month, Evan had managed not only to meet but to marry one Carlene Lundy, the woman who now gave him short shrift.

Despite my disappointment, I chose to remain friends with Evan. Who knew how long this marriage would last anyway? And it didn't take a rocket scientist to figure that in order to remain friends with Evan I had to be friends with his wife. And so I did, as much as anyone could be friends with the unforthcoming Carlene. As for Evan, except for the annual turkey dinners he and Carlene hosted in early December to usher in the holiday season before the rush of other parties, I rarely saw him. And yes, five years later I still lived with Lucy or, as I preferred to put it, we lived *together.* It put a whole different spin on temporary.

I watched as Carlene arranged plates and dishes on the dining table and, after casting a critical eye on the result, rearranged them. I shook my head and laughed to myself over such fussing. The simplicity of the rest of the house didn't reign in Carlene's small dining room. A carved pumpkin holding a riotous assortment of fall flowers and greens served as a table centerpiece. With the early October weather being so warm, the fall decor seemed out of place. I piled the brownies on a plate and put them and the carafe amid a display of smaller pumpkins, orange candles, baby squash, gourds, acorns, and scattered leaves. It looked like Martha Stewart had run amok.

What was going on with Carlene and Evan? Were they permanently separated or, in Evan's parlance, on a "break"? Would the turkey dinner go on as usual in December? Maybe some of the issues that had plagued my marriage to Evan were raising havoc with the Carlene/Evan union some thirty years later. I remembered my chance encounter with Evan at Target the week before. I took him up on his offer of coffee at the Starbucks concession, where he told me about the separation, but not his second offer — dinner at Lemaire restaurant. Hard as it was to turn down dinner at Richmond's most elegant restaurant, I didn't date married men. And separated was, in my view, still married. Taking a so-called break even more so. So I'd collected my purchases and stood to leave, saying, "No, Evan. Thank you, but no. Not while you're married to Carlene." And I'd walked away. In truth, my fantasies of a reunion with a single Evan had dimmed to the point of extinction, so I couldn't claim to be resisting temptation. Still, I regretted not sticking around to hear what had brought on this trouble in paradise — assuming that Evan would share such details.

Little did I know that in a very short time their paradise would become a lot more troublesome.

The group drifted into the small dining room, a spirited discussion about Sudoku puzzles in progress. They loaded miniature plates with brownies and apple slices, some taking care to avoid the goat cheese. Annabel looked alarmed at Linda's blow-by-blow description of her recent colonoscopy. I realized with something akin to despair that I'd reached the age where medical procedures and conditions were discussed in full and complete detail at every opportunity. Sighing, I fixed myself a cup of decaf but found the pitcher bone dry. I carried the creamer and my cup to the kitchen where Carlene poured water from the kettle into her mug.

"Carlene, do you have milk or half-and-half?"

She looked blank, then said, "Yes. In the fridge. Didn't I put it out?"

Sarah appeared in the other kitchen doorway. "Carlene, there're no towels in the upstairs bathroom." Then she grinned. "Jeans work just as well." She rubbed her hands over her thighs in demonstration.

"Oh, dear," Carlene heaved a sigh. "Sorry about that." She left her mug on the counter and went upstairs, presumably to locate towels.

We looked after Carlene's retreating form. Sarah lowered her voice and asked, "Did you find out what was with her earlier?"

I hesitated and wagged my hand back and forth. I could only assess the "huge mistake" discussion as well as the Linda one as vague and unsatisfying. And even if I had something concrete to report, I didn't feel comfortable talking about Carlene in her own house. "Not really" was the best I could come up with to explain my conversation with Carlene.

"Let's go down to the family room and I'll show you a few exercises you can do at home," I heard Kat suggest to Art. She walked, swaggered actually, through the kitchen to the family room beyond. A belly

36

diamond winked at us over her jeans with thigh cutouts. Art, looking like a lovesick puppy, trailed behind her. Sarah and I turned to each other and laughed.

Sarah said, "The guy's so *skinny* — I can't see him lifting even ten-pound weights." Art was on the lean side. His lankiness combined with his height and concave chest reminded me of a folding lawn chair.

Sarah asked, "What about Linda? What's the story with her?"

I kept my voice low and my eyes on the kitchen doorway. It shouldn't take Carlene long to find a towel. "Carlene says she doesn't remember Linda, so she had nothing to say about her." *Not verbally, anyway.* A phone sounded in the dining room and a second later, Annabel appeared in the kitchen, clutching a tiny phone to her ear. She smiled at us and walked down the steps to the family room.

I poked around in the refrigerator and finally located a small carton of 1 percent milk. I surreptitiously sniffed it before dumping some into my cup and the rest into the creamer. Sarah and I walked into the dining room and I resolved to do no more work. I saw Linda regaling Helen with an anecdote involving her dermatologist. A couple of minutes later Carlene, mug in hand, came into the dining room.

Sarah pushed up her oversized glasses and began. "Anyway, Hazel, I need your opinion about this nonprofit." Sarah volunteered for a couple of local organizations. As I clocked in many volunteer hours myself, I was frequently consulted for my opinion about various groups. We chatted for a couple of minutes until I picked up the words "stem cell," "misguided liberals," and "Bush" behind me. Uh-oh, Helen on her soapbox. I turned to find her preaching to Annabel and Carlene.

"Oh, no, she's at it again," Sarah muttered. "She already worked that subject half to death tonight."

Deciding to rescue them from Helen's clutches, I held up a finger to Sarah in a wait-a-minute gesture. But Art beat me to it. Standing in the kitchen doorway with Kat, the body-building demo apparently over, he exhorted the "author contingent" to give progress reports on our work. I noticed Annabel's grateful smile along with a flash of annoyance on Helen's face. But, presumably remembering her manners, she smiled as she turned to Annabel and said, "You start, Annabel."

"Oh, I'm on a brief hiatus from writing. But *Sunset Over Monticello* is due out in

February." Annabel set her police procedural series featuring Gloria Shifflett, a hard-bitten and hard-living homicide detective, in Charlottesville. I gave an update on my baby boomer sex romp. I didn't look at Helen, who no doubt was fighting an urge to make faces at my subject matter.

The group's real interest was in Carlene, as the new kid on our block in the publishing world. She had recently sent her second book, *Graveside Death,* to her agent. The story started with the murder of a widow at her husband's graveside service. The widow had been, by several accounts, faking her grief.

"What are your plans for a third book?" Sarah asked. I remembered our earlier conversation in the den when Carlene alluded to a woman meeting up with her past.

Carlene picked up an apple slice and took a dainty bite before saying, "I'm thinking of setting it at the Fountain Bookstore. I need to run it by Kelly Justice." Kelly owned the independent bookstore located in Richmond's historic cobblestoned Shockoe Slip area.

"Tell us about the story line." Annabel made "come on" motions with her hand.

"Well . . . it's about a woman who's been a fugitive for years. Not from justice, but from — *love.*" Carlene paused, perhaps for effect, then laughed and said, "And that's all I'm telling right now." She picked up her tea and tried to take a sip. When she grimaced, I thought maybe the new tea wasn't a hit, but the problem was the temperature. She said "Too hot!" and set the mug back on the table.

"What gave you the idea?" Sarah asked amid a chorus of protests.

"Oh, Carlene, I saw the most glowing article about you," Helen gushed. "I brought it with me tonight. Art, honey, bring me that magazine. It should be right by my purse."

"Art, honey," still standing next to Kat by the entrance to the kitchen, obeyed his mother. But he yelled back that he couldn't find it. Helen called, "Well it *must* be there." Helen started for the living room when Art came in waving a magazine.

"Oh dear. This is *AARP*. I *told* you to take the other magazine, the one on the counter."

"This is the only one I saw." Art stabbed the magazine with his finger. "Why don't you ever make yourself clear?"

"You're such an idiot!"

Art flushed. The rest of us looked at each other and shook our heads in dismay. This wasn't the first time Helen had hurled abuse at Art while he ineffectually tried to defend himself.

Helen huffed and said, "Well, I'll just scan the article and e-mail it to everyone." Turning to Carlene, she touched her arm and said, "So sorry for the interruption. Sarah asked how you got the idea for your new book."

Our attention returned to Carlene. She took a larger bite out of the apple slice and thoroughly chewed it before she responded. "It was a movie . . . a movie I saw years ago. I can't remember the name of it or who was in it. And I'm not sure what made me remember it . . . Anyway, I thought it would make a good story." She picked up the mug and walked toward the kitchen. "Excuse me, this tea needs some ice."

"Fugitive from love," Linda said, seeming to be trying out a foreign phrase. "What do you mean by that, Carlene?" I wasn't sure, but I thought I detected a mocking tone in the question. The phrase did have a melodramatic ring. Recalling her huge-mistake question, I entertained the notion of Carlene being on the lam — lam from love? A huge mistake could get a person on the run.

Now Carlene paused and looked thoughtful, as if she was trying to figure out what she did mean. Finally, she settled on a weak "It's hard to explain" and made no attempt to do so.

"I'm sure your story will be great, Carlene," I assured her. "Are you keeping the characters from your first two books?"

"Yes, Minerva Mazarek and her dysfunctional family." In *Murder à la Isabel,* a man had been crushed to death in Isabel, the hurricane that had devastated Richmond in the fall of 2003, when a tree crashed through his bedroom wall. The relatives suspected he'd been murdered before the crash and hired private investigator Minerva Mazarek to unearth the truth.

"Okay, that's enough about me." Carlene grabbed another apple slice. "Should I make another pot of decaf?" A couple of acceptances enabled Carlene to successfully escape into the kitchen and dispense ice from the gizmo in the refrigerator door into her tea mug. Then the phone rang and she disappeared from view to answer it. A second later she closed the pocket door.

Annabel now turned to Helen. "Helen, what did you decide about designing a website for Sam?" After taking a number of courses at a local community college, Helen had become a freelance Web designer and from all accounts did well, rapidly gaining a reputation in the area. In fact she designed Carlene's author site for her class project.

Sarah pulled on my sleeve like a little kid, eager to resume our discussion about non-profits. I tried to recall the name of someone I knew who volunteered for the one in question, but found the bombardment of conversational fragments around me — Cuban food, jewelry, websites, Richmond Symphony — distracting. I spotted Linda chatting with Kat and Art. Like me, Kat didn't brook discussion of medical procedures, so I guessed Linda had to curtail her doctor-related tales. Apparently that was too much for her as she soon grabbed her jacket and purse, waved, said, "Nice to meet you all," and left. I noticed she made no effort to look for Carlene — likely she felt hurt after being ignored by our hostess.

The rising decibel level in the dining room suddenly shifted to the living room, as everyone moved in there to sit. "People have way too many names," Sarah cried. What was she talking about? I must have looked puzzled, because she explained, "Here I'm trying to process all these employer-matching contributions from the Alzheimer's Association Memory Walk. John Smith makes a donation but he submits it to his company as Albert Smith. And he's just one of many. You expect women to change their names, at least their last names.

43

I never did, mind you. But everyone these days goes by multiple first and last names, interchanging middle names. If they want their companies to match their donations, use consistent names. That's all I ask."

Annabel glanced at her watch and exclaimed, "Goodness, it's ten o'clock," and got up to leave. Looking around, she asked, "Where's Carlene?" When I said I thought she got a phone call, Annabel looked uncertain, then shrugged. "Well, I have to get my jacket." She tried to open the pocket door from the dining room to the kitchen, the one Carlene had closed earlier. But it stuck and Annabel had to jiggle it to get it open a crack.

Seeing the last brownie in the dining room — someone said they were pumpkin brownies — I looked at Sarah and said, "Want to split it?" At her eager yes, I started to ask, "Do you know who brought —" A shriek sent the group rushing en masse to the family room, this time through the door from the hall to the kitchen that Carlene had closed as well. We ran past Annabel, who stood at the top of the steps, still shrieking.

Carlene had taken her tea to the family room to talk on the phone. Now she sat slumped in her chair, hand draped over the arm. Perspiration and a deep flush covered her face, a bluish froth at her mouth. The mug lay upended on the floor, the tea soaking into the carpet. Kat checked Carlene's pulse, setting off a cacophonous bangle-on-bangle tinkling that cemented my hatred of those danged bracelets from that moment on. A disembodied male voice yelled from the cordless phone on the floor next to the chair.

"Someone call 911," I ordered, my voice dry and raspy. Kat shook her head, looking grim, saying there was no pulse. I covered Carlene with an afghan that Helen handed me. Or was it Sarah? It seemed like everyone was everywhere. An almond odor hung on the air. Either it was the tea or — cyanide? Did that mean I had the gift? I spotted a folded sheet of paper on the floor behind the chair. Even in the stress of the moment I remembered one warning drilled into me by the crime novels I'd read and that was not to contaminate the scene. I didn't know if it was a crime scene but it didn't hurt to exercise caution. The dim light did not lend itself to reading so I turned on a tabletop lamp with a tissue I found in my jeans pocket. Then I knelt on the floor and, using the same tissue, unfolded the note, and read.

Soon the place teemed with paramedics and police. In the ensuing pandemonium, I think I remember stricken faces, mouths making "O"s of horror, hands making signs of the cross . . . and the hope and prayer I felt sure we all shared that we would wake up and find this to be the nightmare to end all nightmares.

And then realizing that we *would* wake up. Unlike Carlene, for whom there was no awakening. Ever.

CHAPTER 3

"I can't believe it was cyanide." Lucy Hooper shook her head in bewilderment. "Cyanide poisonings don't happen in the real world, Hazel. Only in Agatha Christie's world."

I wiped my eyes, blew my nose, and regarded Lucy. "I wish that was true. Then last night would be . . . not true."

Lucy worked away on her latest knitting project, likely an afghan involving varying shades of teal. She asked, "Do you want to keep talking about this, Hazel? Maybe you should get some sleep. After the trauma you've been through —"

"I'm fine," I interrupted. "Well, not fine, but I'd rather talk about it. Talking beats thinking." Lucy had been waiting up for me when I'd returned home at 11 p.m. the night before. Beyond a little babbling, I'd been too tired to debrief her on the dramatic events of the evening. Sleep had proved fitful and now, at nine, I felt worse for the effort. We sat in our morning room with Daisy and Shammy, our feline companions. A basket of muffins sat on the wicker table in front of me, but so far I'd only managed a few sips of coffee.

I blew my nose again and added the tissue to the impressive pile by my side. Lucy had a similar but smaller pile next to her. She rarely attended book group, but knew Carlene. If asked if she'd liked her, her honest response would echo that of the other members: "She's all right." The shock and drama of Carlene's death explained our tears, not any real affection for her.

Lucy said, "I bet Annabel's in a state, finding her the way she did. Annabel may write scenes like that, but writing's a far cry from the real thing." After a pause, she said, "Tell me about your interview with the police. You didn't say much about that last night."

"There's not much to tell. It was pretty much like it is in books. They searched our purses and pockets. There were two detectives — one was a cute young guy who looked like he was still in high school. He herded us into the living room and made sure we didn't talk to each other. The other was this stern-faced woman, Detective Garcia, who interviewed us individually

48

upstairs in Carlene's den. She asked for our contact information, what we ate and drank, who brought what. I had no idea who brought the refreshments, so I wasn't much help there."

"What were the refreshments?"

"Oh . . ." I racked my brain for a minute and came up with, "Apples. And, um, goat cheese. And there was something else." I snapped my fingers in triumph. "Pumpkin brownies."

"Okay, so what else did the detective ask?"

"She wanted our accounts of the evening, if anything unusual happened. Since I talked to Carlene the most, I imagine that I had the most to say. Not that anything I said was illuminating. What else?" I looked heavenward as I dredged up recollections. "They issued the usual directive not to leave town without letting them know and let us go."

"So it sounds like the police don't believe it was suicide."

"I don't know what they believe, but I'm sure they have to consider all possibilities."

"Well, it's hard to believe that Carlene committed suicide. And the note said, 'I can't do it anymore'?"

I nodded. "Whatever 'it' is. Was, rather." I thought back to the folded sheet of paper

I'd found behind Carlene's chair. I read it in disbelief and pointed it out to the police when they arrived with the paramedics. The rest of it went, 'I'm sorry, but it's best this way. May God forgive me.' "

"I wonder why she needed forgiveness. To commit suicide it must have been pretty serious."

"Maybe it had something to do with the huge mistake she brought up. I can't begin to imagine what that was all about. But suicide doesn't make sense. If I felt suicidal, I'd be too despondent to get myself all worked up over bad writing, like Carlene did." I sipped from my mug. "And with her being so private, and so vain, I can't see her killing herself in a group setting. I see her arranging herself in an attractive pose in her perfectly decorated bedroom, hair fanned out on the pillow, makeup flawless. She'd be found with an empty container of sleeping pills at her side. Very ladylike and pretty. Like the Lilly Bart character in *The House of Mirth*. However . . ." I paused again, trying to marshal the thoughts churning around in my sleep-deprived and traumatized brain. "We're talking about Carlene here. The mysterious, inscrutable Carlene. All bets are off if we try to guess what she was thinking."

I shifted focus. "And Evan — I'm just sick thinking about him. I wonder how he's taking this. Despite the separation and his hitting on me, I'm sure he still had feelings for Carlene."

"Can you call him?"

"How? I doubt that he's staying at the house. And I don't have his cell number or even an e-mail address."

Lucy narrowed her pewter eyes. "That discussion about cyanide is really bizarre. Carlene brings up the subject of cyanide right before she plans to ingest it? It's macabre. And it requires a pretty black sense of humor. And she never struck me as having much of a sense of humor, black or otherwise."

"True, but like I said, it's useless to try to guess her character and state of mind when we're clueless about either. Of course, cyanide was in that book she was so up in arms about, so her bringing up the subject isn't that weird."

"We need to get a copy of that book — it might provide a clue. What was the title? — *Murder in the Keys*?" Lucy asked and answered her own question.

"And another thing . . ." I told Lucy about Carlene and Georgia's Costa Rica plans and how we had arranged a coffee date with

Georgia so they could get travel tips from me. I slapped my forehead. "Oh, no! I forgot all about Georgia. I hope Kat or Evan called her, but somehow I doubt it. I'll call her. In a few minutes," I said, procrastinating. "It's probably not in the paper yet. Too soon."

"Probably not," Lucy agreed, looking pensive. "The case against suicide is pretty strong. Plus Carlene was on a roll with her writing. But if we don't buy the suicide theory, we have to consider the alternative . . . that someone killed her and planted the note. You said it was handwritten — did it look like her writing?"

I thought. "I'm not sure I ever saw her handwriting. We always e-mailed."

"Well, Hazel, I hate to say it, but this points to someone in the book group — one of you. Of course, it could have been an accident . . ."

For an instant, I felt hopeful. An accident didn't implicate anyone in the group. But I couldn't hold on to that hope. "Accident? Lucy, are you serious? How does cyanide accidentally end up in someone's tea?"

Not having an answer, Lucy shrugged. "You said you smelled bitter almonds, right?" When I nodded she went on. "I wonder who passed on the almond-smelling gene. Since our mothers are sisters, I wonder if I have it or if it's from your dad's side."

"Hopefully you'll never have to find out."

"What do bitter almonds smell like?"

"Like — I don't know — almonds. But somehow different. *Bitter.*"

"What did Detective Garcia say when you told her about the almond smell?"

"Nothing. But as reactionless as she was I did catch a hint of amusement when I mentioned the smell."

"Maybe she suspected you'd read one too many Agatha Christies — or that conversation you all had earlier made you suggestible."

"I wouldn't doubt it." I finished my coffee and put the mug on the table beside me.

"So — since Carlene had that tea, and likely no one else did, I guess we can assume the cyanide was in that." Lucy attended book group often enough to know about Carlene's infamous teas.

"It could be that the tea smelled like almonds. I'm sure it was bitter enough. We'll just have to wait for the pathology folks to do their testing."

For a couple of minutes, we sat silent, Lucy's needles clicking in rhythm. Daisy jumped into my lap. Then Lucy said, "Back to the suicide question, let's not forget about the separation — she could have felt despondent over that. What about her nervousness last night? Did that have to do with the separation or something else entirely? And her ranting about that book? And this Linda showing up? Did you mention Linda when you talked to Detective Garcia?"

"Oh, didn't I say that?" When Lucy shook her head I said, "Yes, I told her about Linda." Daisy snuggled close to me and I petted her as I considered Lucy's questions about Carlene. "She was nervous, out of sorts, unlike her usual poised self. Linda could well explain her nervousness to *some* extent. But it's a huge leap from nervousness to suicide." I ran my hands through my hair as I thought some more. "It'll take more than a note, something a five-year-old could produce, to convince me otherwise."

Lucy nodded. "So, okay, if we rule out suicide and an accident as possibilities, we're talking deliberate, premeditated poisoning — in other words, murder. And my money's on this Linda. She and Carlene knew each other in L.A., they meet up here, Linda shows up at the book group, Carlene didn't seem thrilled to see her, Carlene winds up dead. It's a no-brainer. It all ties in with the huge mistake that came back to haunt her, meaning Carlene. Wait — I remember something from the signing, something sort of . . . funny."

Lucy paused for a moment like she was calling up a memory. Impatient, I made a go-on motion and she started. "After Carlene signed my book, I was standing near the door, talking with Bonnie Stiller. Art Woods came by and said, 'Do you see that woman there?' and he pointed to a woman who was leaving the store. He told us about her standing in front of him in the signing line, insisting that Carlene knew her and her husband in L.A. Carlene was equally insistent that she didn't know them. The woman was quite put out about it, said she was sorry that Carlene had already signed the book, else she'd return it."

"Hmm." I pondered this for a moment. "Interesting. Did you get a good look at this woman?"

"Not really. Like I said, she was leaving, so I just saw her from the rear. But her hair was heavily highlighted."

"I'd sure like for it to be Linda, being an outsider. But, in Linda's defense, Carlene was agitated anyway, and possibly Linda's being there was nothing more than a co-incidence." I thought some more. "I'll give

Art a call and see what he has to say about this."

I stroked Daisy's silky fur and went on. "It has to be premeditated. It's highly unlikely that someone came up with the idea to spike Carlene's tea based on a chance discussion, a discussion Carlene herself initiated, and just happened to have cyanide on her — or his — person. Who carries cyanide around, who even possesses it, where do you even obtain it?" The very questions Carlene had posed. But the answers were simple enough — research, either via the Internet or the old-fashioned way, the public library.

"Oh!" Now Lucy sounded excited. "Could the cyanide have been added to the tea beforehand? Someone could have put something in the tea sometime during the day. That way it doesn't point to one of you."

I shook my head. "It wasn't in the tea. The tea was new, something she'd never tried before. In fact, I saw her take the cellophane wrapper off the box. So unless we're talking about some clever mass murderer armed with cyanide-laced tea it does point to someone in the group."

"But what about putting something in the mug ahead of time? Where was the mug, anyway?"

I closed my eyes and visualized the virtually empty kitchen. "On the kitchen table. On a tray."

"Do you know how long the tray had been there?"

I shrugged. "So you think someone came over earlier? Someone outside of the book group?" I heard the hopeful note in my voice. Any possibility that the culprit was a non–book group person was welcome. "But let's not forget that this hypothetical person who visited earlier may be a book group person. Or," I added as an unwelcome idea occurred to me, "there's Evan."

Lucy cringed. I gazed out the window, biting my lip. The idea of a past marriage to a future wife killer rankled, although I was to find that thirty-plus years is a long time, more than enough time to form and reform characters.

I regarded Lucy. "Who knows about Evan and me?"

"Everyone knows you were married to him."

"But do they know about . . ."

"Why you moved here in the first place?" When I nodded, she said, "I don't know . . . Well, I think I told Sarah."

I sighed. "When did you tell her?"

"It was before you arrived from California.

57

Once you got here and found out that Evan was married, I said nothing, hoping she'd forgotten. She did ask me about it once, and I said you had a change of heart, and left it at that. After all, she didn't even know Carlene back then — I don't think so, anyway — she didn't know her until the book group started."

"Who else?"

"I don't remember telling anyone else. Did you tell anyone?"

"No one in book group. Let's hope Sarah didn't say anything."

"What are you worried about?"

"Looking like a suspect — like I was out to get rid of Carlene so I could have another go at Evan."

"Well, it's unfortunate that you spent so much time in the kitchen. But, really . . . you a suspect?" Lucy shook her head in disbelief. "Unless I'm in denial, not willing to face the scary realization that I've lived with a killer relative for all these years. Tell me this: who knows about your conversation with Evan at Target?"

"No one. Just you. And Evan."

"If I were you I'd keep these speculations between the two of us. As far as anyone else is concerned, especially in the book group, we completely accept the suicide verdict.

Otherwise you run the risk of making the killer, assuming there is one, uncomfortable enough to kill *you.*"

"Yeah, you're right, Lucy."

Lucy gave me a puckish look. "What about Vince as a resource? I'm sure his cronies in the police department keep him in the loop."

Lucy was referring to Vince Castelli, a retired Richmond homicide detective turned true crime writer, my sometimes friend, sometimes more-than-friend, sometimes much-more-than-friend. A petite redheaded woman named Molly had accompanied him to Carlene's signing at Creatures 'n Crooks, confirming our current status to be in the "friend" category. Lucy's mission in life was to get me married off to Vince.

"Forget the matchmaking, Lucy. You saw his new girlfriend at the signing."

Lucy waved a well-manicured hand in dismissal. "Probably won't last."

Once again we lapsed into silence, but not for long. "This whole thing is so — creepy," I said, not able to express my feelings better. "But who did it? And why? And how?" I sounded like a journalistic owl.

"I need more coffee." Putting her knitting aside, Lucy got up and refilled her mug. "If we knew who we might know why. And vice versa. Coffee? And have one of these zuc-chini muffins," she ordered. "I got up at seven and made them." So as not to incon-venience Daisy, who now blanketed my lap, Lucy let me sit while she filled my mug with the arabica brew and handed me the basket of muffins.

After obediently accepting her offerings, I suggested, "Let's look at each person's con-nection to Carlene. And how she — or he — came to be in the group. I need paper. Will you hand me that pile of mail?" I asked, pointing toward the counter that separated the morning room from the kitchen. In practicing my recycle/reuse policy, I'd developed a penchant for writing on the backs of envelopes.

Envelopes and pen in hand, I started. "We know how I met Carlene — through Evan." I felt my nose wrinkle at the memory of be-ing jilted by my ex. Even after all these years, this inaccurate memory persisted.

"When did you and Carlene form the group?"

"Three, almost four years ago — early in 2002." For some time before that, Carlene and I had attended the same library mystery group. Over time we found fault with the group and had our own ideas about how it should be conducted. So one day we said to each other, "Let's start our own and have things the way we want them."

I asked, "How about Sarah?"

"We told her about the group at a neighborhood watch meeting." Lucy snagged a nail on her knitting. As she took an emery board from the pocket of her robe, she asked, "Did she and Carlene have any association outside of book group?"

I thought. "Don't think so."

Lucy held up a hand to check the progress of her filing. "Did you talk to Linda at all? We need to learn more about the Linda/Carlene connection."

"No, I wanted to, but she was telling Annabel about her colonoscopy, so I steered clear of her." Lucy smiled, knowing my aversion to medical topics. "Then she told someone, I think it was Helen, about some skin condition she had."

I picked up my muffin and split it in half. "Carlene worked as a computer programmer in L.A. As a contractor she worked at a lot of companies. The IT community is small, even in a megacity like L.A. Using the theory of six degrees of separation, someone I know is bound to remember her. Maybe Linda as well, as they could have worked together."

"So I take it you're going to get your L.A.

buddies working on this?" Lucy asked.

"Sure thing." I added the item to my to-do list. "I wish I'd thought to ask Linda for her e-mail and phone number. Maybe Kat has it. It sounded like they'd talked at the signing."

Lucy looked thoughtful. "I wonder if Carlene had a lot of secrets . . . secrets that hold the key to why she died."

A flurry of squirrel activity on the patio galvanized Shammy into action. Fur bristling, she raced from one side of the room to the other, while Daisy remained on my lap, oblivious to the commotion.

"Maybe rereading Carlene's book would help."

"Possibly," Lucy agreed. "You're thinking of looking for buried clues?"

I nodded. "And I'd love to get my hands on anything she's written for her third book." I recalled the laptop in her den. Maybe Evan would give it to me. I wrote down a reminder and reviewed my notes. "Who's next?"

"Helen and Art."

"Hmm. Carlene and Helen may have met at the gym."

"So, we need to know how Helen and Art came to the group, and if either of them knew Carlene before."

I wrote that on my growing list. "I dread getting buttonholed into a family values lecture. Helen was really on a tear last night."

"Let me guess — pro-life?"

"You got it — with an emphasis on the stem cell aspect." I rolled my eyes. "And now, who's left? Ah, Annabel. She also started at the group's beginning and definitely had a Carlene connection, being former Fan neighbors."

"Were they close friends?"

"I'm not sure. Carlene invited her to join the group, but that doesn't necessitate closeness. And I know they went on a house and garden tour together last spring. I never heard of Carlene being close with anyone, except Georgia. And I don't even know how close they were, even though they'd known each other for years."

I twirled my pen like a baton as I mused. "I always thought it was funny how close-mouthed Carlene was about L.A. She admitted to living there, but that was as far as she'd go." I looked up at the ceiling as if seeking heavenly inspiration. But the heavens were ignoring me. "Maybe the secrets, assuming there are secrets, can be traced to her L.A. days."

"That brings us right back to Linda. When

you call whomever you're going to call out there, you might come up with something. Hopefully something concrete, not just gossip."

"Sometimes gossip's a good starting point."

Lucy yawned in response. "Do we know anything useful about Carlene's marriage?"

"Nothing. Except that there appear to have been problems. My few, and brief, conversations with Carlene were limited to mysteries and writing. If I broached anything personal, like I did last night, she cut me off."

"This is where Georgia would be a good resource. Hopefully she confided in her."

"I'll call her now," I said, reaching for the phone on the end table. I noticed the blinking voice mail light, but decided it could wait. I reactivated the ringer that I'd put on "do not disturb" the night before. I searched for Georgia's number in the directory, trying the office first. Knowing how she loved her work, I figured that's where she would seek solace, distraction.

Our conversation was short and tearful. Thankfully, Kat had already called her with the news. "She said the police found a suicide note. I can't believe it! Suicide? That's *nuts*. Why, we spent this past weekend at a spa. It was her birthday." I remembered Carlene's stunning haircut and French manicure from the night before. Another no-suicide vote. For what seemed like a long time, but was probably no longer than a minute, all I heard was Georgia's sobs. Finally, she said, "I've got to go. I have a doctor's appointment. Let's talk tomorrow at the office. Will you be here?"

"I'll be there," I assured her. I volunteered for Georgia at the Richmond Women's Resource Center a couple of days a week. "Take care of yourself, Georgia," I said, and ended the call.

I told Lucy about the spa trip, ending with, "So that reinforces our hunch that Carlene didn't kill herself." Lucy agreed.

"So what about Kat?" I looked blank for a moment, still in a reverie about the spa trip. Lucy explained, "We know how she come to be in the group — she was another founding member, likely at Carlene's invitation."

I petted Daisy and considered Kat in suspect terms. "Vince says that in real life, as opposed to murder mysteries, the killer usually is the obvious one. And a family member to boot."

"They could have had stepsister issues," Lucy mused. "It seems like whoever did this had the perfect window of opportunity when Carlene went off on her towel-finding mission and left her mug in the kitchen. I know you told me before, but let's go over it again. Who — besides you — was in the kitchen at the time?"

I thought. "Sarah. A few of us went in and out. Annabel had a phone call and went down to the family room. Kat and Art cut through the kitchen to go down to the family room." We smiled at the vision of Kat showing exercises to a love-struck Art.

"So — that means that five people had ample opportunity. Four, when we exclude you. Would Sarah have a motive to kill Carlene? Remember, she was the reason Carlene left the kitchen."

I spread my hands to indicate being at a loss for a reason that Sarah would poison anyone's tea. "I could see it more with Annabel, what with professional jealousy over publishing."

"But Annabel's pretty accomplished already. She had a head start on Carlene."

"Don't forget Annabel's the one who found Carlene and could easily have deposited the note by her chair. And" — I shook my finger when I remembered yet another reason to implicate Annabel — "there was the business with her husband."

"But she was never tried for that or even arrested —" The sound of the doorbell startled us. Lucy stood and walked through the kitchen to the hall. "It's Kat."

I removed a protesting Daisy from my lap, stashed the envelopes under a cushion, and walked to the front door. Just before Lucy opened it, I stage whispered, "Let's be careful what we say, in case she did it."

"So who the hell killed Carlene?" Kat demanded as she charged through the doorway.

Then she burst into tears.

CHAPTER 4

"Kat, we're so sorry," I said. Lucy echoed my sentiments. We exchanged hugs before Lucy shepherded us into the morning room. "Coffee?" I offered. When Kat nodded wordlessly I went to the kitchen to get a mug. Kat's willingness to accept refreshment struck me as pretty trusting. After all, coffee served the same purpose as tea as a vehicle for poisoning. Of course, if Kat poisoned Carlene's tea she had nothing to fear from anyone else's beverage offerings. If she was innocent, maybe any danger hadn't yet occurred to her.

"I'll get more tissues," Lucy said as she headed for the downstairs bathroom. I poured coffee into Kat's mug and handed it to her, thinking as I caught her miserable expression that if she was the killer, she was either racked by guilt or a consummate actress. I admonished myself not to get carried away with this killer business. I couldn't dismiss the suicide conclusion out of hand.

Lucy returned with a box of tissues and placed it next to Kat. As we sat, I took a moment to inventory Kat's wardrobe. I think that anyone who met the woman, regardless of the circumstances, shared my fascination with her flamboyant style. But the first detail I noticed was one made conspicuous by its absence — something leopard. Her usual black prevailed in her leather jacket and leotard with plunging neckline. Tight stretchy pants clung to her slim, well-developed legs and flared at the bottom. Her mass of blond curls seemed slightly flatter, her abundant eye makeup smudged beyond repair after what looked like a lot of tears. Kat was still "out there," just not as far as usual.

Lucy looked her usual elegant self in her periwinkle robe with a satin shawl collar. My contribution to this fashion show of sorts was a pair of sweats purchased long ago at a California swap meet and socks with holes at the heels.

Kat sat on the end of the sofa and looked down at her lap. "I hope you don't mind me barging in on you like this. I'm meeting Evan and Dean at eleven to discuss the . . . arrangements." Dean Berenger was Kat's father, an affable sort whom I'd met at Evan and Carlene's turkey dinners. He'd spent most of his time standing in the driveway with a can of soda and a cigarette. "In the meantime I couldn't bear being alone." At that her voice broke and tears flowed down her cheeks. My eyes filled and soon the three of us were off on a crying jag.

"I can't believe the whole thing. I can't take it in," Kat sobbed. Then she grabbed my arm with a hand decorated with at least ten rings. "So how are you doing after last night?"

I whispered, "I'm okay." Then, my voice restored, "And Evan?"

"Evan doesn't know what hit him yet. As for Dean, he's full of regret about the past — useless regret, in my opinion. Carlene never really forgave him or her mother for all the hurts of her childhood." Kat blew on her coffee. "I tried to get her to go to Al-Anon but she refused."

"What about her parents? Did someone let them know?" Lucy asked.

"Both dead."

"How did Evan find out?" I asked. "Who told him?"

"He found out because he called Carlene and —" Kat's voice broke again. After a ragged inhale, she continued. "Can you imagine, she died right when they were *talk-*

ing." I had forgotten the male voice yelling through the phone.

Kat continued. "When no one responded, naturally he was frantic — he was at a conference in Northern Virginia, two hours away. He called Janet, their next-door neighbor, to find out what was going on. Thankfully, she has a listed number and Evan knew her last name. By the time he reached her, all hell had let loose, what with the ambulance and police and all. Janet called the police, who of course wouldn't tell her anything, but she told them how to get in touch with Evan." Kat grabbed a wad of tissues from the box. "Then he had to drive back here and be interviewed by the police. So he's had no sleep."

Lucy went to the kitchen and came back with a bowl of fresh fruit and placed it next to the basket of muffins. Kat's tears streamed down her face, making the smudgy black spots under her eyes fade. I couldn't remember a time when Kat wasn't fully made up. She looked younger now, almost innocent. Shammy jumped up on her lap. "Cats know when you need them," she said as she stroked Shammy, who rewarded her with an adoring look. "My Leopold is a huge comfort to me right now."

Kat mopped at her eyes and cheeks. "I'm

sure I look a fright," but seemed unconcerned as she sipped her coffee and seemed to take strength from it. "Anyway, Dean's trying to find Hal. We have no idea how to get in touch with him."

"Oh, Carlene's brother," I said, remembering the sullen-looking boy in the family photograph.

"He's more or less a hermit, holed up in a cabin out in Montana, Wyoming, some godforsaken place. At least that's the last anyone heard. He always was a loner." Unfortunately that description recalled the Unabomber, Ted Kaczynski, a hermit who lived in an isolated cabin in Montana until his eighteen-year career of bombing by mail ended in arrest.

"Until last night, I didn't even know she had a brother." I told Kat and Lucy about the photographs in Carlene's den.

"He probably won't show up, but he needs to know, so Dean's contacting the park rangers out there. Hal is, after all, family." Family — I had to remember that Kat was family, and I was not. Ex-family is what I was. But as I felt like family, I felt left out.

"What I want to know is this: who the hell killed her? And don't say it was suicide." When I saw the set to Kat's jaw, I wouldn't have challenged her even if I did believe it was suicide. "You mark my words, someone killed her, and I'm going to find out who it was. It was the tea . . . something in that tea."

For a moment, no one spoke, just ate. Suddenly ravenous, I scarfed down two muffins. Kat bit into one, spraying crumbs.

"Carlene and Evan were separated, you know." Kat looked at both of us in turn. "Judging by your lack of surprise, I guess you knew that."

"Yes, I ran into Evan at Target and he told me." Lucy shot me a warning look but she needn't have worried. I had no intention of offering up details on the Target encounter. "He didn't say for how long — do you know?"

"About a month or so."

"Where's he been staying?"

"With what's his name . . . Warren."

"Oh, yes, Warren Oglesby — a classmate from Rochester and best man at our wedding." And the reason Evan picked Richmond when he took his lottery winnings and left Rochester to launch his teaching career, having visited Warren often over the years. "He's supposed to have a nice place." Warren, a hotshot lawyer, and his family lived in Richmond's prestigious West End, overlooking the James River.

I wondered how often Evan returned to the house he'd shared with Carlene. After all, he might have needed a certain shirt or tie. Or a try at reconciliation. Or a chance to doctor his wife's tea mug — Stop! I ordered myself. The idea of Evan as wife killer was unbearable. And wasn't poison the weapon of choice for women? I chided myself for thinking in sexist stereotypes.

I lit on safer thoughts — why had they separated? Who had initiated the split? All questions I should have asked that day at Target, but Evan's unexpected dinner invitation put the kibosh on further discussion.

I was about to ask Kat about the separation details when she posed her own questions.

"Have you talked to Vince? Or are you guys in off mode?"

"I haven't talked to him."

When I offered nothing about our current mode, Kat shrugged. "So — my question remains unanswered. Who *did* this? Who killed Carlene?" Kat cursed a blue streak.

I held my hands out, palms up, in a beats-me gesture. At this point, the question was rhetorical. I started carefully. "So you're determined that —"

Kat cut me off before I could get out the "S" word. "Don't say suicide! Carlene did *not* commit suicide."

"Georgia agrees." I described my earlier conversation with Carlene's friend, including their recent spa weekend.

"You see? And Carlene and I had our birthday lunch last week. We went to the Grapevine. She was *fine.*" Kat fixed me with a defiant look. "People in my family don't kill themselves." If I needed convincing that Carlene didn't do herself in, that last rationale didn't do the trick.

I tried another tack. "Did you see anyone near Carlene's mug last night? Did you see anything odd at all?"

"No!" she wailed. "Not a thing."

Changing the focus, Lucy asked, "What about Linda? What do you know about her?"

Kat drew her brows together. "You think she did it?"

"Not necessarily. I'm asking because you seemed to know her and the rest of us didn't." Lucy described her sighting of Linda at the signing and Art's account of the conversation between Linda and Carlene.

"I met her at the signing. She said she knew Carlene from L.A. She asked about the book group, and I started to tell her about it but her husband was pacing around outside. So I gave her my card and she rushed off. She called me a couple of days ago, asking where the group was meeting. Then she showed up last night." Kat opened her hands, palms up. "That's all I know about her."

"Did you talk to her last night?"

"No. Art cornered me and I wound up showing him some exercises." Kat gave a long-suffering sigh.

"At the signing, did Linda say how she and Carlene knew each other in L.A.?"

"No. I meant to ask but, like I said, hubby was in a hurry so our conversation was pretty brief."

Lucy picked up her knitting. Looking thoughtful, she asked, "Kat, were you and Carlene always close?"

Kat laughed and that fond tone people assume when they reminisce about the recently departed came into her voice. "We weren't close at all when we were growing up. My brother and I stayed with her family when my mom went on trips with her boyfriends. I was the classic wild child and Carlene the classic Goody Two-shoes. I embarrassed her to no end. Then she went away to college while I went to the local community college. After graduation she moved to L.A. and I stayed in Virginia. We were out of touch for years."

"How long did Carlene live in L.A.?" I asked.

"Twenty years or so." Kat played with the silver earrings — how many were there? Five? Six? — dangling from her right ear.

"She never wanted to talk about L.A. and I always wondered why. After all, I lived there too, and we were both computer programmers, so we might have known people in common. But whenever I'd mention anything about the place, she changed the subject."

Kat shrugged. "Then I guess she didn't want to talk about it. Carlene was a forward thinker, didn't like to dwell on the past."

"Yes, well, that's a good way to be. Still, it struck me as odd." I waved my hand and said, "Go on."

Kat started turning her mug around in her hands as she took up her story. "I didn't know that Carlene was back in Virginia until my mom told me. One day I called her and we started getting together for lunch, especially for birthdays. I think I still embarrassed her, but maybe she figured people were too busy looking at me to notice her. Probably true. We also had family holidays together — Thanksgiving, Christmas. She and my daughter, Stephie, hit it off. Maybe it was being middle-aged, but we both seemed to have discovered the importance of family, however dysfunctional ours was with all the alcoholism and drugs. We still had little in common, but that didn't matter as much anymore. We didn't hang out together, just developed a kind of mutual fondness.

"In 1999 a lot of things changed. First Carlene's mother drank herself to death. Not long after, Dean retired from teaching and moved down here from Fairfax. The two of us finally owned up to our drinking problems and sobered up together. I was busy with him and didn't see Carlene as much. And I met Evan and we started our relationship. We were never really serious, but . . ."

"Evan?" Lucy and I blurted out at the same time. "Evan Arness? You and Evan dated?"

"Yes — oh — I guess you didn't know that. We didn't exactly date — but we had a lot of really hot sex!" She waved her red talons in a parody of a blaze, then covered her mouth with the same talons. "Oh, Hazel, I'm so sorry. I totally forgot that you and Evan were married or I wouldn't have said anything."

I had a vision of Kat and Evan ripping off

each other's clothes in their passion. Strewn on a path to the bedroom would be her leopard prints and black leather with his polo shirt, khaki pants, and penny loafers. I snapped out of my clothing reverie and waved her apology aside. "It's okay. Evan and I are ancient history."

Lucy, now recovered from her surprise, said, "Tell us about you and Evan. I have to say, I'm simply floored. How long did your relationship last? But first, do you want more coffee?" Kat had stepped up her mug twisting.

"Oh, yeah, sure. Thanks." Now with a full mug, Kat went on. "Our relationship lasted about six months or so. Then, on my birthday in 2000, Carlene, Georgia, and I were having lunch at Chez Foushee — you know that place downtown?" When we nodded, she said, "Evan came in with another guy. I made the introductions. A few days later Evan told me he wanted to ask Carlene out, and would I mind. I did mind but didn't want to admit it. Then Carlene called and said Evan had asked her out and would I mind. I still minded and still didn't want to admit it. They got married six weeks later. Small wedding, just family and a few close friends. They had the wedding brunch downtown at the Kent-Valentine House.

"You asked if Carlene and I were close. We weren't, then we were, then her marriage strained our relationship for quite a while, but over the past couple of years we slowly got closer again. The strain was more on her part, guilt I guess. I got over being dumped pretty damn fast. It's not that Evan and I had a future anyway . . . Like I said, the sex was fabulous, some of the best I've had, and I've been around the block a time or two, believe me." We did. "But I guess you would know how good he is, Hazel."

"I never kiss and tell." I tried for an airy tone. While I had fond enough bedroom memories of Evan, I didn't care to compare notes with others on lovers in common. One of my fictional characters engaged in such cheesy behavior, but I believed in discretion.

I couldn't help but wonder how "damn fast" Kat recovered from being dumped. Great sex plus Evan's lottery winnings made him quite a catch. Although I never knew how much he'd won. With my transparent face, I'd best limit my wondering until after Kat left. "More muffins?" I held the basket out to Kat, hoping to distract any attention from my suspicious thoughts.

"Um . . . yes, I think I will. Surprisingly, this whole business hasn't affected my appetite. It occurs to me that you two may be wondering if I was *really* over Evan." I sighed and vowed to go shopping for a poker face. Kat went on, again getting crumbs everywhere. "Like maybe I longed for him all these years and finally just had to have him. Ridiculous. Why wait this long? I'm not a patient woman. Besides, our Evan turned out to be very possessive and domineering."

"You're kidding!" Lucy looked at me. "I never heard you mention that, Hazel."

"He wasn't like that with me."

"Nor with me," Kat said, her tone wry. She dabbed at her mouth with her napkin. "Carlene brought out something in him that should have — I don't know — stayed in."

I remembered my earlier, unasked question. "Do you think that's why they separated?"

"I'm not sure. I can't help but think the reason was sex-related, like maybe Carlene couldn't appreciate Evan's talents in that department. She was a god-awful prude in high school."

"Really?" Lucy asked.

"To an extreme. I tried my best to educate her about the pleasures of the flesh, get her interested, but she just wanted to study." Kat raised her eyes to the ceiling to convey her attitude toward studying.

"And she never married before Evan?"

"No. She was forty-five when they tied the knot."

"Kat, how did you and Evan meet?" Lucy asked.

"At the gym. I was his personal trainer. It's the best job for meeting guys. All that sweat and state of undress." Kat gave one of her bawdy laughs. Then she looked concerned. "Are you sure you're okay with all of this, Hazel?"

"Absolutely," I assured her with great aplomb. "Granted, you threw me for a loop. It was all news to me. But, like I said, Evan and I were married, and divorced, an eternity ago."

"How long's an eternity?"

"We married in 1972. What's that — thirty-three years? We were seniors in college."

"And how long did you stay together?"

"Two years."

"I imagine your parents weren't too happy about your getting married before you graduated."

"That's putting it mildly. Mine weren't crazy about the whole idea, but they accepted it. On the other hand, Evan's parents were very unhappy when we married and very happy when we divorced. At the wedding they wouldn't speak to me or anyone else in my family. I never knew why. Fortunately for Carlene, they both died before she and Evan met so she was spared hostile in-laws." Then I added, "That's assuming their hostility wasn't reserved for me in particular." An image of them meeting Kat sprang up in my mind and I tried to hide my smile.

But Kat seemed to divine my thoughts. Giving me a shrewd look, she said, "I'm sure you're thinking 'What if Kat met Evan's parents?' I know I'm not the kind of woman a guy brings home to Mom. But we live with our choices, don't we?" I reminded myself that I'd best cease thinking in her presence. Or in any book group member's presence. She laughed, then asked, "If you don't mind my asking, why did you and Evan split up? Was it the hostile parents?"

"They contributed somewhat, but I didn't see them very much even though they didn't live far away. The real reason, I guess, was . . . youth." I was going to leave it at that. I limited discussions of my past, preferring, like Carlene, to move forward. But I found myself continuing. "I'm serious — we were too young. And, like I said before, he wasn't possessive when we were married.

Quite —" I stopped before saying "quite the opposite." I didn't want to get into Evan's open-marriage phase.

Kat and Lucy waited for me to continue, but I didn't satisfy their curiosity. Finally Kat asked, "But you and Evan are friends now. Did you stay in touch over the years, or did you meet up here in Richmond?"

How much did I want to reveal? If Kat was so gung-ho that Carlene hadn't committed suicide, I didn't want to give her any reason to suspect me of doing the evil deed. If I could suspect Kat, she could examine my motives as well. I caught Lucy watching me with her pewter eyes. Would she come to my rescue and change the subject? But she just clicked away with her needles, and I couldn't wait indefinitely, so I said, hoping I wouldn't let something slip, "We always kept in touch. Like I said, I lived in L.A. for years, so we only saw each other when I came back east to visit. Dinner mostly. We sent each other Christmas and birthday cards, and occasionally talked on the phone." I didn't add that the cards had stopped once Carlene came on the scene. As had almost any contact with Evan.

Kat wore a "well, that's interesting" look on her face. "I'm sure it's none of my business, but I have to ask. Did you ever want to get back together?"

I felt like agreeing that it was indeed none of her business, but I controlled myself. "I thought about it from time to time, but always came to the conclusion that we were meant to be just friends — definitely not married."

Lucy offered, "Hazel's mother always liked Evan. She wanted them to remarry." She continued. "She didn't like any of your other husbands, especially that one you were married to for thirteen years. Then there was that other guy you went around with in L.A. She didn't like him either."

"Bill Mason. Funny, I thought she did like him. She confided her true feelings to you more than to me." Funny, because my mom never really got along well with Lucy. "But let's move on. We don't need to rehash my failed marriages."

But apparently we did, because Kat asked, "How many husbands have you had, Hazel? And why didn't your mother like the thirteen-year guy?"

Seeing Kat as she leaned forward, looking her usual animated self, I reconsidered my reluctance to discuss my sorry marital history. If I could divert this discussion from Evan and the events of last night, I'd best grab the opportunity. I briefly summarized my marriages, starting with Bobby Dee, my second husband. We lived together for three years until I got fed up with his philandering and moved out. As neither of us were in a hurry to remarry I didn't bother to divorce him for twelve years. At age thirty-eight, I decided to get my life in order, which meant that hubby number two had to go — legally, that is.

A couple of years later, I married Dan Ricci. That happy union lasted for one year and twelve days. I lost no time in divorcing him.

"What happened there?" Kat asked.

"Cabin fever." Not surprisingly, my terse response didn't work. This time I caved in to Kat and Lucy's expectant looks. "We went to Yosemite and stayed in a cabin. Let's just say it was too close for comfort. However, to his credit, Dan was faithful at least."

"Okay: Evan, Bobby, Dan. Anyone else?" Kat's ticking off the names of my exes on her fingers left me feeling unsettled. Did Elizabeth Taylor ever feel like this?

"The Republican with the earring." Lucy was enjoying herself.

"Yes. Richard." I laughed as I remembered him. "Despite the earring, he turned out to be way too conservative for me."

"The earring fooled you, huh?" Kat chuckled. "Tell me about him."

"There's not much to say about Richard. He was your average trendy Republican." I laughed and shrugged at the same time. "We filed for divorce, but he died before it became final."

"Died? How?"

I described Richard's death during a skiing weekend at California's Mammoth Lakes when he'd managed to wrap himself around a tree, leaving me a widow. He and some sweet young thing had been celebrating our impending divorce. I ad-libbed the sweet part, but as she'd had the temerity to show up at the funeral as the bereaved, um, *mistress,* I could attest to her youth.

Kat looked closely at me. "I can't tell if you're sad or not, Hazel. You're so — I don't know, matter-of-fact about it."

"Yeah, well, it was just another one of those married-today, divorced-tomorrow deals. Widowed, not divorced. Not that I hated him, but still . . ." I trailed off, eloquence eluding me. In truth I had a soft spot in my heart for Richard, mainly because his untimely death had left me financially secure. He'd kept his net worth a secret during a marriage so brief that he died before we could file a joint tax return.

After a pause, Kat pursued a different line of questioning. "So, Hazel, what made you decide to move to Richmond?"

"All those marriages took a toll on me. I found myself at loose ends and needed a change. Lucy had lost her husband recently as well, so she invited me to stay with her for a while." If I went with the long version of the story, and usually I didn't, I'd go on to say that after Richard died I reviewed my options. I no longer needed to endure my high-stress job as a systems analyst for an L.A. publishing company, but I had only three months to go until I was fully vested in my company's 401k plan. The "only" three months turned out to be very long, but they finally came to an end. With great satisfaction I gave my resignation to my Generation X boss — or was it Generation Y or Z? I never got a grip on those alphabetic designations for generations. But he *was* young.

I instantly regretted my decision to skip the long version, as Kat's next question was, "Did Evan know you were moving back here?" I guess it was inevitable that the conversation would turn back to Evan, no matter how many stories I told to delay the moment.

I sighed. "Yes, he did know. As I mentioned earlier, we talked occasionally." I didn't tell Kat that during that pre-move conversation with Evan, remarriage with him seemed like a possibility. A possibility never realized. It occurred to me that Kat and Evan's torrid affair coincided with that same conversation. So Kat and I shared an Evan-related loss at about the same time.

"How did he react?"

"React? He said it would be great to see each other more often."

"And did you?"

"Not really."

Kat raised her eyebrows but didn't comment further on Evan. "Well, Hazel, I didn't realize you had such an interesting past." Kat seemed to have new respect for me now that I'd joined the ranks of those with an "interesting past."

Lucy looked at the cat-shaped clock on the kitchen wall. "Yes, I always enjoy visiting Hazel's interesting past. But I have to cut my visit short — I have a lunch appointment at noon." She put her knitting away in a bag by the sofa and stood. Lucy managed a placement agency in downtown Richmond. She'd canceled an earlier appointment in favor of a debriefing of the events of the night before.

Kat glanced at a leopard bracelet watch

that had until now been hidden under her jacket sleeve. I knew she had to have a leopard item somewhere on her person. Now she said, "I've got to get going too. It's almost eleven." She and Lucy hugged before Lucy sprinted up the stairs. Then Kat rooted through that bag of hers that was large enough to hold all her worldly possessions and maybe even mine and checked her cell phone for messages.

"Let us know about the funeral," I said, again feeling the vague hurt that I wasn't family. If I were, I could be involved in the funeral arrangements. "By the way, do you have a cell number for Evan?"

She gave me a look, like she was debating with herself whether she could trust me. I guess I passed muster because she pulled her phone out of her pocket, checked her contact list, and read off a number that I jotted down on a napkin, my envelopes still under the cushion. I wondered what her reluctance was about — a possible reigniting of their relationship offered a possible explanation.

Kat gently dislodged a reluctant Shammy from her lap. As we walked to the door, she pronounced, "We need to find out who killed Carlene. If we ask around, someone might remember something that's significant. Someone killed her, and I for one am going to find out who it was." She slanted a look at me. "I'd love to have your help with this, Hazel."

I gulped. "Kat, that's a very bad idea. If someone killed her, we don't want to be the next victims."

Kat looked heavenward. "Oh, spare me the mother hen bit. You need to hook up with Vince again. Get him to ditch that red-haired woman. And I guess I'll have to give in to Mick. With the two of them in our back pockets, we'll have access to information *and* protection."

At my questioning look, Kat explained about Mick Jairdullo. "He's this cop I know from the gym and he's been bugging me to go out with him. He's great-looking, body to die for, sexy, the whole bit. But he's got this crazy girlfriend who he claims he's trying to break up with. Beverly. Real nut job. I don't want to get in the middle of that relationship. But" — she threw up her hands — "you gotta do what you gotta do — it's all in the name of justice."

I thought to myself that Kat might also see getting in good with the law as a way of shielding herself if she wound up a suspect in her stepsister's murder. As for Vince, I didn't know if I could "get him" to ditch the new girlfriend, Molly, and I wasn't about to get involved in ferreting out killers. "Yes, well, you need to be careful with the cops as well. Pillow talk will only protect you so much." Kat responded by leveling a look at me with smudged and reddened blue eyes.

"Kat, maybe you can locate Linda. Find out something about her and her relationship with Carlene." Best to let Kat think I suspected someone other than her. Naturally, Linda came to mind as the someone. "You said she called you — was it on your cell phone?" When Kat nodded, I went on. "Is the number in your incoming calls register?"

She got her phone out of her pocket again and checked her log. Then she shook her head. "No, I was afraid of that. I delete my calls right away." I silently cursed the neat freaks of the world with their compulsions to keep even their phone logs tidied up. I went to the kitchen and grabbed the phone book, turning to the listings for the needle-in-a-haystack name of Thomas. I found a number of "Lindas" as well as "L" initials.

"Why does she have to have a name like Thomas?" I griped. "What about her husband? The listing could be under his name."

Kat thought. "I don't think she mentioned

his name. Just called him 'husband.' Hazel, don't worry, I'll track her down. It will give me something to focus on. When I find her, I'll tell her about Carlene. Since she left early last night, she might not know."

When Kat suggested we program each other's numbers into our phones, I went upstairs and retrieved mine. We spent a couple of minutes assigning speed dial designations. For good measure, I suggested that she program Lucy's number as well.

I asked, "Should we send an e-mail to the book group about what happened last night — especially for the folks who weren't there, like Trudy Zimmerman?"

"Is she still even a member? Doesn't matter, I guess. As soon as I know about the funeral arrangements, I'll let everyone know."

After teary good-byes, Kat left and I went back to the morning room. I knew I should check my voice mail, but I stared into space, reviewing the conversation with Kat. It struck me as odd that we hadn't mentioned cyanide, or any poison for that matter. And, despite being fired up about finding Carlene's killer, Kat hadn't presented any candidates for the killer role. Unless I was her candidate of choice . . . Sobering thought.

Had Kat really gotten over Evan's dumping her to pursue Carlene? It was, after all, a long time ago. Wouldn't she be over it by now? How long did one hold a grudge, anyway? When had she found out about the recent separation? Did she know from the start, a month ago? If so, maybe she saw an opportunity for another try at a relationship with Evan and, not wanting to chance that he and Carlene would reconcile, had eliminated the competition. On the other hand, her grief and sorrow seemed genuine enough. Besides, the same speculations could apply to me. I imagined someone posing the argument that following my encounter with Evan at Target, I'd fantasized about getting back together with him and had taken my own measures to avoid being thwarted a second time — and that meant that Carlene had to go.

I resolved to let *no one* in on the details of the Target encounter.

CHAPTER 5

The first voice mail I listened to was from Art. "I'm so sorry about Carlene. *Shattered* is a better word for how I feel. She had a lot of class." Art really did sound shattered. "Call me. I need to talk about this — with someone besides my mother. And I don't want to bother Kat at a time like this." I wrote down his cell number.

"Hazel dear, I heard what happened last night and that you were there." I felt surprised by my relief at hearing Vince's voice. Why did I break up with this nice man? Was he just too nice to wind up on my roster of husbands? "Call me anytime. I'm in San Diego until Thursday. Roseanne's wedding." Roseanne was his daughter. I wondered if Molly had accompanied him to the big do. I didn't need to note the cell number he gave me — after a series of break-ups and makeups, it was easier just to keep his number on my speed dial. I had a one-sided conversation with him via voice mail, assuring him of my well-being — all things being relative.

I punched in Art's number. "Hi, Hazel. How are you doing today?"

"Okay. At least I'm alive."

"Terrible about Carlene," he said. "Just terrible. Do you really think she did it herself?"

Yet another person doubting the suicide. Remembering my promise to Lucy to tread carefully, I said, "Well, there *was* a note." Maybe a hint of skepticism combined with a seeming acceptance of facts struck the right balance of believing yet not believing the suicide idea.

"Art, do you remember at Carlene's signing when you pointed out a woman, saying she was mad that Carlene didn't remember her or her husband?"

"Sure. It was Linda. I couldn't forget that striped hair. No, not striped — two-toned!" Art exclaimed, triumphant in grasping an elusive hair concept.

"It's called highlighting, Art. In her case, violently so."

"And those eyes. The woman looked like a tiger had his — or her — way with a raccoon."

I laughed at the rather apt description. I

asked, "Were you surprised to see Linda last night?"

"I was, considering the conversation she and Carlene had at the signing. But then I thought maybe they'd talked since and Carlene had invited her."

"Hmm. Maybe. But they weren't too chummy."

"So do you know what happened? How she . . . died?"

"I don't. But she had a new tea; I saw her take the cellophane off the box. God only knows where she got the stuff, but I wouldn't be surprised if it had something weird in it." It would be nice for all of us suspects and would-be suspects if the tea purveyors were at fault. But I doubted it.

"Art, do you mind going over what was said between Carlene and Linda at the signing?"

"Okay. The first thing I heard was, 'You don't remember us? You don't remember P.J.?' Carlene said, 'I'm sorry, but I don't,' and she was trying to look around Linda, reaching for my book. So Linda said, 'I wish I could demand my money back, but you've gone and signed it. It's probably crap anyway.' "

"Did you have the impression that Carlene did recognize her?"

With no equivocation, Art said, "Yes, I did."

Interesting. "Then what happened?"

"Linda walked away, stomped away, actually. Carlene signed my book. Her hand shook a little, so she had trouble writing. I tried to make a joke to put her at ease and she gave me a pained smile. A few minutes later, I saw Linda leaving. That's when I mentioned the incident to Lucy and Bonnie Stiller."

"Did anyone else hear this conversation?"

"I don't know. Carlene is — was — so soft-spoken, but Linda wasn't. But it was pretty noisy in the store."

"Who was behind you in line?"

When Art said he didn't remember, I moved on. "And you said Linda referred to someone as P.J.? As in initials?"

"Yeah. Could have been P.G."

"Who do you suppose this P.J. or P.G. could be? You don't suppose she meant something innocuous, like a peanut butter and jelly sandwich?"

"It was a pretty heated exchange. So unless Linda gets intense about sandwiches . . ." Art trailed off.

We reviewed the previous night's events but Art didn't remember much except for Kat and Linda, and only vaguely recalled the cyanide discussion even though he'd participated in it. Not an ideal witness.

"Art, do you remember how you came to join the book group?"

"Yes, Mom told me about it. Can't remember how she heard. She thought we should do something together. Mother-son thing." Art sounded amused.

Art and I talked a few minutes more until he had to leave for his job at Walmart. I sat staring at my phone, like I expected to divine the answers to my questions via technology.

I recalled the conversation Lucy and I had started earlier about Annabel, a conversation aborted by Kat's arrival. Annabel's husband had been shot and killed several years before and the case remained unsolved. His killer was never found, but Annabel had been, and likely still was, a "person of interest" in the investigation. Annabel was not only a spouse, but a published crime writer with an impressive knowledge of murder weapons. But her husband, Greg Mitchell, had been a homicide detective in Charlottesville, Virginia, so the list of possible suspects ready and willing to gun him down was likely a long one.

Annabel's mysteries were gritty fare, set in Charlottesville. The main character, a homicide detective named Gloria Shifflett, mirrored Annabel's experience. After her own husband's unsolved murder, Gloria began specializing in cold cases. The killers invariably turned out to be women killing the abusive, philandering men who'd wronged them. Annabel published a new mystery annually.

So what could all this have to do with Carlene?

"What if Carlene came upon some damning information about Annabel having to do with her husband's murder? What if she used that information to blackmail Annabel? Blackmail is always a good motive for murder."

"Blackmail?" Lucy looked incredulous. "That goes along with cyanide in being a staple of fiction. Blackmail on top of those B.J. initials Art told you about, it all seems like make-believe —"

"It's P.J. or P.G."

Lucy looked askance. "Oh, well, Ps and Bs sound alike. Let's talk about this later. I've got to go." Looking around, she asked, "Did you see my keys?"

"It's something to consider, that's all. Let's be open-minded." I handed Lucy her keys. She was the most organized person I knew — except when it came to tracking her keys.

She picked up her slim-line briefcase. How did she fit anything into that skinny thing? Blowing me a kiss, she said, "Get some rest," and her power-suited figure disappeared through the door.

I started up the stairs, en route to the shower. But the sound of the phone thwarted my plans.

"Hazel. It's Helen."

I held back a sigh. Of course, she could have something illuminating to offer — I just had to steer her away from her soapbox.

She got right to the point. "So do you think Carlene committed suicide?"

As I had with Art, I acknowledged suicide but allowed an element of doubt. "Well, I . . . I don't know. There *was* a note." Once again in the morning room, I plopped down into a rattan chair. "But it's funny . . . Saturday was Carlene's birthday and she and her friend Georgia went to a spa for the weekend, must have spent hundreds."

"That doesn't sound like something you'd do just before you kill yourself." Helen heaved a sigh. "Unless she was worried about looking good — she was so particular about her appearance."

"Exactly. So why pick such an ugly way to

die?" I told Helen my picture of how Carlene would stage her own death: beautifully.
Then, remembering to hold on to the note
of doubt, I added, "But all bets are off when
it came to Carlene. Who could figure her
out?"

"Maybe it has to do with that incident at
the library. She could have felt guilty enough
about that to kill herself." I waited for Helen
to explain her cryptic statements. "Last
week, Tuesday it was, our fiction group met
at the library. Art and I started going there
recently."

Lucy and I had decided a while back to
boycott the fiction group. The members
spent little time discussing books and much
time ranting about bad writing. Not unlike
Carlene's trashing of *Murder in the Keys.*

"Don't they just read contemporary fiction? I thought Art preferred historical set-
tings."

"He's steering them in that direction. He
picked our next book, *A Farewell to Arms.*
But let me get back to my story." Taking a
deep breath, she launched into what turned
out to be quite a tale. "When Art and I first
arrived, we were walking through the parking lot and saw Carlene sitting on a bench
with a . . . *man.*" She paused, like she
expected me to react with horror.

"Well . . . so what? Why can't she talk to a man?"

"It's just that, um, well, there's more." Helen took another deep breath. I hoped she got through this story before she hyperventilated. "Carlene never came in to the group. We waited for a few minutes, then started without her. It was nine by the time we left the library, and we'd forgotten all about her. Art and I stood outside for a while chatting with a couple of women and by the time we walked to our cars, hardly anyone was left in the lot. We saw Carlene's car in the back row, in a dark corner. You can't miss her license plate, it says CARLENE plain as day. So" — Helen stopped, perhaps for effect — "as we walked by the car, we saw two figures in the backseat. First we saw a bare foot propped up against the window of the rear passenger side. Then a figure moving up and down, like . . . you know . . ."

"They were having sex?"

"Yes! Disgraceful. And Carlene a married woman. Art and I were so embarrassed. We moved quickly past the car, trying not to stare."

I felt sure they tried to see whatever they could. I said, "Well," and, not able to come up with another word, said, "Well," again.

Finally, I rallied enough to ask, "When Carlene and the man were on the bench were they sitting close together? Did they seem . . . intimate?"

"No, there was plenty of space between them. I don't think they were even talking. He was sitting kind of bent over, with his elbows on his knees, and his chin in one hand."

I pictured Rodin's famous *Thinker* sculpture. "It sounds like they were having a serious discussion, or an argument."

Helen's tone dripped with sarcasm. "Obviously they resolved whatever it was."

"So, what did this guy look like?" I asked. "The one on the bench?"

"Dark hair. Longish."

"Facial hair?"

Helen thought. "Don't think so, but not sure. It was evening and I couldn't see that well."

"Did you meet him?"

"No, Carlene just said hi before turning back to him. He looked up briefly, then away."

"Did you think it was Evan? He has dark hair. Maybe —"

"Maybe what?"

I tried for a dithery tone. "Oh dear, I lost my train of thought." I'd been about to sug-

gest that they were trying for a reconciliation, but caught myself in time. It sounded
like Helen didn't know about Evan and
Carlene's separation and I didn't want to
enlighten her, at least not yet. Such knowledge could temper her outrage and make
her less eager to share other interesting information.

"Besides, Evan knows us. He would have
said hello."

"Did anyone else see them?"

"No one's mentioned it to me."

"Maybe the guy on the bench and the one
in the car were two different people. And
that allows that Evan could have been the
man in the car."

"No, the one in the car had the same long
hair."

It sounded like she got a good look
through the window despite her claiming
that the car was parked in a dark corner
and that they tried not to stare. But I let it
go.

We mined the cyanide discussion, wondering if we'd missed an indication that Carlene harbored plans of suicide. Something
that made us cry in regret, "We should have
known," "We should have seen it coming."
But nothing came to mind.

Helen muttered something that sounded

like, "Imagine her doing that to my boy." What was she talking about? What had Carlene done to Art? I didn't find out because the policy of not speaking ill of the dead occurred to Helen and she scolded herself. "But one last thing . . . You know, Hazel, God would have forgiven Carlene for her adultery. She didn't have to take her own life. If she'd only been a churchgoer, all this could have been avoided. We'll have to pray for her salvation."

Lest I get grilled about my religious habits, I asked Helen how she and Art first heard about the book group.

"Let's see, where was it? I think at the gym. Carlene posted a flyer."

"So you didn't know Carlene from before?"

"No."

I wasn't getting anywhere with Helen or Art using this avenue of inquiry. Both were vague about their introduction to the group. But sometimes such details were elusive and their not remembering wasn't necessarily significant.

I had paused long enough for Helen to steer the conversation to her favorite subject. "Speaking of flyers — there's a woman speaking at my church next week on stem cell research. A *very* important topic. Do come, and bring Lucy."

I envisioned a church full of Helens descending on us like vultures. We wouldn't get out of there alive. To appease Helen, I asked, "Did you say you have a flyer?"

"I do. I'll e-mail it to you. Let me educate you about stem cell —"

"Got to run, Helen. Someone's at the door." I lied, not up to being educated. After assuring her that Kat would let us know about the funeral, I hung up.

I was fast overloading and shorting out. Too little sleep, too much talking, too much death, plus I was knee deep in maybes and wonderings.

CHAPTER 6

"What's with the sex hair?"

I put my hands on my head and felt matted tufts going every which way. I regretted that the prosaic reason for my tangled mess was sleeping on wet hair. Normally, my hair brushed my shoulders in chestnut waves.

"Oh, I washed it and fell asleep before it dried."

"You must have slept for a long time. It's seven thirty now." Lucy smiled at Shammy and me. Daisy looked up from her seat on Lucy's lap, yawned, and went back to sleep.

"Since about one, I guess. After you left, Helen called. Then I took a shower, started rereading *Murder à la Isabel,* and drifted off."

"Did you glean anything from your reading?"

I sighed. "Not a thing." I'd had hopes of unearthing a clue that might explain Carlene's death. But I felt none the wiser for having read her book, if in fact I read it at all before sleep took over. "Unless I registered some insight at a subconscious level. But who knows when, or if, it will surface."

I'd awakened from my long nap with Shammy tucked behind my knees. Now she stood by my side in the morning room. She probably figured that I needed watch-cat services. I picked her up and scratched her ears.

Lucy's fingers flew through the same teal afghan from that morning. This time her robe was a deep eggplant. She didn't have a separate closet for her at-home wear, but it was just a matter of time before she'd need one. Mendelssohn's Violin Concerto emanated from the CD player. I liked classical music, but the Mendelssohn piece was one of the few I could identify with confidence.

Lucy's brows drew together. "What about those roots?"

"I know, I know. I'm calling Rhea in the morning."

"Hungry?"

"Starving."

"How about some scrambled eggs?"

"Yes, comfort food. Thanks." Somehow I thought it would take more than eggs to regain my comfort level, but I'd take what I could get.

"Let's talk while I fix them. I called you earlier but I guess you were already out cold." Lucy eased Daisy off her lap and set her knitting beside her chair.

Lucy broached her favorite subject, Vince. "He left several messages." When she paused to check my reaction, I kept my face blank. "I didn't want to wake you, so I called him. He says to call anytime. I guess he told you he was in San Diego for Roseanne's wedding."

"He did." I sat at the table and regarded the Norman Rockwell plates bordering the room.

Lucy opened the refrigerator and took out an assortment of egg-related items. Giving me a sly look, she said, "Maybe some good will come out of this whole sorry mess if it brings you and Vince together again."

Did I hope something would come of it? Okay, I did, but hesitated to openly admit it. "Cool it on the matchmaking, Lucy. Besides, that fiery-looking Molly is probably with him."

Before Lucy could come back with a rejoinder, I asked, "Why did you call me earlier?"

"To see how you were doing and to find out if you'd heard anything interesting. Any word on Evan?"

"Not yet. But Kat gave me his number. Reluctantly, I might say. I'll call him after we eat."

"Speaking of Kat, she sent an e-mail to the book group. The memorial service is on Friday at eleven, at St. Bernard's."

"Why St. Bernard's? Did Carlene go there?"

"Don't know."

"I didn't think churches held services for people who weren't members."

"Depends on the church I guess."

"And you said memorial service. Does that mean no funeral, as in . . . no body?"

"Correct. She's being cremated, either tomorrow or Thursday. As soon as they finish with the autopsy and toxicology tests. Apparently she and Evan drew up wills when they married and she specified cremation." The idea of cremation made me wince. It was fine in theory, but I didn't like thinking about it.

"And the church is okay with her committing suicide? A lot of churches frown on that." Wouldn't God have compassion for someone despairing enough to commit suicide?

Lucy had nothing to offer on church attitudes toward suicide. "Back to Evan. I went by the house and saw the crime scene tape. This tiny blond woman named Janet was getting her mail from in front of the house next door. We recognized each other from the turkey dinners."

"Was she the one he got in touch with last night?"

"Yes, she said she was. When I asked if she'd talked to him she said she had and that he was staying with a friend. We talked a bit about last night, but I didn't learn anything new. She did mention that the police had talked to her and the other neighbors. Oh, and that Sarah had just been by with a casserole that she left with Janet. And so —" Lucy said with a hand flourish, "What did Helen have to say?"

I recounted Helen and Art's coming upon Carlene and the "man in the car." Even if I ever learned his identity, I would probably continue to think of him as the "man in the car."

Lucy and I looked at each other for a moment, clearly admiring the impropriety of the very proper Carlene. I said, "It's sure funny how the same actions that get you branded a floozy at sixteen give you sex goddess status at fifty. Middle age has its perks."

"I guess there's an element of excitement in doing it in a car, in a public place," Lucy allowed. "Doesn't one of your characters, someone in our age bracket, do it in a car?"

I smiled. "On the hood of a car. And yes, she and her lover are in their fifties." When I started my romance-writing career the year before, I heard a lot of pooh-poohing of my plan to feature characters enjoying sex in middle age and beyond. Time would tell if they were right, but I was determined to prove it didn't take elastic breasts and a wrinkle-free complexion to enjoy sex. "Carlene's definitely going into my next book. In fact, she has recurring character potential."

"I can just picture prim and proper Helen coming upon that scene."

I laughed. "She was quite indignant." Yawning, I said, "The man could very well be Evan. Even though Helen claimed it wasn't based on the fact that the guy didn't say hello. Maybe he and Carlene were reconciling. At least temporarily."

Lucy whisked eggs in a glass bowl and added shredded cheese and roasted red peppers. She held up four slices of bread. "Toast?"

"Sure." I stifled another yawn and got up to fix some herbal tea. "I want to know who these mysterious people are — P.J./P.G., the man in the car, Linda . . ." I trailed off. "And what did you think about that stuff Kat told us about Evan?" Without waiting for Lucy's response, I went on. "First Evan dumps Kat in favor of Carlene. Then, adding insult to injury, he marries Carlene, becoming Kat's step-brother-in-law. And possibly Kat envied Carlene her book success. Very classic. You don't suppose . . . ?"

Lucy poured the egg mixture into a pan sizzling with olive oil. "Well . . . she was quite open about her relationship with Evan and how he dumped her. Would she do that if she'd just done Carlene in the night before? However, you're right — she certainly had powerful motives of jealousy and revenge. And who knows what their childhoods were like, with all that alcoholism. Lots of grudge potential there."

"Want some Sleepytime?" Lucy nodded and I dunked teabags in two mugs of water and placed them in the microwave. "But after all this time?" Wasn't there a statute of limitations for grudges? Granted, I held somewhat of a grudge against Evan for going off and marrying Carlene, but it was a low-level and passive grudge, as grudges go.

Lucy continued. "But you know something? I tend to think Kat didn't do it. She seems so genuinely sad. And I don't think she's a good enough actress to fool us. She's too out there. And if she killed it would be in a physical way, something with her hands, like strangling, stabbing, not poison. Poisoning's a sneaky way to kill."

"She could probably kill someone with a well-placed karate chop. She does have a black belt."

Lucy nodded. "You have to match the person to the crime."

When the microwave beeped I took the mugs out. Lucy set two plates on the table. With a sour-lemon look at the mugs, she asked, "Isn't it kind of creepy to drink tea so soon after last night?"

I looked at Lucy. "I didn't even think of that. And I won't start now."

We tucked into our food and ate in silence. I felt ravenous, like I hadn't eaten in days, and restrained myself from licking the plate. "Thanks for the great food, Lucy."

"Back to Kat, I'm pretty sure she didn't do it, but I'm not a hundred percent sure — so be careful."

"I will. I will." I held up my hands in mock surrender. I wasn't entirely convinced of Kat's innocence myself, so I'd give it further thought.

Lucy ignored my look of wry amusement. Then, trying for a casual tone, she asked, "Are you going to call Vince tonight? It's three hours earlier in San Diego."

"I'm aware of the time difference, Lucy.

Don't worry, I'll call him. After I call Evan."

I turned the conversation in a different direction. "You know, Lucy, I need to find out who did this."

"I hope that doesn't mean you plan to play amateur detective."

"Lucy, the woman died right in *front* of me. The two of us started the book group together, so I feel a responsibility to at least try to get some answers. Granted, I wasn't crazy about her, but she didn't deserve to die like that." Finished pleading my case, I shrugged and smiled.

"You always did have a strong sense of justice. I remember visiting you when you were only ten and you'd be outraged at something you read in the paper about a bad deal someone got." Lucy sighed. "And just how do you intend to get these answers?"

"Talk, snoop around, ask questions. The usual."

"The usual," Lucy snorted. "Hazel, my dear, dear cousin, the 'usual' can get you killed."

"I'll be careful, I promise. Tell you what, I'll act at all times like I don't know anything. I can't be a threat if I don't know anything."

Lucy gave me a long look. "If you're hell-bent on doing this, promise me you won't be alone with anyone from the group. *Ever.* If you have to meet face-to-face with anyone, I'll go with you. Just call."

"Oh, so now you're my official bodyguard."

"Damn right."

I thought Kat would make a better bodyguard. Another reason to drop suspicion of her — I could take advantage of her muscle.

I hunted for the napkin I'd used to scribble Evan's cell number and headed back to bed. I stifled a scream when his electronic voice exhorted me to leave my name, number, and a brief message.

"Evan, I'm so sorry. Carlene was a lovely woman." I sounded like someone's elderly aunt, but I felt strapped for sincere platitudes. I thought about trying him at Warren's house since I knew he was probably there, but decided that calling him on one number was sufficient. I speed-dialed Vince.

He answered immediately. "Hazel! How are you holding up?"

"Frankly, I've been better. I keep seeing poor Carlene, the way she looked . . ." I trailed off and shuddered. "But I've been so busy — or so asleep — that the whole thing hasn't hit me." Shammy joined me on the bed. I adjusted the pillows behind my head. "How did you hear about it, Vince? I'm sure it didn't make the San Diego news."

"Dennis called me. He knew I'd want to know." Dennis Mulligan and Vince were long-time partners in the Richmond Police Department. "He remembered when Carlene consulted with me about her book. And he knew you were there last night."

"You've probably already heard, but the memorial service is on Friday at eleven. Will you be back by then?"

"Yes, I'll be back on Thursday night." He paused. "How's Evan doing?"

"Don't know. I tried calling his cell but wound up leaving a message. Kat says he's staying with his friend Warren."

Vince turned the conversation in a direction I'd hoped to avoid. "According to Dennis, Evan and Carlene were separated."

I vowed to keep my responses short, hopefully to one syllable. "Yes."

"So you knew about that?"

"Yes." Then my mouth disengaged from my brain and I heard myself adding, "I ran into Evan one day. At Target. He told me then." I prayed my brain and mouth would synchronize before I spilled the beans about the Lemaire proposition. For a distraction, and because I did want to know the answer,

I asked, "How long will the house be a crime scene?"

"Hard to tell. Probably not long."

"The place is so clutter-free it should take about thirty minutes to process it."

A long pause followed. Vince, while retired, hadn't forgotten about the silence tactic police used in interrogations. The human tendency to fill the silence with talk often works to police advantage. The real problem for me was Vince's soft-spoken Brooklyn accent, an accent that invited confidences, the baring of souls, the baring of . . . No lascivious thoughts, Hazel, I admonished myself. Focus on the matter at hand. I doodled on my envelope and scored a mini victory when Vince broke the silence. "How's Kat taking this?"

"She's pretty shaken up." Should I tell Vince about Kat and Evan's past relationship? I stopped doodling and made a note to think about it.

"Did I tell you I saw Kat and Evan at Chipotle's over at Stony Point?" Was the man reading my mind? Scary thought.

"And?"

"Well, that's it. I saw them."

"When was this?"

"Last week. Maybe the week before."

"What were they doing?"

"Eating."

"So?"

"Just thought it was curious, that's all."

"They couldn't have been doing anything intimate with all those windows at Chipotle's." As much as I like Chipotle Mexican fast food, I didn't find the fishbowl atmosphere conducive to a rendezvous.

"No, they probably just ran into each other." Based on my earlier conversation with Kat, I felt a stab of skepticism about the just-running-into-each-other idea. As I'd wondered earlier, when did Kat find out about Evan and Carlene's separation?

"Did you talk to them?"

"No, I didn't have time. We just waved."

The Chipotle sighting was interesting, but I still didn't feel comfortable talking about Kat and Evan. Redirecting the conversation, I asked, "You said you talked to Dennis. Any word on what it was that . . . killed Carlene?"

"Not yet. Hopefully tomorrow we'll know. You gave the pathologists a good lead with the bitter almond smell."

"Detective Garcia didn't seem impressed. It's nice to know she gave my nose some credence."

"Detective Garcia is a woman of few words, but she's a damn fine detective."

Let's hope so, I thought. Aloud, I said, "Anyway, I hope no one gets any ideas about calling me in to assist at autopsies."

Vince snickered. I had a mental picture of him, and a pleasant picture it was: tall, broad-shouldered, shock of white hair, slate-blue eyes. Easy to get along with — except that somehow we didn't get along. Hmm — did that make me the difficult one? The Dr. Phil intervention would have to wait. There were more pressing matters at hand.

I asked, "Where was the cyanide? In the tea? Is it like sugar?"

"We won't know for sure until they finish with the toxicology testing. Cyanide is a white powder, but I'm not sure if the consistency's like sugar."

"This is all pretty fast, isn't it? The autopsy and results."

"Unless there's a backlog, it doesn't take long."

"And Carlene's being cremated as soon as the results come in — gives me chills just thinking of it." I felt myself choking up and took a deep breath. "By the way, where do you get cyanide?"

"It's used in pest control, gold plating, photography, jewelry cleaning. When I say photography, I mean the darkroom type. Of course, a chemist might have it."

Who in our group would have such a chemical on hand? Or access to one? No one had confided in me about a pest control problem. I mentally scanned the interests of the members, trying to recall any avid gardeners, jewelers, or photographers. Helen used a digital camera for her website work, so didn't need darkroom chemicals like cyanide.

"Does anyone still develop in darkrooms?" I jotted down another note, this time to consider cyanide possession possibilities.

"I'm sure plenty still do." Then Vince asked, his voice gentle, "Do you feel like talking about last night?"

"Sure." I took a couple of deep breaths. Where to begin? At the beginning, I guess. And so I launched into the unbelievable tale of my first, and hopefully last, death experience. "Well, last night our book group met at Carlene's and . . ." A disjointed mess of facts, "and-thens," "what-ifs," and just plain angst came tumbling forth at breakneck speed. Vince listened and, save for an occasional uh-huh, didn't interrupt. His long career as a homicide detective hadn't been in vain — he was up to untangling such all-over-the-place accounts.

By the time I finished, I'd managed to cover every detail from my arrival at Carlene's to my much later arrival home. I described Carlene's tirade about the book, the ominous cyanide discussion, Linda's appearance, my discussion with Carlene, the "huge mistake" bit, the logistics of the tea mug, the love fugitive plot of Carlene's third book, Annabel's shrieking, and a host of other details, large and small. After all, the solution could be hidden in a point I deemed unimportant.

"I really think Linda is a key figure. The woman just shows up and Carlene dies. I believe in coincidences, but this is too much of one."

"Are you questioning the suicide?"

"Well . . . there was that note."

"Yes. And I'm sure that doesn't convince you." Like a mere note was proof? I never bought the easy answers; I expected complications and difficulties. Vince knew that about me. The book group members did not, a fact that could work in my favor when I pretended to buy the suicide with the attendant note.

"Anyone could have left that note — Annabel, of course, since she found Carlene. But we were all down there in the family room running around like chickens without heads."

A back-and-forth about the suicide question followed. Vince snorted when I presented Carlene's spa day from Saturday as an argument against her killing herself. "You've always claimed you didn't know her, that she refused to disclose much of herself, but now you're reading her mind."

"No, I don't claim to know, or even guess, what Carlene thought or felt about anything. I do know that she looked better than ever last night. That is, until the end." My voice caught on that last, but I plowed on. "A woman hell-bent on suicide doesn't invest in herself that way."

"Maybe she wanted to look good when she died. If Evan's the one who precipitated the split, she wanted to send a message: look what you gave up."

"That's assuming the split was Evan's idea."

"Well, that really doesn't matter. Regardless of whose idea it was, she may very well have been distressed about the breakup. It's hard to say what will drive someone off the deep end."

"And why pick cyanide? She couldn't have looked worse." I shuddered again. "But maybe she didn't realize how she'd look. In detective stories, they never mention how someone looks. They just slump over their tea or whatever. And then I have this *House of Mirth* theory . . ."

"*House of Mirth?*" Vince groaned. "You mean that interminable movie you made me sit through?"

"It was a great movie." I outlined my idea of how Carlene would have picked Lily Bart's suicide method and be found prettily dead and alone in bed, as opposed to how she was found: flushing and foaming at the mouth like a menopausal, rabid dog while hosting the book group. I failed to impress Vince.

"I was just glad that she, meaning the character, did die and the damn movie ended. You *may* have a point about Carlene's vanity determining her choices, even in death. But you said she brought up the cyanide topic during the book group. And that she seemed distressed."

"People get distressed and don't do themselves in. Besides, distressed isn't quite the right word. Agitated is more accurate. As opposed to her usual calm, serene self. Besides, there's her book success. Despite the thing with Evan, things were looking up — oh, I forgot about the Costa Rica trip." I told Vince about Carlene's travel plans and how she asked me to have coffee with her and Georgia. "She wanted travel tips about the country. Does someone plan a trip and then turn around and kill herself?" Vince allowed that suicide didn't follow.

"Of course, I don't want to get carried away here. It's certainly possible that she did commit suicide. Who could figure the woman out anyway?" I moved on to share the conversations I'd had earlier, starting with the man in the car.

"Sounds like this was an ongoing relationship," Vince noted when I finished. "Maybe ongoing encounter is a better word."

"Why, I didn't think of it that way. I had an idea he was someone new." I resolved to start thinking outside the box and wrote it down to be sure I remembered. "Do you think he was the reason for the separation?"

"Could be. Just speculation, of course. What other conversations did you have today?"

I told him about Art's description of Linda and Carlene at the signing. Despite my earlier decision to keep quiet about anything to do with Kat and Evan, I wound up spilling the beans on their hot affair. Other than agreeing that it was a funny combination, strange bedfellows and all that, Vince had little reaction. I imagined that as a cop he'd seen and heard it all.

After a pause, Vince asked, "Did Carlene and Linda talk to each other last night?"

"Not that I saw. I'm sure Carlene was avoiding Linda. She seemed puzzled that Linda remembered her so well when she didn't remember Linda. Personally, I think she remembered Linda very well, and that she wasn't a pleasant memory. I never saw Carlene so rattled. Of course, she was rattled before Linda showed up . . . That could mean that she knew ahead of time that Linda was coming . . ." I trailed off, trying to collect my thoughts. "I thought Linda and the huge mistake might be connected."

"Did you talk to Linda?"

"No. She was in the dining room describing her colonoscopy to Annabel. I didn't want to interrupt." Vince hooted. "She left early, way before anyone else did, so the police don't have any contact information for her, and no one else does either." I told him about Kat's deleting Linda's number from her incoming call register.

"You say you were all in the dining room when Carlene closed the pocket doors to take her call in private. Did Linda look for Carlene to say good-bye?"

"No. I distinctly remember that because I thought it was funny that she didn't ask where Carlene was, or say, 'Well, tell her I said good-bye,' something like that. She just left by the front door. Of course, Carlene had ignored her, so she might have been miffed about that."

"And now a word of caution, Hazel." Vince, in police mode, echoed Lucy's earlier words. "Don't discuss this information with anyone, especially not with your group members."

Sniffing, I said, "Well, since I was there last night, I have a vested interest in anything to do with what happened."

"Not if it puts you in danger. Keep in mind that if Carlene didn't die at her own hand, she died at someone else's, likely someone in your group." Vince issued the expected warnings about not being alone with any of them, avoiding eating or drinking anything with them, and so on.

"Okay, let's wrap this up. You must be exhausted. Will you send me a list of names and addresses — snail mail addresses — of everyone in your group? I'll run background checks on them."

"And are you going to share your findings with me?"

"Only if appropriate."

"Will you at least give me Linda's number? To welcome her to the group and all."

He ignored me. "By the way, did you ever figure out how to use the camera on your cell phone? Are you even using your phone?"

"Um, well, not too much. But I did take a picture of Daisy and Shammy." Shammy, nestled against my thigh, looked up at the sound of her name.

"And how long ago was that?" I had no idea, but hastened to assure Vince that I knew how to use the camera and that besides, I had a manual. Vince said, "Remember, if you have a killer in your group, you'll need protection."

"And taking pictures of this would-be killer will protect me?"

"Just humor me, Hazel. Use your phone. You may need to use it quickly." Vince paused for a moment. "Again, be careful. You're too curious by half."

"Is curious a euphemism for nosy?"

He laughed but didn't disagree. Echoing Lucy's earlier remark about my concern for justice, he said, "You do have a vigilante streak." Now he became earnest. "Hazel, I don't want to lose you. Keep your phone on and with you at all times. Familiarize yourself with the camera feature so you can take a picture at a moment's notice. Is my number on your speed dial?" It was, but I didn't want to admit that. "Uh, no. But don't worry, I'll take care of it." After he gave me Dennis Mulligan's numbers to assign on speed dial, he said, "Call me tomorrow?"

I assured him that I would, and we hung up. I got out of bed, trying not to disturb Shammy, and walked down the hall to my den where I turned on my computer. After sending the book group directory to Vince, I read e-mails from Kelly Justice at the Fountain as well as Lelia Taylor from Creatures 'n Crooks, both of them offering glowing tributes to Carlene as an up-and-coming author. I looked at the e-mail that Kat sent:

As many of you already know, my sister, Carlene Arness, passed away last night at her home from unknown causes. She was hosting Murder on Tour. All who were present are devastated at the loss of this talented woman. Evan is inconsolable.

As the group's cofounder, she offered unique insights into our reading selections. And her recent publication of *Murder à la Isabel* was a huge success, the start of what promised to be a long and successful writing career.

A memorial service is scheduled for

Friday, October 14, at 11:00 at St. Bernard's Episcopal Church.

Fondly,
Kat Berenger

Various replies followed, along the lines of "Just awful," and "I still can't believe it," "Poor Evan," "I'm so sorry for your loss." Helen said she'd pray for Carlene's soul.

Annabel sent a message to the group, omitting Kat as a recipient. "Does anyone know what Carlene ingested?" No one had responded, not even with a speculation.

I opened Helen's e-mail with the attached flyer promoting the lecture on stem cell research. Above a photo of a woman wearing pearls and hair sprayed to within an inch of its life read the caption: "Stem Cell Research: What You Need to Know." I hit the delete button.

Lucy and Daisy came up to my den and plopped down on the day bed. Lucy said, "Tell all."

"I didn't talk to Evan, just left a message. As for Vince . . ." When I got to the part about Vince's sighting of Evan and Kat at Chipotle, Lucy looked thoughtful. "Well, that either means something or . . . it doesn't. It's possible they just ran into each other and talked." She petted Daisy, who

131

gazed at her with adoring eyes. "But in view of what she told us this morning, it might very well mean *something*."

"I wonder if Kat got an invitation to Lemaire?" We shared a laugh when we tried to picture the stir she'd cause if she walked into that traditional restaurant in one of her leopard getups.

Lucy was disappointed in my lack of progress in getting back together with Vince. "You just have to look smashing at the memorial service."

The unwelcome specter of Molly loomed. What was the point of putting energy into developing, or redeveloping, anything with Vince if he and Molly were an item?

"Don't forget Molly."

"All the more reason to knock his socks off on Friday."

CHAPTER 7

I loved Richmond's northside, with its historic neighborhoods and beautiful mansions dating from the turn of the twentieth century. Much of the area had been developed by Lewis Ginter, a philanthropist who had made his fortune in the tobacco industry. Remarkable architecture abounded in neighborhoods like Ginter Park and Bellevue. A brick Georgian Revival mansion, complete with stone gates and expanse of lawn, housed the Richmond Women's Resource Center. With earplugs I could imagine the original beauty and tranquillity surrounding me. Otherwise I had to endure the present-day reality of RWRC's noisy neighbor, Interstate 95.

The Women's Resource Center's stated mission was to plant the seeds for girls and women to grow and succeed in life and in their careers. To that end we provided counseling services, along with career and personal development services.

The house stood flanked by magnolia trees; Ionic columns supported a wide veranda. Even recent events couldn't take away the delight I always felt when I approached the postbellum mansion that RWRC had appropriated ten years before. In the early 1900s a new set of owners added a third floor as well as an "East Wing" in the Colonial Revival style that blended well with the Gothic Revival style of the original "West Wing." In the latter part of the twentieth century the house was updated to be handicapped accessible by adding a tower to the east side of the house. The beautiful result ensured that the house would remain a community treasure for years to come.

Georgia Dmytryk pulled into a parking space just as I started up the steps leading to a small wooden veranda. I waited for her and we hugged before proceeding into the house. A woman sitting at the reception desk took off her reading glasses and set them on the newspaper she had spread on the desk. She greeted us in warm, dulcet tones. I guessed her to be the temp filling in while the office manager was out on maternity leave.

"I'm Vivian Durand. And you must be

Hazel." I shook the ringed hand she offered me. Vivian arranged her golden-going-on-gray hair in the long-ago fashion known as the Gibson Girl, a poufy updo not unlike a mushroom, albeit an attractive one.

The phone rang and when Vivian answered I noted her professional and soothing phone manner. Georgia nudged me and said, "Let's go to my office and talk."

Not for the first time, I admired the way Georgia carried herself. Georgia and Carlene had shared not only a childhood, but a commitment to perfect posture. I'd often teased them, asking if they'd spent giggly girlhood sleepovers walking around with books on their heads. In fact they had done just that, with Georgia winning their contests to see who could walk the longest without dropping her book. With her regal bearing and statuesque figure she reminded me of a ship's figurehead. Her dark hair swung in a harmony only found in an expensive cut — likely the result of the spa weekend she'd shared with Carlene.

We walked into Georgia's office. RWRC may be a nonprofit operation, but it was a classy one. A crystal chandelier presided over the large space with its floor-to-ceiling windows, just-for-show fireplace, and Oriental carpet. Georgia motioned for me to close the door. I did so, then sat next to a potted something-or-other. Georgia's haggard and drawn face revealed at least one sleepless night. "Can I get you something?" I asked. "Tea? Oh . . ." I started rummaging through my tote bag. "I brought some banana bread. Courtesy of Lucy."

"No. No, I'm fine." Not a convincing fine, but as my nurturing talents were limited, I let it go.

Then Georgia wailed, taking her glasses off and setting them, lenses down, on a desk the size of my dining room table. Not the time to tell her how damaging that was to the lenses. She mopped the tears that streamed down her face and put her head in her hands. Tears were contagious and soon we were crying together, sharing the box of tissues on her desk.

When our tears subsided, Georgia asked if I'd seen the obituary in the paper. I nodded, but didn't comment on the brevity of the piece. "Beloved wife of Evan" and the memorial service logistics were included, but nothing on her family or background. I guessed that Evan had provided the information and either didn't know his wife very well or chose to honor her tight grip on privacy.

Georgia started to reminisce about Carlene, aka Carly. That suited me, as I wanted to get going on my so-called investigation. I deemed Georgia to be my best source for Carlene-related information. Reminiscing was a good way to start and could turn up something unexpected.

"Carly and I met in first grade, up in Fairfax. My family was loving and close-knit, so Carly spent a lot of time at our house. Her parents were always drinking, occasionally fighting, but usually they were passed out, so things were quiet. They pretty much ignored Carly and her brother, Hal. Eventually they divorced and her mother married Dean Berenger. You know him, don't you?"

"Yes, I've met him at the turkey dinners." The same place where I'd met Georgia, who had lost no time in enlisting me as a volunteer for RWRC. *No more turkey dinners,* I thought, feeling disappointed and a little selfish.

"Did you and Carlene go to the same high school?"

"Yes. We were good students, nerds actually, always with our noses in our books. Neither of us dated much in high school, we weren't even interested, although we did go to the prom with equally nerdy guys. We were curious about sex, and my mom told us a little, admonishing us to wait for marriage. Kat told us a lot, but she didn't suggest waiting. As it happened, neither of us waited for marriage, but we were well into college before we, let's say, succumbed.

"And Carlene didn't just succumb, she got so into sex that she worried me to no end. I was always concerned she'd get into trouble with her freewheeling lifestyle." Fresh tears streamed down her face unchecked. At least Georgia didn't have to worry about ruining her makeup, because she never appeared to wear any, a grooming choice at odds with her high-maintenance hair and nails. I admired her bronze polish, a departure from the burgundy shades most women favored.

Georgia continued. "It was almost like she led a double life. She was always and forever the perfect lady. From the time we were little kids she was polite, refined, soft spoken. When she discovered sex she remained that same lady and became a hedonist at the same time."

"How *did* she discover sex?" This business with a sexual alter ego was intriguing, as I'd only known Carlene in her perfect lady mode.

"When Carly was a senior at the University of Pittsburgh, she had an affair with a married professor. Until then, her experience was limited to one boy from college, who wasn't exactly sexually inspiring. But the professor took his teaching responsibilities into the bedroom and showed Carly a world of pleasure. After graduation she moved to L.A., where her college roommate lived. She embarked on a sexual odyssey that lasted for years. She and the roommate lived together for a while but had a falling-out over Carly having breakfast sex in the kitchen.

I tried to stifle a laugh, but didn't succeed. Georgia started to laugh too, that cleansing laughter that often follows sadness, shock, tragedy. We laughed until our stomachs ached, then laughed some more.

The more I learned about Carlene's adventures, the more I felt like a voyeur. But my plans to immortalize her by making her a character in an upcoming book provided a ready rationalization. Georgia said, echoing my thoughts, "She definitely belongs in the pages of your book, Hazel, or the next one, anyway."

It occurred to me that Carlene's book contained no sex scenes or sexual references. Why would such a sexually adventurous woman populate her book with squeaky-clean characters? When I asked Georgia for her take, she shrugged.

"All kidding aside, Carly was pretty reckless and I often feared for her health and safety. She had a lot of partners, and would try anything, at least once. I don't even want to think about some of the things she told me." Georgia blotted her eyes. "I hope I don't sound like I'm antisex, because I'm not. I just think she used it to seek validation."

Maybe, maybe not, I thought. It could be that the woman just plain liked sex. "I don't mean to question her truthfulness, but did you believe all her stories?"

"Yes, unfortunately. I wish I could say she was spinning fantasies — but she was always truthful when we were growing up, so I have to say that I think her tales were true." Georgia's face clouded. "What I *don't* believe is that she committed suicide. Was it that tea that she drank? Is that what did it? I never trusted that stuff — wouldn't touch it with a ten-foot pole."

"It probably was the tea." As gently as I could, I told Georgia about the possibility of cyanide in the tea.

"Cyanide! That's nuts. Carly wouldn't take cyanide. I think I told you that we spent the weekend at a spa. We had a wonderful time. It was Carly's fiftieth birthday, you know." Georgia smiled at the memory. "Of course, I just got the basics: facial, massage, mani/pedi. Carly got all that plus an herbal wrap, mud bath, and a few other things. Spent a *fortune.* On the way home, we went to a jewelry store where she got diamond studs and a second hole pierced in each ear. And that *still* wasn't enough — we had to stop at a tattoo parlor where she got a toucan tattooed on her ankle."

"Oh, for your Costa Rica trip. I remember the toucans from when I went there." The large-billed birds populated the rain forest in great numbers. "You know, on Monday night Carlene and I arranged to meet with you and talk about your upcoming trip."

Georgia shook her head in disbelief. "I ask you, Hazel, does this sound like a woman about to commit suicide? Does it?"

Naturally, I agreed with Georgia's stance, but still wanted to play both sides of the suicide argument. "Was Carlene upset about anything? Was the separation weighing heavily on her mind? Was she in despair?"

"Oh, so you know about the separation." With a wry tone, Georgia said, "She was happy enough about that." With a start, she backpedaled. "I'm sorry, Hazel. I forgot that

Evan was your ex. And you two are still friends, I know." *Were we still friends?* That question hung in the balance. I assured Georgia that she could speak freely.

"Kat said there was a note . . . was it handwritten or typed?" When I said handwritten, Georgia said, "Well . . . anyone could write a suicide note and copy Carly's writing." Then she looked stricken. "But that implicates . . . one of you. And I'm sure none of you would do it. It's too scary to contemplate."

"Let me tell you about the other night." I recounted Carlene's edginess, the ranting about the book, then the question she posed to me about making a huge mistake. I included the love-fugitive angle planned for the forthcoming book.

"And this Linda . . . did Carlene ever mention a Linda Thomas?" When Georgia looked blank, I told her what I knew about Linda, both from the signing and from the other night.

Georgia shrugged her eyebrows. "I missed all that drama at the signing. I do remember someone who looked the way you described. But —"

"That's another funny thing — sorry for interrupting. Carlene was reticent about all things L.A.-related. Why do you think that was?"

As she was already nodding, I took it that Georgia knew about the L.A. ban. "Your bringing up Los Angeles takes me back to when Carly moved back here. She was afraid of somebody, although she was never specific. She mentioned a stalker and a doomed love affair. And a fiancé. I don't know if the fiancé and the stalker were one and the same. I assumed the fiancé was the other party in the doomed love affair. But I couldn't say for sure.

"So she moved back here, I guess to flee from the stalker. She wanted to start over and be respectable and she saw disassociating herself with L.A. as a way to do that. She never even went back to visit."

I shifted in my chair, wondering where to start in this dizzying array: fiancé, stalker, doomed love affair. "Tell me about the fiancé."

"Beyond his being a lawyer, I never heard much about him. He didn't last long, just one of those here-today-gone-tomorrow deals." Georgia spread her hands in a helpless gesture. "That's all I remember."

"Okay, how about the doomed love affair that may or may not have involved the fiancé? What did she tell you about that?"

"Other than that it had occurred, not much. Funny thing, she was closemouthed about it, even when it must have been going on. What I remember is this: in 1996 Carly told me she was moving to Richmond. She didn't want to go home to her alcoholic parents, so I insisted she stay with me until she found a place. Like I said, she was unhappy and needed, as she put it, a complete overhaul. Unusual, because she didn't usually take the end of love affairs to heart. In all honesty, she was rather shallow, but that may be due to her upbringing. At any rate, something, or someone, was troubling her. But, aside from tossing about hints and innuendos, she wasn't inclined to discuss any of it."

"So it sounds like she was a fairly open person until these events that immediately preceded her moving back here."

"That's right. Then she became just as closed as she'd been open before."

"What about the P.G. or P.J. that Linda brought up? Does that ring any bells?" Georgia looked down for a moment before shaking her head. I added, "It was likely someone they knew, or at least Linda knew, from L.A." But that didn't help, as Georgia continued to move her head from side to side, reminding me that Carly didn't like to talk about L.A.

"And what about this big mistake? I tend to think it's tied in with Linda."

"Based on what you've told me, Linda could be a pissed-off wife or girlfriend. Her showing up like that the other night makes me mighty suspicious."

I agreed. "But I don't see how she managed to put something in the tea. And we don't know how to get in touch with her. No one has her phone number, e-mail address — nothing."

"Maybe Creatures 'n Crooks has her information in their customer records." I grabbed one of Georgia's Post-it notes and made a note to follow up on her suggestion. Lucy's office was near the store. They weren't likely to give out contact information, but Lucy might be able to stop in and ferret out something helpful.

"Did Carlene have any other close friends?"

"Not here. Maybe in Los Angeles, but I doubt it."

"Did she mention anyone in particular from out there? I might know someone."

"That's right, you lived there too." She pressed her lips together in concentration. Slowly shaking her head, she said, "Can't think of anyone."

"What about the stalker? Any clues about him?"

Georgia placed her hands palms up in a "beats me" gesture. "She just mentioned it in passing one time and then clammed up." When I noted that a stalker was a funny thing to mention in passing, Georgia agreed. "But she didn't seem upset about it, just matter-of-fact. I figured he was back in L.A., so she felt safe here."

Like a stalker couldn't find her in Richmond? In this age of technology, it would be child's play. Aloud, I said, "I wonder if she planned to draw on her experience with this stalker for her next book." Stalker and love fugitive struck me as being twin concepts.

When Georgia shrugged, I left the stalker topic. "So, you said she stayed with you when she moved back here . . . How did that work out?"

Georgia gave a short laugh. "Oh, it was interesting. She surprised me by wanting to go to church with me. Carly had never been religious. After my divorce a friend took me to this wonderful healing church. They provided a lot of support and activities for the kids and me. It was much more fundamentalist than I was used to, but that didn't seem to matter. They frown on sex outside of marriage. I wasn't having sex anyway so it was a nonissue."

Georgia paused before going on. "As it turned out, Carly had attended a similar church in Los Angeles with the fiancé. She liked our church and got involved in the activities. She deemed the sex taboo a good idea and decided to be celibate until she married. I was highly skeptical, but kept my thoughts to myself. Just in case she was sincere, I didn't want to discourage her."

We didn't speak for a moment. Georgia opened a desk drawer and took out a box of tissues, replacing the now empty one on her desk. I tried to marshal my thoughts about the "new" Carlene.

"How long did she attend the church? Or was she still attending?"

"No, she only went for a while. Her mother died from alcoholism and she found solace at church. But after she got a place in the Fan she lost interest. I think it had to do with that Randy." From the way Georgia's face clouded, I surmised that Randy didn't top her list of favorite people.

"Randy? That's a new name . . . tell me about him."

"I don't remember much, not even how Carly met him. From all appearances they had a stormy relationship. She complained about him being possessive and domineering, bossy."

Hmm. Another possessive and domineering guy. Perhaps Carlene was drawn to such men. Or she brought out those qualities, I thought, steadfast in my belief that Evan did not come by such traits by nature.

"Sounds like it had to do with sex." When Georgia looked confused, I explained, "You know, makeup sex."

"Maybe. But she wasn't sharing details of her sex life with me anymore. Maybe she thought the church had made me judgmental. I never thought it had, but maybe she saw things differently. Like I said, our church takes a stand against sex outside of marriage. It doesn't *necessarily* follow that the members obey the rules. Still, she may have felt uncomfortable in church if she was having sex and stopped attending for that reason."

"Did you ever meet Randy?"

"Once. For the life of me I couldn't see the attraction. Middle-aged bald guy, pug ugly. Full of himself. When Gary and I got married, Carly didn't bring Randy to the wedding. He wouldn't have mixed well with our fundamentalist group. Surprisingly, she came alone."

"Was he married?"

"Yes, but separated. Long divorced by

now. In fact, his ex-wife, Trudy, is in your book group."

"Trudy! Trudy Zimmerman was married to this Randy character?"

Georgia nodded, looking puzzled by my reaction.

Now things were getting interesting.

CHAPTER 8

Like most book groups, we had a contingent that attended for a while before moving on. Some found our practice of discussing multiple books rather than a single one too radical. Scheduling conflicts provided an effective all-purpose excuse — one that may or may not be true. The truth could be that they didn't care for the people, the books, or how the group was conducted. The scheduling conflict excuse that Trudy Zimmerman cited for dropping out of the group was a case in point.

At the time, I took the excuse at face value. I had thought Trudy was content enough with the group. As expected of a librarian, she displayed an impressive interest in and knowledge of books. If we'd given prizes for the best book summaries, she'd have won hands down every time. She was less forthcoming on a personal level, revealing little beyond being divorced with no children. As Carlene was equally reserved, I didn't attribute Trudy's manner to any dissatisfaction with the group. But with Georgia's bombshell, I wondered if Trudy's defection had to do with Randy and Carlene.

"When Trudy started going to your group, Carly wasn't sure if she was Randy's ex. She never met Trudy or even saw her, but did know she was a librarian. And Trudy had a different last name from Randy. But, after all, how often do you hear the name Trudy? Especially Trudys who are librarians in the Richmond area? Naturally, Carly didn't want to ask, so she just figured it was the same Trudy."

"And we don't know if Trudy was on to the fact that Carlene was Randy's former lover?"

"No, Carlene couldn't tell. She said Trudy was decent enough to her. Not exactly friendly, just decent."

I mused. "I bet Trudy found out when Carlene's book was published. Carlene used the author name of Carlene Lundy Arness. So back in the Randy days she was Carlene Lundy?"

"No. Carla Gennis. When she moved here she changed from Carla Lundy to Carla Gennis. Gennis was a family name."

"Still, Trudy could have found out — maybe Carlene or Annabel mentioned something."

Georgia's eyes widened and she covered her mouth. "I just had a horrible thought. You don't suppose . . ." Her voice trailed off.

". . . that Trudy did it?" I finished her sentence. "She wasn't there. Hasn't been in a while. And she's on her honeymoon and not due back for another week."

"Really? She got married?"

"She did. On board an Aegean cruise. Kind of a whirlwind deal — according to Sarah, who sees her a lot, she met her husband about six weeks ago."

"Well, good for her. I hope she's happier with him than she was with Randy."

I asked, "By the way, where did Carlene work? Before she became a full-time writer?"

"Different places. She did a lot of contract work."

"So, getting back to Carlene and Randy — how did their relationship play out?"

Georgia put her fingers on her forehead, striking a thinking pose. "I don't recall all the details. She was still seeing Randy when she met Evan. I was there when Kat, who was dating Evan at the time, introduced them." Georgia paused and slanted a look at me. "Did you know about Evan and Kat?"

"Yes, Kat told us yesterday." Realizing that Georgia was the perfect witness to the Carlene-Evan-Kat triangle, I asked, "How did Kat take it at the time?"

Georgia thought. "I don't remember her having a problem with it. But she pretty much has an easy-come, easy-go attitude about life in general and men in particular."

"So you don't think she could have done it?"

"Oh, heavens, no. She showed up at Carlene and Evan's wedding with a date and seemed unperturbed. And she wasn't one to hide anything or pretend . . . If she was pissed with you, you knew it. Like anyone, she probably didn't like being dumped, especially for her stepsister. But I think she just let it roll off her back and moved on."

With Lucy's tepid vouching for Kat and Georgia's more wholehearted endorsement I felt ready to declare Kat suspicion-free. "Well, Lucy and I don't really feel like she could have done it." I omitted the back and forth we'd had on the matter.

Redirecting the conversation, I asked, "So what happened to Randy?"

"He got dumped. And he didn't take being dumped graciously. He caused a scene outside Carly's house in the Fan a couple of times when Evan was there. One time the police came. It was in the paper."

We shook our heads in amazement. I felt hard-pressed to reconcile the taciturn and low-keyed Carlene with this vixen of sorts. "Do you think she was faithful to Evan before they separated? Did she mention another man?"

"No, no one. And as far as I know, she was faithful."

When I told Georgia about the man in the car, she sighed. "Like I said, she didn't mention anyone, but anything was possible with that woman. And the backseat of a car would fit right in with her need for adventure."

"Maybe the man in the car was the 'big mistake'!"

"Maybe. I just hope it wasn't Randy. He'd sure qualify as a big mistake."

"Hmm." I had nothing to add to Georgia's somewhat rhetorical statement, so I switched over to Evan. "Tell me about the separation. I have to say I was surprised to hear about that."

"I wasn't." Georgia looked grim. "Gary and I had dinner with Carly and Evan a couple of times. Are you sure it doesn't bother you if I speak frankly about Evan?" When I shook my head, she said, "I never liked him because he watched Carly like a hawk, which she didn't like either. And I think he was jealous of her book success — he wanted her all to himself, didn't even want to share her with the reading public. Gary thought that Carly came on to him, meaning Gary. I never saw any indication of that, but frankly I didn't trust her with men. She wasn't malicious, just loved men much too much. I got so I'd rather see the two of them in group situations, or Carly alone.

"Anyway, Carly said she felt smothered. She was too free-spirited for a possessive guy. And the fact that Evan was supporting her financially didn't help. She was glad to be able to write full time, but was planning to return to her, as she put it, 'day job.' "

"Yes, it takes a while to make a living as a writer."

Georgia carried on with her story. "One day in September, I met her for lunch. She said she and Evan had separated on a trial basis. Actually, she considered it permanent; the trial part was just to soften it for him. He called and stopped by the house constantly. Carly was fed up with him and I think she worried she had another stalker on her hands."

Again, I felt denial rising in me. It was bad enough to consider Evan as domineering and controlling, but to add killer and stalker to the mix was going over the top. And hadn't Georgia described Randy in similar terms? "You said that Randy was domineering as well. It sounds like Carlene was attracted to such men."

"Could be. Although she always said she wasn't." I resisted the temptation to comment on Carlene's psychology. "After they separated, I didn't say much to Carly about Evan. It's best not to in these situations. I just said I'd be supportive. About three weeks later, she had her signing at Creatures 'n Crooks. We met at a restaurant in Carytown for dinner. She seemed more relaxed that evening, said she hadn't seen or heard from Evan in a week. But toward the end of the evening she became rattled and edgy. Not terribly so, but it was enough of a contrast to how she'd been earlier." Must have had to do with Linda. Georgia drew in a deep sigh and new tears welled up in her swollen eyes. "I'm so glad I got to spend her birthday with her."

Her voice broke and I reached out and touched her hand, assuring her that she was fortunate to have had that time with her lifelong friend. We talked for a few more minutes until Georgia said she had to get some work done. "I have to do something normal."

As I gathered my purse and overstuffed tote bag, I asked, "How's Vivian working out?"

Georgia waggled her hand back and forth. "Oh, she's a mixed bag. Great on the phone — that voice, you know. But if she's not reading the paper, she's going on and on about her wonderful son. Calls him 'baby boy.' " Georgia rolled her eyes. "This so-called baby works in the state Attorney General's Office. The other day she showed me an article about a woman who found her birth mother after a search of twenty-five years."

"Persistent, wasn't she?"

"I'll say. Vivian said she didn't agree with this business of searching for birth mothers. Then she proceeded to tell me what 'baby boy' — who apparently is adopted — said when she told him about the article: 'Mom, you're my mother and you're the only mother I've ever known. Maybe my birth mother is out there somewhere, but I have no desire to find her. After all, she gave me up, didn't she?' Of course, she looked quite pleased to have such a loyal son.

"Oh, she's a good person and I'm sure

her son's wonderful, but still. A little less talk about him would suit me just fine. She doesn't say much about her husband at all."

I left Georgia to her various tasks. After leaving the banana bread in the staff kitchen, I proceeded to the volunteers' desk. Most of the staff had arrived by then.

After fielding questions about Carlene's strange death, I called Lucy and asked her to go over to Creatures 'n Crooks and see what information she could assemble about Linda from the signing. She agreed and said she had an errand to run in the area at lunch and would swing by the store then. She'd pick up a copy of *Murder in the Keys* if they had one. I told her I'd fill her in later on my conversation with Georgia. I didn't want to conduct a private conversation with several sets of ears in hearing range.

I mailed out donor acknowledgment letters and managed some routine database maintenance, but my mind refused to focus on my work. Not surprisingly, it focused on Carlene and her mysterious sex-laden past. I felt convinced that her huge mistake had its roots in L.A. and that Linda was either involved in it or at least knew about it. The fact that Carlene's relocation to Richmond marked her transition from openness to reticence, a reticence that lasted until two days ago, indicated that something went awry on the West Coast. The mistake likely had to do with the doomed love affair, stalker, fiancé, and God only knew what else. Any one of these dramas held mistake potential. Taken in combination, they added up to trouble — in other words, a "huge mistake." I hoped to enlist Susie Abbott, my friend and former coworker from my own L.A. days, in getting information about Carlene's past.

At one o'clock I gave up trying to be productive, at least as far as the center was concerned. I decided to swing by the library even if Trudy was away. It might be interesting to survey the site of Carlene's parking lot rendezvous.

Georgia was on the phone, so I mimed a good-bye and see you tomorrow.

I walked to my car, my head spinning with Carlene minutiae. Was Georgia right in thinking that sex was Carlene's undoing? Georgia's description of Carlene's sexually active lifestyle suggested that her death was punishment for sexual "sinning." My mouth twisted in distaste at the notion, but a number of people held such beliefs. Was Georgia one of those people? Did her fundamentalist church teach along the lines of divine retribution?

Divine retribution . . . now that was scary stuff.

CHAPTER 9

Based on Helen's account, Carlene's back-seat assignation with the man in the car took place in the farthest corner of the back row of the library parking lot. As I headed that way I barely missed a collision with a woman in an SUV. Her simultaneously lighting a cigarette and wedging a cell phone between her ear and shoulder as she steered hampered her progress in backing out of her space. Not for the first time, I rued the day that multitasking became a valued skill. A skill few people possessed.

I dodged a few more oblivious drivers and pedestrians before reaching my destination. Once I nosed into a space I sat and reviewed my surroundings. Oak trees provided heavy cover for the spaces in this back row where the lighting was sparse at night, making it an ideal trysting spot. I considered Randy a viable candidate for the mysterious lover. Georgia's description of him as bald didn't eliminate him as a candidate — a toupee or hair plugs were easy enough to come by. I smiled at a vision of the toupee falling off in the backseat. A character in my book has a similar experience.

A tinny rendition of "Fly Me to the Moon" sounded from my phone. Realizing that Vince was right about my phone, I'd turned it on that morning and tucked it into the deep side pocket of my purse. My challenge was remembering to recharge the battery before it pooped out. I also remembered my promise to get up to speed on taking pictures. I'd practice on the cats when I got home. And there were those numbers Vince had given to me to add to my contact list. No question about it — I had to spend time with my cell phone later.

Vince's name showed on the tiny display screen. He dropped the news that wasn't news at all. "I wanted to tell you about the test results — the tea was full of cyanide."

"Oh. Okay. Not exactly a surprise." I took a deep breath. "So I guess the cremation's next." We said nothing for a moment, perhaps honoring the gravity of the situation.

I related the highlights — and lowlights — of my conversations with Georgia, including the very, as the British put it, randy

Randy. We ended the conversation with Vince saying he'd call the next day from the airport. For a few moments I sat in my car, gazing into the middle distance. The stress of the past couple of days descended upon me in a cloud and I felt weary to my bones. This investigating business required energy. It was time to head to the gym for some recharging.

I turned my key in the ignition, drove out of the lot, and headed south.

I saw Kat before she saw me. Like the day before, her outfit was solid black, save for her leopard-print shoes. She chatted with the young woman who worked behind the check-in counter. "Hazel!" Kat exclaimed. "I'm so glad to see you." The young woman, Amy, smiled a hello.

As I returned my scanned card to my gym bag, Kat said, "Let's talk." Before I could say yea or nay we were sitting at a wobbly table in the café area. "Want anything?" Kat gestured toward the counter. I shook my head.

Kat's reddened eyes indicated bouts of crying, but her heavy makeup appeared to be intact. She said, "I'm trying to get Amy to do something different with her hair." Amy habitually pulled her curly hair into a tight bun on top of her head. It looked painful.

"Good idea. But you know, Kat, if I'd adapted her style thirty or so years ago, I might have avoided this facial sagging. I'd likely be bald . . . But, looking at it from the bright side, I could wear a wig, not have to worry about my roots, and have a sag-free face to boot."

We laughed for a moment before Kat ended the small talk. "Mick and I are having coffee later."

I tried to recall someone, anyone, named Mick. "Oh, Mick. Your police friend. With Beverly the crazy girlfriend."

Kat snickered. "Yeah, I've got to watch out for that one. Anyway, Mick told me about the autopsy results." She gave me a meaningful look. "Cyanide."

I nodded. "Vince told me."

"Vince! Does that mean you two —"

"No. It doesn't mean a thing. We just talked, that's all."

Kat gave me a measuring look before going back to Mick's report. "He says the results confirm that the cyanide was in that wretched tea. I wonder if it was in that crap all along — God only knows where it comes from."

Kat drew a deep breath. "So . . . the

cremation is tomorrow."

"It's all going so fast." At Kat's perplexed look, I explained. "The autopsy, testing, cremation, memorial service. I just expected it to take longer. And the church —"

"It's all Warren's doing. St. Bernard's is his church, so he got us in there. And the medical examiner goes to the same church and is Warren's great pal. It's who you know, and Warren knows a lot of people."

"Are you going? To the . . ." The very word stuck in my throat. ". . . cremation?"

"Not me, I couldn't take it. Evan and Warren are."

After a pause, Kat said, "I want to find out from Mick what the cops are saying about this, if they really buy the suicide bit. And if they have any suspects." Kat's eyes filled with tears. "Hopefully not you or me. It's bad enough that I to have cope with Carlene's death, but being a suspect on top of it would be too, too much."

"No, it's not a thrilling prospect."

Kat produced a tissue from her cleavage and dabbed at each eye. "Damn! I don't want to cry now."

"It's okay to cry, Kat." I tried to sound soothing.

"No it isn't," she said with gritted teeth. "We need to find out who did this, who

165

killed my stepsister."

"I'm still wondering about Linda."

Kat looked thoughtful. "I'm coming up with zero on her. I searched for her online but, like we said yesterday, there are lots of Linda Thomases out there. And I called all of them, along with the L. Thomases. I wish we knew the husband's name."

I shot Kat a look of admiration. She'd acted like a real detective, calling the names in the directory. Besides not being a real detective, I was a lazy one. Kat spread her hands on either side of her face in an unwitting imitation of *The Scream,* that famous painting by a Swedish — or was it Norwegian? — painter. Instead of screaming, she settled for a sigh. "We have to find her."

I asked, "What did the husband look like?"

"Tall, skinny, blond hair going gray." Another one of those descriptions that fit thousands of men in Richmond alone. Why couldn't I get a description of someone with turquoise hair and a limp? Kat continued, "And he wore a knit shirt, the kind with those two-toned panels." Kat's curled lip indicated her opinion of that fashion choice.

"Did you hear any conversation between Linda and Carlene at the signing?"

"No. I only met Linda when she was leaving."

"Well, let me tell you what Art told me." When I finished, Kat said, "It sounds like Linda deliberately sought me out to pump me for information about Carlene."

I shrugged. "Could be. Did you tell her about the book group or did she bring it up?"

Kat thought. "I think — I think *she* did, said she heard that Carlene had a book group and asked if I belonged to it. So I told her about it and gave her my card. Then she left."

"And she said that she knew Carlene in L.A., right?"

"Yeah, she did. But she said nothing about Carlene not remembering her."

"Funny. Because if she was leaving when she talked to you she must have already had the conversation with Carlene. Did she seem pissed at all?"

"Not that I recall." Kat rested her chin in her hands and pressed her lips together. After a moment, she said, "But you don't kill someone for not remembering you. Do you?"

"No. But I suspect that Carlene did remember her. And the memory wasn't pleasant. I think that explains her agitation from the other night."

"We have to find Linda. That's all there is

to it. I'll call Creatures 'n Crooks."

"Oh, Lucy was going over there at lunch-time. Let me give her a call." I looked around. It was a little after two and few people worked the machines and the group exercise rooms were empty. But Kat was popular and no telling who might interrupt us once members started pouring in. Talk of murder required privacy. "Can we go next door to Starbucks? It's easier to talk there."

Kat told Amy she'd be back in "a few." In Starbucks, Kat opted for a vanilla Frappuccino. I wasn't hungry but I hadn't had lunch, so decided on a blueberry muffin and a latte, remembering in the nick of time to specify a ceramic mug. I usually made the effort to bring my travel mug for coffee occasions, but didn't feel like making the trip to my car. As usual when I found myself buying coffee I gritted my teeth at the exorbitant amount of money I handed over to the server — excuse me, "barista." Oh, those pretentious terms born of the Seattle coffee invasion. I joined Kat at a table by the window, away from the other patrons.

I took my phone out of my purse and speed-dialed Lucy. I dispensed with hellos and dived right into my purpose for calling. "Did you go to Creatures 'n Crooks?"

"Well, hello to you too. Where are you?"

"At Starbucks, next to the gym. Talking to Kat."

"Okay. Yes, I did go. I got *Murder in the Keys* and talked to Lelia Taylor. When I asked her if she was aware of an altercation between Carlene and a customer, she said she'd been pretty busy, but did remember this woman with bizarre highlights." If Linda took up a life of crime, assuming she hadn't already, she'd do well to rethink her hair-coloring options. Lucy went on. "The woman left the signing table but went back a few minutes later and said, 'So, Carlene, or whatever your name is now, maybe you should write a book about death by drowning. True crime, of course.' Then she winked and walked away again."

"Sounds like a threat to me. What did Carlene do?"

"She left shortly after that, said she didn't feel well. According to Lelia, she looked pretty stunned."

"I'll bet she was. Did Lelia have a customer record for Linda?"

"No, nothing for a Linda Thomas. She didn't recall ever seeing her before. And Linda's a person you'd remember. So either one of the shop assistants sold the book to her and she paid cash, or she got the book someplace else and brought it into the store for the signing. Kind of crass if she did that."

"Okay, thanks. See you at the house."

When I told Kat, she sighed in frustration. And when I asked if she'd ever heard of anyone named P.J. or P.G. she screwed up her face in thought. But the initials didn't ring any bells and she slowly moved her head from side to side.

Kat asked, "Have you heard anything else?"

One sticking point remained for me in clearing Kat of suspicion: the Chipotle lunch. Going for the direct approach, I said, "Vince said he saw you having lunch with Evan at Chipotle's."

Kat looked first startled, then exasperated. "So? Oh, I suppose that means that Evan and I plotted to kill Carlene so we could live happily ever after?" Kat put her head in her hands and groaned. "It was *Chipotle's,* a frigging fishbowl. Hardly a place for romance." She said romance with the accent on the second syllable and a flourish of her hand, tipped by red leopard-print nails.

I found her reaction over the top, but tried to mollify her. "No one said it meant anything. Vince just mentioned it when we talked last night." Trying for a casual tone, I asked, "So, how did you happen to be hav-

170

ing lunch with Evan?"

"I ran into him at the T-Mobile kiosk. I said I was headed for Chipotle's and did he want to join me. He said yes. That simple."

"When was this, anyway?"

"At least a month ago. Maybe three weeks, I dunno."

"Did you know that he and Carlene were separated at the time?"

"Yes, he told me that day. He kind of hinted around that we should get back together, but I pretended not to take the hint."

"You weren't even tempted?"

"Not really." Her eyes twinkled, and she revised her claim. "Okay, I was. Like I said before, the sex was to die for. But it occurred to me that the whole separation thing could be very temporary and then, once again, I'd be dropped like a hot potato. *Not* appealing."

Kat didn't add anything more about Chipotle and possibly there was nothing more to add. I had no choice but to give her the benefit of the doubt, at least for the time being.

I nibbled on my muffin, finding that I was hungrier than I'd thought. Before I could introduce Helen's man in the car sighting, Kat said, "I talked to Georgia earlier."

"Yes, I talked to her as well."

"Anything interesting?"

"Well . . . Carlene had some trouble when she lived in L.A. Did Georgia tell you anything about that?"

"No. We didn't get past reminiscing about high school. What kind of trouble?"

"No one really knows." I ran down my conversation with Georgia, hoping that I didn't sound insulting or judgmental of Carlene. I felt like I was violating Carlene's privacy, as everything I said seemed to be news to Kat. If she'd wanted Kat in on her drama, she'd have shared it with her. As Kat sipped she alternated between concern, alarm, and delight with Carlene's sexual hijinks.

"Fiancé, stalker, doomed love affair, fundamentalist church? I never heard about any of this. Who on earth could the stalker be? And why didn't she ever tell me about her riotous sex life? I thought she was a prude."

"You said you fell out of touch with her until she moved back here. By that point she was closemouthed. Remember how I said that she didn't want to discuss L.A.? She didn't want to the other night either, when Linda arrived."

"Linda again." Kat gritted her teeth. "She

172

must be involved in this L.A. story."

I agreed and sighed. "There's more. Helen called."

Kat's face clouded and her voice took on an edge. "And?"

I told Kat Helen's tale about the man in the car. Kat took it in, looking grim. When she spoke it was only to say, "My sister was no prude, was she?"

"Definitely not," I said as I finished my last crumb.

Tears welled in Kat's eyes and spilled over. As they streamed down her cheeks, I looked for tissues, but Kat grabbed a napkin from a pile on the table. "I'm glad she discovered sex and enjoyed it so much — but it sounds like it had something to do with getting her killed. Now Helen would say that was true, she'd call her a sinner." Her voice bitter, she went on. "Helen was here earlier and asked me if I thought Carlene had committed suicide. I said, 'Oh, Christ, no.' Of course, I got a chiding look for taking the Lord's name in vain. Then she asked, 'So do you think someone *poisoned* her?'

"I said it certainly looked like it. I asked Helen if she saw anyone hanging around in the kitchen. We got into a cagey discussion with Helen claiming that she wasn't, after all, on kitchen patrol and didn't want to finger anyone, although she managed to finger several of us. She said Annabel got a call and went out to the kitchen. And you and Sarah were by the refrigerator, whispering."

I explained to Kat how I went into the kitchen for creamer when Carlene was fixing her tea. "When Sarah showed up saying there were no towels in the bathroom, Carlene went to find some. She probably left the tea unattended in the kitchen. I mean, why would she take it with her?"

Kat said, "And Art and I traipsed through the kitchen so I could show him those exercises in the family room. Helen didn't mention that as it would implicate her dear son, although it's possible she didn't see us. She didn't see Linda in the kitchen, and neither did I — still, Linda's an unknown, so she wound up in first place on Helen's likely suspect list."

Kat pounded the unsteady table, making it bounce. "We've got to find Linda."

We sat for a few moments, listening to our own thoughts as we downed our coffee concoctions.

When it was time for Kat to lead her group exercise class, we went back to the gym and headed for the locker room. She repaired her ravaged face as best she could and I donned a long T-shirt and leggings, the same outfit I'd worn for ten years. I found a treadmill where I could watch CNN. But my news watching was short lived, as I heard an appreciative "Hi, Hazel" and turned to find one of my favorite gym denizens on the treadmill next to me.

"Joe!" I exclaimed with delight. "It's so good to see you." I tried not to stare at his muscles, very evident in his tank top and shorts. Dark hair lightly salted with white trailed from the bottom of his baseball cap with "Cincinnati" emblazoned across the front. A tiny diamond stud sparkled from one ear while a wide gold ring decorated the third finger of his left hand. Sigh. Once again my thoughts strayed to my hair. By my best estimate, Joe's age was close to mine. Men could be sexy, hot, at any age, but women didn't enjoy the same perks. Sixty is the new forty, the media proclaimed. But the media was full of it. I felt skeptical enough of the media's news coverage, so why trust them with age perceptions? Did people believe the hype?

Joe asked, "How's the writing going?"

"I'm working on the final draft." It felt nice to talk about normal stuff, not death.

"Speaking of writing, did you know that

woman author who died?"

So much for the normal stuff. I looked at Joe and nodded. "Carlene Arness. Not only did I know her, but I was there when it happened." At Joe's amazed reaction, I gave a bare-bones account of Carlene's harrowing death.

Joe shook his head. "What a dreadful experience. Cyanide, huh? Suicide?"

As Joe wasn't involved in the group, I figured I was safe in airing my views with him. "No one knows yet. But I don't buy the idea of suicide." I didn't go into Carlene's past with the murky characters, love fugitives, lovers, and so on, or even her recent past with the man in the car. I did present her publishing success, spa day, and upcoming Costa Rica trip as arguments against suicide.

I heard strains of music, the kind of dance music Kat played for her class. When I turned I saw a latecomer to the class closing the door behind her. "Do you know Kat? The trainer here?" When Joe smiled and said, "Oh, yes," I told him about the connections she and I had to Carlene.

"Amazing! Stepsister. Ex-wife." Joe shook his head again. "How's her husband holding up?"

"From what I understand, he's devastated." I sipped from my water bottle. "They were separated, but still . . ."

"Any children?"

"None." I put my hand up at that point and said I'd just as soon not talk about it anymore. Joe said he understood and started to run on the treadmill. I resumed watching CNN, but had no idea what I saw. Whatever it was paled in comparison to the drama in my own world.

Joe interrupted my reverie. "Got to get back to work." He stopped the treadmill, cleaned it off, and said, "Take care of yourself, Hazel." I watched him as he walked away, sweat pouring down his face, and envisioned him in the pages of my book.

I smiled.

CHAPTER 10

Lucy and I sat in the kitchen, twirling linguine topped with Lucy's award-winning marinara sauce. The particulars of the long-ago award had faded into obscurity, but not the wonderful taste and aroma. When I finished updating her on the day's conversations, Lucy said, "I'm relieved that we decided to trust Kat."

"Yes, nobody can fake tears like that. I really feel bad for her. It's hard to suspect someone you pity."

Lucy looked thoughtful as she speared a lettuce leaf. "And she's going out with Mick to keep in the information loop?"

"And maybe for protection. Since she's as against the suicide verdict as I am, she realizes that someone killed Carlene and may not stop at one death."

Lucy grimaced at that. "Well, let's move on." Shaking a finger at me, she started. "What about your cell phone? Vince was right about the camera."

"Okay, after dinner, you and the felines can pose for me. And quit shaking that finger at me."

We sat in silence for a few minutes. I finished my pasta and put my fork on the plate. Lucy put her elbows on the table and folded her hands under her chin. Her plum polish was the exact shade of her blouse. "So," she began, "let's see where we are now. We have Linda and Annabel . . . Trudy would've been a good suspect, but this marriage of hers puts a damper on that idea. That bit that Georgia told you about Carlene having an affair with what's-his-name was interesting."

"Randy," I supplied.

Lucy stood to clear the table. "So far Art, Helen, and Sarah look innocent. But maybe we'll come up with something on them."

"At this point, my money's on Linda. I wish I could get a handle on this P.G./P.J. person. Somehow it seems important. I hoped Georgia might know, but she didn't. Neither did Kat."

"Are you sure it refers to a person?"

I hadn't considered that possibility. "Well . . . no." I remembered my decision to make "thinking outside the box" my new mantra.

Once the kitchen was tidied up, we went upstairs, where I took photos of Lucy and the cats. It didn't take more than a minute to refamiliarize myself with my phone's camera feature, and the results were acceptable, even recognizable. But the point of the exercise was to become a quick draw, meaning I couldn't fumble with the danged thing, looking for the right menu options.

I set to adding Dennis Mulligan's numbers — office, cell, home — to my contact directory along with speed-dial designations. When the landline rang I jumped.

"Annabel," I mouthed to Lucy. The only words I could get in were "sure," "okay," "see you then."

"She's coming over."

"When?"

"Now. She's in the area and needs human contact with someone from the book group. She didn't explain why we're the humans she picked, but I guess we're as good as anyone."

"Well, I'm glad she did. Maybe we can get something out of her. Remember — let her do the talking. Don't tell her a thing." I agreed as the doorbell rang. To arrive so quickly, Annabel had to be coming here by intent. Lucy and I weren't on the way to anywhere and didn't live by a main street.

She came through the door, looking as crisp and pristine as ever in a charcoal gray pant-suit. I could never figure out why she dressed like a lawyer. She was a full-time writer with little need to turn herself out so well. I guessed that wearing professional clothing was a personal preference. As for me, I admired the clothing but did not miss the days when suits and three-inch heels were my daily uniform.

After a round of awkward hugs Annabel presented a bakery box filled with an assortment of cookies: oatmeal raisin, chocolate chip, peanut butter, and macadamia nut. "Coffee?" Lucy offered. "Don't worry, at this hour, it'll be decaf."

We agreed to decaf and Lucy headed for the kitchen, cookies in hand. Annabel sat on the edge of the armchair seat, back straight with legs together and slanted to the right. I plopped down on the sofa and put my feet up on the table.

"Poor Evan," Annabel said. "*Such* a nice man. Have you talked to him?"

"No. I left him a voice mail, but haven't heard back. According to Kat, he's coping. It has to be a horrific shock."

"Any word on what it was that killed her?"

"No." I lied, holding to my resolve to keep inside information under wraps.

I wanted to get Annabel going on the reason for this impromptu visit but figured Lucy would be furious if I started without her. So I forced myself to be patient as Annabel eased herself into the chair and set to twirling a lock of hair behind her ear. If Lucy didn't show up soon, I'd have to resort to small talk about the weather. As it turned out, the cats saved me from bland conversational efforts. The reserved Shammy hovered at the edge of the room, observing our visitor from afar, while the extroverted Daisy sniffed the toe of Annabel's sling-back pump. When she jumped up onto Annabel's lap and Annabel shrieked I shooed the cat away. She gave each of us a reproachful look before she joined Shammy and they trotted off.

"Sorry about that," Annabel said as she brushed at her pants. "I'm not a cat person." I remembered that Annabel had a preference for toy poodles.

Annabel went back to twirling that lock of hair and tapping her toe to a rhythm only she could hear. The dark circles under her eyes told of at least one sleepless night. When Lucy finally showed up with a tray laden with a carafe of decaf, mugs, and cookies, Annabel looked as relieved as I felt.

We went through the rituals of adding

182

cream and stirring, leaving the sugar un-touched. Lucy and I picked our favorite cookies — macadamia nut for her and oatmeal raisin for me. I felt a moment of unease, wondering if we had an antidote to any poison in the cookies. That begged the question: what was the antidote? As if by mutual agreement, Lucy and I waited for Annabel to eat her peanut butter cookie before taking tentative bites of our own. Then Annabel turned to me and, voice overly bright, began. "I wonder if I should talk to your friend Vince." Her voice broke and tears spilled down her cheeks. "That is, if you still communicate — I saw him with that redhead at the signing."

Lucy grabbed the box of tissues from the end table and handed it to Annabel. I waited a moment for her to collect herself before prompting, "How could Vince help you?"

Annabel didn't answer. Instead she hemmed and hawed for a full minute. Heaving a sigh she said, "I *guess* I can trust both of you. Right?" She looked at each of us in turn. When we agreed with her assessment of our trustworthiness, yet another sigh came forth. At last she began. "Do you remember Ronnie, that horrible woman Trudy Zimmerman brought to book group

183

last summer?"

I nodded and, for Lucy's benefit, described Ronnie as a petite woman with oversized glasses who worked as a librarian at the University of Virginia in Charlottesville. She'd seemed pleasant enough to me, but Annabel's use of the word "horrible" suggested a darker side.

Annabel said, "She came up to me that night and said she remembered me from the library at UVA where I did research when I lived in Charlottesville. At first I thought she was a fan, but she quickly disabused me of that notion. You *won't* believe this, but she said that maybe I did that research for purposes other than my writing — for example, maybe for killing my dear husband."

Annabel always referred to her late spouse as her "dear" husband, never as simply *husband* and never by his given name.

The tears started falling again and Annabel said, "She laughed but you don't kid around about things like that."

Lucy asked, "Why would she think you killed your de— your husband?"

Again, Annabel didn't answer. She blotted her eyes and blew her nose. I considered that Annabel tested a murder method at book group. I read a mystery where a writer poisoned someone to try out the method for authenticity in her writing. The method had worked for that writer and, if Annabel did the same thing, it had worked for her as well. I set aside the what-if scenarios for later — I didn't want to miss any tidbits Annabel might drop.

"Last night she called and started right in with her needling. I guess Trudy told her the news about Carlene." I didn't let on that Trudy was out of the country — but I imagined that Ronnie had other ways of getting information.

Annabel reenacted the conversation with Ronnie, giving herself a normal voice and Ronnie a chipmunk one. "She said, 'Funny thing, Ms. Annabel, you're involved in not one but *two* suspicious deaths.' I reminded the twit that Carlene committed suicide. 'Yeah, right! According to whom?' 'According to a *note* that she left.' 'How do we know she wrote the note? I can't help but wonder about you, Annabel . . . I mean, you know so much about killing. You spent hours here at the library poring over books about murder methods and I'm *sure* that your fingerprints remain. Wasn't your first book about a woman killing her husband? It sure would be interesting to match the prints on all the books you handled here at the library with the ones on the note. But maybe now you're too smart to leave your prints. Too bad you weren't so smart years ago.' By this time the woman was *cackling.*

"Like I'd have killed my dear husband. I *loved* him!" Annabel blew her nose again.

Had she? Was her husband really "dear"? Was Annabel using her killer characters to write obliquely about herself? Did she have personal knowledge of a killer's mind?

I asked, "How long ago did your husband die?"

"Ten years next month. I've never gotten over it. *Never.*" She continued to weep and rail. "Can you believe the gall of that woman, the total lack of feeling?"

"Would your prints still be there on the books? How long do they last? And wouldn't other people have used the books in the meantime?"

Annabel held up her hand in a wait-a-minute gesture. Somewhat composed, but with her face still scarlet with emotion, she said, "I don't know how long prints last on paper. As for other people using the books, there are plenty of mystery writers in Charlottesville, so I imagine some of them have availed themselves of the same books." She took a fresh tissue and mopped her eyes. I hoped our supply would last, but there was always toilet paper. Maybe Annabel was the last of the weeping women we'd have to console. With all the tears of late I regretted not buying stock in a tissue company.

"So, anyway, I think she intends to blackmail me."

Unfortunately I had a mouthful of decaf. Choking, I managed to swallow it without spitting any on myself. "Blackmail?" I asked with alarm and more than a little disbelief. I remembered posing the question to Lucy about Carlene blackmailing Annabel — but I was just pulling ideas out of thin air. Did blackmail even exist in the real world? I realized that it did, but I'd never known it to touch the lives of anyone of even my remotest acquaintance. But I'd never known murder to touch their lives either. Had I read one too many murder mysteries and now found myself passing eternity in the pages of one, à la *The Twilight Zone*? "What do you mean she *intends* to blackmail you? Why didn't she do it when you were on the phone?"

"The blackmail was *implied.*" Annabel's pressed her lips in a grim line. "She broadly hinted that she could be persuaded not to call the police about the prints. I told her I'd sue her for libel or slander. Whatever."

I still felt stunned about the word "black-mail," but Lucy took up the slack. "Frankly, I'm missing something here . . . Why does this Ronnie think you killed Carlene?"

Annabel groaned. "Oh, no doubt it all goes back to the whole thing between Carlene, Randy, and me. I'm sure Trudy told Ronnie the whole sordid story. Or as much of it as she knew to tell — I was never sure just what Trudy knew. So now Ronnie's intimating that I killed Carlene out of revenge. Over Randy! The guy's *nothing.* That's when she went into the wild thing about my fingerprints. She said she'll notify the police about my fingerprints, and that they'll take her seriously because of my close connection with two deaths."

"Whoa! Let's back up a bit — who's Randy?" Annabel didn't have to know that I already knew about him.

"Yes, um, Randy. Well, he wasn't any big deal. No real loss at all. Despite what *he* thought about himself." Annabel tossed her already well-tossed hair.

"So, who *is* he?"

"Randy Baker. Trudy's ex. No real loss," she repeated. Despite her airy tone, I caught a hint of pain and wistfulness crossing Annabel's face. Perhaps Randy was a bigger loss than she cared to admit. Annabel's speech got pressured as she continued, "But another woman might not have taken it so lightly when her man was snatched away from her."

I thought of a twangy country lament about tragic love. "It sounds like . . . first you were seeing Randy, then Carlene was seeing him. Is that right?"

Annabel huffed a sigh and said, "Okay." She poured more decaf, added milk, and sipped. Fortified, she began. "You know that Carlene and I were neighbors in the Fan, don't you?" She didn't wait for us to affirm before going on. "We rented the same duplex where I live now." She took another sip of her decaf. "Anyway, Randy and I met at a signing for *Jack Hit the Road*. He claimed he was a big fan of mine. And so we started dating."

Lucy asked, "How long did you two date?"

"Oh, a couple of months, I guess. Until the night we went out to dinner with Carlene and her man of the moment. The next thing I knew Carlene and Randy were seeing each other and I was out in the cold. Along with the man of the moment. What was his name?" Annabel looked at us like she expected us to provide the answer. Then she snapped her fingers in triumph. "Tom. Tom something."

Any regard I had for Carlene was taking a serious nosedive. "Well, that was a crappy thing for them to do! I'm so sorry, Annabel."

Annabel waved a hand in dismissal. "All in the past. At the time I was pissed, I'll tell you that right now. Not because I especially liked Randy. Truth is, I was about to dump him and he beat me to it. It was the principle of the thing. You know, we never even slept together. I have morals, I don't just jump into bed with men willy-nilly," she sniffed. "I make them wait. What's all the fuss about sex anyway?"

From her sniffing I guessed she was putting herself above someone who did jump into bed with men willy-nilly. And I had a good idea who that someone was. "And Carlene?"

Annabel, involved in converting a tissue into an origami creation, laughed. "She most definitely didn't make men wait, and Randy was no exception. I heard that headboard banging against my wall the same night as the double date. I thought she was with . . . what did I say his name was?"

"Tom. Tom 'something,' " Lucy supplied.

"But the next morning I saw *Randy* leaving." Annabel paused, perhaps to emphasize the implications of her statement. Lucy and

I looked appropriately appalled and Annabel gave a harsh laugh. "I could write a book based on the woman's sex life."

I felt tempted to advise her that writing about vicarious sex didn't work. It might work for some writers but most needed to have a sex life or at least enjoy sex. As far as I knew, Annabel didn't fit in either category. As for myself, I fit in the second category and hoped that soon I'd fit in the first.

"The walls in those Fan duplexes are thick but not thick enough. Oh shoot!" Annabel spilled decaf on her jacket and we devoted the next couple of minutes to cleaning up the mess. Between Daisy and the decaf, Annabel's dress-for-success outfit wasn't faring well.

"Now where was I?" Annabel asked.

When Lucy prompted with "the walls in the duplex not being thick enough," Annabel said, "Right. Her bed was on the other side of the wall from mine, so night after night, I had to listen to them. I wound up changing bedrooms. And then," she said with a dramatic flourish, "one day, it was around dinnertime, I went to Carlene's kitchen door to ask if she'd feed my dog while I went out of town." As she leaned forward and lowered her voice, I could tell she was enjoying herself. "Did you two see

Fatal Attraction?"

"Ah, the famous kitchen scene," I said. We laughed as we recalled the intense kitchen sex between Michael Douglas and Glenn Close. It brought to mind the kitchen sex scene Georgia had told me about, the one that sent Carlene's L.A. roommate packing.

"Randy and Carlene could have been reenacting that scene. There they were, Carlene up on the edge of the sink and Randy's naked behind facing me."

We laughed all the more. Tears running down my face, I asked, "Did they see you?"

"I don't think so. They were too . . . involved. And I think he was standing on a stool or something. He was quite short."

"What did you do?"

"Do? Why — I walked away and resolved *never* to approach her door unannounced. The next day I called her from work and asked about my dog. I didn't mention the scene from the night before. She agreed to take care of Yvonne and that was that."

Lucy said, "So, it sounds like you remained friends with Carlene. If not, you wouldn't ask her to take care of Yvonne. Hazel and I wouldn't let anyone we didn't like tend to Daisy and Shammy."

At the mention of their names, the cats

appeared. They made their way to my side, giving Annabel a wide berth. Lucy checked her watch. "It's nine o'clock. Treat time." Lucy got up to dispense the treats. "Can I get anything else while I'm in the kitchen?"

We shook our heads and I turned back to Annabel. "Yes, not only did you remain friends with Carlene, but the two of you went on tours, attended exhibits, stuff like that. And you came to the book group because of her."

"Yes, well, we had common interests. Like mysteries. And the arts. But that didn't make us close." It occurred to me that if I wanted to kill someone, I'd manage to be in that person's company on a regular basis. That way I could plan my murder strategy and wait for the optimum time without being pressured. Lucy returned as Annabel said, "And you know something . . . I believe in forgiveness. I'm not a grudge holder." This she managed with such a pious tone that I was hard-pressed to keep from laughing.

To appease her, I said, "I'm sure you're not." Privately, I wasn't so sure. Just as I wasn't so sure Annabel was the forgiving soul she claimed to be. She had a powerful motive for killing Carlene, regardless of how many years had passed since they'd shared that Fan duplex. Apparently, grudges run deep and long with some folks. And Annabel wouldn't be the first person to be in grudge denial. But my musings about grudge holding distracted me from Annabel's recounting of Carlene and Randy's tawdry relationship. I cautioned myself to stay focused.

"Carlene asked me if I minded if she went out with Randy, I'll grant her that much. Not that they went *out* much." Annabel arched an eyebrow at this. "I assured her I didn't mind in the least. Of course, I did mind, but I didn't want to admit it." Annabel and Kat operated by the same set of dumpee rules. Mind, but don't *ever* admit it.

"So how long did Carlene and Randy see each other?" Lucy asked.

Annabel raised her eyes like she expected to find the answer on the ceiling. "Oh, I don't know. Six months? Real hot and heavy, then Evan came along and Randy got dumped on his behind." I thought about Kat getting dumped by Evan at the same time. A whole lot of dumping going on. And musical beds.

"Then what happened?" Lucy and I looked like children listening to stories around a campfire.

Annabel grabbed a chocolate chip cookie

and took a bite. "Randy didn't take well to being dumped and kept coming around to Carlene's place, even when Evan was there. Maybe especially when Evan was there. One night there was a big brouhaha because he was banging on the door, yelling things like, 'You f-ing bitch,' and worse. It went on and on, and finally one of the neighbors called the police. The first time Randy left before they arrived. The second time, he didn't manage to escape, or maybe didn't want to, and the incident ended up in the paper."

"What happened after that?" Lucy asked.

"Randy showed up a few more times, but he was much quieter. Evan and Carlene got married quite soon after they met, about six weeks, and they moved to where they live now. Lived," she amended in a rueful tone.

In keeping with my ask-don't-tell policy, I didn't want to reveal that Carlene and Evan had separated or that she'd been seen with another man. So I tried an oblique approach. "I wonder if Carlene and Evan were happy. Did she confide in you about that or if she was seeing another man?"

If I had any doubts about this being a silly question, Annabel's gales of laughter set me straight. "Are you joking? Carlene confide? In *me*? No way, recently or not. Carlene was not a confider and didn't suffer personal questions." She laughed again.

Lucy asked, "Did she ask you for advice on writing?"

Annabel waggled her hand back and forth. "Sometimes about publishing, agents, that kind of stuff. But not writing per se." That struck me as odd. But maybe Carlene didn't like Annabelle's writing.

I moved on to Trudy. "When Trudy showed up at book group, did you recognize her as being Randy's ex-wife?"

"Oh, yes, we knew each other from the library. Neither of us ever mentioned Randy. As for Carlene, I don't know if she recognized Trudy. You see, Carlene and I never referred to that . . . *time,* or anything or anyone associated with it." Annabel scowled. "We pretty much kept our conversations to small talk."

Annabel had no more information and no memory of other men in Carlene's life, although she assured us there were plenty. Carlene didn't go long without male companionship. And Annabel had nothing to add to the meager knowledge we had of Linda Thomas — she remembered her from the signing but nothing of any ruckus with Carlene.

"Of course, I know *way* too much about the woman's colonoscopy." Annabel rolled her eyes. "Honestly, between her and Helen, it was tough avoiding the two of them the other night. *Every* time I turned around, there was Helen, or there was Linda, nattering on about something I didn't want to hear."

Annabel frowned at her fancy watch. "Goodness, is it nine thirty already? I must dash." She slanted a look at me and asked, "Now do you see why I need to talk to Vince? How can I get in touch with him, Hazel?"

"Well, let's see . . ." I hesitated. I thought that a lawyer would be a better choice than Vince. Aloud, I said, "I'll give you his e-mail address. Wait a sec while I go upstairs and look it up." Annabel didn't need to know that I had it in my head.

When I returned with the address on a Post-it, Annabel said, "Thanks so much!" She picked up her satchel bag, started to stand, and then, as if the effort was too great, she sat down again. "I just hope that Ronnie doesn't show up at the service. I'm just so upset about this whole thing. Plus I'm devastated about poor, poor Carlene." The "poor, poor Carlene" part sounded like an afterthought if ever I heard one.

"Did Carlene ever mention a person named P.G. or P.J.?" Catching Annabel's exasperated look, I said, "I know, I know, she didn't confide in you. But you never know . . ."

"I understand. But, once again, I can't help you. Sorry."

This time Annabel managed to stand, smoothing her pants and adjusting the straps on her sling-backs. "Well, gotta go! See you on Friday." We walked her to the door.

Lucy and I waited until Annabel started her car and drove off. Then, in perfect synchronization, we turned to each other. Lucy mimed wiping her brow and said, "Whew! Do you believe her?" From Lucy's skeptical tone, it didn't sound like she herself did.

I waggled my hand back and forth. "Not sure. Not sure at all. But she's definitely gained a top spot on the suspect list. Unlike Kat, she didn't voice any doubt about Carlene's committing suicide. That could mean that she poisoned her. What better cover for murder than a suicide verdict?"

"And just yesterday we talked about how Annabel found Carlene and could easily have left the note by her chair."

I nodded. "I wonder if Carlene did, or said, something recently to piss off Annabel and dredge up the old feelings. Something that stoked Annabel's dormant rage. Or maybe not so dormant."

"The woman is — what would be a good word — fraught?"

"As good a word as any. I sure wouldn't want to get on her bad side. I can just see her sitting at home sticking pins in voodoo dolls."

Lucy said, "And my guess is that two of those dolls resemble Carlene and Ronnie. Ronnie sounds like the devil incarnate. As for Carlene, she didn't respect relationship boundaries, did she?"

I considered the recent reports of Carlene as a sexually provocative woman who made a practice of appropriating other women's husbands and boyfriends. Did she finally piss off the wrong woman? It may have been just a matter of time before she got her comeuppance. A very deadly comeuppance.

Lucy said, "All this talk about blackmail . . . Remember how the other day we wondered if Carlene knew about Annabel's husband and maybe . . . blackmailed her?"

"As I recall, I wondered about it and you dismissed the idea out of hand."

"Yes, well, you may have been on to something."

"So Annabel could have more than one

motive."

"She very well could."

CHAPTER 11

At ten o'clock I left Lucy, reading *Murder in the Keys,* and went upstairs to my den. I had felt exhausted and talked out before Annabel's arrival. Her visit, while enlightening, hadn't energized me. But I didn't want to put off my quest to dig up dirt from Carlene's L.A. days. It was seven in L.A., and unless she was sitting in freeway traffic, I had a chance of finding Susie Abbott at home.

I hoped the number I had for her was a current one, as she moved a lot. So did many others in my address book, judging by the crossed-out entries in the AB section alone. I could barely make out the number squeezed onto the edge of the page. When would I learn to use a pencil?

I wound up leaving a message on Susie's machine. It was probably just as well, as a conversation with her could run into hours. I told her I'd send her an e-mail and that we could talk the next day. The e-mail I composed outlined the bare bones about Carlene's death and a description of Linda. I included a link to Carlene's site.

Her website photo was backlit, so I hunted around for some better ones. The previous Christmas Lucy had given me a digital camera, and for a while I had snapped pictures every chance I got. I found a folder on my computer called "Book Group" with three good pictures of Carlene, including one of the two of us, looking chummier than we ever actually were. I attached them to the e-mail and asked Susie to send them around to people in the IT community. I figured that if she sent them to enough people and they in turn sent them to enough people, someone was bound to remember Carlene. I wished I had a photo of Linda to include.

Later that evening, I lay back against my pillows, petting Daisy as she nestled up against my thigh. Usually Shammy was my buddy, but every so often the cats switched allegiances. I had just finished *Murder à la Isabel* but felt none the wiser for having reread it. No buried clues. Carlene's second or third books might be more insightful. Maybe eventually I could take a look at her computer.

Carlene's author photo on the back cover was a duplicate of the one on her website. It showed her posing beside a dogwood tree, backlit by the sun. She wore a black leather coat over slacks and a turtleneck, and stood with arms raised and spread apart, like she was doing the yoga sun salute.

Her author biography was a sketchy one. She was a programmer analyst in another life. She wrote mysteries at an early age, reading installments to her friends on her way home from school. Nancy Drew and the Dana Girls were her biggest influences. She lived in Richmond with her nameless husband and was hard at work on her next Minerva Mazarek adventure.

I continued to study the photo that was little more than a silhouette and her to-the-point biography. "Hiding," I said aloud. "Why's she hiding?"

Hiding. And who hides?

Fugitives.

Love fugitives.

CHAPTER 12

"Coffee. I need coffee," I groaned to myself. Either coffee or twenty-four hours of uninterrupted sleep.

I was back at the Women's Resource Center, trying to proofread a grant proposal, but fatigue was having its way with me. But I perked up considerably when Vince, waiting for his plane to board in San Diego, called.

After the preliminary inquiries — "How are you?" "How are you feeling?" — I found myself telling him about Annabel's visit.

His reaction was predictable enough. "Annabel came to your house? Hazel, I told you to be careful. Like it or not, everyone in your book group is a suspect. And that includes Annabel."

"I *was* careful." I practically bit off my words. "Lucy was with me, we were armed with cell phones, and I've been taking pictures madly." All two of them. "Now let me tell you what Annabel said. Without the interruptions."

"Okay. Calm down. Proceed." I gave him a run-down of Annabel's revelations, including her version of the Randy saga and Ronnie's hints of blackmail in the matter of Annabel's dear husband and his unsolved murder.

When I finished he said, "I remember hearing about those incidents with Randy. As for Greg Mitchell, when I was running through the names of your book group members, I refreshed myself on the details of his murder. The man wasn't dear. He was a philandering cop who enjoyed 'special' relationships with scores of women. So many that prevailing thought had it that an unhappy woman or her husband had killed him. Annabel may have taken advantage of that theory. She was certainly a suspect herself. As you know, they never did catch the person who shot him."

"Maybe Annabel hired someone."

"Maybe." Vince sounded skeptical. He went on, "The neighbors had a lot to say about Greg and Annabel. A lot of fighting and yelling. No one would have been surprised if Annabel did it."

"Just supposing it was Annabel, why shoot him? Why not just divorce him?" The very question Laci Peterson's mother asked her son-in-law, Scott Peterson, during his trial for murdering her daughter. It was a rhetorical question — I neither expected nor received an answer.

"Greg helped her with her writing. She wrote her first two books before he died — one was a poisoning, the other a shooting. In both, a woman killed her husband. Ironically, Greg may have been participating in his own murder."

"Cheery possibility to ponder."

After a pause Vince said, "And now she's bringing up all this stuff about the library and her fingerprints. Interesting."

"Yes, it seems kind of dumb, but I think she wanted to get all her dirty linen out in the open. That way, she'd look like she had nothing to hide and could make Ronnie reconsider her blackmail scheme. Assuming she had blackmail in mind."

"Could be, but it doesn't gain Annabel much as far as Carlene is concerned. She had as much of a motive as anyone."

Vince had a point. Annabel belonged to the swelling ranks of Carlene's romance victims. As did I. At least I knew I was innocent.

"Is the house still a crime scene?"

"Oh, no. Not since yesterday."

"So what happens now?"

Vince paused, then an edge crept into his voice. "It's an open case."

"For how long?"

"I can't say."

I sighed. I interpreted Vince's testy responses to mean that the police had nothing to go on and would probably declare Carlene's death a suicide. Which meant that we had to come up with something for them to go on.

When Vince's flight was called for boarding we ended the conversation and agreed to talk the following day at the memorial service.

I left the center at three and resolved to put all thoughts and discussion of Carlene and her untimely death on hold for the rest of the day. I got my roots touched up and let Rhea talk me into coloring my hair with a zippier shade of chestnut than my usual subdued one, accentuating the reds and golds against the brown. I even splurged on a manicure and pedicure. Lucy brought home Thai takeout and I broke the Carlene moratorium long enough to catch her up on Vince's latest about Annabel and the dear husband. I broke it again when Susie Abbott called and I gave her a blow-by-blow account of Carlene's suspicious death. Susie said she'd already sent the photos around and would let me know when she heard anything.

Then Lucy and I curled up with the cats to watch *The Turning Point,* one of my favorite movies, one I'd seen at least five times since its release in 1977.

But not for a sixth time — I didn't make it through the first scene before sleep took over.

The beauty of sun beaming through the mullioned windows of St. Bernard's Episcopal Church almost made me forget why we were assembled there. Also the fact that this church was quite — what would be a good word? — unchurchlike. With its yellow walls, vaulted ceiling, gold chandeliers, and the not-stained-glass windows, we could have been in an upscale home. I couldn't even locate a cross. Only the pipe organ and pews hinted that we were indeed in a church, awaiting Carlene's memorial service.

When the minister appeared, I spotted his toupee from my seat in the back of the church. Shouldn't a man of God be unconcerned with such worldly effects as hair? Half a dozen bouquets and wreaths, attached to easels or sitting on pedestals, flanked him as he stood at the front of the church. He welcomed the family and opened the service with a prayer of remembrance. Not a personal remembrance — he didn't know Carlene from Adam. Eve, rather. He delivered a generic every-dead-person-was-wonderful kind of eulogy, rhapsodizing on Carlene's literary success. I thought literary a bit overstated, but . . . whatever. Despite his faux hair and limitations of not knowing his subject, he lent an eloquent and sincere tone to the service.

Much sniffling and rummaging for tissues accompanied Eric Clapton's "Tears in Heaven." When the minister invited family and friends to speak, Kat, flinging her shawl over her shoulder, went forward first. She kept her eulogy subdued, sharing a couple of childhood anecdotes involving her stepsister. Her voice broke several times, but she pressed on. Like Kat, Georgia didn't let her tears stop her from sharing memories of the lifelong friendship she shared with Carlene. I smiled as I imagined someone getting up and regaling us with the carnal adventures of Carlene's "other life."

Carlene's brother followed. Hal was well spoken, reminiscing about childhood with his older sister. I had noticed him when he walked down the aisle with the family, a scruffy but handsome man wearing a mish-mash of ill-fitting clothes. I had correctly guessed him to be Hal the hermit. Kat had called earlier with the news that Dean had located Hal and flown him out from Colorado — or was it Wyoming? "He arrived late last night," Kat had said. "I haven't had a chance to talk to him. Georgia told me that he lived with Carlene for a while in L.A., but she doesn't remember when. If you talk to him after the service try to get something out of him." We'd see how my getting-something-out-of-people skills were holding up.

Before Hal finished, I heard a minor commotion behind me. Two men and a woman came in and slid into the pew behind where I sat with Lucy and Vince. One of the men bumped my hat, making it tilt over one ear. When I turned to see who the offender was, a tall, thin man sporting sunglasses, a dark suit, and stylish blond-turning-gray hair mimed a profuse apology. To my surprise, Linda stood next to him, her own wide-brimmed hat not quite covering her high-lighted glory. I guessed that she'd seen the obituary. Out of the corner of my eye, I noticed a second man, dark haired, standing off to the side. His well-tailored suit and sunglasses duplicated those of the blondish man, who I figured was Linda's husband. But who was the nonhusband? I didn't want to crane my neck or turn all the way around and peer at them. As I righted my hat, I resolved to be patient and buttonhole Linda after the service.

Evan remained in his seat and did not offer a eulogy for his wife. I wondered if that was due to grief, ambivalence, anger, or all three.

Readings from the Old Testament, New Testament, Twenty-third Psalm, and a soprano of all sopranos singing "Pie Jesu" failed to hold my attention. I scanned the printed program with Carlene's author photograph and an image from *Murder à la Isabel* gracing the cover, my thoughts drifting as I regarded the assemblage from my vantage point at the back of the church. Lucy and I had arrived early to claim the best people-watching spot, with Vince showing up shortly afterward, taking a seat on the other side of me.

Of the mystery book group, all of us were present with the exception of the globe-trotting Trudy. Helen's military bearing was on display, contrasted with Art's slumped one. Sarah's braid, usually hanging down her back, now coiled around her head, coronet-style. Her husband, Den, a Vietnam paraplegic and flirtatious as all get out, positioned his wheelchair in the aisle next to his wife.

Many of the arrivals had waved and I'd waved back whether or not I recognized them. Some looked familiar, while others didn't. There was a contingent of regulars from the turkey dinners, and no doubt some were Carlene's former coworkers and Evan's present coworkers. I recognized faces from the fiction group. I wondered if any of the men present numbered among Carlene's former lovers.

The soprano reappeared, belting out the Lord's Prayer. Then we riffled through the pages of the hymnals for "Amazing Grace," one of my favorite hymns.

All in all, the service was a moving one and I regretted not fully appreciating it. Once we were dismissed, I turned to find Linda and her entourage gone. How had I not noticed them leaving? I knew I should wait for the family to leave first but I couldn't pass up my opportunity to speak with Linda, assuming I even had one. So I made a beeline for the door, scanning the area in front of the church as well as the street. Not a soul. Lucy, with my purse in hand, appeared by my side with Vince. Both asked what I was doing. Agitated, I vented my frustration at having Linda so close only to vanish into thin air.

Vince asked, "That was Linda behind us?"

I nodded, continuing to fume. "One of those guys was probably her husband. The blond one. As for the dark-haired guy, I couldn't tell who he was. Not with the shades."

The family was spilling outside followed by the rest of the mourners. I ducked back into the church to look at the guest register. Since Linda had arrived late, I started at the bottom. No Linda. But I wasn't giving up hope of her showing up — for all I knew she was using the facilities.

Evan, wearing a charcoal gray suit with a blue striped tie, shook hands at random. If pressed to identify the emotion indicated by his demeanor, I'd say somber, but it wouldn't be quite right — lack of emotion would be more accurate. A tall man with enough hair to cover two heads stood next to him. Who could he be? Kat's brother, I guessed by the process of elimination. Kat and Dean walked arm in arm. Kat's daughter, Stephie, and her husband, Ted, completed the very small family. That smallness surprised me until I remembered that both Carlene and Evan had lost their parents and I didn't think there were many other relatives. Again, I felt that pang at yet another reminder that I was not a member of this family. With its dwindling size, the family should welcome even ex-members.

From the surprised looks I guessed my dramatic, noir style startled people. I'd always wanted to wear one of those big hats, the kind that could double as a serving platter in a pinch — or a Frisbee. The hat covered the updo I'd had Rhea arrange the day before. An ensemble of sophistication to match the hat was in order, starting with the form-fitting black suit and moving on to large gold disks at my ears and sky-high heels — a rare turnaround of my belief that comfort trumped style any day. No question about it, I looked great, like a femme fatale who shows up in a seedy office of a down-and-out detective created by Raymond Chandler or Dashiell Hammett. With a large-brimmed hat shading her face, she spins a tragic tale of a missing husband.

For once I looked better than Lucy. And that was saying something as she stood out from the crowd in her eggplant suit. As I looked around, I saw every color on the spectrum, including pastels. Somehow black for funerals, or a very dark color, was ingrained in me, but these days anything went. Georgia had opted for a tan pantsuit.

A young man who looked like the actor Ralph Fiennes accompanied Annabel. Lucy and I looked at each other. "Son?" Lucy ventured, with a lascivious look.

I shrugged. "Probably." Unless Annabel was taking up with young men. Except for the brief and, by her account, sexless relationship with Randy, I'd never known her to be in a relationship. A short, bald man who had sat in front of us in the church sidled up to Annabel. She returned his mischievous look with one I could only describe as civilly polite. The couple of crab steps she took to put distance between them spoke volumes in body language. I wondered if he was Randy.

Vince worked the crowd, smiling and shaking hands as he did so. Like me, he was on the lookout for signs of guilt, culpability. Unlike me, he knew what he was doing. Vince's heady combination of Brooklyn and southern gentleman served him well in law enforcement and in romance. Especially since he wasn't *always* a gentleman . . . not when it counted. I sensed an imminent reunion with his ungentlemanly side. Then I remembered Molly and a crankiness descended on me like a shroud. Shroud? Appropriate enough, I guessed, given the occasion.

Kat weaved in and out of the crowd, handing out flyers. She had reserved the clubhouse of her town home community for the post–memorial service lunch. I was about to suggest to Lucy that we head on over there when I saw her chatting with a petite woman who looked familiar. In a flash it came to me who she was — Janet, Evan's next-door neighbor, the one who had gotten word of Carlene's death to him.

If pressed to describe Janet, I'd say she was a middle-aged version of the classic girl-next-door. Cheerleader was written all over her — blond hair cut in a pixieish style, charming overbite with a gap between her front teeth, perky manner. I wouldn't have been a bit surprised if she executed a cartwheel right there on the sidewalk. I remembered wearing her shade of bubblegum-pink lipstick in the sixties. I introduced myself, perhaps unnecessarily. While I had seen her at the turkey dinners, I didn't recall if we had actually met. When she spoke I caught a whiff of tobacco breath that didn't square with the cheerleader image.

"It was good of you to come." I sounded like an undertaker. Appropriate enough under the circumstances, but still.

Lucy still held my quilted chain bag. I

didn't think the femme fatales of film noirs carried shoulder bags, but my need to emulate the sirens of stylish forties-era crime dramas only went so far. Besides, this bag held a number of essentials, including the digital recorder I'd started at the beginning of the service, hoping to catch some incriminating scraps of conversation. I took the bag from Lucy and looped it over my shoulder.

Lucy said, "Janet was just saying that Evan's moving back to the house tonight."

"Oh? Surprising." I didn't add that I also found it macabre.

"Yes," Janet explained. "He's having the house cleaned today. The investigators messed it up a bit." She pressed her lips together before going on. "I'm just *sick* about this whole sorry mess. And so sorry for poor Evan. He and Carlene were *such* nice people. I couldn't have asked for better neighbors. So quiet, so considerate —"

I cut her off. "So you're the Janet who contacted Evan . . . that night?"

"Yes." Janet looked wistful. "It's impossible to believe that Carlene committed suicide. I'm just glad I wasn't there when it happened."

I asked, hoping that I sounded casual, "Janet, did anyone visit Carlene on Monday before the book group met? Early in the evening?"

Her eyes widened. "Yes! Someone *did* visit her on Monday. About six thirty or so. I was in the kitchen fixing dinner when I heard a car pull up. My kitchen looks out on their driveway. I didn't see anyone, just a car. A few minutes later, I heard a door slam and the car backed out of the driveway."

I could barely contain my excitement — this might make up for Linda's slipping through my fingers.

"Was it a man or a woman?"

"I never saw." Janet cringed, like she thought we'd hit her for botching her responsibilities as nosy neighbor. Perhaps hoping to redeem herself, she added, "But I'm sure it was just one person. I'm sure only one car door slammed."

"And you said this person stayed for only a few minutes?" Lucy asked.

"I'm not sure exactly how long. Not as long as a half hour. I don't *think.*" The apologetic look appeared again.

Janet wasn't the best witness. Although why should she be? The poor woman was innocently preparing dinner, not spying on her neighbors. Who could the mysterious visitor be? Even if the person stayed only a minute, a minute was all it took to sprinkle cyanide in Carlene's mug. The hyper-organized Carlene likely had all her dishes laid out for the group. I remembered a time when our refrigerator conked out and I had to take some sort of dessert, one that required refrigeration, over to Carlene's early on book group night. All the dishes were laid out on the dining room table, testimony to her preparedness. It was easy enough to pick out her mug with the "C" swirled across it. Did whoever provided the refreshments the other night bring them over early?

I shifted from one foot to the other as we stood on the sidewalk. I asked, with little hope of a definitive answer, "Did you see what kind of car the person drove?"

"No. It was small. And dark." I stifled a groan. Small, dark car, indeed. My patience for Janet's substandard observational skills took a nosedive.

Lucy, probably sensing my dwindling tolerance, asked Janet, "Back to the suicide and just how unbelievable it seems . . . Did you notice any problems between Carlene and Evan?"

Janet started, like she'd just been struck by a thought. Hopefully a helpful one. She leaned forward and lowered her voice like she had state secrets to reveal. "Well, they were separated." For show, we assumed you're-kidding expressions. Janet went on, "So sad for Evan . . . he lost her twice."

"I guess Carlene initiated the separation?" I prompted.

"I would imagine so — but don't quote me. Between you and me Evan was the one in love with her. She could take him or leave him." And she had opted for leaving. Janet's assessment was consistent with Georgia's.

The three of us were among the few remaining from the earlier crowd. Vince waved and said he'd see us at the lunch. As we started walking toward the parking lot, Janet stopped. "Now, I'm wondering about something — something that struck me as being kind of funny when I heard about it."

"What's that, Janet?"

"Well, it's this . . . I hadn't seen much of Evan since he moved out. But last weekend he was over, doing yard work. He said Carlene was out of town for the weekend, at a spa with her friend. When I heard about the suicide, I thought it very odd that Carlene would go to a spa and then come home and commit suicide." Janet looked from me to Lucy, and asked, "What do you think?"

"We think it's odd too," I said. Lucy nodded in agreement.

"Another thing that's odd . . . Carlene

told me she was going to Costa Rica with a friend. Frankly, it sounded like hell to me. Not Costa Rica, just travel. I hate to travel. Anywhere. I'm a widow, you know." How would I know that? And how was it relevant? I guessed it was a speech affectation. Now Janet said with a nervous laugh, "But my point is, why plan a trip like that if you have suicide in mind?"

Why indeed?

Lucy asked, "When did Carlene get back from the spa?"

"Sometime on Monday. Or maybe Sunday night." That left Evan at the house, with Carlene away. Hmm. Lots of opportunity to plant cyanide. But wasn't poison a woman's crime? Sexist thought, but better than thoughts of Evan as wife killer. If he did it, it meant someone from the book group didn't do Carlene in after all and we were off the hook. That was the positive view. But it also meant that I had a killer ex-husband and at one time came close, at least in my fantasies, to having a killer present husband. No, I didn't like what I was thinking. Not at all.

But like it or not, I was stuck with the thought.

CHAPTER 13

At the clubhouse Lucy and I surveyed the buffet table laden with deviled eggs, lunch meats, tomatoes, breads, salads, fruits, and that staple of southern buffets, ham biscuits. Stephie and Ted greeted us with hugs. Between them, they wore enough metal piercings to bring airport security to its knees for days. I hoped I'd never have to travel on the same flight with them.

"It's awesome that so many people came out for Aunt Carlene." Tears smudged Stephie's abundant eye makeup. Of course, that could have been the way she wore it anyway. "Do you know my uncle Kenny?"

The tall man with the mega hair whom I'd noticed at the church planted a kiss on Stephie's cheek. "Ken Berenger, Kat's brother," he said. He shook hands with Lucy and me in turn. He took a long pull from his beer bottle. "Try the ham biscuits," he invited.

"Yes," Ted agreed. "They're awesome."
Awesome was the word of the day. Lucy and
I filled plates with a little of this, a little of
that. Several bowls contained what I imagined were pasta salad, potato salad, and the
like — the thick layers of mayonnaise made
it hard to tell. We eschewed them along with
the ham biscuits.

As the room filled up, the low ceiling of
the room trapped sound, creating an unbearable din. Shades of the seventies, I
thought as I took in the shag carpeting,
orange Formica counters, and harvest gold
appliances in the kitchen. The furniture was
upholstered in that plaid, nubby fabric that
no cat in the world could resist scratching.

I spotted Evan standing under another
seventies icon, a faux-Tiffany swag lamp.
Warren Oglesby, our long-ago best man and
Evan's port in the storm following his
separation from Carlene, had his arm
around Evan's shoulder while another man
of Evan's age — and mine — stood with his
hands in his pockets. I recognized him as
Arnie Jeffers, an usher from our wedding.

Evan and I embraced in a tentative manner, like we were breakable. I felt a twinge
or two of guilt for even thinking he would
kill his wife. But I had little time to indulge
in guilt — or college war stories, for that

matter — and so, after a few minutes I excused myself and carried on in my self-appointed investigator role. I came upon Vince and a sandy-haired man with raffish good looks who turned out to be Detective Mick Jairdullo, Kat's inside information source. After making introductions, Vince again admired my ensemble but said I should have kept my hat on. I rejoined that the hat made eating difficult, if not impossible. Mick and I cast appreciative eyes on each other's outfits. An elderly relative channeled an outdated expression to me: "He cuts a fine figure . . ." Which Mick did in an impeccably tailored and likely Italian black suit, shoes shined to within an inch of their lives.

Aside from commenting, verbally and nonverbally, on my attire, the two were in cop mode, their attention on the crowd and not on me. Perhaps Vince gave my reservations about Carlene taking her own life more credence than he let on and had everyone under scrutiny. And likely Kat had won Mick over to her side with her own doubts about suicide. Of course, their law enforcement careers had instilled observation habits. At any rate, I wasn't about to get in their way and would seek more forthcoming conversation elsewhere.

Before I did so, I scanned the room. "Linda and company don't seem to be here."

Vince offered a simple no. Mick nodded, seemingly up to speed on the Linda aspect.

That was that. Time to move on. I circulated around the room, asking people if they had noticed Linda and the sunglassed men. No one had. Not surprising, as the trio had arrived late, sat in the back of the church, and cut out early, escaping the attention of the present gathering. It occurred to me that the man in the car could be in the room, but Helen's vague description of someone with longish dark hair applied to several men. Allowing for recent haircuts added to the difficulty in spotting the elusive figure.

Kat and Janet were deep into what looked like a heartfelt and tearful discussion. I hadn't had a chance to talk to Kat. I felt bad interrupting them, but I made it short. When I told her about Linda being at the service and then slipping through my fingers, Kat exclaimed, "Dang! So close. We just *have* to find that woman."

Annabel looked less than happy to see me. No doubt she regretted being so indiscreet two evenings before. Unless her scowl was directed at the two middle-aged and hungry-looking women who stood nearby, chatting up her son. Annabel denied seeing Linda with more vehemence than necessary. I looked askance as she walked away.

Kat grabbed her stepbrother by the hand and introduced him to Janet. Hal had a feral look, with his full dark beard and mustache and collar-length dark hair. Feral and gorgeous, an intoxicating combination. So what if he looked like a bum, I thought, taking in the jacket with the too-short sleeves, pants with the too-short legs and too-big waist, and scuffed loafers. I guessed that he'd put together an outfit preowned by a short, fat man during a thrift store run. He and Kat left Janet and weaved through the crowd toward the back of the room.

I found Art balancing a plateful of ham biscuits and took the empty seat next to him on the sofa. I was hoping to eat the food I'd been toting about uneaten for the past fifteen minutes. Art added his "no" to the tally of those who'd seen Linda. I launched into my debunking-the-suicide routine. "Art, you know I found that note and all . . . but I still have trouble with this whole suicide thing. Especially the *way* she did it." I added a shudder for effect. "Too creepy."

Art gave me a quizzical look. "People commit suicide all the time."

"No, Art, they *don't* do it all the time. At

226

least not in my world. And it definitely doesn't seem like something Carlene would do."

Art bit into a ham biscuit. "I couldn't say, Hazel, I barely knew her. I mean, we were acquainted for a while, but as to what made her tick, I haven't a clue." I finished my turkey sandwich and put my plate down on an end table. Art took a large bite of his biscuit and chewed thoroughly before asking, "So, if not suicide, then what . . ." He lowered his voice. "Murder?"

Thank you, Art, I said silently as he provided the opening I needed to discuss murder as an option. "Well, yeah, but" — I cringed for show — "I was thinking more along the lines of an accident."

Art raised his eyebrows and regarded me with amusement. "Accident?"

"*Probably* not an accident. I'm just considering the full range of possibilities."

"So, if we're talking murder . . . who's your candidate of choice?"

I laughed. "Goodness, I couldn't hazard a guess. I like to think we're all fine people . . ." I trailed off when I saw Art staring at me with his dark, penetrating eyes. I felt spooked. Maybe these suicide vs. murder debates weren't such a good idea. After all, one of us wasn't so fine, and that one could be Art. But I couldn't resist asking, "And yours?"

Art guffawed and parroted my earlier remark disqualifying the book group members. "Like you, Hazel, I think we're all *fine* people."

I sighed. "It's all just speculation anyway. And, like I said before, there was that note. So, like it or not, we may have to accept the fact of suicide." I did my best to sound airy and nonchalant. I shot a look at Art to gauge my success. He gave me that same unnerving look as before. What was up with that look?

He asked, "Was the note handwritten?"

"It was."

"Maybe the killer composed it."

"Assuming there was a killer." I felt like we were going around in circles.

"No one really knew Carlene, so how can we know if she committed suicide or not? God knows Mom tried to get to know her, but couldn't get anywhere. They fought a lot."

"Fought? About what?"

"The website." With a lofty tone he added, "Artistic differences."

"Artistic differences?"

"Mom wanted to be more creative. I mean, she *is* an artist." I recalled Helen's vivid paintings covering the walls of her apartment. "But Carlene wanted a simple design. Of course, Carlene won, but they had a lot of set-tos about it. Mom grumbled that Carlene just didn't want to spend the money on a knockout design."

Would Helen murder a client over artistic differences? How would she get her hands on cyanide? Was she so hell-bent on producing a stellar site that having to settle for a ho-hum one sent her over the edge? Speaking of going over the edge, was I? The thought of Helen killing was preposterous. She was so pro-life — it just didn't compute. But what did I know about Helen beyond her stand on social issues? What did I know about Art?

Seeing that lack of knowledge as an opportunity to steer the conversation away from murder, I asked Art about his background. He described an array of jobs that ran the gamut from convenience store clerk to telemarketer. After a bout of unemployment, he got his current job selling electronics at Walmart.

"Have you always lived in Richmond?"

"No, in Rochester."

"Rochester, New York?"

When Art nodded, I said, "I wonder why I didn't know that. Because Evan and I went to school there and lived there when we were married."

Art shrugged. "I guess by the time Mom and I met you we'd been here for a while. Rochester wasn't uppermost in our minds."

"What did your mom do in Rochester?"

"She was a stay-at-home mom until I went to school. Then she had lots of jobs: art teacher, rug sales, insurance sales, magician's assistant, secretary, clown, you name it."

I almost laughed out loud. I had only been listening to Art with half my attention, distracted by a man with a shock of white hair talking to Helen and Annabel. I didn't think he'd been at the church but I had seen him before, maybe at the signing. But I did catch the clown bit and tried, and failed, to conjure up an image of refined Helen as clown. Going for a change of subject, I asked Art, "How did you come to be here in Virginia?"

"Mom was a fan of Jerry Falwell."

I imagined that Helen would be drawn to the controversial religious conservative. Jerry Falwell had built a virtual empire, including a mega church, university, and political organization, in Lynchburg, Virginia. Puzzled, I asked, "Then why Richmond? Falwell's in Lynchburg, over a hundred miles away."

Art shrugged his bony shoulders. "It's closer than Rochester."

"Yes, well . . ." I didn't pursue that illogical logic. "Do you share your mother's religious convictions?"

"Hell, no." So Art wasn't a true mama's boy, at least not in all areas. I caught another one of those disconcerting looks. But now I thought I knew what it meant. He wanted me to say something, ask something, *do* something. Since I hadn't a clue as to what the something could be, I turned the conversation to romance, or the possibility of romance. "Is your mother seeing anyone?"

Art's "Oh crap, it's the complaining dominatrix" followed by "Hi, guys" put that conversational gambit on hold. The "guys" were Phyllis Ross and Janice Singleton from the fiction group. Phyllis was wearing a flowing black dress that appeared to be scarves connected together — whether knotted, pinned, or stitched, I couldn't tell. I remembered her as the group's chief complainer and the reason that Lucy and I had developed "scheduling conflicts" as our excuse for leaving the group. It was easy to peg Phyllis the "complaining dominatrix." Janice favored close-cropped hair and earrings long enough to give her a good smack if she turned her head too quickly.

The two women complimented me on my outfit and, remembering Lucy and me from before our defection, suggested that we return to the group. I offered a vague "maybe we will," but they had moved on to discussing the group's next book with Art. In no time, Phyllis was grumbling about having to read *A Farewell to Arms.* "Never could stomach Hemingway." I remembered Helen telling me that Art had picked that book. Taking this as my cue to leave, I smiled at the three of them and got up from the sofa.

After disposing of my plate and utensils, I scanned the room, looking for more prospects for my Linda search. But Kat, with Lucy in tow, put the hunt on hold when she rushed up and said, "Lots to tell. Let's go to the garden," and hustled me out a back door.

The garden was a weed-choked affair surrounding a nonfunctioning fountain and boasting one weather-beaten bench. In deference to my screaming feet I perched on the edge of the bench, taking care to avoid the bird droppings. Kat and Lucy opted to stand.

Kat's reddened and smudged eyes revealed recent tears. The day being warm, she removed her shawl and draped it over the fountain. A belt covered in fake leopard circled the waist of her black sheath dress. "I was just out here with Hal. We had a good cry."

Kat stopped and took a deep breath. "Well, like I told one of you, can't remember who, Georgia said that Hal and Carlene lived together for a while in L.A. I never knew that. So I asked him if he remembered any names of her friends from out there. After all, they probably don't know what happened and I offered to get in touch with them. But he said he never met any friends."

Catching a breath, Kat went on. "He said it was difficult living with her and that now he wishes he'd been more patient. He didn't care for her lifestyle. He started getting cold feet about saying negative stuff, but I could tell he needed to unload, so I just waited."

I felt the warmth of the day seeping through my black ensemble. But the only clothing I wore under my jacket was a bra. Granted, it was a knockout bra and I'd feel no embarrassment if I had an accident that landed me in the hospital. But present circumstances and propriety dictated that I sweat it out.

"He said Carlene was engaged to one guy

and seeing another one, that one married. And suddenly the engagement was off and she wouldn't talk about it. Or anything else for that matter. But after an incident with the married guy's wife, Carlene ended that sordid affair.

Lucy asked, "What was the incident with the married guy's wife?"

"She came by one night looking for her husband, demanding to see Carlene. To protect Carlene, Hal said she didn't live there, but the woman said then why was her name on the mailbox? He finally convinced her that no one except for him was in the apartment. So she sat by the pool and smoked. After a couple of hours, he heard commotion and screaming. Lots of cursing, 'stay away from my husband,' stuff like that. Hal went outside, but not soon enough. Carlene wound up in the pool."

Lucy and I looked alarmed at this revelation, no doubt both of us thinking of the death-by-drowning comment Lelia Taylor had overheard someone fitting Linda's description make at the Creatures 'n Crooks signing. Did the comment relate to this long-ago pool incident? It would be too coincidental if it didn't. "Did the woman throw her in the pool?"

Kat said, "I asked that very question. He

said he wasn't sure that she *threw* her. It could have been an accident. It all happened so fast."

At least Carlene's reticence didn't run in her family. I asked, "What did this woman look like?"

"Skinny with dark hair." Kat heaved a sigh. "You know men with their descriptions. And it was a long time ago."

Skinny with dark hair — not a current description of Linda. But take away the highlights and a few pounds and Linda could well be a skinny, dark-haired woman.

Lucy, apparently deciding that her own feet needed a rest, carefully lowered herself to the other end of the bench. "It sure ties in with the drowning remark Lelia Taylor overheard at the Creatures 'n Crooks signing, wouldn't you say?"

Glumly, we nodded. Kat said, "When Hal wondered why I had so many questions and what any of this long-ago stuff had to do with what's going on now, I gave him a rundown on Linda, including the death-by-drowning comment.

"Apparently Carlene was pretty shaken by the whole pool thing. Scared. And a few days later she got something in the mail that upset her."

Lucy asked, "What was it?"

"He didn't know. She wouldn't say." After a pause, Kat continued, "He said she was planning on moving to Wyoming with him, then decided she'd just move to another part of L.A. where this guy and his deranged wife couldn't find her. Hal felt skeptical about that, and didn't like the idea of leaving her there, but she was adamant and he was losing patience with her. So he helped her move and then left for Wyoming."

Lucy pulled some tissues from her purse and handed them to Kat and me. We blotted the sheen from our faces and necks. I asked, "Where did she move to in L.A.?"

Kat shrugged. "I didn't think to ask."

"Did Hal say he'd ever met the married guy?"

"Yes, once. Said he had the shiniest and widest wedding band that he'd ever seen. Like a halo on his finger. He obviously didn't have one on his head." Kat snorted and said, "I asked what the guy looked like and, naturally, he had dark hair, dark eyes, average height."

I held back a scream of frustration. "I don't suppose he remembered his name?"

Kat shook her curls. "And he never heard of a P.G., a P.J., or a Linda Thomas."

Lucy mused, "Not much to go on. Still, we need to come up with a Linda-finding strategy."

"That's the rub — finding her. If she was up to no good, she may have given us a phony name. And she might not even live around here."

Kat groaned. "You're right, Hazel. She could be a — a Tilly Poindexter from Alabama. Probably even a PI couldn't nail her down."

Lucy reined us in. "Let's try finding her as Linda Thomas in Richmond before we go further afield."

Kat returned to the Hal conversation. "Eventually we talked of other things, catching up, that sort of thing. Consoling each other. Georgia had told him that Carlene became religious after she moved back here. I didn't tell him otherwise."

Yes, I thought, there was no need to tell him that the whole religious quest hadn't taken with Carlene and that she'd returned to what some would call her wicked ways — Randy and the man in the car capers being prime examples.

Kat ended her report with a sigh and looked at each of us in turn. "Any news on your end? Hear anything interesting?"

Lucy and I told her about Annabel's visit and our conversation with Janet.

Kat nodded. "Pretty much the same stuff

Janet told me earlier — except she didn't mention the mystery visitor. I do remember that article in the paper about Carlene and Randy. So now we have to add Annabel to our list." Kat looked beleaguered at the thought of another suspect. "At least we know where she is."

We went back inside and the first person we ran into was Hal, sipping a yellowish beverage.

Kat introduced me and Lucy to Carlene's brother. I found myself looking into a familiar pair of money-green eyes. Just like Carlene's.

"I understand you live in Wyoming," I said, fervently hoping I didn't have food on my teeth.

"Montana," he corrected.

We talked about his life in Montana until he smiled at a point behind me and I turned to find Evan, eyes red, and maybe feeling the effects of too much wine. Lucy and Kat had drifted off, probably pulled into other conversations.

Evan put his arm around me and said, slurring his words, "This woman was a good friend to Carlene. A damn good friend." Hardly. But Evan no doubt found solace in believing that his wives were friends, so I simply smiled and didn't correct him.

Hal said, looking from me to Evan, "Weren't you two married to each other?"

"Yes," I confirmed. "Long, long ago."

"Weird."

"Yes."

The three of us reminisced about Carlene. Then Hal checked a battered watch. Another borrowed item? "Georgia and Gary are taking me to the airport," he explained.

He shook our hands solemnly, adding a hug for me, and turned to greet Georgia and Gary Dmytryk. Gary was garbed in a suit the color of blue ink, reminding me of the Hitchcock movies of the fifties where the men were suited in the same blue hue. Georgia pulled me aside and confirmed my guess that it was Randy sitting in front of us in the church and talking to Annabel outside. "Thankfully, he didn't say anything to me."

When Georgia asked me to come into work on Monday if I could make it, I agreed. Then she and Gary left with Hal in tow.

The place was thinning out. Evan urged me to take his business card. After a moment's hesitation, I did. I noted his e-mail address, and thought it would be preferable to communicate with him electronically than via phone. I didn't trust him to observe

239

a proper mourning period for his wife, whatever a proper mourning period was these days. I thought about Janet's revelation that he was moving back to the house he'd shared with Carlene and wondered if I should mention it. But I held my tongue — it was none of my business. The tight embrace he gave me was a far cry from our earlier sort-of hug. I hoped the wine was responsible and that another Lemaire invitation wasn't imminent. Helen and Janice Singleton, the "earring lady," stood next to me, waiting to talk to Evan. I didn't relish being the subject of rumors and accusations of making a play for Evan at his wife's memorial service, so I stepped aside and let them take my place. When Evan turned to Helen, the same get-me-out-of-here expression I'd seen countless times on faces of book group members came over his face. I smiled.

I rounded up Lucy and we looked for Kat to say good-bye. We found her in the back of the room, curled up on a sofa, talking to her brother and to Mick. Shoes with heels even higher than mine toppled over on the floor in front of her. After introducing Lucy to Mick, Kat stood and wrapped each of us in tight hugs and we made a bloodless pact to find Linda. "I can't believe she was this close." Kat used a purple-tipped thumb and index finger to measure off a half-inch of distance. "Damn!"

We moved through the room, stopping along the way for good-byes, hugs, kisses, more reminiscences about Carlene, a tear here and there, what have you. I thought that this whole business of detecting was not as easy as it looked. Plus it was potentially dangerous and I wasn't a brave person — my vigilante streak hadn't come packaged with courage. Even though the police were probably satisfied to deem Carlene's death a suicide, I resolved to leave the matter in their hands. Let me get on with my life.

Great idea in theory, but I didn't welcome the prospect of living in a perpetual limbo of not having answers about Carlene's death. Not knowing was infinitely worse than knowing. Every time I saw someone from the book group, I'd wonder: "Did she do it?" "Did he kill Carlene?" "Did Carlene kill herself?" Something like being a love fugitive.

And what about those high-minded ideas I had about exacting justice?

There was no turning back. I had to soldier on.

So much for the getting-on-with-my-life idea.

CHAPTER 14

Once outside, I kicked off my shoes. Enough was enough. So what if I wrecked a pair of panty hose and a pedicure? Even with walking on asphalt with an occasional sharp stone impaling my feet, my relief was palpable. Lucy and I rehashed Kat's account via Hal of an enraged woman throwing Carlene into her pool with our guess that Linda was the enraged thrower. Our rehashing being unproductive, I moved on to Helen, relaying Art's tales about the website disputes. Lucy looked blank. "Is that all?" When I said, well, yes it was, she said, "So *what*? Are you saying that Helen poisoned Carlene over website differences?"

"I'm not saying that at all. I'm just telling you what I heard."

"Carlene was paying her, even if it wasn't as much as she wanted. Plus, we're talking about Helen — the most religious, conservative woman we know. Murder is a *sin*."

"But religious people —"

"Yeah, yeah, yeah, they've been murdering for centuries for a good cause. But a website is hardly a good cause. Now if Helen was interested in Evan — uh-oh!"

Lucy and I were so involved in our pow-wow that we were startled to find Vince and Helen standing between Lucy's Honda hybrid and the open trunk of Helen's car, some indeterminate model. Hopefully our voices hadn't carried.

Helen's navy suit flattered her slim figure. A string of pearls and pearl teardrop earrings completed her simple yet elegant ensemble. She looked 100 percent lady. The tones of her hair, fashioned in a smooth pageboy, alternated between blond and silver, depending on the play of light. With the halolike effect she looked younger than she was — not that I knew her age. I thought Art was about forty — so, regardless of the fact that Helen didn't look a day over fifty, she had to be at least sixty. The cheekbones helped — I had a theory that prominent cheekbones held up the skin, keeping it from sagging.

"Helen was just showing me her digital camera. Quite impressive." Vince held a flyer in his hand, the same stem cell research one Helen had sent me earlier in the week.

"Yes, come and see. I just got it this morning."

"Where's Art?" Lucy asked.

"He went to work."

I suspected that the camera was a ruse to get us over to her car to promote one of her causes, all of which she touted via a collection of bumper stickers. She proclaimed herself a "Bush Woman" and an NRA supporter. Sure enough, the inside of her trunk was piled high with brochures and flyers. A lot of library books, many with Agatha Christie titles, were fanned out over the floor of the trunk. Also Raymond Chandler and Jill Churchill. It looked like she'd raided the "CH" section.

I recognized some titles from the Murder on Tour selections. Sarah had talked up *Deadly Harvest* with great enthusiasm when we "toured" Washington State. If memory served me the book featured a detective priest. I wondered if Helen read these books or if they just remained stashed in her trunk.

Helen lovingly lauded every detail of her camera. Apparently it did everything but wash dishes. Sales pitch over, she picked some flyers off a stack and urged them on us, but I pushed them back at her, reminding her that Lucy and I already had one.

Sensing that Helen was about to amplify

on the event advertised on the flyer, I planned an exit strategy. Just then I was gifted with one — the stack of flyers toppled over in the trunk and my attention fell on a plastic see-through envelope that had been under the pile — specifically on the photograph visible inside it.

I asked, leaning in for a closer look. "Is that Evan?"

All eyes went to the photograph, showing a smiling Evan. The image looked familiar and no more than ten years old. I thought it could be the one our alumni publication had included with an article on Evan when he'd retired from his job in Rochester and headed south to Richmond. The envelope's thickness suggested other photos besides the visible one.

Helen made a dismissive gesture. "Oh, those are some photos I scanned for Carlene a while back. When I took a Photoshop class she gave me this envelope and asked me to digitize them and touch them up if necessary. She wanted to create a DVD for Evan for their anniversary. I wonder if she ever did." Helen gave a short laugh. "I forgot all about them. You know how bad I am about keeping stuff in my car. I guess I should give them to Evan."

Lucy looked toward the clubhouse down

the street. "He might still be there."

"Goodness, I won't bother him now." Helen straightened up the sheath of flyers now spread out across the trunk. "Well, I do hope to see all of you at the stem cell presentation. You know, don't you —"

Vince cut her off. "Would you ladies care to go to Crossroads?" he asked, referring to a neighborhood coffee house on Richmond's Southside, near downtown.

Helen spoke up. "Thanks for asking, but I have to get going. First stop is the library — I find myself there every day — always seem to have research to do."

"Which library?" Lucy asked.

Helen closed her trunk and shrugged. "Mostly Westover Hills, just because it's the closest. But my favorite is the main city library downtown."

"Yes, I like that one too. But don't you research online? I'd think a computer-savvy person like yourself would."

"Oh, I do both. I don't want to see the printed word go by the wayside. And then, speaking of the Internet, I have an appointment later with a new website client. Then Bible study. I just never stop!"

After citing a list of errands, projects, and appointments that filled her days, Helen turned to me. "Hazel, what do you think about . . ." Then she looked at Lucy and Vince and said, "Oh, I'm holding everyone up. We'll talk later, Hazel. I'll call you." And so I was saved, at least temporarily, from having to think.

After Helen left, Vince looked at Lucy. "How about you, Lucy? Crossroads?"

"Oh, you two go. I'm going to the office. You'll give Hazel a ride home, won't you, Vince?" Her nonchalant manner didn't fool me. She was delighted with this turn of events. Like a stage mom. I halted her hasty retreat long enough to retrieve my purse and a travel coffee mug from her trunk. As part of our commitment to saving the environment, we each kept a stash of re-usable shopping bags, coffee mugs, and take-out containers in the car. Reluctantly, I eased back into my shoes. When Vince suggested I wear the hat, Lucy plunked it on my head and fussed with it a bit. Then she drove off, waving gaily.

Vince and I traveled along Forest Hill Avenue to Crossroads, officially called Crossroads Coffee & Ice Cream. As I stepped out of the car, Vince again remarked on my outfit. "Very sexy," he said with an appreciative look. I felt a little self-conscious and very, well, sexy.

I said, "So what did you and Helen talk about?"

"Stem cell research," Vince smiled. "Oh, and her digital camera."

A converted gas station, Crossroads was a funky and comfortable place with big purple couches and mosaic-topped bistro tables. Vince and I stood out in our dressy attire — but the jeans-clad customers were too involved with their newspapers and laptops to notice us. I produced my travel mug for my latte and urged Vince to specify a ceramic mug for his. I opened my purse, making a flirtatious show of looking for money that I knew wasn't there. Vince fell in with my plans and insisted on paying.

After sprinkling cinnamon on our coffee concoctions, we went to an adjacent room — probably a former waiting room — and settled in by a window. I lost no time in slipping off my shoes. For a few moments, we sat in a silence that looked to be companionable, but was really expectant. Finally Vince asked, "So, Hazel . . . tell me about your conversation with Carlene's brother."

I looked at Vince, trying to gauge whether jealousy or an ingrained investigative instinct drove his question. But he wore that inscrutable expression mastered by cops everywhere. I mentally shrugged and said, leaving out my observations on his attractiveness, "Our conversation was very short. But Kat had an interesting talk with him." I launched into Kat's description of the pool incident. "It had to be Linda. After that remark she made to Carlene at the signing, it would be too much of a coincidence otherwise. We have to find her. Did you find an address for her?"

"With a name like Linda Thomas she's not the easiest person to find. But let's back up for a minute — what remark did she make?" Vince's blue-eyed gaze was intense.

Realizing that I'd forgotten to tell him about the death-by-drowning remark, I filled him in on that reported exchange. He raised his eyebrows and nodded but made no comment. "Makes sense. Bears looking into." He wrote something in a notebook that he produced from his pocket. "Anything else?"

It didn't escape my notice that he'd evaded my question about Linda's address. But I let it go and went on to summarize the rest of Kat's conversation with Hal. "Thankfully, he didn't share his sister's reserve. He sounds much more straitlaced than she was, rigid almost. Full of moral rectitude."

"Moral rectitude, huh?" Vince looked

amused. "That's what I get for taking a writer to coffee. Speaking of writing, how's yours going these days?"

"It's taken a hit this week. But I'm gathering some excellent material. Thanks in large part to finding out all this stuff about Carlene. And yours?"

Vince updated me on his latest research into the true crime story of the Lattimer sisters. Patty and Nancy Lattimer had stunned Richmond three years before when they shot and killed their wealthy parents. This tragic story always got me thinking about the dynamics of the obviously dysfunctional Lattimer family. Were the daughters born "bad" or was their environment responsible for their decisions? What kind of parents had the Lattimers been? Vince was doing his best to find out but may never arrive at a satisfactory answer to the nature vs. nurture question.

When he finished, he asked, "Who was that young man with Annabel today?"

"Her son."

"I wondered. All those middle-aged women fawning over him. What's the attraction? I didn't think he was so great-looking."

"No, but he's sexy as all get out. He looks like that actor, you know — Ralph Fiennes."

"*The English Patient*." Vince's tone conveyed his opinion of that movie. "That was three hours of my life that I'll never get back."

"Yes, well, I long ago made it up to you with all those action films," I retorted. "Anyway . . . speaking of Annabel, did she talk to you today? Or send you an e-mail?"

Vince shook his head. "Maybe she had second thoughts." I'd given Vince a heads-up that Annabel wanted to talk to him, probably about the whole Ronnie thing with the fingerprints. It occurred to me that what Annabel really had wanted to know was how tight I still was with Vince. Maybe after being seen with him today, I'd be hounded with requests, the go-to person for inside information.

Vince sipped his latte and gave me a long look. "I'm telling you, Hazel, you could be in harm's way with these people. Annabel certainly has a motive. Carlene stole her man. And if Annabel was doing all that library research . . ."

"But why wait this long to seek revenge? Don't people get over anything?"

"Many don't. Not ever."

Vince proposed that Carlene may have incited Annabel in other ways when they lived next door to each other. Maybe Carlene stole other men from her, waylaying them as they came up the walkway. I had a vision of Carlene appearing on one of those Fan verandas in a filmy peignoir and feathery high-heeled mules, luring men from Annabel's door.

"Carlene stole Trudy's man too. But Trudy wasn't at book group. She got married and is on her honeymoon as we speak."

Vince took notes when I told him Janet's account of Carlene's mysterious visitor on Monday evening, but he looked skeptical. "Or maybe Janet was the visitor."

I looked stunned. "Why — I never thought of that." My skepticism skills were undeveloped.

"She gave you a lot of vague details. I always wonder about these sightings."

"Lucy and I wondered if Carlene had reason to think that Annabel killed her husband; if so, Carlene might have gone in for a bit of blackmail herself." When Vince looked doubtful, I said, "Hey, she could have heard all kinds of stuff when they were neighbors in the Fan."

"I do remember something — when Carlene consulted with me, she mentioned Annabel and her husband. She thought his unsolved murder would be a good idea for a future book."

A thought struck me so hard I wondered how my hat stayed on. "What — what if she decided to interview Annabel about it? And what if Annabel didn't want Carlene to write about it and decided to nip that problem in the bud by killing her?" My words collided in my excitement.

Vince allowed that it was a possibility but, not surprisingly, reminded me that we had no proof and there was little likelihood of getting any. He fell to reviewing his notes while I twisted my napkin into various shapes. I got up and looked at the flyers tacked to the walls: lost pets, music lessons, Bible study groups. I considered telling Vince about Helen and Carlene's website disputes. It all sounded lame, but after a lightning-quick hemming and hawing session with myself, I decided to tell him anyway and went back to the table.

When I finished, his look confirmed the lame judgment. He closed his notebook and put it on the table. "I wonder why your book group attracted so many people who had an axe to grind with Carlene." When I didn't respond to this provocative statement, he went on, "Annabel, Linda . . . maybe Kat and even Helen."

"Well, I'm glad you don't include me with that bunch. Or Sarah. Or Art."

"I forgot about Sarah and Art. As for you, I don't see you as a killer, Hazel. Oh, maybe in a moment of passion, but premeditated murder . . ." He shook his head. "Plus, I never felt there was any great feeling between you and Evan. I imagine he was the reason you moved to Richmond in the first place, but still." I couldn't think of a good enough comeback, so I finished my latte and tried to affect an allure that suited my noir persona.

"Would you like to have dinner with me?"

I waited a couple of beats before saying, "Sure." Then Molly appeared in my mind, unbidden. Much as I wanted to ignore her, I knew I had to deal with the woman, the sooner the better. "But what about Molly?"

"Molly?"

"Yes, Molly. I thought you two were an item."

"Hardly. I think she's a Nazi."

"A *Nazi*?"

"Yes. She has some very authoritarian views. I introduced her to Bill Hall."

I laughed. "They might get along." Bill Hall was one of Vince's former police colleagues. Vince and I once tried to fix him up with Helen and she found him too conservative. Go figure.

"So, how about that dinner?"

With Molly out of the picture, I had no trouble agreeing. "Yes, I'd like that. When?"

"Well, I guess next weekend. I'd like to see you tomorrow night, but don't want to be asking at the last minute."

"Well . . ." I made a show of mentally reviewing a hectic social calendar. Should I play hard to get or at least challenging to get? Nah — we were too old for those games. "Let's say tomorrow at seven."

"Seven, it is."

We looked at each other then quickly looked away. We could have been fifteen.

"Vince, did I tell you about Carlene's love fugitive idea?"

"*Love* fugitive? You mentioned something along those lines the other night."

When I described Carlene's plans for the third installment of her series, Vince asked, "Why didn't she talk about this love fugitive idea at her signing?"

"I think she recently came up with the idea. I wonder if something happened that made her come up with it. When she consulted with you, did she mention it?"

"No."

I outlined my reasons for thinking that Carlene was hiding from someone or something, citing her author photo, sketchy biography, and general opaqueness as lend-ing credence to my suspicions. "Then there's the L.A. contingent: the fiancé, the stalker, the 'doomed' love affair. Whether we're talking about one person or three people is anyone's guess. And that brings us back to Linda."

"Maybe someone in L.A. knows something. Or knows Linda."

I brightened at the opening Vince provided. I had omitted any mention of talking with Susie. Talking with book group people was one thing — as friends and witnesses it was natural for us to discuss Carlene's death. But Susie was an outsider. Of course, Carlene's L.A. friends — assuming there were any — would want to know of her death, so it was reasonable that I would try to contact someone out there. I decided to wait until Susie came through with something substantial before introducing her into any conversation with Vince. I made a show of having a sudden epiphany. "Yes, I could ask some people in L.A."

But my acting skills, such as they were, didn't fool Vince. "I'm sure you're already working your L.A. contacts," he noted with a shrewd look.

"Well, I know people who might have known Carlene. We did the same kind of work, you know. And the same people might have known Linda."

"Did you ever think the person Carlene was hiding from could be Linda?"

I felt stunned. Linda already tied with Annabel for top place on my personal suspect list. But as for being the cause of Carlene being a love fugitive, no, I hadn't even considered her.

So sexist of me to assume that Carlene was hiding from a man.

CHAPTER 15

Vince and I eventually left the murder subject and spent the rest of the afternoon sharing pastries and catching up on each other's lives. When he dropped me off at home he kissed me, a simple kiss that promised more to come. Much more.

I had a message from Lucy, champing at the bit to hear about my coffee date with Vince and demanding that I call her on her cell phone the minute I got her message. I wished Lucy would temper her enthusiasm about Vince until I felt on more solid ground with him. Then I laughed. I might as well wish time would stop.

Naturally, she was delighted about my dinner plans. "I just knew Molly would turn out to be a nonproblem. It's all falling into place, Hazel." Then the fussing started: What did I plan to wear? The house needed a good cleaning. What about breakfast? Rolling my eyes, I assured her that I'd come up with something presentable to wear and that I'd devote some time to cleaning before the big event, emphasis on "some." As for breakfast, we'd eat out. I wanted to talk about Carlene and, when finally allowed to do so, Lucy was intrigued by the idea of her being in hiding for all these years not from a man, but from a woman — specifically Linda.

"That could mean that Linda searched for Carlene and found her. Which makes sense — if Carlene was hiding from Linda, then Linda was looking for Carlene. Not an easy task with Carlene's frequent name changes."

I agreed. "Unless it was a coincidence that Linda showed up at the signing. But, if they did have an adversarial background, a co-incidence is doubtful. Linda showing up at the signing of a first-time author whom she just happened to know in California and just happened to have thrown into a pool?"

"I wish we knew Linda's searching tech-niques so we could use the same ones to find her. There's the Internet, there are private investigators, professional data-bases . . . but why would she go to all that trouble?"

"And, like we said earlier, if Linda was up to no good the other night, she probably was using a phony name." I groaned at the daunting obstacles in the cat-and-mouse game with Linda.

Lucy's heaved a heavy sigh. "We need to put on our thinking caps."

"Are there enough thinking caps in the world for this task?" Needing a change of subject, I noticed a paperback on the counter. "What did you think of the Keys book?"

"Oh, it's dreadful. Carlene was right, it has no ending."

"I'm going to read it tonight."

"Don't bother. It isn't helpful as far as Carlene's death is concerned."

Lucy said she had to go and meet her friend Maxine for an early dinner. When we hung up I thought an early dinner sounded like a good idea, so I fixed a salad sprinkled with Gorgonzola cheese. I needed a rest from all my talking of late and so relished the quiet that I didn't even play music.

I knew I should work on my writing, but *Murder in the Keys* was calling me. Despite Lucy's negative review of the book and warning that it wouldn't help to unravel the mystery of Carlene's death, I curled up with the cats on the sofa in the morning room and opened the infamous tome.

■ ■ ■ ■

"Drivel. Pure drivel!" I proclaimed as I tossed the book onto the floor. Carlene and Lucy were right in their assessment of the poorly written story, especially the non-ending. The author, perhaps going for realism, left the murder a cold case. Someone needed to alert her that this was the fiction world and mystery readers wanted closure. Mercifully, the story was short and skimmable.

I turned my thoughts to my main reason for reading the book by the author with the unpronounceable last name: seeking clues to Carlene's demise, whether by her own hand or by another's. Not coming up with a clue, I considered the cyanide theme that had permeated Carlene's last evening on earth . . . cyanide in the book, cyanide as a major discussion topic, and cyanide in the tea. The fact that Carlene initiated the topic was natural enough since she'd just read about it. But the fact that cyanide killed her an hour later was too coincidental.

Did someone come up with the spontaneous idea to kill Carlene based on that discussion alone? If so, that someone would have been carrying cyanide around, waiting for a chance to use it. I thought of the Nazi war criminals who kept cyanide at the ready in case they needed to expedite their earthly departure to avoid prosecution for their World War II crimes. That was twice in one day for the Nazi subject — I thought of Vince's assessment of Molly's ultraconservatism. I mentally scanned the group for Nazi tendencies, but thankfully came up with nothing. Helen and Sarah were conservative, but I thought — hoped — they drew the line at Nazism.

I tabled the cyanide subject and turned my thoughts to Susie — had she forgotten about me? As if on cue, the phone rang.

Without preamble, Susie said, "Hazel, I have a great source for you. Quite a few people recognized Carlene from her photo but couldn't remember her name, just that Carlene Lundy didn't sound right. But Jeanette Thacker worked with her at Soyars Publishing and says her name was, get this, Carlotta Gennis. How did she come up with that one? Anyway, Jeanette's one of those people who knows everything about everyone. For some reason people confide in her even though she's a blabbermouth who never forgets a thing."

I was sure Georgia had said that Carlene changed her name from Lundy to Gennis when she'd moved to Virginia. But apparently she used the Gennis name on the West Coast. Deciding that the name issue amounted to either my misunderstanding or Georgia misremembering, I put it aside and said, "Great! That's exactly what I need, a blabbermouth with a long memory. Can I talk to her?"

"Yes, she's expecting your call. She's home now." I displaced Shammy from my lap, found an envelope on the kitchen counter, and took down Jeanette's number. Susie said, "I need to warn you about Jeanette. She's a bit — let's just say she's earthy." In my experience, earthy was a euphemism for crude. "I know — I worked with her for a few years. So be prepared for a salty discussion. Anything new? How was the memorial service?"

I told Susie about the service, about Janet's report of Carlene's pre–book group visitor, and Kat's conversation with Hal. No doubt I was missing something.

"So this is like *Murder, She Wrote*. Lots of suspects. And the murderer is always the one you least suspect."

"Remember, Susie, this may be a suicide."

Susie snorted. "But you don't believe that, do you?"

"No."

"Well, I'll let you go so you can catch Jeanette. And keep me posted."

"Hi, Jeanette, this is Hazel —"

Jeanette cut to the chase. "So what's this business about Carlotta or whatever she was calling herself these days?"

"Carlene."

"She went by Carlotta when I knew her. She still looks pretty good — I guess I should say *looked* good. I'll have to read this book of hers. Lots of sex?"

It took me a second to realize that she was asking a question. "No, not really." Not for the first time I wondered why Carlene had spared the sex in her book, in view of her lifestyle.

"Humph. When I knew her she was quite the round-heeled woman." Susie was right, this woman didn't pull any punches. "You can't imagine my surprise when I saw on her website that she was married. Carlotta *married*? To *one* man?"

"One man," I confirmed.

"So, Hazel, Susie thinks I can help you. But first tell me how Carlotta — if you don't mind, I'm just going to call her Carlotta, it's easier. Anyway, how did she manage to get herself killed? Susie says suicide, but also says you don't buy that idea."

265

"Well, I —"

"The Carlotta I knew would *never* have committed suicide. The woman had no depth. You need depth to kill yourself. Tell me how you got mixed up in this. Friend of hers?"

I gave Jeanette some background on me, Evan, "Carlotta," and Carlotta's suspicious death, with Jeanette making occasional exclamations of "Wow," "Unbelievable," and the like. When I finished my hellacious tale, I said, "So, tell me about the Carlene — sorry, Carlotta — that you knew."

"Well, the woman was just something else. Gorgeous. Bright. Hardworking. All the women envied her, especially when she regaled us with tales of her sexcapades."

"I can't imagine her telling sex tales." I described the reticent Carlotta I'd known.

"She wasn't reticent when she worked here, I can tell you that right now. I'll never forget the desk incident. She and some guy did it on her desk during our company Christmas party. She told me this while I sat in her office working with her on a project — yuck! All I could imagine . . . well, you can imagine what I could imagine. And, get this, her fiancé was at the party."

The fiancé again. "Tell me about the fiancé."

"He was a hotshot lawyer. Spiffy-looking guy. He showed up at the party in a pinstripe suit and wingtips. He looked ready for the friggin' Biltmore, but had to settle for So-yars's lunchroom. The guy was a born-again Christian, didn't believe in sex before marriage. If there are two things that didn't go together, it was Carlotta and celibacy. But she said she was in love and wanted to honor his religious convictions. So she had a quickie with someone else. She wouldn't say who. She *claimed* she was coming out of the ladies' room and ran into this guy —" It was clear that Jeanette doubted Carlene's claim. "— and got *sidetracked.* She was quite pleased with herself." Jeanette stopped, perhaps to draw a breath.

Her tale sounded like others I'd heard about Carlene over the past few days. The open Carlene, the Carlene who bragged of her exploits, staggered me. I guessed that her fugitive status had put a damper on the sharing of her illustrious love life — or on anything personal.

"What did the fiancé do while all this was going on?"

"How would I know? I guess he nursed his drink, waiting for his beloved to return from the ladies' room with a powdered nose. Instead, she showed up with after-glow."

"So what happened with the fiancé? She didn't marry him, did she?" I felt enormous sympathy for the hapless guy.

"No, not long after that party he broke off the engagement. She said he found out about an affair she'd had. '*An* affair?' I'd asked. Funny thing was, she didn't want to discuss the whole thing — suddenly she was, in your words, reticent. And shaken. Normally she had an easy-come, easy-go attitude about men. She left Soyars shortly after that and we lost touch. At some point I heard that she'd left the state."

"Well, let me tell you about this Linda. Maybe you know her." I proceeded to describe Linda and her behavior at the signing, at the book group, and at the memorial service. For the sake of simplicity, I kept her name as Linda Thomas from Richmond and didn't get into other names, other places. I was about to launch into the tale of the poolside dunking when Jeanette interrupted.

"B.J.? She mentioned a B.J.?" I detected heightened interest in Jeanette's voice and hoped it wasn't a figment of my hopefulness. I noticed that she, like Lucy, heard "B.J." when I'd said "P.J." Maybe Ps and Bs did sound alike.

"Does B.J. ring a bell?"

"Kind of . . . There was this guy, Ben Miller, who worked with us at Soyars. By 'us' I mean Carlotta and me. I heard his wife call him Benjy. Although she could have been saying B.J. — hang on a second, someone's at the door."

While I waited, I pondered the names. Benjy sounded like B.J. Like P.J. as well. Amid the din of an author signing, it was easy enough to hear variations. I felt like I was getting somewhere at last.

When Jeanette returned, I asked, "Do you remember Ben's middle name?"

She snorted. "Middle name — are you serious?" Actually I was, and while I was not hopeful of an answer, this was no time to leave stones unturned. She went on, "Anyway, I was about to tell you that Ben had a weird-looking wife named Linda."

"Linda, huh?" I reminded myself that the world was full of Lindas. "Did you ever meet her?"

"Yes, indeedy. At the very same Christmas party as the infamous desk incident."

"And you said she was weird-looking?"

"I think she was going for a Morticia Addams look." When I urged her to tell me more, she said, "Yes, what's now called

Gothic — or is that an outdated term? Who knows, who cares. She had long black hair, looked like she'd dumped a bottle of ink on her head. Skinny. Dressed in head-to-toe black. Lots of makeup. Ben used to make fun of her — of her looks but also her lack of intellect, so maybe that's why it's hard for me to imagine her reading books, anything other than a tabloid."

I described the current Linda. "Her last name isn't Miller. It's Thomas. Tell me about Ben."

"He was terrifically sexy, had those bad-boy looks, real swaggery type. Dark, wavy hair, dark bedroom eyes."

"Hmm. This Linda's married to a tall blond guy. At the memorial service she was with him and another guy with dark hair and sunglasses. I'm thinking she's the same person based on your description. She just gained weight and highlighted her hair. And managed to get divorced along the way."

"All doable. Especially the change in body mass — don't I know it!" Jeanette hooted. "It's been years since I saw Ben or Linda. They moved away and I lost track of them. They could have split at some point — their marriage didn't strike me as one made in heaven. I'm pretty sure that Ben had a thing with one of the Soyars receptionists. And that's just the one I know about; there could have been others. And so, for Linda, it's not a quantum leap to highlights and remarriage to the blond guy."

"Do you think Carlotta and Ben had an affair? Or, at the very least, a flirtation?"

"Carlotta didn't usually fool around with the guys at work. She had few principles, but that was one of them. But that doesn't mean that she didn't make an exception for Ben. He was pretty hot."

"Maybe he was the desk guy."

"Could very well be."

Jeanette laughed when I told her Hal's account of the pool incident. "I never heard anything about that. I'm sure I'd remember something that dramatic. And funny." Now Jeanette's voice softened. "I do, however, remember Hal. Carlotta brought him to the office one day. Simply gorgeous. A bit scruffy, but a guy that good-looking can dress any way he wants."

"Does it seem plausible to you that Linda pushed Carlotta into the pool? Hal's description of Linda is roughly the same as yours."

"Sure, it's possible. Plus, the woman did say, 'Stay away from my husband.' But Ben was hardly Carlotta's only lover, assuming they were lovers at all. Carlotta could have pissed off any number of wives and girl-friends."

Like she continued to do in Virginia, I thought.

"You know something, Hazel, I think I have pictures from that Christmas party. Don't worry, none of the desk incident," Jeanette chortled. "But first I have to find them."

"Would one of them be of Ben? And Linda?"

"Probably. I tried to include everyone. Give me your e-mail address."

I did. "How soon can you get them to me?"

"Well, I'll do it as fast as I can, Hazel. Gimme a break! I said I have to find them first. I've moved twice since that party. Then I have to deal with this friggin' scanner; in fact I may have to get my mother over here to do it. She just lives next door. Do you believe it, she's over eighty, and she's a whiz with computers. It's kind of embarrassing. But don't fret, Hazel, I'll get right on it. I *know* this is important."

"Okay, I appreciate your help, Jeanette," I said, hoping to mollify her. Control freak that I am, I hated to wait for other people to do things. I hoped Jeanette was the follow-through type.

"Is there anything else you can tell me about Carlotta? Anything about her other lovers?"

"I never met any of her conquests and don't remember any names, and I probably never heard last names in the first place. Way too many to keep track of anyway. I just listened to her lurid tales. There was this one guy — I never knew his name, so don't even ask — who videotaped their trysts. She used words like trysts, can you believe it? But anyone who'd pick a name like Carlotta . . . Anyway, they got into some kinky stuff, according to Carlotta. Marty's Hideaway closed down after she left town. Seriously."

"Marty's Hideaway?"

"Her after-work meeting spot — trysting spot I should say. One of those rent-by-the-hour places."

"Why not use her place?"

"Her brother. He stayed with her for quite some time."

"What else can you tell me?"

"What else — I don't know . . . let's see, Carlotta fled. I don't know where she went, but apparently she ended up in Virginia. Literally *ended* up."

"I wonder about the órder of all these events. Like, was the pool incident before or after the Christmas party? And how soon before or after?"

"Who would know? Besides Linda, of course. Do you think Linda did Carlotta in at your book group?"

"I'm inclined to think so. But there's no proof that she did. No one saw her in the kitchen or anywhere near Carlotta's tea. And there's another suspect." I told Jeanette about Annabel. "And let me tell you this . . ." I described the pre–book group visitor. "And then there's this . . ." and I launched into the man-in-the-car scenario.

"Sounds just like our Carlotta," Jeanette said in a singsong voice. "That woman belongs in the pages of some lurid romance."

I said that Carlene was indeed inspiring me in my writing. Not wanting to get sidetracked by talk of writing, I said, "I'm puzzled about all her names." I listed the names I'd learned to date: Carla, Carlene, Carly, Carlotta. "They're not that different, just variations of the same name. Carlotta has a noirish ring."

"She got the name from an Agatha Christie character in *Thirteen at Dinner.* Carlotta Adams. That Carlotta died as well . . . I don't know if that means anything."

"Well, she was a big Agatha Christie fan

and probably liked the exotic sound of the name so she used it for a time." I told Jeanette about the love fugitive subject of Carlotta's next book, musing that Carlotta's varying names and her becoming taciturn stemmed from her being a love fugitive.

"Love fugitive. Oh, please."

"I know, I know, it sounds fanciful. But still." Then, remembering my conversation with Vince, I said, "Maybe she was fleeing from Linda."

"Well . . . it's possible. I thought her moving had to do with the broken engagement, but maybe not. I imagine if some wild woman threw me into a pool, I'd be a tad disconcerted. I'd have called the police." After a pause, Jeanette said, "As for Carlotta's name, I think she just changed it a lot, got bored with the same one for too long. I recall her using the name Carolina for a time."

"Yes, well, changing names is another way to hide." I sounded like a country-song writer. "I wish I could locate Linda. She appeared and disappeared at book group and at the memorial service like a genie in a bottle." Jeanette offered the usual suggestions like contacting the bookstore, Googling, or white pages. "We tried the bookstore with no luck. As for Googling or the phone book, we tried that, but her name is Linda Thomas. Linda Miller wouldn't be much better. And no one knows her husband's first name. Plus" — I remembered the unwelcome possibilities we'd bandied about earlier — "Linda may not even live around here. You said she and Ben moved away years ago. Any idea where they went? And did they move before or after Carlotta?"

"I'm not sure about the chronology. Ben and Linda moved to Chicago. Or Cleveland. Some cold-assed place that started with a 'C.' " I pondered the idea of looking for Linda Thomas/Miller in Chicago or Cleveland and shuddered.

"And so, can we wrap this up, Hazel? I want to start hunting for these photos. Of course, I'll expect an autographed copy of your book."

"You got it." I thanked Jeanette for her input and she assured me that she'd send the photos ASAP. With that, we ended our whirlwind conversation.

While dark-haired men with dark bedroom eyes weren't exactly in short supply, I felt confident that Ben Miller and B.J./Benjy were one and the same person — and a good contender for the man in the car. I felt equally sure that Linda Miller and

Linda Thomas were different names for the same person. How did the two of them come to move from Chicago or Cleveland to Virginia? Was it to hunt down Carlene?

As matters stood, I possessed more information. But I still had more questions than answers.

CHAPTER 16

As she'd promised earlier, Helen called, wanting to know how I felt about moving the next book group meeting up a week to the following Monday. She had to go out of town on the scheduled day and felt that we needed to discuss our future, the sooner the better.

"As for me, I'm probably leaving the group. The fiction group, as well. I just have too much on my plate these days, Hazel. I can't handle it all."

Surprised, I managed, "Oh, but —"

Helen cut me off, saying that she'd e-mail everyone. Then she more or less hung up on me without getting my input about re-scheduling.

When Lucy came home the cats raced downstairs and accompanied her back upstairs. After recounting her dinner at Mosaic's with Maxine, I told her about my conversation with Jeanette.

"That Carlene . . . what a *woman.* Do you think she had the desk sex in a cubicle or did she have her own office?"

"I couldn't say. But with what we now know about her exhibitionist tendencies, I'd say a cubicle. It wouldn't even have mattered if it was hers." We laughed as we pictured the scene.

Lucy got up and said she was going to bed. She planned to get an early start for Northern Virginia the next morning to visit her daughter and granddaughter, not returning until Sunday evening. When I said this trip was news to me, she insisted that she'd told me about it, just had forgotten to put it on the calendar. I suspected she'd hastily arranged it once she learned of my upcoming date with Vince and said as much.

"I did nothing of the kind, Hazel. But it does work out nicely, doesn't it? You and Vince will have the house to yourselves, and . . ." She trailed off, leaving me to end the sentence. Easy to do, with my imagination already working overtime.

Early Saturday morning found me again at my computer, checking my mail every five minutes to see if Jeanette had come through with the photos. I knew it was unlikely that she'd be up at 5 a.m. Pacific time, but I persisted. I responded yes to Helen's question about rescheduling the book group meeting. By the time I'd finished deleting an accumulation of junk mail, Lucy left for her trek to Northern Virginia, clad in a brown and black "weekend" outfit from Chico's, saying as she carried her overnight bag down the stairs, "Let's be thinking about finding Linda. Except, of course, when you're with Vince."

I promised myself to limit e-mail checking to once an hour on the hour and use the in-between time for my writing. The week before I'd labored over a sex scene and given up in defeat. I hadn't been going for Stepford Wife sex, but my characters had the same robotlike dimension as the ones populating the pages of that enduring tale by Ira Levin. But today, using my reveries involving Vince as a muse, I managed to produce a more than passable scene. Thinking of what I'd learned about Carlene's exploits helped as well.

Then my mind lit on images of a lifeless Carlene. I shook my head to dispel the unwelcome pictures. If I wanted to produce a book, I had to put this whole sorry mess behind me. And I wouldn't, indeed couldn't, do that until I had answers as to how she died.

So much for my short-lived enthusiasm for writing. I'd have to be thankful for the one scene being so good that time had flown by and it was eleven. I groaned in disappointment when Jeanette persisted in being a cyberspace no-show. Resigning myself to being patient and resisting the urge to bug the prickly woman, I decided an early lunch was in order — the cats agreed and accompanied me downstairs to the kitchen. After feeding them, I fixed chicken salad for myself. When I went back upstairs, I forced myself to do something other than check my mail.

The cats flanked either side of my monitor, sitting on their briskets. As they gazed at me with half-open eyes, I thought back to Monday and the cyanide discussion. Using the Dogpile search engine, I looked up cyanide, Tylenol murders, Seattle murders, and famous cyanide murders in general. Agatha Christie figured prominently in the results. Cyanide was often her weapon of choice, featured in *And Then There Were None, A Pocketful of Rye,* and *The Moving Finger,* among other works.

I studied pages about the Seattle murders someone had mentioned during the book group discussion about cyanide. Stella Nickell had added a lethal dose of the poison to Excedrin capsules — not Tylenol — killing her husband along with another woman. She was nailed from the fingerprints in the library books she'd used as reference for her nefarious activities. The pages that detailed cyanide had the most fingerprints. I marveled that the police solved cases in this day and age using such Agatha Christie–ish methods of detection — fingerprints in books.

I thought of Trudy's friend Ronnie threatening to turn Annabel over to the police, citing knowledge of Annabel's fingerprints in several library books. Two similar fingerprint stories in one week had to be more than a coincidence. I located the account of Stella Nickell's case, *Bitter Almonds,* in the library database and reserved it online. More searching on the cyanide subject turned up accounts of Nazis, the Peoples Temple of Jonestown, and James Bond movies among others.

The ringing of the doorbell startled the cats and me. I went to the window and looked down at the front door, seeing only the back of a wheelchair and a long gray braid. That was enough to identify my two callers as Sarah Rubottom and her husband, Den. I couldn't recall Den's last name but it wasn't Rubottom. I wondered what prompted their unexpected visit.

When I opened the door, Sarah got right to the point. "I just *know* this shindig at Helen's is going to be a memorial service. We *had* a memorial service. At the church. And I just *know* Helen will have a Bible at her side and want to read passages, lead us in prayer with our hands held."

I asked if they'd like to come inside. "No, no, no, no, no," Sarah protested, waving her hand from side to side. "We just stopped to say hi. Your car was in the driveway so we figured you were home. Right, honey?"

"Right, honey," Den agreed, but his eyes didn't leave mine. As usual, his mischievous smile hinted at sexual invitation. He was a man who loved women; regardless of age, race, size, hair color, he loved them all. No matter how unattractive a woman considered herself, she was bound to feel special when Den bestowed that smile on her.

I doubted they stopped just to say hi. True, they lived down the street so their coming by the house wasn't unusual. But Sarah's need to vent was a more likely reason. Not wanting to let the cats out, I popped the latch and closed the door, standing on the front steps in my socks. "Please excuse my appearance." Why did I need to ask unexpected visitors to excuse me for wearing sweats and no makeup in my own house? Sarah and Den's sweatshirts and jeans fared little better on the classiness scale.

"Why would we care?" Sarah echoed my thoughts. "Getting back to Helen, I have no idea why the woman even bothers to attend book group. Our politics just aren't compatible."

"We've all wondered about that." The rest of the group ran moderate to liberal. I considered myself to be moderate, but if I toppled off the political fence I'd land on the left side. "She might regard us as personal challenges."

Sarah went on, "Even though I'm a Republican too, Helen and I are light-years apart. We agree on fiscal issues, but we never talk about them. No point, I guess. It's the social issues — I can understand her pro-life stance because I'm on the fence about that — but how can she think the way she does about stem cell research? And she doesn't want to discuss her opinions, or defend them, just wants to make proclamations and that's it. Period." Sarah paused to take a breath. "Of course, I suspect she's one of those women who doesn't think anyone of our gender knows anything. Likely she gets her opinions from men, like her minister, or from cable TV."

I remembered Art's puzzling revelation that his mother had moved to Richmond because of Jerry Falwell. That spokesman for religious conservatives had an authoritarian manner. And maybe Helen's husband had been a bossy sort, although I knew nothing about the man. Had she ever mentioned him? Had Art ever referred to his father?

Aloud, I said, "Another reason it's curious that she comes to our book group. Except for Art, we're all women."

"Go figure." Sarah rolled her eyes. "But getting back to politics, I was quite liberal in my youth, during my years at Berkeley. But somewhere along the way —"

Thinking that if Sarah wanted to chronicle her political passage we could do it indoors over tea and maybe she'd reveal something useful about the investigation into Carlene's death, I repeated my invitation to come inside.

"Oh, no. We have to get going. Just wanted to get out and enjoy the beautiful day."

"Well, getting back to the praying, I wouldn't worry about it, Sarah. We can suggest having a moment of silence and say our own prayers. Or not." I wasn't the most religious of persons, but I believed in the power of prayer, thought it a good practice. Sarah, on the other hand, branded herself an agnostic.

When I said the meeting's purpose was to discuss the group's future, Sarah said, "Yeah, well, I doubt that we have a future." I suggested that she forgo the meeting, reminding her that it wasn't, after all, a command performance. She shrugged.

Wanting to move on, I asked, "Was there anything in Carlene's second book that hinted at suicidal thoughts?" Carlene hadn't cared for critique groups, but trusted Sarah for thorough and constructive criticism and proofreading.

Sarah touched her fingers to her forehead, a classic thinking pose. "I don't think so, but I'll give it some thought."

"Have you seen anything of Carlene's third book?" At her no, I said, "I'm intrigued about the love fugitive idea."

"Me too. But she never showed anything to me — probably hadn't reached the critiquing stage." We described the love fugitive idea to Den.

Den turned the conversation to the memorial service, with each of us agreeing it was lovely, a nice send-off, so to speak.

"Carlene was one beautiful woman." Den shook his head in sorrow, but the hint of a playful smile remained. "I'll miss her."

I wondered at Den's choice of words, *I'll miss her.* Apart from the turkey dinners, when had he and Carlene seen each other?

Sarah rolled her eyes. "Yes, I'm *sure* you'll miss her, honey."

Sarah's edgy tone wasn't lost on me. Had there been something between Den and Carlene? Was he another notch on Carlene's bedpost? If so, it sounded like Sarah was not only on to it, but grudgingly accepting. At this point, *Carlene* and *affair* went together. The question was, despite Den's charm and provocativeness, could he, um, *deliver?* I didn't know the extent of his injuries, and Carlene had been one adventurous woman. And so, yes, Den could deliver *something.* Feeling that a paraplegic character with alternative sexual gifts would add spice to my work-in-progress novel, I hoped to hold on to the idea long enough to record it once I got back in the house.

"We have to go," Sarah announced. "We're having in-laws over for dinner." I stood watching them walk and roll down my walkway, wondering what the abrupt departure was all about. Maybe Sarah wasn't crazy about her in-laws. I thought of Evan's cold parents. The parents and siblings of my other husbands had been considerably nicer, but our acquaintance had been too brief to get to know them. Then I realized what prompted the hasty good-byes — Sarah might have realized that despite the brevity of our conversation, she and Den had revealed too much. If Carlene did have an affair with Den, that provided Sarah with a motive to kill her. And Sarah had told Carlene that she had no towels in her bathroom. Easy enough to arrange an outage and remove Carlene from the kitchen for as long as it took to sprinkle white powder into her mug. I sighed at the prospect of adding yet another book group member to my suspect roster, but I couldn't ignore the fact that Sarah had just cast even more doubt on the suicide verdict. For the time being I made her an "understudy" suspect, to borrow theatrical lingo.

I toyed with the idea of going for a walk. The temperature hovered at about seventy-five degrees, my cutoff point for comfort. But walking required shoes — too much trouble. Back inside the house, I remembered my idea for a paraplegic Don Juan and looked around for my recorder. Keeping track of the recorder, intended to aid me in my writing, presented a perpetual challenge. As I jotted down the Don Juan idea on the back of a receipt, I remembered using the recorder, tucked away in my dressy purse, at the memorial service. I'd had a lofty notion of capturing someone's murder confession. But I didn't want to take the time to listen to at least three hours of recording and, besides, I needed a diversion from death and its aftermath. At the moment, cleaning loomed as a viable, if not welcome, one.

Even though Vince and I didn't stand on ceremony, the place needed at least a light cleaning, and light it would be. Starting with the important rooms, my bedroom and bath, I spent the better part of an hour sprucing up the place. My next e-mail check still yielded nothing from Jeanette, but the messages from the book group had multiplied. The general consensus on the book group meeting was that Tuesday worked better than Monday. My eye fell on Helen's home address. Something struck me as being familiar about it. Of course, I'd been to her place many times over the past couple of years. But something else prompted the recognition. I laughed at my need to find significance in the smallest detail. The smallest detail could break this case wide open. That's the way it worked in murder mysteries. The fictional kind, I reminded myself.

As she had a few days before, Annabel sent an e-mail that didn't include Kat as a recipient. "Yesterday, Kat told me that Carlene ended her life with cyanide. It was in her tea. How very, very sad." Annabel was likely paraphrasing because I doubted that Kat used the phrase "Carlene ended her life." Just how sad did Annabel find Carlene's death? She ended her missive with "And weren't you all talking about cyanide at the book group right before I got there? Where would she get the stuff?" So far no one had replied. I didn't either.

Jeanette finally came through. Looking at the photos, I realized she was right — Linda's midnineties persona recalled Morticia Addams, with her Gothic-looking long, dark hair and tight black dress. If I had Photoshop, it would be child's play to produce a present-day Linda. It was a simple matter of painting white stripes on her hair and adding digital meat on her bones.

As for the man sitting next to Linda, B.J. Miller, Jeanette was also right about his bad-boy looks and bedroom eyes. His look stirred a feeling of familiarity, but I couldn't place him. Besides, he could be anywhere and may or may not still have the mustache and beard. My efforts to remove hair and add years via mental Photoshop fell short.

Besides, for all I knew he might still be in Chicago, or wherever he and Linda moved to all those years ago.

Carlene, aka Carlotta, wearing a glittery holiday sweater, stood off to the side, auburn hair flowing over her shoulders in Art Nouveau–type waves. Age-wise, she looked much the same as she had five days before. While Linda chose not to smile, Carlene wore a big grin, whether from precoital anticipation or postcoital bliss depended on whether the photo was taken before or after the desk incident. B.J.'s similar smile fueled my suspicion that he was the desk guy. Jeanette had included a photo of Carlene by herself and one of her with the suited and celibate fiancé.

I sent the photos to Kat and asked her to call me when she got them. I debated with myself about sending them to Helen and Art, asking them if B.J. could be the man in the car. But how would I explain Linda's presence in the photo? They probably wouldn't even recognize her, but I took the precaution of cropping her out of the picture before sending it to them. Maybe I'd get a break and get a match on B.J.

But the break wasn't coming that day, at least not courtesy of Helen and Art, with whom I exchanged a few rounds of e-mails.

291

Neither of them could identify B.J. as Carlene's parking lot companion with any degree of certainty. "Art and I barely saw him when he was sitting on the bench. And when they were in the car we couldn't actually see him."

Art asked the inevitable question: "How did you get this photo?"

"I was talking to this friend of mine from L.A. who knew Carlene years and years ago. She thought I'd be interested in some photos of Carlene and e-mailed a few to me. When I saw them, something made me think the guy with her could be the man you and your mom saw her with that night." Apparently my explanation sufficed, as I heard nothing further from Helen or Art.

When Kat called I gave her a lightly edited version of my conversation with Jeanette. I figured she'd appreciate the desk sex bit.

I was right. "Still amazes me," she said with a chuckle. "These are good pictures of her. She hadn't changed a bit over the years. Ageless." I heard a catch in her voice. "Really ageless now," she said ruefully. "As for Linda, she looks, I don't know . . . anorexic? And B.J.'s her ex, you say? He looks familiar. I think. But you said this picture was taken nine or ten years ago, so it's hard to be sure."

"Yeah, and he might have a lot of gray now, or maybe he's bald. And he may not have the beard and mustache anymore either."

Kat turned away from the phone to blow her nose. "I just can't put a name with his face. But I know one thing — I wouldn't mind taking a tumble with him. Maybe I did — maybe that's why he seems familiar." I "heard" a smile through her tears.

I had to face it — the man in the car could remain an eternal mystery.

"Well, Carlene certainly didn't change over the years." Vince echoed Kat's assessment. "You say this is from 1995?"

"Thereabouts. Maybe ninety-six."

Vince sat next to me at my computer. Both cats competed for his attention, Daisy walking around on his lap, with Shammy licking his hand. As we studied the photograph describing the triangle formed by B.J., Linda, and Carlene, I gave him a rundown of my conversation with Jeanette. When I got to the part about the desk sex, Vince looked at me and I looked at him.

Our dinner plans fell by the wayside — unless we counted the pizza we had delivered and ate in bed, scrutinized by cats looking for handouts.

When I told Vince about Sarah and Den's visit much later, I took care to qualify my remarks. "Of course, we don't *know* that Carlene and Den had an affair."

"But what's the likelihood that they did?"

"Pretty good," I sighed. "And that makes Sarah another suspect." Then I hastened to recite the mantra, "If it wasn't suicide, that is."

As I had earlier, I speculated about what Den could do. When I asked Vince for his take on the matter, he had a suggestion.

And a very interesting suggestion it was.

On Sunday morning we enjoyed a late breakfast at Joe's Inn. Then, after a lengthy good-bye, Vince left to work on his writing and I sat at my computer, determined to get cracking on my own. I put all thoughts of Carlene's death out of my head but kept the erotic ones generated by the previous evening. I expected to produce steamy scenes by the dozens. Sex had never been a problem for Vince and me. Although, unlike Carlene and her penchant for sex in uncomfortable places like desks and cars, I wasn't quite so adventurous, preferring the comfort of a bed. I contemplated my newly resurrected relationship with Vince — what direction would it follow? What direction did I want it to follow? Deciding to dispense with the relationship what-ifs and put my re-charged sex muse to good use, I opened my latest chapter.

But neither my muse nor my characters got to first base. The phone rang, with Kat Berenger's name scrolling across the display window.

"Hazel, you'll never guess who's here at the gym!" Not waiting for my guess, she exclaimed, "Linda!"

CHAPTER 17

"I didn't realize she was a member, but she said she just joined recently. And not a minute too soon — the woman's thighs are pure cottage cheese! She was *not* pleased to see me, I can tell you that. Anyway, she did offer her condolences before she tried to give me the brush-off. I told her we'd been trying to find her, wanting to include her in the book group. She said she wasn't interested.

"She did ask how it happened. When I said cyanide, she immediately jumped to the suicide conclusion. Painful as it was, I didn't bother correcting her. She couldn't get away from me fast enough, so I didn't get to grill her." After a sharp exhale, Kat continued. "You might have better luck with her, Hazel, being as you're more . . . sedate. How soon can you get here? I doubt she's the sort who clocks in much time at gyms. I got her address and phone number from the database here, but it would be *much* better if you confronted her in person."

"I don't know about confronting her, but I do want to talk to her. And you're right, it would be easier if I just 'happened' to run into her than if I called her."

I sprang into action, throwing clothes and shoes into my gym bag. As I opened the kitchen door, the phone rang again — Lucy, according to caller ID, no doubt expecting a debriefing of my date with Vince. I let her leave a message. I wasn't about to let Linda slip through my fingers.

Kat met me at the door to the gym. Her getup of the day, unconventional even for her, involved yellow patent leather and leopard velvet. How did all that patent leather "breathe"? Kat launched right into an update on Linda. "She just left the Jacuzzi. I was right, she didn't spend much time exercising, just strolled on the treadmill for five minutes. So go. Meet her in the locker room. I'll scan you in."

"What about you?" I sounded like a toddler on her first day of nursery school, clinging to her mother's skirt. Now that I was about to meet Linda face-to-face, I wanted Kat's comforting muscle. The exercise area looked sparsely populated and mostly by men, making me doubt that the locker room contained women in significant numbers. This investigation business was fast losing its appeal. In books, silly amateur detectives put themselves in dangerous situations with not even a token regard for the consequences. The fact that I didn't live in the pages of a book was never clearer to me than now. But Linda wasn't likely to pose a danger in the locker room. Was she? My contrary mind itemized the potential danger zones — showers, sauna, lockers, just for starters. What about my promises to Lucy and Vince that I'd avoid being alone with anyone from the book group?

"What *about* me? She already blew me off. Besides, I have a personal training session in a few minutes. Call me if you need me. You've got your phone, right? Put it in your pocket. And you've got me on speed dial, right?"

"Yes, we took care of that the other day." I checked the assigned number as I transferred my phone from my purse to my jacket pocket. "Eight."

"Good. Well . . . just go. You'll be fine." I shot Kat a doubtful look.

"You're just having a casual chat with her, nothing more." Kat made shooing motions with her hands. "You'd better get a move on."

Casual was not a word that I'd use to describe my feelings at that moment. More like terror when imagining myself folded into a locker. Looking for a delaying tactic, I asked, "How's Mick? I haven't heard anything about him."

Kat looked exasperated. "Just *go.*"

Thinking fast on my feet was never my strong suit. With more advance notice, I'd have invested time planning my strategy. Yet another aspect of investigating that detective fiction glosses over is the need for improvisational skills. But planned conversations weren't likely to work anyway. I needed to establish myself as a trustworthy confidante and hope that Linda responded with an outpouring of Carlene-related angst. I ignored Vince's voice telling me to turn tail and run.

Herbal shampoo and sweat permeated the locker room. I caught Linda in the act of peeling off her wet suit. Not stellar timing on my part. Kat was right — Linda needed to spend some quality time at the gym.

I couldn't see or hear anyone, confirming my fear that Linda and I were alone. Not even the sound of a shower promised the eventual appearance of someone. Fortunately Linda was close to the locker room entrance so I could make a hasty exit if necessary. Resolving to remain calm and matter-of-fact, and hoping I'd remember my resolve to remain calm and matter-of-fact, I put on my brightest smile and gushed, "Linda! How wonderful to see you. I'm Hazel Rose. Remember me? From the book group."

"Yeah, I remember you." She sounded underwhelmed. She finished removing her suit and stood there, naked, looking at me.

Despite feeling more than a little disconcerted at her display, I maintained a bubbly manner. "Kat and I have been looking for you, but we didn't have your phone number or e-mail address."

"Yeah, yeah, yeah, I know. Yellow Bird jumped on me the minute I got here." I took it that Yellow Bird was Kat. An apt description.

Linda's long streaked hair hung around her head in wet ropes. The Jacuzzi had melted off her thick eye makeup and now it settled in creases under her eyes. Had she forgotten that she was naked? As if she heard my question, she draped her towel around her neck. I toyed with the idea of suggesting she cover other parts as well. No, just ignore the whole thing, I decided. And maintain eye contact.

Linda didn't ask why we'd tried to reach her, but that didn't stop me from explaining. "We wanted to welcome you to the book group and invite you to a special planning meeting on Tuesday." I ad-libbed our agenda, leaving out the part about the group possibly disbanding. "Can you join us?"

Linda looked blank for a moment before realizing that I'd asked a question, putting the ball in her court. "Uh, Tuesday?" When I nodded, my smile starting to feel frozen, she said, "Sorry, can't. Tuesday's Bingo night."

"Oh well, another time perhaps. We so enjoyed meeting you, despite the circumstances." Then I went from gushing to sympathetic. "I'm so sorry about your loss." I reached out a hand but didn't touch her. Even though it would have just been her arm, that was attached to her naked body. Off limits.

"Loss?"

"Carlene. Weren't you two friends in L.A.?"

Linda gave a derisive snort. "Not hardly. But she was obviously a friend of yours, so I won't say a word." She gave me a coy look.

I took that as my cue to stand up and count myself one of the legions of women who had lost out in the romance department to femme fatale Carlene, thereby establishing a common bond with Linda. "Well —" I drew out the well and tried for my own coy look. "We weren't exactly *friends.*" I looked around, acting like I had confidences to share and didn't want to be overheard. "Just between you and me, I'll tell you something I *never* talk about — Carlene stole my fiancé right out from under my nose! Not to speak ill of the dead, of course."

"You're kidding!" Linda looked delighted.

I told her how I had moved from L.A. to Virginia to marry my fiancé, but my plans got derailed when Carlene stepped in and married him before I'd even arrived. I left out unimportant details, like the fact that neither my so-called fiancé nor Carlene knew of my marriage plans.

I definitely had Linda's attention. "Nothing that woman could do would surprise me."

"Sounds like you had a bad experience with her as well."

"You might say that." Linda slanted a look at me, perhaps debating with herself if she could trust me.

Prodding her, I asked, "Was that back in L.A. or recently?"

"L.A. Years ago."

Everyone had a story to tell, and I expected that Linda was no different. I waited a couple of beats before my next prod. "So how did you know Carlene? Did you work with her?"

"No, my husband worked with her. Carlotta, that's what she called herself then." Scowling, she added, "I met her at their company Christmas party."

"Carlotta?"

"Yes, Carlotta. Fancy-assed name. Maybe she changed it to Carlene after the incident with the fiancé and the tapes."

"Fiancé? Tapes?" Maybe I was about to hear an expanded version of Jeanette's fiancé story. Jeanette had alluded to tapes that one of Carlene's lovers had made.

Linda laughed. "Sorry. I'm getting ahead of myself. Where was I?"

"The Christmas party."

"Ah, yes. The infamous Christmas party." Linda took a deep breath and began. "Carlene had her fiancé with her, a lawyer. He was actually very nice, but for some reason felt he had to tell us that he and wifey-to-be didn't have sex 'cause they were born-again Christians. I mean, why did I have to know that?

"Anyway, the four of us kind of hung out together at this party. On the way home, I noticed that B.J. reeked of perfume. When I asked about it, he said he'd danced with someone who'd gone overboard with the stuff. I was suspicious but didn't really know what to think. Well, I *did* know what to think, just didn't want to. I didn't remember him dancing with anyone. I came to realize that he and that floozy Carlene took off somewhere for a quickie. So much for her being a born-again Christian."

I wanted to cheer in triumph at the confirmation of B.J.'s identity. I hoped my feigned amazement at Carlene and B.J. having a quickie masked my elation. "You're kidding! A quickie? Did they leave the party at any point?" I doubted Carlene was a born-again Christian on either coast, so I left that aspect of Linda's account alone.

"I'm sure they did, but all I would have thought was that they were going to the restroom. I mean, it was a party, who really pays attention?" Linda's expression turned hard. "Maybe they did it in a stall."

Or on a desk. Aloud, I asked, "You said you came to realize that they went off somewhere. How was that?"

"It was the tapes that I found in B.J.'s desk. Tapes of him . . . and Carlene. You can just imagine what they were doing." A note of pain crept into her voice, replacing the previous hostility.

"Oh, Linda, I'm so sorry —"

With an impatient gesture, Linda dismissed my expression of sympathy. "I started following Carlene home from work. I expected B.J. to show up but I never saw him. Maybe they went somewhere else. One night I went to her apartment and, get this — there was another man there! He said she didn't live there, but I didn't believe him and said I'd wait. I sat by the pool, one of those apartment complexes with the courtyard, pool, the whole Southern California bit. And, finally, she came home." She paused in her narration.

Jeanette had mentioned Marty's Hideaway as Carlene's "trysting" spot when Hal was visiting, which might explain B.J.'s not showing up at the apartment. Should I tell Linda it was Carlene's brother Hal in the apartment? And ask if she'd recognized him at the memorial service? No, I concluded. She'd wonder how I had that information. "And then?" I asked.

"I told her to stay away from my husband. Or she'd regret it."

"How did she respond to that?"

Linda shrugged. "Don't remember. I do remember neighbors opening their doors, watching us, and the guy from Carlene's apartment coming out and escorting her inside."

So Linda was leaving the pool incident out of her tale. I nudged her some more. "I guess your confrontation was pretty loud to get the neighbors outside." She allowed that the exchange was heated but didn't offer additional information.

"The next day I sent copies of the tapes to her. *And* to the fancy lawyer. Thankfully he had given me his card at the party."

I felt my sympathy for Linda slipping away. It was bad enough to send the tapes to Carlene, but sending them to the lawyer was over the top. Linda had no doubt suffered pain over B.J.'s infidelity and the tapes might have been too much to bear. But still. As for B.J., where was he in all of this? Had he emerged unscathed from this tragedy of sorts? Trying to sound neutral, I asked, choosing my words and tone with care, "When were the tapes recorded?"

"According to the date stamp, exactly one week before the Christmas party. I guess the tramp wasn't cut out for celibacy."

No, Carlene and celibacy were not a match made in heaven. Aloud, I asked, "Did she know it was you who sent the tapes?"

"As opposed to who? B.J.?" She laughed. "Why, I never thought of that. So I guess

she never knew for sure *who* sent them."
She sounded pleased with the notion.

"Did Carlene stay away from B.J. after
that?"

"I don't know. I continued to follow her
for a while until B.J. told me she'd left the
company. I watched out for any new tapes,
but never found any. Of course B.J. probably noticed that they'd disappeared and
couldn't very well ask me about them. So if
there were others he'd certainly stash them
somewhere where I couldn't find them. As
for Carlene . . . I don't know if she wound
up marrying the celibate lawyer. He certainly didn't deserve a woman like her," she
sniffed. "Unless he was the forgiving sort."

"What was the lawyer's name?"

Linda made a show of summoning the
name from her memory before shaking her
head. "Can't remember."

Likely story. I felt sure his name was
seared on her brain for eternity and her
lapse owed to contrariness. "Did you ever
confront B.J. about the tapes?"

"Nope." She shook her head emphatically,
spraying water on me in the process. It
dawned on me that we were still standing
and that, aside from the towel she wore like
a scarf, Linda was still naked. Should I sit
on one of the wooden benches and give my

feet a rest? No, that would place my line of vision somewhere I didn't want it to be. I started shifting from one foot to the other and continued to look straight into Linda's smudged eyes.

She went on. "So, like I said, Carlene left the company. And then, let's see, B.J. and I moved to Cincinnati. His dad was sick, so we decided to be dutiful children. I had an idea that moving back to our roots would help our marriage. By that point I was blaming the L.A. environment for all our problems. But they got even worse in Cincinnati."

Cincinnati. *I recalled Jeannette's saying they'd moved to a "cold-assed place that started with a 'C.'" Cincinnati qualified on both counts.*

"And how did you end up in Richmond?"

"After B.J.'s dad died my mom got sick. She lives in Richmond, so again we did the dutiful children bit and moved here. B.J. continued to tomcat around. My mom and sister urged me to get a divorce. After all, the kids were grown. And so I did. Then I married Lloyd. And B.J. married his bimbo of the moment."

"Bimbo?" Then I realized that I was missing my prompt to act stunned and confused at Linda's revelation that she and B.J. were no longer married. Acting confused wasn't a problem, it was remembering to act confused that could trip me up. "You mean . . . you're not married to B.J. anymore?"

"Well, no," Linda rolled her eyes. "Why on earth would I be, after the hell he put me through?"

"Yes, well, you have a point. So that wasn't B.J. with you at the memorial service the other day?"

Linda sighed. "Actually, it was. When Lloyd and I showed up, B.J. latched on to us. Most unfortunate. Lloyd can't stand him."

"That's right, now I remember. You were with *two* men. Which one was B.J.? The tall blond one?" I figured that guessing the wrong one added credence to my not knowing who was who.

"The dark-haired one in the shades. Brooding, kind of. Cross between a gangster and the guy in *Wuthering Heights*, what's his name?" Linda snapped her fingers. I always wondered why people used finger-snapping to summon up stray bits of information.

"Heathcliff," I offered. From what I'd gleaned of B.J., I thought him too shallow to compare him to a bitter, tortured, and fictional Victorian romantic. But lest we got sidetracked by literary characters reinvented as modern-day sleazebags, I asked, "So it sounds like you and B.J. are on good terms. Despite Lloyd's feelings."

"I suppose. We have to be for the kids and grandkids. Plus we live in the same area, so I run into B.J. and the bimbo more often than I'd like. Like here." She wrinkled her nose in distaste.

"Here? At the gym?"

"Yeah. I haven't been here on a Sunday. And believe me I won't be again. First I run into Kat, then B.J., and now you."

"B.J.'s here — now?"

"I just *said* he was."

I wanted to meet the now infamous B.J., but it struck me as unseemly to ask Linda to introduce us. It shouldn't take me long to find someone who resembled the image in the photo. But I still had issues to iron out with Linda and didn't want to let her go. If I missed B.J. I could always ask Kat to look up his address and phone number. But as with Linda I preferred to approach him in person. "What does B.J. stand for?"

"Benjamin Joseph."

Linda was starting to fidget, so I stepped up the pace of our conversation. "How did you come to meet up with Carlene again?

At the signing?"

"Sometime before the signing, I got an e-mail from Creatures 'n Crooks announcing that Carlene would be there. Of course, I had no idea it was my old enemy, what with her name being different and all. When I saw her, I couldn't believe my eyes. It was like it was yesterday — she hadn't changed one bit. When she claimed she didn't remember me or B.J. — that *really* got my goat. Of course, I knew she was lying."

"She was probably afraid of you."

"As well she should have been," she said, barking a laugh. "I got to talking to Kat and she told me about the book group and Carlene's website. She gave me her card and said to let her know if I wanted to come to the group and she'd give me directions. Which I did."

"But why? Why did you show up when you loathed Carlene so much?"

"To make her *squirm.*" Linda noted my discomfort and looked amused. "Actually, I thought she and I could chat a bit. Maybe work out a financial arrangement. Know what I mean, Hazel?" She gave me a provocative look.

What could she mean? Then it hit me. "The tapes! You still have the tapes!"

"Bingo! You win the prize!" With yet

another amused look, she said, "I'm sure Carlene wouldn't have wanted her husband to see them."

I felt stunned. I'd certainly opened the floodgates. Either I was good at this stuff or simply lucky enough to approach someone who was ready to open up about Carlene. It made sense — I didn't pose a threat, and so far my agenda for ferreting out Carlene's killer remained hidden. I hoped. I wish I'd thought to bring along my recorder. All the gadgets in the world did me no good if they weren't at hand.

"But Linda, that's — that's blackmail."

She pretended to recoil in horror. "Oh, Hazel, blackmail's such an ugly word. So distasteful. But yes, I was planning to lean on her a teensy bit. A simple business arrangement. I'm always a little strapped for cash . . ."

I narrowed my eyes. "How did you know she had a husband?"

"It says on her author blurb that she and hubby lived in Richmond. Gotcha, Hazel!" After yet another harsh laugh, she went on. "Remember how I said she looked the same after so many years? Those tapes could have been made yesterday."

"Meaning that if her husband saw them, he'd think they were made recently."

I wanted to smack the smug look off Linda's face, but I opted for bringing her down several notches. "What about the date stamp? You said it was a week before the Christmas party." The now years-old date would make the tapes an unpleasant viewing experience for Evan but far from a show of infidelity.

Linda stopped and looked uncertain for an instant before she recovered her aplomb. "Oh, you *must* be able to remove the date stamps. With today's technology, I'm sure that's not a problem. Speaking of technology, in 1996 I wasn't into the Internet like I am now. I could've gotten even more money from her if I'd threatened to digitize the tapes and upload them."

The downside of the Internet — it opened up countless ways to humiliate people on a global scale.

Linda said, "But there's no point in discussing it now, is there? She's dead. Killed herself, according to Kat. I had a tape right in my purse. But when I couldn't manage to talk to her alone, I left, thinking I'd try another time." I had an image of Linda going through her purse and pulling out her book. But she'd pulled out a number of other items as well — a VHS tape among them. Had Carlene seen it? If so, her already elevated anxiety level likely ratcheted up several notches. At last I had a bead on what Carlene meant by a "huge mistake." Her history with Linda and B.J. qualified in the mistake arena.

Linda said, "She probably couldn't handle her guilty conscience any longer. Seeing me again was just too much for her, so she doctored up her tea and . . . bye-bye. Thankfully, she did *herself* in, else I guess I'd look like a pretty good suspect."

You look like a good suspect to me, I thought. I paused to take a deep breath, trying to marshal my thoughts.

Linda's eyes took on a nasty gleam. "You think I killed her, don't you, Hazel? I bet you don't believe she committed suicide." I was getting on shaky ground. Linda's buying the suicide verdict and feeling safe in revealing her uncharitable feelings toward Carlene had given me a feeling of security that I now realized was false. And still no one in the locker room. Should I call Kat? I reached into my pocket and pulled out my phone. Acting nonchalant, like any person obsessed with her cell phone, I pretended to check messages, placing my finger over the speed dial button for Kat. Just in case.

"Sure I do, Linda. The police ruled it a suicide. And she did leave a note. That's good enough for me."

"I bet it *is* good enough for you. Seeing as you had a motive for killing her as well."

Hearing Linda's goading tone, I felt it best not to respond. My tale of Carlene stealing my faux fiancé had served me well in getting information from Linda; on the other hand, it cast me as a viable suspect in Carlene's murder. I just met Linda's raccoon-like eyes and kept my own counsel.

She moved closer to me, looking menacing. I pictured headlines: "Local Romance Author" — okay, aspiring author — "Killed in Smelly Locker Room by Overweight Naked Woman." Maybe she'd take that towel from around her neck and wrap it around mine. "Let's just say that I did in fact do it . . . Just how is anyone going to prove it?"

How indeed?

With a self-satisfied smile, Linda backed off, grabbed her cosmetic bag, and slipped her feet into a pair of flip-flops. How did I miss the black polish on her toes and fingers? Easy answer — I'd been focused on maintaining eye contact. The malevolent gleam returned to her eyes. "Yes, well, I didn't kill her. Granted, I had a motive, but a living Carlene was potentially too valuable to me. And now, if you don't mind, I'd like to take a shower and get the hell out of here."

Linda turned toward the shower area, but I had a few more questions. I doubted I'd have another chance to ask them so I'd have to risk her impatience. "Wait a minute, Linda. Did B.J. and Carlene keep in touch over the years?"

"Don't know. Don't care."

"Well, if they didn't, how did he know about the memorial service? For that matter, how did he even know she lived in Richmond?"

Laughing, Linda said, "Why, he had *me* to tell him."

"When? When did you tell him? And what did you tell him? After all these years, did you call him and tell him that his former lover killed herself at a book group that you attended?"

"Well — yeah, but that wasn't the first time I called. I called him after Carlene's book signing to tell him that I'd seen her. Let me tell you, he was surprised. He laughed when I said she didn't remember us."

"Did he get in touch with her?"

"I haven't the faintest — wait, do you think B.J. killed her?"

I huffed my impatience. "Like I said

316

before, I have no problem with the suicide verdict. But tell me this, Linda: why did you all show up at the service? I mean, after all you've told me, I can't help but wonder. I can understand B.J. wanting to go, but why you and Lloyd?"

Linda glowered at me for a moment before answering. "To pay our respects, of course. And now can I *please* take my shower?"

I swept my hand out in a be-my-guest gesture, leaving Linda to her ablutions. Not bothering to change, I stashed my gym bag in the nearest locker and made a beeline for the exercise area, hoping for a showdown with B.J. Now that I knew he lived in Richmond I had him pegged as the man in the car.

CHAPTER 18

As I made my way around the gym I carefully scrutinized the men, fervently hoping to ID one of them as B.J. — if, in fact, he was still there and looked at all like the ten-year-old photo Jeanette had sent. If that test failed, I'd visualize the men in suits and sunglasses to come up with an approximation of the man at the memorial service.

I remembered Kat's glowing promotion of the gym as the perfect place to meet men. "All that sweat and state of undress" was the way she'd put it, with her hallmark lascivious cheer. No doubt true, but I wouldn't know from personal experience. If things didn't work out with Vince this time around, perhaps I'd invest in a fashionable exercise wardrobe and put the gym idea to a test.

I found Kat guiding a plump young woman through a weight-lifting routine. Kat waved and said, "Later." I continued my search for B.J. And just what was I going to say to him? Not to worry, I told myself — while unnerving, I'd survived my chat with the naked Linda.

My gym friend Joe waved as he jumped off his treadmill. He grabbed a bottle of cleaner and a towel from a bin and wiped down the machine. Again I thought of the sweat and state of undress phrase as I admired his well-developed muscles, show-cased by a loose-fitting tank top. His signature Cincinnati cap crowned his head.

Cincinnati. B.J. Benjamin Joseph. The propensity that some had to use their middle names.

"Hi, Joe. Or should I call you B.J.?"

His smile faltered. "No one's called me that in quite some time."

"Then I guessed right, you *are* B.J." I went for a carefree laugh, feeling like a talk-show host. As with Linda, putting him at ease seemed the best way to acquire infor-mation and remain safe during what were amounting to high-wire acts. "I just ran into Linda, your ex, in the locker room. She calls you B.J. and said that you once lived in Cincinnati. The hat" — I glanced up at his head — "tipped me off."

"I bet she gave you an earful about me."

"Actually, we were talking about Carlene."

319

In response to his "Who?" look, I clarified, "You know, the woman who died last week at my book group. Linda was there. And, interestingly enough, Linda said you and Carlene worked together in L.A."

"Oh, right. *Carlotta*. That's how I knew her back in L.A."

I wasn't up to dealing with the multiple names at the moment. "Well, I knew her as Carlene, so that's what we'll call her." I didn't wait for his yea or nay on the matter. "That explains why you came to her memorial service the other day. Linda said it was you sitting with her and her husband, right behind me. I didn't recognize you — the different clothes and shades made it hard to tell." I felt my nervousness rising. For all I knew B.J. and Linda were in cahoots. "So how did you find out about Carlene's death? From Linda?"

"Yeah, she told me. And like she told you, Carlotta — excuse me, *Carlene* — and I worked together, so she thought I'd be interested in knowing about it."

We spent a moment shaking our heads, assuming the grim looks people assume when faced with the reality of death. Cutting the commiseration short, I started, "Tell me about Carlene. How long did you work together? And where?" I explained that

I had spent many years in L.A. working in the same field. B.J. told me about Soyars, a midsize publishing company, where he and Carlene had been coworkers during the 1990s. His description of Carlene as an attractive, bright, professional coworker made me wonder how many of my professional coworkers had done it on an office desk.

B.J.'s eyes darted around. I imagined he was looking for a way out of this conversation. Before I managed a follow-up question, he smirked and said, "Maybe Linda told you this — she likes to tell anyone who'll listen what a crappy husband I was. Carly and I — uh, we were more than coworkers. We, uh . . . we had an affair."

This was going better than I'd dared hope. Prompted by my cool "Really?" B.J. gave a sketchy account of the affair, adding little to what Linda had told me, except more about the desk encounter than I needed to know. He left out the part about the tapes. When I asked why the affair had ended, he hesitated before saying that Carlene had suddenly stopped speaking to him. "Then she just as suddenly left Soyars and moved away. I had no way of contacting her and I couldn't locate her online, either using her last name of Gennis or her fiancé's name, which I've already forgotten."

Like Linda, B.J. had managed to forget the fiancé's name. Recognizing my cue to pretend I didn't know something that I did in fact know, I put on my best wide-eyed look and asked, adding a note of incredulity, "Fiancé?"

"Yeah. She was engaged." He had the grace to look embarrassed at that last admission, but I suspected the look was for show and didn't alter the fact that he was a sleaze. But sleazes of both sexes populated this tragedy. "Some really religious guy who didn't believe in sex before marriage. Carlene brought him to the Soyars Christmas party. How she wound up with someone like that . . . I dunno, pretty amazing. Oh, he was a nice guy and all, just didn't seem like Carlene's type. It wasn't long after that party that she vanished and I knew nothing of her until the other day."

"Funny how you all wound up in Virginia." B.J. allowed that it was funny, adding that he and Linda lived in Cincinnati for a while. He touched the bill of his cap and said, "Hence the cap."

"And you've had no contact, no knowledge of Carlene for all these years?" I couldn't keep the note of skepticism out of my voice. "Nothing at all until Linda told you about her death?"

322

"Well . . ." He drew out the "well," probably to gather his thoughts. "Actually — actually Linda told me about her a few weeks ago."

I said nothing, just waited for him to continue. I wondered how closely his and Linda's accounts would match. "Linda told me she saw Carlotta — I mean Carlene — at a book signing. She'd changed her first name to Carlene and her last to Arness."

"It's interesting that you and Linda are still close." When B.J. looked puzzled, I clarified. "Well, Linda told you about seeing a woman you had an affair with during your marriage. I would think it would be a bad memory for her."

"Oh, Linda never knew about our affair. She just thought we were good friends, that's all."

"Ah." I smiled.

B.J. said with a shrug that emphasized his muscles, "At least I don't *think* she knew."

"So what did Linda tell you about Carlene?"

"That she didn't remember us. *That* sure didn't sound right." He looked smug and pleased, confident that no woman could forget him. "Linda said this Carlene looked so remarkably like the woman we'd known that she, meaning Linda, couldn't possibly be mistaken. So when Linda told me she was going to Carlene's book group, she gave me her website name."

"So then what happened?" I glanced at the shiny gold band on his left hand, but didn't comment on his marital status.

Not answering my question directly, he said, "There was a number to call on the book group site. And so I called. From a pay phone."

"Pay phone?" Did pay phones even exist anymore?

"I didn't want my wife checking my calls. She does that when I'm in the shower. She's suspicious as all get out."

I could well imagine why she'd be suspicious, but I silenced the sarcastic responses that came to mind. I settled for a mild, "And what happened when you called Carlene?"

"She agreed to meet me at the library. We talked for a long time."

"And when you ran out of things to talk about, you wound up in her car."

"Well . . . yeah." I caught the pleased look on his face. Then it struck him that I had unexpected knowledge. His eyes narrowed and he asked, "How did you know that?"

"Several people from Carlene's book group saw the two of you in her car." I rushed to add, "They didn't see your faces, but they knew her car, so they figured it was her — with *someone.*" Again, the pleased look. Part of me wanted to smack it off his face. But the man was temptation itself, I granted him that. Jeanette was right, he had that bad-boy appeal that draws some women like a magnet.

"It was amazing to see her again. It was ten years or so since I'd seen her, but she looked the same. I had to agree with Linda about that." This squared with the testimony I'd heard from others. "It was like she was, I don't know — frozen in time." He looked dreamy, perhaps thinking of other ways in which he'd found her to be the same.

"Did you ever go to her house?"

"No." He looked cautious. "I don't even know where she lived. I only saw her that one time. After that, she wouldn't return my calls or e-mails. I didn't even know she was married until the other day at the service."

Somehow I doubted that — in fact, I'd told him she was married just a few days before at the gym — but it wasn't an important enough point to pursue. "What did Linda tell you about the book group? About how Carlene died?"

B.J. gave me another wary look, then

looked behind me and muttered, "Speak of the devil."

I turned to see Linda, blowing kisses in our direction, her jacket a blinding orange color rarely seen outside of prisons. As she pushed open the door and left the gym, she shot us an impudent look.

When I turned back I caught B.J. disappearing into the locker room. I called out but either he didn't hear me or he pretended not to. Likely the latter. He'd seen his opportunity to bolt and had taken advantage of it. Oh well, I told myself, I probably got as much information from him as he was going to give. Maybe he'd even told me the truth as he knew it. As for the tapes, he'd probably deny their existence, but his reaction could be interesting.

I knew that a treadmill session would help to order the thoughts spinning out of control in my beleaguered brain. It didn't. At one point, I caught B.J. slinking out the door. After forty-five minutes of walking nowhere my brain was nowhere as well. Even David Bowie's "Modern Love," usually a sure energizer, didn't help.

Kat finished with her training session and we sat in the café. When I told her the latest revelation in Carlene's abundant sex life, her thrilled reaction was as expected. "Sex tapes? Carlene? You're kidding me! My sister gets wilder by the minute. So . . . Cincinnati Joe, B.J., and the man in the car are all one and the same. He hit on me, more than once. Believe me, I was tempted, but I have a rule about married men — strictly off limits." Then she pronounced, "Linda did it. You mark my words, Hazel." Kat looked mutinous. "So how are we going to nail her?"

"With proof, Kat. So far we haven't a shred of that."

"We'll get proof, Hazel. We're so close." Close? It felt immeasurably far to me.

I asked, "But why would Linda kill someone she was planning to blackmail? Wouldn't it defeat her purpose?"

"We don't know that she was ever going to blackmail Carlene. She's conveniently using the blackmail story to fool you into believing she didn't kill her. But she did. She *did.*"

I finally left the gym and sat in my car. I called Lucy, who listened agog as I summarized my date with Vince. I refused to share all the details, but assured her that he'd stayed the night. Then I tried to move on to recounting my conversations of the past two days.

"Not so fast. Where did you have dinner last night?"

I tended to keep anything about Vince to myself. That was due to our erratic history and because Lucy was so intense about our relationship, whatever stage it happened to be in at any given moment. But I did cave in and confess that we never got to dinner. "Got right down to it, huh?" Lucy chuckled. "So, when are you two getting together again?"

"We didn't make plans." Feeling exasperated, I pleaded, "Okay, now can I tell you about my conversations?" When Lucy agreed and I filled her in, she exclaimed, "Blackmail? How many times has that word popped up? And how bad could the tapes be, anyway?"

"Well . . . I don't know. Bad enough, I guess. Jeanette said Carlene and some guy went in for kinky stuff. I don't suppose Carlene wanted Evan or the religious fiancé to see her having sex, kinky or not, with someone else."

"You're probably right," Lucy admitted. "Well, I'll see you in a while. About ten." Sounding sly, she added, "Unless of course, you and Vince —"

"Good-bye," I sang as I ended the call.

Back home, I sat in the morning room,

sipping green tea and writing down all the bits and pieces of information I'd recently acquired: sex tapes, celibate fiancé, desk sex, love fugitive, man in the car. Identifying the man in the car was an accomplishment, but my least valuable one, as it only satisfied my curiosity, doing nothing to pinpoint Carlene's poisoner.

Now what?

I thought back to the fiancé portion of my conversation with Georgia. Georgia thought that someone other than the fiancé had fueled Carlene's return to the East Coast. I now could name the someone, or *someones*: Linda and B.J. Possible remorse over the broken engagement no doubt contributed to her decision to move. And, thinking of Carlene's name change, she had an opportunity for a fresh start — in other words, reinvention.

Funny, tradition had it that people moving to L.A. to reinvent themselves started over from scratch. They hoped to escape their pasts in Wichita, Pittsburgh — or, in Carlene's case, Northern Virginia. For those who didn't fancy L.A., San Francisco and San Diego offered the same reinvention opportunities. Few chose the more traditional cities of Bakersfield or Fresno. Many succeeded in their mission to start over, living happily ever after. For others, someone who knew them from their pre-reinvention days might show up on their doorstep and blow their cover.

For Carlene, that process reversed itself, with her flight from L.A. to Virginia. She changed her name, toyed with religion, resumed her pleasure-seeking ways, and took up marriage, again changing her name. But eventually, Linda and B.J. showed up on her doorstep, metaphorically speaking.

For the first time since the onset of this exercise in futility, I sensed the pain and fear that Carlene must have carried around with her. No wonder she'd been so reserved. I pictured her looking over her shoulder all these years, not knowing if she was fleeing from B.J. or from Linda. Unless she actually *knew* who sent her the tapes, I was right — she could as easily have been fleeing from a woman as from a man. And to see Linda at the signing . . . I shook my head. I thought back to the night of the book group when Carlene went on about the love fugitive. Had Linda suspected that Carlene was talking about her? I remember Linda saying, using a mocking tone, "What do you mean, love fugitive?" More or less a harmless remark on the face of it, but seen through the light of recent revelations, it loomed in significance. Was she taunting Carlene for sport?

Without the no-proof hurdle thwarting me at every turn, I'd feel confident in naming Linda my number-one choice for killer.

I wrote down the top suspects: Linda and Annabel. Matching them to the motive-means-opportunity triad yielded no surprises — both had motive and both could have acquired cyanide. How they acquired it I couldn't answer, but motive supplied means — a paraphrasing of the adage "Where there's a will, there's a way." As for opportunity, both had that as well. It took nerve, but likely nerve wasn't in short supply with this pair.

I sat there, letting my mind wander until it came upon the recording from the memorial service — I still hadn't listened to that. I nudged Daisy off my lap and went upstairs to get my quilted bag. Back in the morning room, I spent the next three hours listening, with the lofty hope of hearing a confession. But if anyone had confessed, it was in tones too low for my unsophisticated gadget to catch. One word did strike me as having significance: "insurance."

When Art had recited the list of jobs his mother had held over the years, I hadn't noticed the insurance one. I'd been so floored at learning she'd been a clown that the rest of her jobs had escaped my notice. And insurance is, after all, a boring topic.

But now a connection occurred to me: Evan worked in the insurance field in Rochester for many years before he retired and moved to Richmond. Could he and Helen have worked for the same company and known each other? If so, was that significant? I reminded myself that there was no shortage of insurance companies and that Rochester, a fairly large city, likely boasted several of them.

Still, something sent me to my address book to look up the number for Donna McCarthy, a friend from college who worked for the same insurance company as Evan. Donna and I exchanged Christmas cards and talked on the phone every so often.

After leaving a message on her machine, including my home and cell numbers, I pondered the possibilities beyond the book group. Someone, supplied with the deadly white powder, visited Carlene during the day of the book group. Like the mysterious early-evening visitor. Or, as Vince had speculated, was the visitor a hoax, fabricated by Janet? I entertained the idea of Janet as perpetrator, seeking revenge for an affair between her husband and Carlene — then I remembered Janet's proclamation that she was a widow. But for how long? Had Carlene and the husband had an affair before his death? Had he died during the "act"? That would supply Janet with plenty of motive for killing Carlene.

Looking at my notes, I realized that it boiled down to the same theme: Carlene liked sex and she took advantage of all opportunities to have it — wherever, whenever, with whomever those opportunities presented themselves, leaving a trail of lovers and scorned women, some of them mighty unsavory, in her wake. And the betrayed fiancé — why would she even have been with the man? Could he have showed up on Carlene's doorstep on that fateful Monday, abandoning religious principles, seeking revenge? A crime of passion perhaps? No, poison is not the weapon of passion crimes.

When considering the problems that plagued Carlene — separation, her love fugitive status, Linda's resurfacing in her life, a possible guilty conscience from stealing other women's men — suicide was looking more likely. Maybe her conscience became a burden.

Assuming she had one.

■ ■ ■ ■

I heard a scratching sound and followed it to the living room. Daisy and Shammy used their scratching posts to good avail but fancied a nice piece of furniture on occasion. Shammy was indeed applying her paws to the chair, working at something behind the cushion. I reached around her and pulled out a MasterCard in the name of one Annabel M. Mitchell. I remembered her sitting there during her so-called impromptu visit on Wednesday.

I put Annabel's card in my purse, making a mental note to let her know that I had it. I punched Vince's speed-dial button. After fulfilling his professional duty of admonishing me for talking to Linda and B.J., he said, "At least now you can stop going on about that man in the car."

"Well, it seemed worth going on about, as you so charmingly put it. I just wish it had turned out to be a more significant discovery. Instead the guy's just a garden variety ne'er-do-well." Then I brightened. "But Linda's looking more and more like a suspect. Actually cosuspect. There's still Annabel."

"Don't be too sure," Vince cautioned.

"Your findings are interesting, but inconclusive. We don't have enough to go on, Hazel. Not enough to move forward."

"Yeah, yeah, yeah. No proof." Even after looking at this thing six ways from Sunday, I still couldn't come up with proof.

Vince expressed interest in the tapes, going so far as to propose watching them together. "No way, Vince, just forget it. Even if we had the tapes, which we don't, I'm not about to watch my ex-husband's deceased wife having sex with some — some low-life lothario."

"Just a thought." Vince sounded unruffled.

"Besides, I wouldn't relish being compared to Carlene."

As Vince rushed to reassure me of my carnal talents, I laughed to myself.

Was I really envying the sex life of a dead woman?

Chapter 19

Monday turned out to be a quiet day at the Richmond Women's Resource Center, allowing us to get caught up. I didn't usually volunteer on Mondays, but with Georgia being without an assistant, her development director on vacation, and the emotional distress of losing her lifelong friend, she was running behind. Vivian handled the few calls that came through, leaving her time to thoroughly read not only one but two newspapers. In my opinion, she could help with the clerical work too, but that wasn't my call.

While I merged donor acknowledgment letters my cell phone rang. Donna McCarthy.

"Hi, Donna." Not wasting time with preliminaries, I asked, "Did you hear about Evan's wife?"

"I sure did. Arnie told me and I spread the word here. Acer sent flowers for the memorial service and we sent a group card. I've been meaning to call you. Just a second, Hazel." After having a muffled exchange with someone Donna came back on the line. "How's Evan doing with all this? What happened anyway?"

"Evan's about how you'd expect." After filling Donna in on the details of Carlene's death, I got to the real purpose of my call. "Donna, there's this woman in our book group, Helen Adams, and I just found out that she worked with you and Evan at Acer Insurance." I wasn't above fibbing for a good cause. "Did you know her?"

"Sure, I knew Helen. Gosh, she left here a long time ago, at least ten years. She had a different last name then — was it Riley? Something like that. She got divorced shortly before she moved to Richmond. I hadn't heard that she remarried. Carol never said."

"She's not married now. Who's Carol?"

"A friend of Helen's. She hears from her occasionally."

"Does Carol work at Acer?"

"No, I know her from church. In fact, I'll see her tonight at Bible study. She's kind of a gossip. She and Helen grew up together, same schools and all. Carol once told me that Helen went away for a while when she was about fifteen and everyone thought she had a baby in secret. Those were the days when you went to a special home and gave your baby up for adoption."

I did some quick math in my head. If a fifteen-year-old Helen had a child, I figured it would be about forty-five now. Assuming that Helen was in fact sixty. If she was my age, fifty-five, that dropped the child's age to forty. Art's age. Interesting.

"Did Helen and Evan know each other at Acer? I ask because I don't remember either of them ever mentioning it."

"I don't know. They were in different departments, he in operations and she in claims."

"But wouldn't they run into each other in the cafeteria, or at the company Christmas party?"

"I guess." A note of exasperation crept into Donna's voice. "Hazel, why don't you just ask them?"

"Oh I will. Like I said, I just found out about it . . . I forget who told me."

"It's possible Evan wouldn't have noticed Helen because she was a bit frumpy, over-weight. Not exactly a head turner."

"Really? She's quite attractive now. And slim. Maybe she had a makeover when she moved to Virginia."

Donna had a meeting, so we ended the call. I sat looking out the window at the leaves fluttering in a gentle breeze, reflecting on this new information. It couldn't be a coincidence that Helen and Evan had worked for the same company.

Could it?

I went back to my acknowledgment letters, only to be interrupted by Annabel calling on the center's line. "Oh, I'm *so* glad you're there. I left a message at your house, and I don't have a cell number for you." She rushed on without pausing. "By any chance did I leave a credit card at your house?"

"Yes, you did . . . Sorry, I meant to call and let you know. I just found it last night, wedged behind the cushion of the chair where you were sitting. I have it in my purse."

"Oh, thank goodness. I didn't miss it until today when I tried to use it. I hate to inconvenience you, but . . ."

It wasn't hard to guess in what way she hated to inconvenience me. Not that I minded — the Fan district where Annabel lived was a stone's throw from the RWRC and one of my favorite areas of Richmond. The Fan was so named because the roads that radiated westward from its eastern

339

border adjacent to downtown formed a fan shape. It was known for its locally owned restaurants, active nightlife, and post-Victorian architecture. The eastern end of the Fan, or Lower Fan, was home to Virginia Commonwealth University, dubbed VCU by the locals. The Upper Fan, or western end, was one of Richmond's most desirable neighborhoods for young professionals.

"I'd be happy to bring it by your house. I'm working here until four, so I can be there about four fifteen or so."

"Thanks so much, Hazel. I don't know if I'll be there, I have a *ton* of errands today, but my friend Sam might be. He's stopping by to assemble a computer chair for me and then we're going out for dinner. If he's not there you can just stick the card through the mail slot."

We chatted for a few minutes. Annabel's gorgeous son had left that morning to return to Charlottesville and she sounded wistful. She said nothing about Ronnie or blackmail and I followed suit. After assuring each other that we'd both be at Helen's the next evening, we hung up.

At four, I grabbed my keys, logged off the network, and said my good-byes to Georgia and Vivian. Vivian, finished with her newspapers, now flipped through a magazine.

■ ■ ■ ■

Parking was scarce on Annabel's street and I had to settle for a spot a couple of blocks away. Fortunately I always welcomed exercise so I didn't mind hoofing it a bit. Plus it gave me a chance to look at the Fan's charming homes along the way, many adorned with bay windows, stained glass, and turrets.

Crape myrtle trees presided over monkey grass plants on the postage-stamp-size lots that fronted Annabel's duplex, a mustard-colored brick. Plants trailed verdant leaves from the hanging pots placed at two-foot intervals around the perimeter of the porch. White columns supported the veranda that spanned the length of the house. The porch railing posts suggested bowling pins. From the almost identical glider swings with flowered cushions and wrought-iron tables, it looked like Annabel and her neighbor had coordinated their decorating efforts, unlike the individual approach taken by most Fan denizens. The whole setup conjured up images of evenings spent watching the world go by with a mint julep in hand. Did Annabel glide away the hours in one of her power suits?

As I climbed the steps, I noticed a plump older woman sweeping on the other half of the porch. She looked like a grandmother straight out of central casting with her white hair gathered into a bun, bib apron tied around a shirtwaist dress, and orthopedic shoes. I pictured a batch of cookies baking in the oven while a pot roast simmered on the stove.

"I'm returning something of Annabel's," I said when she eyed me with friendly curiosity. I held up the envelope that contained the credit card. "She said I could put it in her mail slot. She accidentally left it at my house the other day . . ." I trailed off as I caught myself overexplaining.

"Oh, sure, honey, go right ahead. Annabel's been so upset over the business with that poor woman getting killed. Did you know her?" She stopped sweeping and pointed at her half of the house. "You know, she used to live right here." This she whispered, like it was a state secret.

"Yes, I did know her. In fact, Annabel and I were both there when it . . . happened."

The woman looked distressed as she shook her head. "Oh, by the way, I'm Mabel Crenshaw. My daughter and her family live here. I come over during the day to take care of the girls. And you are . . . ?"

"Hazel Rose."

"Hazel Rose. Pretty. Well, like I said, Annabel feels just wretched about — what was her name, Carla something?"

"Carlene Arness," I supplied.

Mabel nodded. "Yes, she wrote a book. I read it and so did my daughter. Not as naughty as we expected." Mabel looked disappointed at the lack of naughtiness. "Annabel had a terrible time with her." Again, she lowered her voice to a whisper. "Apparently Carlene seduced Annabel's son." She stopped, gauging my reaction.

Suppressing a smile, I tried for a shocked demeanor. "Seduced?"

"Yes, seduced. Although that probably wasn't hard to do, men being what they are. And these days the young ones aren't as innocent as they were in my day. And he's an awfully handsome man. So polite. Sylvia — that's my daughter — says he looks like that English actor with the funny name."

"Ralph Fiennes," I said, using the correct pronunciation, "Rafe Fines."

"That's it! Anyway, Frankie was nice enough to come here from Charlottesville for Carlene's memorial service. His former lover. So sad." When Mabel placed her hand over her heart, I irreverently listened for the wail of violins. "He just left this morning."

"Yes, Annabel told me. So, she said that Carlene *seduced* Frankie? When did this happen?"

"Let's see, Sylvia and Roy moved here in 2000 — or was it 2001?" Mabel looked off like she expected a passing motorist to yell out the answer.

I didn't care what year the big seduction took place. My interest in the Carlene/Frankie affair was in its possible long-term consequences — like Carlene's death. "Did Frankie live here with his mother then?"

"No, as I understand it he was visiting his mama. He lived in Charlottesville with his grandparents. I don't know why he didn't live with his mama and I don't like to pry, of course."

"So, he was visiting," I prompted, trying to keep Mabel on track.

"Yes, summer vacation or break. According to Annabel, she hardly saw him. He was over here the whole time." Now Mabel went back to her whispering. "Upstairs. In the bedroom."

"Annabel must have been mad."

"Oh, honey, she was mad as a wet hen. She's still mad about it to this day and it was a good long while ago."

Interesting. Very interesting. Aloud, I asked, "How old was Frankie?"

"Oh, young," she said, waving a hand. "College age. After all, he's not very old now. Carlene was at least twice his age if not more." Mabel shook her head in wonderment. "Lands sakes alive! In my day you didn't see goings-on like that." She tsked and then laughed. "I guess I sound like an old lady."

Her laughing allowed me to let go and have a good chuckle myself. "How long did the affair last?"

"Well, until he went back to Charlottesville. And then, and this is what made Annabel really mad, Carlene took up with someone else immediately. I'd have felt the same way if some hussy had gone after my Walter. He's my son," she explained with pride.

Mabel smiled in delight at a point behind me. "Hi, Sam." I looked up to see the white-haired man who'd been talking to Annabel and Helen at the memorial service.

"Sam, this is Hazel Rose. Hazel, Sam Smith."

"Oh, yes, Annabel said you'd be here to assemble a chair for her." We shook hands. Sam appeared to be on the far side of middle age. Oh, wait, *I'm* on the far side of middle age and Sam had a good ten years on me if not more . . . so that made him, well, the near side of old age. "I recognize you from the memorial service the other day. You were talking to Annabel and Helen."

"Ah, yes, Helen. Wonderful woman." Despite his hearty manner, I caught something fleeting in Sam's blue eyes that made his bonhomie ring false and made me doubt that he found Helen quite so wonderful. He continued, "And one tough businesswoman, I'll tell you that. Annabel wanted her to do a website for me. I already have a Tripod site but Annabel wants me to have a better one. More professional."

I vaguely recalled overhearing Annabel asking Helen about doing a website for someone named Sam. It must have been at the book group. "And is Helen going to do the site?"

"We talked about it, but couldn't come to terms on price. And the Tripod one is fine with me. Lots of banner ads, but I don't mind. It's free."

First Carlene objected to Helen's prices, and now Sam — I wondered what the woman charged, or overcharged, for her Web designs.

"Tell me about the site."

"It's for my photography. Something I dabble in." My ears perked up. I remembered Vince saying that cyanide was used in darkroom supplies.

Mabel proclaimed, "He takes beautiful pictures. Simply gorgeous. You have to see them, Hazel."

I decided to get Sam going and look for an opening where I could ask a question about cyanide without being too obvious. It was a long shot, but I had to grab my investigative opportunities when I could. "What are your subjects?"

"Still lifes, landscapes, European military history. That's my field, European history."

"Sam's a retired professor." Mabel beamed like a proud mother. "VCU." Then she looked like an unwelcome realization struck her. "Oh, my goodness, I'm forgetting all about my roast." I was right, she had a roast going in the kitchen. If only I could apply my food-related intuition to solving this mystery. "It was nice meeting you, Hazel. I hope I see you again. And good seeing you again, Sam." She dashed into the house, broom in tow.

I asked Sam, "Do you do digital photography?"

"Oh, absolutely. It's the only way to do it these days."

"Did you ever do it the traditional way, darkroom, mixing chemicals together?"

"No, I just started a few years ago. Digital was well under way by then." Sam produced a card from his pocket and handed it to me. I read "Sam Smith, Photographer," with a Charlottesville address.

I almost stamped my foot in frustration. I'd hoped to nail Sam as Annabel's perhaps unwitting cyanide source. I put the card into the side pocket of my purse. "You live in Charlottesville?"

"Yes, on a farm between Charlottesville and Scottsville, right off Route 20." I nodded like I knew exactly where he meant. In truth I knew nothing about Scottsville or Route 20.

"It's funny you asking me about darkroom processing, Hazel, because I've been thinking about trying my hand at that — there's a darkroom in the farmhouse. The previous owner set it up."

And maybe the previous owner left behind a gift of cyanide. Perfect opportunity for Annabel to get her mitts on the poison. Had she been to the farmhouse? The only way to find out was to ask. I smiled and gushed, "Really! I just know you'll enjoy it, Sam. People tell me photography without the darkroom just isn't the same. Doesn't have the artistic . . . signature." No one had told me any such thing, but Sam didn't have to know that. "Tell me, has Annabel visited your farm yet?"

"Oh, yes. Several times."

Hmm.

I asked Sam if he'd been at Carlene's signing. He had, but didn't recall Linda, anyone of her description, or anyone clashing with Carlene. We exchanged a few remarks about Carlene, the usual what-a-shame-so-talented sort of thing, before I left him to his chair-assembly task. Realizing that I still held the envelope with the credit card, I entrusted it to Sam.

Walking back to my car, I reviewed my conversations with Sam and Mabel. I laughed aloud at Mabel's revelations, drawing strange looks from passersby. But not everything I'd just learned was funny: Annabel was mad about Carlene seducing her son.

Just how mad was she? Enough to kill? Enter Sam with his possible cyanide connection. Motive, means, opportunity: Annabel had all three in spades. Factor in the Randy-related motive and things were definitely looking up as far as working out this puzzle. But — always a "but" to keep me humble — I still had that proof issue to nail down.

■ ■ ■ ■

At home, I climbed the stairs to my den, the cats darting ahead of me, determined to win the race to the top. They did. Checking the address on Sam's card, I pulled up his Tripod site. Tripod might charge nothing to design a Web page, but the banner ads created the cyberspace equivalent of ants at a picnic. The still lifes and landscapes in Sam's portfolio were fair, not exceptional, but showed potential.

His real interest showed in the military history section. One collage of black-and-white photos struck me with its power — a grouping of Nazi paraphernalia: hats, armbands, uniforms, magazines, bullets, pins, badges, coins, whatnot. I wondered if Sam had photographed the collection, which included a tattered-looking copy of *Mein Kampf,* at a museum, so professional was the display. Why did these Nazis keep popping up? I looked at the collage again for something, anything that I could tie to Annabel.

When Lucy opened the kitchen door I went to the top of the stairs. "I'm up here," I yelled. "Looking at Nazi stuff."

Lucy came into view, the cats in her wake.

"Nazi stuff?"

But the ringing of the phone put the subject on hold. Lucy answered and all I heard was, "Hi, Annabel," and, "Yes, sure, of course, we're here."

"Annabel," Lucy explained. "She's coming over. Again."

"Why?"

"I don't know. She said she needed to talk to us about something."

My guess was that Annabel was on a damage-control mission — probably Mabel told her about chatting with me about Frankie. "Oh, wait until I tell you about her neighbor."

But the doorbell ringing stopped me before I started my tale. Annabel came through the door in a panic. Her charcoal gray suit and red pumps looked as pristine as ever, but her unsettled state showed in the deer-caught-in-the-headlight look in her eyes.

"Would you like to join us for dinner?" Lucy's cheerful manner contrasted with Annabel's agitated one.

"No. Thanks, but no." Annabel walked to the sofa and perched on the edge of the seat cushion. "Sam's waiting for me; we're going out. I'll get right to the point. I know you talked with Mabel today. Oh, and thanks for bringing my credit card. Anyway, I so regret telling her and Sylvia about Carlene and Frankie. The thing is, they're both such sweet and engaging souls, always giving me tea. Especially Mabel. On the other hand, they're *hopeless* busybodies.

"Anyway, I don't want the business about my son getting around because, well, frankly it makes me look like a suspect. I didn't want to reveal any more than was necessary. Not with the unsolved murder of my dear husband . . . and with that damn Ronnie on my case."

"Did you hear anything more from her?" I asked.

"No."

"What was the business with your son?" Lucy asked.

Annabel looked suspicious. "Lucy Hooper, do you mean to tell me that Hazel didn't tell you? I don't believe it."

"I haven't had a chance to tell her, Annabel. You called not five minutes after Lucy got home."

Annabel took a deep breath. I assumed she was about to launch into the saga of her son and Carlene. But she sat silent, literally wringing her hands. Lucy murmured something about tea and went to the kitchen, leaving me with Annabel and an uneasy silence for company. Daisy showed up but beat a quick retreat when she saw Annabel, remembering their last encounter.

Lucy reappeared with a tray of steaming mugs and a plate of cheese and crackers. "Try some chamomile tea. It's relaxing."

I felt impatient to hear this latest installment in Annabel's soap-opera life, but forced myself to wait while she blew on her tea, trying to cool it down. I flinched at the memory of Carlene standing in her dining room, sipping her too hot tea. Was it poisoned at the time?

While we waited for Annabel, Lucy and I sipped our own tea and munched on the cheese and crackers. Annabel finally set her mug down on the coffee table. She looked first at us, then away, pressing her lips together. Taking a deep breath, she began, "My Frankie was one of the scores of men Carlene managed to seduce. He was only twenty-one years old, and Carlene was more than twice his age." She picked up the mug and resumed the blowing process.

"So Frankie and Carlene had a relationship?"

Annabel snorted. "Relationship! That's a good one, Hazel. It was hardly a relationship. He visited me for two weeks one summer. My first mistake was in introducing them. In no time he was spending all his time at her place. It started out with her asking him to help her carry a chair into the house. He was smitten from the get-go. I was outraged."

Annabel held up a hand. "Now I know what you're both thinking: Was I outraged enough to kill her? If so, why wait all these years? I've had opportunity aplenty. But even in my wildest rages, I had to admit that they were consenting adults, although in his case, just barely. And neither was married. I couldn't police his sex life. But I just hated the idea of him being that woman's boy toy, or toy boy, whatever the hell you call it."

"How long did they see each other?"

"Two weeks. Frankie went back to UVA and in no time Carlene took up with that Tom somebody who I told you about before. And then Randy." Annabel snorted again. "At least they were in her age group."

"What was your relationship with her like after that?" Lucy asked.

"Strained. For a while. But, like I said, I could hardly be mad. Oh, I could be, and was."

According to Mabel, you still are, I thought.

Annabel sipped her tea. "Like I said, they were adults. So I resolved to be one too.

354

What I went through with that woman, I just can't tell you." But she did anyway. "For over a year, I endured that damn headboard banging against my wall. And the screams! Thankfully I had changed bedrooms before she got her claws into my baby boy." First Vivian with the baby boy bit, and now Annabel.

"So, what happened with Frankie after he went back to UVA?"

"Oh, he moved on. He's engaged to a nice girl. Unlike Carlene, who wasn't at *all* nice."

Nice. Such an inexact adjective. I used to think Carlene was nice. Not very exciting, but nice. But Annabel was right, she wasn't nice at all. Oh, she had a nice manner and I felt certain she didn't torture animals or trip old ladies. But she had wreaked havoc in the lives of any number of people. An unbidden thought came to me — was the Annabel/Frankie/Randy trio Carlene's huge mistake? I was starting to think Carlene's past harbored huge mistakes by the dozens. I put that thought on my mind's back burner.

"*And* Jennifer is three years younger than he is." Annabel sounded triumphant, liked she'd scored a coup.

No one spoke for a minute. Annabel busied herself with the cheese and crackers.

Looking pleased, she said, "So there you have it. I fall into the category of those who could have done it, but where's the proof? I know I'm not eliminated as a suspect, but it needs to be proven, now doesn't it?" With that she popped a cheese-laden cracker into her mouth.

Lucy assumed a puzzled look. "Why would anyone suspect you, Annabel? Carlene committed suicide."

Annabel looked crestfallen, like she enjoyed being a suspect. "Well, yes. But we don't know that for sure."

I asked what might have sounded like a non sequitur: "Annabel, tell us about Sam. How did you two meet?"

Annabel brightened, but finished chewing before answering. "I met him at an exhibit he had here in Richmond. I asked Helen if she wanted to do a website for him. She said she'd think about it. But when I asked her about it last week, she said she was too busy. *Too busy?* What's she busy doing anyway? She should jump at the chance. Sam's so good and . . ." Annabel went on about how good Sam was and how he needed a professional-looking Web presence. "Sam says Helen wants too much money and won't negotiate. If you ask me she's getting full of herself. Well, if she doesn't come through, I'll get him in touch with a woman from Charlottesville, someone I know from high school. Sam lives out that way anyway." She waved her hand vaguely in an easterly direction. As Charlottesville was northwest of Richmond, I assumed she wasn't striving for accuracy.

Annabel finished her snack and wiped her mouth with a napkin, leaving a bright red lipstick smudge. "Well, I'll be going now. I didn't mean to interrupt your dinner. Thanks so much for letting me unload. I feel much better." Despite her words, Annabel still wrung her hands. Her unloading was clearly not a cathartic experience. "See you tomorrow."

"Lucy's coming too."

We talked for a few minutes about mundane, ordinary, non-Carlene matters. As I closed the door when she left, all I could think was that the woman screamed guilty from every fiber of her being. She toppled Linda from top-suspect position.

"So — what did you think about that story?" I asked.

"Well, I suppose it's all true. But combine that with what she told us the other night, and I'd say that Annabel's a nutcase. Which makes me wonder if she was a nutcase before she met up with Carlene."

"Probably a nutcase in the making. Especially when you factor in her husband's murder and her possible culpability in that."

"The question is, did she do it? Kill Carlene, I mean?"

"She had motive, opportunity, and Sam the photographer possibly gave her access to cyanide. Oh —" I remembered with a start that I'd started to tell Lucy about my visit to Annabel's house before Annabel herself interrupted.

When I finished, Lucy thought for a moment. "So you say there's a darkroom at the farmhouse that Sam hasn't used . . . You think there could be cyanide there?"

"It's a possibility."

Lucy looked skeptical. "But would the stuff still be potent?" When I said I didn't know, she said, "I'm inclined to think that Annabel, or whomever, got cyanide elsewhere, not from a photography source — that's just not reliable anymore. Everything's digital now, isn't it?"

I shrugged. "I'm sure everyone hasn't embraced digital technology. Just like some writers still use typewriters." I shook my head in amazement, but word-processing holdouts weren't a pressing concern at the moment. "Let me show you Sam's website."

We went upstairs where my computer was

in standby mode. When I "woke" it up, the page with the Nazi collage appeared. Lucy was unimpressed by Sam's creative efforts. Even the collage that I found so powerful underwhelmed her.

Then Lucy took a closer look at the page. "That's interesting artwork. I guess it's a book or a magazine." The black-and-white design featured a German title and the inevitable swastika. Lucy scrolled down the page. Sam had transformed the collage to an outline, inserted numbers in the outline of each item, and provided names in a corresponding list. Number one caught my attention: what I thought was a bullet was a brass cyanide vial container.

Lucy and I looked at each other, wide-eyed and open-mouthed. "My God," I whispered like I feared being overheard. "This is where she got the cyanide."

"You think Annabel got hold of that container?"

"It's a good possibility. I don't know how old this photo is, or where Sam got the items, but just suppose he took the photo recently . . ."

"But this could be from a magazine. Or a book. Or a museum. He wouldn't necessarily possess any of this stuff."

"True, and I did wonder if he photographed this collection at a museum. But you have to admit it's the closest we've come to a source for Annabel. Or anyone else for that matter."

"I do admit that. And I'd love to have this mystery solved and behind us. But the container might not have cyanide in it. And even if it did, would it still be effective? We're talking sixty years ago."

I wouldn't be swayed. "You mark my words, Lucy. This is Annabel's link."

"I don't disagree. It's just that — let's do some research." She keyed "cyanide vial container" into a search engine, clicked on the first result, and a magnified version of the container in Sam's collage appeared.

"It looks just like Sam's."

"Yes, but they probably all look alike."

Lucy read the inscription on the cap, "It says 'Tesch U.' on the top line, then those SS initials: 'Hamburg,' '77/42,' 'Stabenow.' Probably manufacturing stamps."

The container was for sale. It had a press-on cap and measured one-half inch in diameter and one and three-quarters inches in length. It accommodated a glass vial of cyanide. The vial was similar to an ammonia ampule used for reviving people who have fainted. I flashed back to a long-ago faint-ing episode on a hot day in an un–air-conditioned church. When the ushers waved that vial under my nose, I came to quickly.

Lucy said, "Interesting, but not conclusive."

"Still, it's something." We sat in silence and watched the cats roll around on the floor. "Oh!" I exclaimed, startling Lucy and the cats. "Guess what I found out about Helen."

When I finished my account of the conversation with Donna McCarthy, Lucy said, "Well, coincidences do happen. And lots of folks move to Virginia from up north. Helen and Evan probably met up here at a turkey dinner or while Helen was designing Carlene's website. They likely discussed Rochester and Acer Insurance at that time and then forgot about it. It's not that amazing, Hazel."

"Yes, well, I still think it's funny." Daisy jumped into my lap, circled around, and settled down. "You know something, Lucy? There's lots of mother-son stuff going on here."

"Mother-son stuff?" Lucy knit her brow. "Besides Annabel, who do you mean?"

"Well, there's Vivian with her baby boy. I know, I know, she's just one other person. I can't explain it, I just have this feeling . . . about mothers and sons." I stopped, not knowing where this thought was taking me.

"Lots of women have sons. I have a son."

"I'm just saying, that's all."

We hashed over Mabel and Annabel's accounts of the Carlene/Frankie affair, comparing the two. "In Mabel's words, Annabel is angry about the whole thing to this day."

To this day . . . to this very day.

CHAPTER 20

Lucy and I continued talking until we realized we were going around in circles. And when I called Vince to relate the latest Annabel tale, the meeting with Sam and Mabel, and the Rochester association involving Helen and Evan, he was definitely interested. Who wouldn't be? We had the ingredients of a soap opera. But, as usual, he cautioned me about jumping to conclusions. When I noted that our Saturday-night dinner plans had never materialized, we settled on the coming Saturday for the replacement dinner and agreed to meet for coffee after the Tuesday book group meeting at Helen's.

I knew I should call Kat to get her up to speed on the latest brouhaha but didn't feel up to another conversation. On Tuesday morning, I left a message on her voice mail. Then I sat at my computer and waved a hand over my face, symbolically erasing thoughts of murder and suicide. I called up my memories of Saturday night with Vince and produced an especially titillating sex scene. I worked steadily until Daisy tapped me on the arm, reminding me that it was lunchtime. I glanced at the computer clock and realized she was right — it was noon. Who needed clocks with cats around?

After feeding the cats, I fixed a lunch of whole wheat toast and peanut butter and took it back to my den. The short break put a damper on my writing. My characters' energy had fizzled out and I had to wrestle with them before concluding that I was fresh out of literary Viagra. I briefly checked my e-mail and saw a notice from the library that the copy of *Bitter Almonds* I'd ordered over the weekend was ready for pickup. Thinking that a walk to the library would recharge me and my characters, I took my backpack and walking shoes out of the closet.

I reached into the side pocket of my purse where I usually kept my keys. Not finding them, I hunted around and found them in a different pocket and pulled out a ratty envelope. I scanned a scribbled list of mystery titles on the envelope, titles we'd discussed at book group . . . *when Carlene was still alive,* I thought with a pang of sadness. I pictured Helen waving her hands about as she raved about John MacDonald's color-coded series. Carl Hiaasen's *Strip Tease* and *The Ice Maiden* by Edna Buchanan — the titles seemed remote now. Maybe I'd read them eventually, but not until the memory of that ill-fated evening faded.

As I locked the door, a thought hovered at the edge of my conscious mind. I laughed, thinking how gnawing intuitions were a staple of murder mysteries. A brisk walk might propel the elusive thought into the part of my brain that could produce the classic "aha" moment. All the more reason to get out of the house.

At the library, I loaded my backpack with books. The walk didn't give me any insight into the Carlene mystery, but it did revitalize my characters. Back at home I worked without stopping for the rest of the afternoon. I was in the kitchen pouring apple juice when Kat called.

"I just got your voice mail even though you sent it hours ago. Dumbass cell phones. You had a busy day yesterday. I'm sorry I'm not doing much, but I had back-to-back training sessions all day yesterday."

Kat's not doing much hadn't escaped my

notice. But I did seem to have more connections, I didn't overwhelm people with an outsized persona, and Annabel chose Lucy and me to be her confidants. I gave Kat credit for calling all those L. Thomases.

"So tell all."

I told her all: about meeting Sam and Mabel, about Annabel's visit, and about Sam's collage with the cyanide container.

"So you think Annabel did it?" Kat sounded grim.

"I don't know."

"Wait! Oh, God, I can't believe I didn't think of this earlier. The other day you said Janet saw someone arrive at Carlene's about six thirty. That must have been Annabel."

"How do you figure that?"

"Those pumpkin brownies —"

I cut her off. "You mean the ones from last week?" I now remembered reaching for the last brownie, planning to split it with Sarah, when Annabel's shriek sent us racing to the family room. And I'd told Detective Garcia about them when she'd requested an inventory of food items, but I'd had no idea who'd brought them. Somewhere along the line I'd forgotten all about the brownies. "Annabel brought them?"

"Yes. I asked Carlene about them when I first got there and saw them on the kitchen table. Carlene said Annabel had an appointment and thought she'd either be late or not be able to make book group at all, so she came over with the brownies earlier."

A bad feeling was coming over me as I slowly realized the implications. Annabel kept appearing at every turn in this whole sorry mystery. And not in a good way.

Kat said, "So you think . . . But wait, the cyanide couldn't have been in the brownies because we all ate them."

"No, no, no. I'm thinking that Annabel . . . did . . . something . . . when she arrived the first time. Put something —"

"She put cyanide in Carlene's mug! Wait'll I get my hands on that little —"

I rushed to say, "We don't know that Annabel did any such thing — it's only a possibility and we're still hampered by no proof. It's that collage . . . so damning but still circumstantial. But Lucy said it could be a museum display or a photograph. So let's just take a few deep breaths."

Kat wasn't ready to concede the point. "I don't know," she grumbled.

I sipped my juice. "How are things with Mick?"

Heaving a sigh, Kat lamented, "Not good. That Beverly is always doing something. Don't get me started on her."

"Okay, I won't. So . . . anything new on your end?"

"That jerk B.J. just got out of his monster SUV." I heard car doors slamming so I figured Kat was in the gym parking lot. She snickered. "He's giving me a sheepish look. Anyway, I talked to Helen earlier. I asked her who was bringing refreshments tonight. She said she'd have decaf and if anyone wanted to bring something to go ahead. Just to be safe I'm sticking a Balance bar in my purse."

"I hate it that we can't trust each other. It doesn't bode well for us as a group."

"Yeah, we don't want to put our lives in jeopardy for something that's supposed to be enjoyable. Hold on a sec." I heard a muffled exchange before Kat said, "Hazel, sorry, but I gotta give a tour."

"Okay. See you later at Helen's?"

"You bet. Annabel better be able to run fast."

"Kat, you can't —"

"Oh, I know, I know. I'll behave myself. But you might have to hold me down."

I'd like to see myself hold Kat down, I thought.

Kat asked, "Do you think the group will survive this whole thing with Carlene?"

"That's what we're supposed to address

tonight."

Our future.

CHAPTER 21

I pondered the new wrinkle of Annabel and the brownies. Her early arrival at Carlene's gave her the opportunity to administer the poison — providing that Carlene's mug was on the table and chances were good that it was. She also needed to have Carlene out of the kitchen, but she could invent some item she needed for Carlene to get for her. Did Annabel have the necessary nerve? She'd displayed considerable excitability during my recent experiences with her. But maybe calmness, or the lack of it, didn't matter if she found herself alone in the kitchen. It took seconds to pour powder into a mug, and the whiteness of both the powder and the mug would escape notice.

I entertained the thought of finishing Carlene's love fugitive mystery. If I got my hands on it, maybe I could write my way to solving the mystery of her murder. Did she back up her writing? Probably — she had the same IT training that I did. Was it too soon to approach Evan about acquiring his wife's computer and finishing her work-in-progress?

Sarah called, asking for Helen's address. "I can't find it and it's not in the book." I kept a hard copy of the book group directory in a folder under the counter that divided the kitchen from the morning room. As I recited the address I was struck anew by the feeling of familiarity I had with it. Of course, I'd been to Helen's place a number of times, but something else, something akin to déjà vu, drifted just below conscious level.

Sarah wasn't inclined to talk beyond a clipped, "Thanks. See you later."

All I could think was that I knew someone who lived in the same area, making the address resonate in my brain. But I couldn't name a single person who lived in Helen's large apartment complex. Then I went back further, trying to think of people who might've lived there in the past. The problem was that I didn't know where my friends and acquaintances had lived in the past. In the five years that I'd lived in Richmond they'd been at their current addresses.

Then it came to me — someone I'd known for longer than five years. Much longer.

Upstairs, I turned to the "A" page of my address book. Bingo! I'd crossed out Evan Arness's old addresses, but I could read one of them — 3576 Brissette Drive. Helen was at 3514 Brissette. When I'd looked up Susie Abbott's phone number I must have seen Evan's address and registered it on some level of awareness where it hovered for nearly a week.

Hmm. First Helen and Evan both worked at Acer Insurance and then they lived at the same apartment complex hundreds of miles away. That those facts were significant was undeniable — but what they signified eluded me.

When Lucy came home I raced downstairs and found her in the kitchen, petting two adoring cats who flanked either side of her chair. I spilled out my latest discovery.

When I'd finished, Lucy looked thoughtful for a moment. "Do you think Helen and Evan had something going on? Maybe still do?"

"Like an affair? Were they in cahoots, planning Carlene's demise?" I shivered at the possibility. Perhaps they were pretending to observe a decent period of mourning, whatever decent meant, before they officially paired up.

"Well, you're running with this, but it's

conceivable that they had an affair. And the other day at her car, with those photos of Evan —"

I broke in. "Oh yes, her cover story for having the photos of Evan in her car . . . I bet she made up that bit about Carlene wanting them digitized for a DVD."

"She did seem nervous, like we'd caught her doing something she shouldn't have been doing." Lucy laughed and said, "If our speculations are true, it means that Evan has an incredible range of taste in women. You, Kat, Carlene, Helen. Think of it."

"Evan's not even religious. Or conservative." Or was he? He wasn't at the time of our marriage. Or was he? We never talked about that stuff, we didn't even *have* views. Aside from our occasionally indulging in marijuana, the hippie movement and the Vietnam War passed us by. I marveled at the things I didn't know about the people closest to me. Only, I remembered, Evan *wasn't* close to me.

I sprinted back upstairs and found the card Evan had handed to me at the memorial service. Back in the kitchen I dialed the number on the card, hit the send button, and waited.

"Who're you calling?"

"Evan. Why sit here and speculate? I hate

to do it, but we have to get him involved." I left a message on Evan's cell, then tried him at home. When prompted by Carlene's voice, I winced and hung up.

"He's not picking up. Let's just go to the house and see if he's there. He could be ignoring the phone. Or ignoring me. If we leave soon, and if he *is* there, we'll have time to grill him about his relationship with Helen before we have to leave for book group. While we're at it, we can ask him if Carlene gave him a DVD for their anniversary."

"Fine with me, but after we eat. Let's have that chili you slow-cooked overnight and a salad."

While I heated the chili and Lucy assembled the salad, I shared my latest on Annabel and her pumpkin brownies.

"So, *Annabel* brought the brownies over earlier. And that means something . . . What does it mean? Oh, she must be the one Janet saw around dinnertime."

"Exactly."

I pointed out how Annabel had a golden opportunity to add the cyanide either when she delivered the brownies or when she arrived the second time and took her jacket down to the family room. I explained, perhaps reexplained, how Annabel and

Linda arrived at the same time and Annabel took her jacket downstairs while everyone in the living room was focused on the newcomer, Linda.

Lucy asked, "Did Linda take her jacket downstairs?"

"No, she kept it with her. I saw her pulling it on when she left." I ladled the chili into bowls. "Of course, we don't know that Annabel did any of this — it's just a possibility." Yet another thing to get all het up about. I felt myself scowling as I again recalled Annabel's arrogant tone on the proof situation from the night before.

"Annabel looks worse and worse all the time." Lucy tossed the salad as she pondered this latest information. "Still . . . no proof."

"Don't remind me," I groaned. "I'm getting tired of those two words 'no proof.' We've got to rustle up some proof. I hate to admit it, but I'm afraid of Annabel. At this point, I'm afraid of the whole damned lot of them."

"That's understandable. They're an unsavory bunch, that's for sure. Annabel absolutely unnerves me. The problem is that we know way too much about her. Of course, it's all stuff she told us herself. Probably regrets it now."

"But then, if she's the killer, why would she be so open with us? She isn't stupid. Is she?"

"Maybe she meant to disarm us so we'd ask ourselves these very questions and not suspect her. At any rate, what can she do tonight? I'm sure she's not bringing doctored pumpkin brownies. If she does, we won't let anyone eat them. Besides," Lucy added, "Annabel might not even show up. After all her revelations, she may be too embarrassed."

"Somehow I doubt that. I think she revels in all the drama." We sat and tucked into our food. "Maybe I can figure out a way to ask her if she brought the brownies over earlier and see what she says."

"Hazel . . ." Lucy's warning tone was unmistakable.

"Don't worry, I'll be subtle."

Lucy's skeptical look told me what she thought of my subtleness, but she changed the subject back to Evan. "You know, we can't just barge in on Evan and pepper him with questions about Helen. We need a good reason for being there — and we need to take food."

"Yes, we never gave him a bereavement casserole."

"There's the chili."

"Okay, fine," I said. Chili didn't strike me as standard bereavement food, but Evan used to like mine, so why not?

As for the good reason for being there — that required thinking. By the time we finished eating, we had a cover story of sorts.

On the way over to Evan's, Kat called, sounding frazzled. "I'm sorry, Hazel, I can't make it. Beverly came to the gym today and started screaming at Mick. Then she started in on me, calling me nasty names. Steve the manager banned her from the gym." Kat paused to take a breath, then rushed on. "When I went to my car later, someone had keyed the whole driver's side and let the air out of one of my tires. Gee, I wonder who that was."

"I'm sorry, Kat. Is there anything we can do?"

"Find some way to nail Annabel. I'm passing on tonight. I'm really sorry, but I have enough BS to deal with."

I stifled a groan. So now Lucy and I will be faced with not one, but two suspects, and without benefit of Kat's bodyguard services. The evening had the makings of a high-wire act.

I decided not to mention our incipient suspicions about Helen. "I understand. I'll let you know how it goes."

"Maybe I'll call you later."

"Don't call on my cell phone. I'm reserving it for Vince." I didn't elaborate on that vague explanation. "If you need to talk to one of us, call Lucy." The night before, Vince and I had worked out a signal. If I called him, I had a problem that required him to hightail it over to Helen's — with backup. Otherwise, we'd communicate with Lucy's phone.

After Kat's exhortations to "be safe, be careful," we ended the call and I told Lucy about Kat's misadventures. By the time I'd finished we were in front of Evan's house. "There's his car!" I sounded like a game-show contestant as I pointed to the Camry parked in the driveway. "He's home."

After the events of just eight days ago, it felt eerie to walk up to the house. After ringing the bell three times with no response, we started pounding on the door. Just as I looked at Lucy and said "I hope he's all right," the door opened. Evan's annoyed look morphed to mild irritation when he saw who we were.

"Hazel? Lucy?"

From his flannel robe, bare feet, and rumpled hair, I guessed that he'd been showering all the time that we were ringing and pounding. Not waiting for an invitation, I pushed the door open further and walked in, Lucy in my wake.

Once we were inside, Evan tightened his robe belt and cast a nervous glance up the stairs. I looked in the same direction, but saw no one. Who was up there? Kat? If so, she'd recovered from the Beverly episode in record time as I'd just spoken with her a few minutes before. That was assuming the story of Beverly's rampage wasn't a trumped-up one. So did that put Kat back in the suspect spotlight? Or was she just trying to get out of going to book group? Not that I could blame her — sex or book group? Hmm.

I half expected her to appear in Evan's shirt, or nothing at all, striking a provocative pose, tousled blond hair going every which way.

Suspicion kept ricocheting from Linda to Annabel, now to Helen and back to Kat, with Sarah as runner-up, in a murderous game of hot potato.

The circumstances made hugging unseemly, so I didn't embrace Evan and neither did Lucy. "We're sorry to bother you, but, you see, we're on our way to book group and . . ." I went into a song and dance about needing to pick up a special book that

Annabel wanted, a memento of Carlene; plus I wanted a few photos to give to Helen for the memorial page on Carlene's website. "We tried calling, but you didn't answer. When we saw your car, we figured you were home. Five minutes. Ten, tops, and we'll be out of your hair and you can get back to . . ." My unfinished sentence hung in the air. "Everything we need should be down in the family room. Helen will make copies of the photos and return them."

A look I couldn't decipher passed over Evan's face and disappeared in an instant. Then, probably realizing the only way to get rid of us was to give us the run of the family room, he waved his hand in that direction. "Yeah, okay, go ahead."

Lucy held up the container she carried. "We brought you some of Hazel's chili."

Despite his prior lack of enthusiasm, Evan brightened. "Your famous recipe?"

"It is. You remembered." I felt just as pleased as I had all those years ago when he'd praised my chili, the one thing I could make at the time. Over the years I'd adjusted the recipe, originally calling for fatty ground beef, using what was "in" at the moment — turkey, bison burger, whatever. "Do you want us to heat it up?" Evan shook his head, saying he'd have it later. I'd never considered chili a postcoital snack. I gave the idea a permanent pass.

Despite my outward bravado, I felt skittish about being in the family room. Lucy sensed my discomfort and squeezed my arm, flashing a look of understanding. Steeling myself, I carefully stepped into the kitchen while Lucy put the chili into the refrigerator. On the table, a half-full wine bottle caught my eye. I smiled at my use of "half-full," the word choice of an optimist.

The family room reeked of tobacco. Who smoked? Certainly not Kat. And I recalled Evan opening windows and waving away smoke from my long-ago cigarettes. I averted my eyes from the chair where we'd found Carlene's body and her poisoned tea, focusing on the two wineglasses and ashtray on the coffee table. Bubblegum-pink lipstick ringed the filters of two cigarette butts. A half crescent of the same shade marked the rim of one of the glasses. It was a shade worn by teenagers back in the sixties, not one favored by mature women in any era, and especially not by Kat. But I'd seen that shade lately, and on a smoker. Janet. I sighed. It was Janet upstairs, waiting for Evan to return to their love nest.

The sight of the glasses and ashtray galvanized Evan into action. He picked them up and headed for the kitchen, passing Lucy on the steps. Remembering his role of impromptu, if reluctant, host, he turned and asked with little graciousness, "Would you ladies care for some wine?" We declined, then exchanged knowing looks before we bit our lips and looked away to keep from laughing.

Lucy and I threw our sweaters and bags onto the sofa and stationed ourselves in front of the bookcase, pretending to study book titles and photographs. This accorded with our plan to do something that took time and ensured that we'd be there for a while. I reflected on Janet, the new addition to this puzzle that was spiraling out of control. Did she kill Carlene to get Evan? My mind formed a picture of Janet calling on Carlene, making a neighborly request for a cup of sugar and, while inside the house, leaving a present of cyanide. Posing as a friendly neighbor provided perfect cover for all manner of skullduggery.

That neighborly friendliness apparently extended to romps with the recently bereaved. Had Janet arrived earlier bearing a casserole and a bottle of wine and one thing had led to another? Assuming today was the first time.

Evan came halfway down the steps and

stood leaning against the banister, taking care to keep his robe closed.

I picked up a photo of Carlene and Evan, clad in swimsuits, walking on a beach. "Oh, Evan, I have to tell you, I talked to Donna McCarthy yesterday. She sends her condolences."

"Yeah, she sent a card."

"She told me something I never knew — that Helen Adams lived in Rochester and worked at Acer." I slanted a look at Evan and asked, "Did you know her up there?"

Evan's face clouded. "No, I met her down here. But she said she'd worked at Acer. Didn't look familiar, though."

I thought of Donna's description of the then-frumpy Helen. Wondering what Evan's dark face signified, I asked, "Where did you meet her?"

"At our apartment complex, off of Jahnke Road. I'm not sure how . . . maybe in the laundry room. Or at school. She was taking courses at Tanson. Still does."

"Did you ever go out together?"

"No, but she invited me over for dinner a lot. Wanted to make sure I got a home-cooked meal. Helen, Art, and me — boring as all get out."

Lucy said, "It sounds like Helen was interested in you — so why have Art there?"

"Beats me." Evan ran his hands through his already tousled hair, making it stand up in randomly placed tufts. "The woman was a pain in the ass. She was *everywhere.* Home, school, you name it. I thought about getting a disguise."

I said, "Maybe she wanted you to initiate something romantically. Like ask her on a date."

"A date?" Evan nearly spat the word.

A floorboard creaked overhead and we looked upward. Likely the bedroom was over the family room, according to the usual plan in these split-level houses. Apparently Evan's paramour was up and about. He excused himself, promising to return in "no time."

Lucy watched Evan go up the stairs and turn the corner to continue up to the bedroom level. She stage whispered, "Who's up there? Kat?"

"No, Janet."

"Janet!"

"Shh. He said he'd be back in no time." Overhead, voices competed with the creaking floorboards and a flushing toilet. I prayed that Evan wouldn't get sidetracked into a quickie.

Lucy chuckled. "Kat's sure missing out on some drama."

"I think she has enough drama with Mick's lunatic girlfriend. Let's look at these photos." The floor-to-ceiling bookcase lined a wall section. Three shelves contained books, mostly hardbacks and oversized art volumes. Two of the shelves were so crowded with framed family photographs that we had to move the ones in the front to see what was behind them. I recognized Evan's parents, dressed and groomed to perfection. Hal, Kat, Carlene at different ages; Carlene's mother, whom I recognized from the photo upstairs in the den.

Tucked behind a large framed photograph I found a three-by-four-inch photo of a toddler-aged boy, standing in front of a house, wearing shorts and a striped top. With his aggressive stance and lips pressed firmly together he looked fierce and determined.

The boy appeared in several other photos; one showed him in a Little League outfit, another wearing a Mouseketeer hat, yet another with missing front teeth. I assumed it was the same boy at different ages. In the next picture, taken in the late sixties judging by the hairstyles, an awkward teenager in a white tuxedo jacket peered at the camera through black-framed Woody Allen glasses. His prom date looked equally ill at ease. By this age he was looking familiar. The senior year photo made me gasp, and with good reason — without the glasses I realized I was looking at none other than my first ex-husband, Evan Arness.

Evan returned, wearing jeans and a sweatshirt. Since he'd changed he was more relaxed, less worried about flashing his family jewels. He sat on the couch and put his bare feet on the coffee table.

I took up the conversation where we'd left it. "So how long did you go to the dinners at Helen's?"

"Oh, I don't know, a few months. The woman gave me the willies — especially after I found those pictures of me in her bedroom."

"Pictures? And what were you doing in her bedroom?"

"I wasn't actually *in* her bedroom, I was in her den. She was showing me something on her computer. The bedroom door was open and I saw this big thing, like a bulletin board, just inside. It looked like all pictures of me."

"Where did she get them?"

"I guess from those dinners. She took lots of pictures then. I couldn't see all of them from the den, and didn't even want to."

Lucy and I looked at each other, then

386

back at Evan. I was speechless, but Lucy managed, "Well, I guess it was a compliment — sort of."

"She's certainly attractive, and it was nice of her to feed me and all, not that her cooking was all that great, but I'm not a fussy eater. And her place was kind of a dump; my butt would get sore from her uncomfortable chairs."

Lucy and I laughed knowingly at that one. We knew all about getting sore butts from sitting on Helen's furniture. Book group usually ended early when held at her place.

Evan said, "It was like there was something else going on."

"Like she was in love with you?" Lucy suggested.

"Yeah, but in a weird way. Not normal. I can't explain it." Using his fingers, Evan raked his hair and smoothed it down. "I started making excuses about coming to dinner and she seemed to take the hint. Then I met Carlene, we married, and bought this house. When I ran into Helen at school, she talked me into giving her my new address so she could send us a gift. Then the dinner invitations started up again, this time for me *and* Carlene. I gave in, thinking that with Carlene it wouldn't be so bad. I was wrong. And when I checked on the photos in the bedroom, they were still there. Helen continued to ask us over, but I told Carlene I wanted nothing to do with the woman. I didn't tell her about the pictures, just said I couldn't stand Helen or Art. If Carlene wanted to invite them to the turkey dinners, I figured there were plenty of people around, so that was okay."

This was the most I'd heard Evan say at one time in years. And I hadn't known him to be so exercised about anything in, well . . . I never had. Regaining my speech, I said, "Evan, you've certainly had a time of it with Helen. I just never dreamed . . ."

"Well, you wouldn't. I never wanted to talk about it — in fact I can't believe I'm talking about it now. Maybe because it's all happening again. She's called me a couple of times since . . . you know . . . leaving messages. I might have to get a new number or give up the landline altogether. At least she doesn't know my cell number. But there's always school." Again, Evan ran his fingers through his hair and over his face as well — his agitation was mounting. "And at the memorial service she invited me to, what else, dinner. At this rate, I'll never get rid of the woman." I recalled his long-suffering look when Helen approached him at the memorial service.

"Did she ever try to get you to go to church?"

"Yeah, that was another thing."

"How about when she was designing Carlene's website? Was she around here a lot then?"

Evan stated, with great emphasis, "Not when I was."

Lucy asked, "Did Carlene give you a DVD for your anniversary?"

"No."

So either the DVD had been intended for their *next* anniversary or Helen was lying. I suspected the latter.

Evan looked at the ceiling. As if on cue, the floor creaked again. "Um, are you almost done? I've got a guest and . . ."

Thankfully we'd collected enough dirt on Helen before we wore out the little welcome we had. I turned to Lucy. "Ready to go?" I grabbed three photos of Carlene at random and Lucy pulled out a coffee table tome on stone houses.

Evan's relief was palpable, and with our departure imminent, he summoned up some charm as he herded us toward the door. We agreed to stay in touch. He said that Kat and Georgia were coming over to either take for themselves or donate Carlene's stuff, like books, clothes, jewelry, and whatnot. If we were interested, we could come over once they finished. Being offered a dead woman's picked-over possessions wasn't exactly appealing, but we said we'd be honored to have a keepsake.

I said I'd like a copy of the book Carlene had been working on. When he said he'd get it to me, I wished I'd asked him at a time when I could get the copy right away. As it was, I had put myself in a position of having to remind him. He'd never remember once he returned to Janet and her distractions. However, the invitation to paw through Carlene's items would furnish an opportunity. I'd arrive at the house with a flash drive in hand.

This time we all hugged, but gingerly. Even with clothes on, touching Evan felt way too intimate.

CHAPTER 22

"Do you believe it? Evan's living a soap opera. Where do we start? Janet? Helen?"

Lucy pulled away from the curb. "Janet. Why do you think it was her upstairs?"

When I told Lucy about the ashtray and the Bazooka Joe–pink lipstick on the wineglasses, she said, "Oh, that explains why Evan came charging up to the kitchen with those glasses. That's when I saw the wine bottle on the table."

"The only person I've seen wearing that shade since 1966 is Janet. Also, there was no car in the driveway or in the street indicating a visitor. All Janet would have to do is walk across the two driveways." I groaned. "And that makes her yet another suspect."

We waited for the light at the Jahnke Road exit off the Chippenham Parkway to change. Lucy said, "Just because Janet and Evan are lovers doesn't mean that Janet killed Carlene. The same holds true for Helen, if she really is, or was, in love with Evan. Granted it casts both of them in a suspicious light. But why . . . for *Evan*?"

"I *know* — why on earth would someone kill over the likes of him?"

Lucy turned off Jahnke Road into the entrance of Helen's apartment complex and drove through a tunnel of supersized pine trees. As she backed into a space and turned off the engine, she said, "As for Helen, Evan did confirm our speculations that she's in love with him. But I never in a million years would have pegged Helen a stalker. What do you think of all that stuff Evan said about her? And the photos in her bedroom?"

I shook my head, the stalker possibility looming large in my beleaguered brain. "I just can't fathom it all. And stalkers — they often kill. So did Helen kill Carlene to get Evan to herself? Of course," I rushed to chant the familiar disclaimer, "Carlene may have died by her own hand. Only thing was, she didn't. If Helen kills the women who stand in her way, then Janet had better watch her step."

Lucy tapped her fingers on the steering wheel. "Why would she wait so long to kill Carlene?"

"Good question." We needed to rethink

this whole thing, I moaned to myself, feeling something akin to despair at the prospect of more thinking. But the thinking would have to wait.

I said, "I'm not looking forward to this evening. At least Janet won't be there. And I don't imagine Linda will show up."

Lucy glanced at the dashboard clock and said, "Gotta go, Hazel. It's seven thirty." We got out of the car. I took a moment with my electronic paraphernalia, muting my phone and stashing it in the deep pocket of my sweater. I added tissues for padding. I had affixed a Velcro patch to Vince's speed-dial button so I could locate it by touch. I tucked the recorder into my bra. Then we started walking toward Helen's apartment.

Speaking in low tones, I said, "I wonder if Helen still has that photo display in her room."

"It's a safe bet that she does. Especially if she's asking Evan over for dinner."

"I'd love to see it. But how can I get into her bedroom?"

We stopped in the middle of the parking lot and brainstormed. It didn't take two minutes to come up with plan A and plan B.

In retrospect, we should have added plan C: turn tail and run.

CHAPTER 23

"Finally! I thought you two got lost." Helen's pique gave way to grudging forgiveness when Lucy and I proffered apologies for our tardiness. I couldn't look the woman in the eye, thanks to Evan's revelations.

Sarah and Annabel were eye-contact challenged as well. Sarah sat with arms crossed under her bosom and a scowl on her face. She nodded at a point behind us. Annabel focused on her cherry-red pumps and ignored us. Art's eyes met mine briefly and I was reminded of that indecipherable look he'd given me at the memorial service lunch. He offered to take Lucy's sweater, but she opted to keep it with her.

Helen waved a hand at two chairs next to her. As we sat, I said, "Kat called. Something came up and she can't make it." Helen's only response was a raised eyebrow, while Annabel smirked and Sarah continued to concentrate on some point on the far wall.

Art folded his lanky form onto the floor.

Helen's many paintings adorned the walls. And that was where her attempts at decorating began and ended. The apartment color scheme ran the gamut of beige to Hershey-chocolate brown. Walls, carpeting, furniture, you name it — brown prevailed in one shade or another. We sat on card table chairs and furniture with wooden frames and foam cushions with a thickness of one and a half inches. Helen had lived here for several years, long enough to purchase decent furnishings, but evidently her attention was on Evan and her social service projects, leaving her little time or interest for creature comforts or aesthetics beyond her artwork. Beige paint covered the one brick wall, where a large canvas showcased an oversized fish. He, or she, regarded the group with a baleful eye.

Lucy began, "Helen, I have a client who's looking for an apartment in this area. Are all the apartments here two bedroom, like yours?"

"Mostly, but they have one- and three-bedroom ones as well."

"And do they all have two baths? This woman has to have at least two baths. Doesn't want to share one with her husband; you know how that is."

Helen smiled in understanding. "The two-and three-bedroom units all have two baths. There are a couple of vacancies now."

"And the second bath is part of the master suite?"

"Yes."

"I'll tell her. Thanks, Helen."

I exhaled, relieved that I now had my excuse to get into Helen's bedroom. "By the way, did Evan ever live in this complex?"

Helen gave me a why-do-you-ask look, but merely said, "I believe so. A long time ago."

Then she looked around the room and said, "Well, we —"

I cut her off. "Annabel, Lucy, and I looked at Sam's site last night. Quite impressive." I hoped my bright and cheerful manner covered my nervousness. I stuffed my hands into my pockets in case they started trembling.

Anabel sniffed. "Yes, he's very talented." She shot Helen a look of reproach.

"Especially that Nazi collage. Where did he find all those items?" Lucy's artless tone betrayed none of the unease that I felt. I felt a twinge of envy for her acting ability.

Annabel narrowed her eyes at Lucy, perhaps suspecting a trick question. Reluctantly, she said, "His uncle was an SS officer."

So did that mean Sam actually owned the items, perhaps bequeathed to a military historian nephew by his doting uncle? That roused Sarah from her reverie. "An SS officer! You're in a relationship with a man related to a Nazi?"

"Sam's *not* responsible for what his uncle did." Annabel's eyes blazed.

Helen put out her hand in the stop position. "Ladies, please. Let's start. Hazel, since you're a cofounder of the group, I thought you might lead the discussion."

Startled, I managed, "Fine." I'd had the impression that Helen was going to facilitate, as she was so intent on having the meeting in the first place. Not that it mattered. "I guess the first order of business is to decide if we want to continue to meet and if we want to continue reading mysteries."

I scanned the faces. Annabel had returned her attention to her shoes, describing circles in the air with her right foot. Maybe I'd misjudged her embarrassment threshold and she did regret her earlier revelations. Whatever the reason, it was fine with me if she avoided eye contact. I felt edgy enough just being in the same room with her, especially after learning of her early arrival at Carlene's the previous week to deliver brownies. And my edginess now extended to Helen. One suspect was more than enough for the likes of me. Two was way over the top. The sooner I expedited this discussion, the sooner I could get into Helen's bedroom.

I asked, "What do you think, Annabel?"

When she managed with an aggrieved air, "Whatever you all decide is fine with me," I resisted the urge to raise my eyes to the ceiling.

After a lengthy exchange the group agreed to wait until after the holidays and see how we felt then. A "cooling off" period as Art put it.

I was about to propose a group vote, but when Annabel asked, "Does anyone really think Carlene committed suicide?" everyone started talking at once. But the speculations they floated echoed my own, with nothing new or helpful.

When the discussion wound down, I thought it was as good a time as any to find out if someone in the group had been the mysterious, shadowy figure Janet claimed she saw early in the evening of the previous Monday. Specifically, I hoped for a reaction from Annabel. But how would I finesse the question?

I never got the chance. Helen, clearing

her throat, started, "I'd like to propose a prayer in memory of Carlene, a woman who gave so much of herself to this group."

I looked at Sarah, who looked mutinous at Helen's suggestion. But Annabel's half laugh turned my attention to her.

"And just what was the 'so much' that Carlene gave to the group?" She didn't wait for an answer before moving along. "I really can't participate in a prayer. I'd feel like a complete hypocrite. You see, I'm not sorry that Carlene is dead. The woman was no frigging saint." Annabel bit her lip before going on. "She slept with my boyfriend and *then* she slept with my son." Lucy and I shot uneasy looks at each other while Annabel ran down Carlene's transgressions, thankfully condensing the account she'd given to us.

Sarah looked astonished. "Goodness gracious. When did all this sleeping business happen?"

"Um, a while back."

"Since you came to the book group?"

"Uh, no, before."

Helen slanted a knowing look at me, probably in a nonverbal reference to our conversation of a week earlier when she'd reported her man-in-the car sighting. Aloud, she said, "But, Annabel, you and Carlene were friends."

Annabel's face contorted into a sneer, but she said nothing. She stood, smoothed her skirt, and picked up her cherry-red handbag. "Yes, well, like I said, I simply can't join you in a prayer. Art, my jacket please."

Art displayed considerable flexibility as he rose from the floor. We waited in an uncomfortable silence until he returned with a short black jacket. He tried to help Annabel into it, but she grabbed it out of his hands and walked to the front door. Turning back, she said, using a formal tone, "I'm glad we've had this time together." With that, she left.

We all looked taken aback, Lucy and I less so than the others. Helen made a show of rolling her eyes and huffing disapproval. *Thank God Annabel's gone,* I thought. But Helen kept me from breathing a sigh of relief.

"Well," said Art.

"Well," parroted Sarah. I half expected Sarah to contribute a story involving Carlene and Den. She didn't, and possibly she didn't have one to share.

Helen started, "So, about that prayer . . ."

Now Sarah leveled a challenging look at Helen. "I agree with Annabel. I don't want to pray. I fail to see how prayers are going to help Carlene now."

"You don't have to pray, Sarah," I said through gritted teeth, thinking that we should be praying for ourselves.

"I'll just be on my way. Then you can pray in peace. Art? My jacket?" Art disappeared again, reappearing with a jean jacket. Sarah left with little fanfare.

"Does *anyone* want to pray with me?" Helen stopped short of calling us heathens, a term no doubt on the tip of her tongue. Lucy, probably feeling the need to diffuse the situation and move the prayer proceedings along, suggested that we simply observe a moment of silence. Helen didn't look happy, but as we indicated agreement with the silent option, she scowled and joined us in a moment that lacked the intended spiritual flavor. All I thought about was what Lucy and I were about to do.

After the moment of silence, we sat, looking uncertain. Helen announced with a sweep of her hand toward the kitchen, "There's decaf, and Sarah brought some éclairs."

Lucy looked at me and smoothed an eyebrow, our prearranged signal to start the action. "Just as soon as I use the restroom," she said.

"First door on your right."

I waited a minute for Lucy to get into the hall bathroom and close the door. Then I launched into my act. Grabbing my stomach, I groaned, "Oh God, I feel sick. Where's your other bathroom, Helen?" I injected as much desperation into my voice as I could.

Helen started down the hall. She opened a door and turned on the overhead light. She turned left, opened another door, and turned on another light. "Right in here." I hoped she wouldn't stay outside in the bedroom, thwarting my plans.

Helen's indifference to interior decor prevailed in the dispirited bathroom with its faint locker room smell. Probably few people ventured in there, if any. The translucent glass of a transomlike window high on the wall above the mildewed shower allowed the only possibility of natural light. A large and threadbare brown bath mat didn't quite hide the worn linoleum. I pretended to vomit, running water in the sink to cover the sound. A couple of gobs of aqua toothpaste clung to the bowl of the sink. I gingerly dried my hands with an uninviting hand towel that looked to be a find from a fleabag motel yard sale. Assuming such establishments held yard sales. I waited two minutes before emerging from the bathroom, trying for a still-sick effect. I was alone.

I looked for the photo collage by the door going out to the hall. Evan had said it was just inside the door and he could see it from the den. I found it about six feet from the door mounted on a pegboard over a faux French Provincial dresser. Either Evan had superior eyesight or he'd lied and *had* been in Helen's bedroom. Or, most likely, Helen had moved the display to a place where she could gaze at it lovingly when she awoke in the morning, because the dresser faced her bed. I had no trouble recognizing the images, as I'd just seen a number of them in Evan's bookcase. The same baby, the same five-year-old, the same Little League player, the same senior yearbook picture, the same awkward-looking teenage prom attendees, the same picture I'd glimpsed in Helen's trunk after the memorial service. In short, the same Evan Arness. At least a dozen pictures showed combinations of Evan, Helen, and Art sitting either on that uncomfortable love seat out in the living room or at the dinette table.

I studied a familiar picture of Evan in a well-cut dark suit accessorized with a boutonniere. Was that taken on his and Carlene's wedding day? I recalled seeing a picture of the two of them just a couple of hours before with Carlene wearing an ivory mid-calf-length dress. Seeing the edge of an ivory skirt in this picture made me realize that Helen had cropped Carlene out of her own wedding picture.

I continued to study the display, seeing a small photo of Evan and Helen that I'd missed before. Helen looked happy, girlish. It looked like Evan and Carlene's family room in the background, so likely they had posed for this shot at a turkey dinner. Either that or Helen had spliced the photographs together, no doubt courtesy of skills she'd picked up at her editing class.

This further confirmed the conclusion I'd already made — Helen was in love with Evan. But this bizarre collection was way too creepy a way for a sixty-year-old to express love. If she was sixteen, it would be normal. Doodling arrow-pierced hearts filled with "E.A. and H.A. forever," long heartfelt conversations with girlfriends, picking apart daisies (loves me, loves me not) were all part of the rite of passage.

Realizing that I had a limited window of opportunity in this room, I got out my cell phone, activated the camera feature, and started clicking. I darted around the room, looking for other pictures. On the same wall as the Evan shrine I found an eight-by-ten photo showing an attractive woman, dark hair fashioned in a fifties-style pageboy. Wearing a glittering evening dress and white gloves, she held a white rabbit. The woman looked somewhat familiar. I tried to imagine her with contemporary hairstyle and clothing, but that didn't help to identify her. A second picture showed the woman with a tuxedo-clad man pulling the rabbit out of a top hat. I looked from the first picture to the second and back again, realizing that the now-blond Helen and the then-brunette woman were one and the same. But wait — Helen wouldn't have been old enough in the fifties. Either this was her mother or Helen was in a retro costume. One other picture featured a dark-haired boy, likely Art, with Helen and a man who looked enough like Art to be his father.

I'd never been in Helen's bedroom and the lack of beigeness surprised me. I found myself in a flower garden, surrounded by a riotous assortment of pinks, yellows, and teals. The same floral pattern repeated itself in the comforter, dust ruffle, pillow shams, bolsters, tied-back curtains, and pleated lamp shades. Even the dresser, which I'd at first thought beige, was a pale pink.

What was up with the nice bedroom and

the not-nice rest of the apartment? Helen herself was always well turned out. I guessed she didn't want to showcase her love for Evan in a squalid room.

I turned my attention to the assortment of books by her bed. A thick Bible with a bookmark stuck in the middle of what looked to be the Old Testament sat atop one of the nightstands. John MacDonald's *Nightmare in Pink* topped a precarious-looking stack in front of the nightstand. Suddenly that pesky thought I'd had earlier in the day came to life full force in my brain: Helen at book group, *The Deep Blue Good-by* spread open across her lap as she waved her arms about — arms covered in long bell-shaped sleeves, sleeves that fluttered about as she emphasized her points. Most of us had learned long ago not to sit next to her at book group — more than one person had been socked by a waving arm. The long sleeves, if I remembered correctly, covered her fingertips when she stood with arms at her side. Too long. Sleeves like those could cover up a lot of deeds. Like poisoning a mug of tea.

A number of the piled books lent credence to the long sleeves and poisoning idea. *Deadly Doses: A Writer's Guide to Poisons* was a case in point. Either Helen was joining the legions of crime writers or she was using the tome as a reference tool for a real-life murder strategy. At this point I suspected the latter and set to snapping pictures of the stacks. I gasped when I saw *Bitter Almonds,* Gregg Olsen's chronicle of the Seattle poisonings at the hands of Stella Nickell — one of the books I had picked up earlier in the day. I gasped again at *Human Poisoning from Native and Cultivated Plants.* Click, click went the camera. Was I at last looking at something that resembled proof, that issue that had weighed me down from the onset of this investigation?

Deadly Harvest. When I'd spotted that title in Helen's trunk, I assumed that it was the traditional mystery that someone had recommended in book group a while back. A Washington — or Oregon — setting. But now I read the full title of *Deadly Harvest: A Guide to Common Poisonous Plants.* Interesting. Since this box was shoved in a corner behind the nightstand, it took minor bodily contortions to digitally capture the book title.

Lucy and I needed to visit Evan again on the way home and pry him away from his bed and Janet. I checked my watch and figured I could call him from the car. Time to get a move on. I pocketed my phone.

There had to be other clues to back my suspicion of Helen as killer. I didn't know what I expected to find: a vial of white powdery stuff with the bitter almond aroma sitting atop her dresser? I looked at the dresser as if to verify the absurdity of the notion. Then I got an idea.

It didn't take long to find Helen's under-wear drawer in the dresser and start rum-maging. People must think that burglars and amateur investigators didn't know about the underwear drawer as a favorite hiding place for valuables and secret items, like safe-deposit box keys, cash, love letters . . .

And, in Helen's case, a brass cyanide vial container.

I found the item in a zippered plastic bag under a pile of half-slips heavily scented with lavender sachets. It so resembled the container in Sam's collage that I felt confi-dent in identifying it. I almost picked up the bag but remembered in time to use a tissue from the box on the dresser and not leave fingerprints. I shook the container out of the bag. The cap was stamped but too small to read the inscription without a magnifying glass. Remembering from our Web research that the cap was the press-on type, I used another tissue to pull it off the container and removed the glass vial. The top of the vial had been snapped off and a few grains of white powder clung to the sides of the glass. I held my breath, not wanting to inhale any fumes.

I stood at the end of the dresser so I faced the door and could see if anyone came into the room. That precaution didn't keep me from nearly jumping out of my skin when the doorknob moved. No time for a mad dash to the bathroom and a groan or two for effect. No time to hide the container with the telltale remnants of a deadly poison.

Helen loomed before me. I felt sure her deer-in-the-headlights look mirrored my own. We had mutually caught each other.

Helen rallied and her expression turned to indignation as she demanded, "Just what do you think you're doing, Hazel?"

My adrenaline charge must have short-circuited my brain because I couldn't respond.

Helen pressed on. "Why are you looking through my things?"

I found my voice — sort of. I choked out, "Just — just curious, that's all." Trembling, I swept the container, bag, and tissues back into the still-open drawer. "I'm so sorry." I whispered. *Sorry on so many levels.*

Helen raised an eyebrow in a questioning

slant, but she decided to play it nice. "How are you feeling?" She moved toward the nightstand.

"Not — not good."

"I'll make you a nice cup of tea." She opened the drawer.

Yikes, I thought. Tea? Lucy and I needed to beat it out of this place pronto. "Thanks so much, but Lucy and I will be going now."

"Not so fast. We need to talk." I caught Helen's menacing tone.

That was when I saw the gun.

CHAPTER 24

Later, when asked what kind of gun, all I could say was that it was small, something easily carried in a purse or pocket. I knew next to nothing about guns and would just as soon keep it that way. Helen pointed the thing right at me, in the vicinity of my pounding heart. A trapdoor opened in my stomach and my whole body succumbed to fear.

Why I stood there like a ninny, not running while I had the chance, not realizing that she was getting a gun out of her drawer, I couldn't explain. It stood to reason that she'd stash her gun in her nightstand drawer — wasn't that where gun owners traditionally kept their weapons? Granted, my window of opportunity had been small, but still. So I was left in the throes of the fight-or-flight response with no resources for fighting or fleeing.

Helen crab-stepped to the door, never taking her eyes or the gun off of me. Opening the door, she barked, "Art, get down here. Something's wrong with the toilet."

A few seconds later, I heard a low mumble of words. Then Helen turned back to me. "Get moving," she ordered, waving the gun toward the door.

I obeyed. Really, what choice did I have? Helen jammed the gun into the small of my back and prodded me into the living room where Art, trying his best to look intimidating, guarded the door that led to the outside. And freedom. Hmm. I wondered if this meant that Helen had enlisted her son to help her kill Carlene. And was he a willing partner or had she bullied him? I suspected the latter.

Lucy sat on the uncomfortable love seat. Per Helen's instruction, I took the matching chair. She kept the gun trained on me. Lucy gasped and I looked over at her. The blood had beaten a hasty retreat from her face and her eyes looked like saucers.

Helen turned the gun on Lucy. "No funny business, you two."

Nothing funny about this business. With a trembling hand, I reached into my pocket for my phone and, finding the Velcro-padded key, pressed Vince's number. I banked on Helen thinking I still kept my phone buried in my purse.

She pounced on me. "What are you do-ing?"

"Just getting a tissue," I said as I pulled out a wrinkled Kleenex. "See?" My voice quavered so much I could barely get the words out. And I wasn't sure I had pressed the speed-dial button firmly enough for the call to go through. Hopefully I'd have another chance. If I lived long enough. I admonished myself to hold positive, uplift-ing thoughts. For good measure, I added a quick but fervent prayer.

"Keep your hands where I can see them." Art spoke for the first time, sounding puckish. "Mom, is that gun even loaded?"

When his mother looked daggers at him, he shrugged. "Just trying to lighten the mood a bit."

Helen sat on the sofa that completed the three-piece "conversational" grouping. "Honestly, Art, you'll have these ladies nervous wrecks, wondering if the gun's loaded or not."

Like we weren't nervous wrecks already, I thought. Lucy and I stole quick glances at each other. What was with the gun, anyway? *Was* it loaded? Was Helen going off the deep end? If so, who knew what she would do. I imagined an unloaded gun could become a loaded one easily enough. Would it help if I emulated Art and injected humor? But even if I could come up with some knee-slapper, humor and guns didn't combine well, and besides, I suspected that Helen's threatening me with a gun, unloaded or not, had to do with one Evan Arness.

It didn't take long for Helen to prove me right. "So, Hazel, what's going on with you and Evan?" When I took a deep breath and glanced at Lucy, she raged, "Don't look at Lucy! Just answer the question."

I had to find a way to disarm Helen — literally and figuratively. I had little talent in the disarming department, but as our survival hung in the balance I had to put forth my best effort. Or as best as I could manage with a mouth as dry as cotton.

"Me and *Evan*?" I rasped. "What would be going on with us?"

"I know you're sleeping with him. I won't have it. You're just like that — that Jezebel, ruining his life."

I took it Carlene was "that Jezebel." I shook my head. "No, not . . . not sleeping together." My voice kicked in. "Not even thinking about it."

"That's not the way it looked last week at the lunch. The two of you looked awfully chummy. I was right beside you." Her eyes narrowed. "If you find him so attractive, you shouldn't have divorced him. It's simply shameful, you getting your claws into the dear man so soon after losing his wife. Although if he only knew what a tramp that woman was . . . First I had to deal with her and now *you*."

I didn't like the sound of that: "dealing" with me. Aloud I said, "Helen, Evan had too much to drink and was feeling rather, um, emotional." Helen looked unconvinced, so I forced a smile and added, "That's all."

Lucy spoke up, her voice hoarse. "Hazel . . ." She cleared her throat and, with a shaking finger, pointed to me. "She's . . . she's back with Vince."

I nodded. "Yes, in fact we're getting married." Where did that come from? I guess one will say anything when facing the business end of a gun.

"Humph!" Helen looked suspicious but turned her attention back to Carlene. "That Carlene was a first-class tramp. Put my boy through all that. You know, Evan used to come over here for dinner and he really enjoyed himself. We had a lovely time, didn't we, Art?"

"Lovely." Art leaned against the wall and rolled his eyes. It sounded like he hadn't enjoyed the dinners any more than Evan had. Helen either didn't catch his sarcastic tone or chose to ignore it — or, the most likely possibility, she was just plain clueless. I caught her use of "my boy." She'd used the same phrase when she first told me about the parking lot incident involving the man in the car. At the time I thought she referred to Art. Now it sounded like Evan, but it was an odd way for her to refer to the object of her affection.

"And then *she* came along and ruined it all. No more dinners. I invited both of them but they only came over once."

Lucy said, "Maybe Carlene was jealous of you. Didn't want the competition."

Helen gave Lucy a rueful smile. She still held the gun but placed it next to her on the sofa. Shaking her head, she said in a small voice, "After that I only saw him at school, but not very often."

Helen's words and pained demeanor made me wonder if Evan had left out key details of his relationship with her. There had to have been more involved than threesome dinners with Art — if the relationship had grown intimate, it would explain Helen's obsession with my — thankfully — former husband. But to the point of killing his wife?

Had it not been for the gun at Helen's

side I might have felt sympathy. Her grip on it had loosened, but not enough to rush her. If I could take on Helen while Lucy kept Art at bay . . . Lucy's knitting needles could do some bodily damage and surely I had a sharp object in my purse, but I doubted that the mother-son duo would wait politely while I unearthed it.

Thoughts of my purse made me look around for it. I didn't see it by the chair where I'd sat earlier — nor did I see Lucy's purse or knitting bag.

"What are you looking for?"

"Um, nothing."

Helen smirked. "Your purses are in a safe place. I didn't want you digging your phone out from the bottom of your purse. And I'm sure Lucy keeps hers in a more accessible place."

With my fledgling overtaking-the-captors plan thwarted, at least temporarily, I sighed. Where was Kat when we needed her most? A well-placed karate chop or two from our missing bodyguard and we'd be out of that apartment in a flash.

Moving on to the next item on her agenda, Helen asked, "And why did you call Donna McCarthy, asking questions about me?"

I braced myself, hoping to sound believable. "Well, it occurred to me that Donna might not know about Carlene, so I gave her a call. After all, she and Evan had been friends back in their coworking days. While we talked, I thought of you. You see, at the memorial service Art said you were from Rochester and that you'd worked for an insurance company. I thought, what were the odds it was Acer? Small world." I added a little laugh, but Helen just stared at me with no expression. "How did you find out, Helen — did Donna call or e-mail you?"

"No, my friend Carol Mobley called and told me about it. She and Donna are in the same Bible study group." Carol, the gossipy high school friend. According to Donna, that friend thought Helen might have had a baby in high school.

Apparently Helen bought my explanation that sounded thin and unconvincing to my ears, because she circled back to her earlier point. "Now back to Evan . . . Stay away from him." She pointed the gun at me, as if to illustrate the consequences of not keeping my distance from lover-boy Evan. "I finally got rid of Carlene and I don't want to have to get rid of you."

I stifled a gasp at her increasing anger. The phrase "I finally got rid of Carlene" had not escaped me. Was she saying that she personally got rid of Carlene? If so, her confession ratcheted up our personal danger an infinite number of notches. And no sign of Vince, confirming my earlier fear that I hadn't pressed the speed-dial button firmly enough. If only I could get my hand in my pocket again — but Helen had me on the hot seat, not taking her eyes off me. She paid little attention to Lucy, making me think that if Lucy could access her phone she could call Vince. I doubted that Lucy had Vince on speed dial, but she could call 911. But Lucy didn't have her purse and, besides, Art could be the watchdog for her. If only we'd developed a contingency plan in case things went awry — and things were very, very awry.

"I was kind of surprised when she actually died." Helen spoke in a matter-of-fact, reasonable tone, like she was discussing the price of milk.

"Mom . . ." Art warned. Helen ignored him.

Lucy matched Helen's matter-of-fact tone. "Why were you surprised?"

"That stuff was so old, from World War II. I didn't know how potent it was. I mean, I did research and all, but couldn't find anything about how long the stuff would last. I didn't know if she'd die or just get really sick."

"Mom, you better not say anything more."

"Oh, they won't say anything. If they do I'll take this gun and go after them. I do know how to use this, you know." I didn't doubt it. The NRA sticker plastered on her car loomed large in my mind. "Just consider this whole evening a warning. Not a word about this conversation. And stay away from Evan."

I squeaked, "No problem." Lucy nodded her agreement.

Did that mean we could go? That Helen wasn't going to kill us? Or was she toying with us, fully intending to consign us to a ghostly eternity haunting her beige apartment? What would they do with our bodies — dump us in the James River at 3 a.m.? I looked from the gun to Art, still at his post by the door.

Figuring it wouldn't hurt to ask, I did so. "Does that mean we can go?"

"Why, not until I've served refreshments." But Helen didn't make a move toward the kitchen. She hadn't produced the tea she'd promised earlier, but I figured that was a good thing. Again I wondered if we could overtake the two of them. If the gun was loaded — and I didn't relish verifying this — its power trumped any collective muscle Lucy and I could summon up. Plus Helen was in good shape. We'd have better luck getting around the undernourished-looking Art, but we had to get past his mother first. Maybe we could just throw a net over the obsessed Helen and get her admitted to a psych ward. Such a feat, of course, required a net. Again, I silently cursed the absent Kat.

A feeling of disembodiment came over me. I couldn't decide if that was good or bad, but given the situation, more bearable. Our best strategy was to keep Helen talking. We knew too much already, so we might as well learn as much as we could and get it recorded. Hopefully my recorder wouldn't make a clicking sound. And I'd keep alert for an opportunity to press Vince's speed dial.

Lucy seemed to be of the same mind. "Helen, I'm curious about something . . . Evan and Carlene got married over five years ago. What made you so upset all these years later?"

Helen recounted the story of her and Art spotting Carlene and the man Lucy and I now knew was B.J. in the library parking lot, apparently forgetting that she'd shared the story with me already. I didn't remind her. "I couldn't believe the woman, performing like that in a public parking lot."

Lucy said gently, like she might to a child, "But Helen, Carlene and Evan were separated."

"Separated?" Helen's startled look turned to a wary one, like she suspected a trap. She pressed her lips together, saying nothing for a moment. "Still, they *were* married and that tramp committed adultery."

This time I asked, trying to imitate Lucy's soft tone. "Are you sure it wasn't Evan in the car with her?"

Art fielded that question. "It wasn't. We saw Carlene talking to a guy earlier. They were sitting on one of the benches outside the library. He wasn't Evan, his hair was much longer. So we assumed the guy in the car later was the same not-Evan guy. I mean, we didn't want to stare at them."

Oh, no, staring was rude. But killing was fine. What it came down to was that Helen had killed Carlene over an assumption. In this case the much-bandied definition of assume, "making an ass out of you and me," took on an alternative and sinister meaning. The fact that Helen was correct in her assumption didn't matter — an assumption it was. It wasn't inconceivable that Carlene could talk to one man and jump in the backseat with another an hour or so later.

"I wasn't going to let her get away with it,

making a fool out of my boy. But I didn't mean to kill her. Really I didn't. I just wanted to make her really sick. You do believe me, don't you?"

"Of course," Lucy assured her with a straight face. I seconded the lie. What choice did we have?

Lucy asked a question that surprised me. "Helen, how long have you been in love with Evan?"

Helen looked aghast. But Art, back against the door, said with an air of resignation, "All my life. And then some."

"All your life?" Lucy looked puzzled.

That was when my brain cells went into such a frenzy I could almost hear the snap, snap, snap as puzzle pieces fell into place. "My boy," the pictures of Evan, Carol, the gossipy high school friend who speculated that Helen had a baby in high school, Vivian and Annabel with their "baby boys." Just the night before I'd suggested to Lucy that mothers and sons permeated conversations involving Carlene and her death. But the significance had, until that moment, eluded me.

But age remained a sticking point. When Donna McCarthy told me about fifteen-year-old Helen having a baby, I'd figured the boy must be about forty-five by now.

Evan was fifty-five.

I regarded Helen, reassessing her age. Could she be older than sixty?

Helen looked affronted. "Why are you staring at me?"

"Helen, how old are you?"

"How rude!"

"She's seventy."

"Arthur! That's enough from you."

Seventy, I thought, amazed. "You certainly don't look it, Helen." Lucy echoed my compliment. Did we think if we buttered her up, she'd let us go, sparing our lives?

Art smirked. "She's had a lot of work done."

If I was in the market for shaving ten years off my face, I'd get a referral from Helen.

With the math worked out so that Helen could have a fifty-five-year-old son, I pressed on. "So, Helen, I'm guessing you're in love with Evan, but not romantically. He's your son, isn't he?"

Helen looked stunned, eyes widened, lips parted.

Then she burst into tears.

CHAPTER 25

While Helen wailed, Lucy looked at me in disbelief and Art broke into gales of laughter, doubled over, clutching his stomach. "I can't believe you guessed," he said one word at a time between laughing fits. "The big secret."

I sat there, shocked at my own revelation. Apparently Evan had been born out of wedlock and given up for adoption. Why was I learning this for the first time? However long ago or short our marriage, it was information I would expect to have. Why hadn't he told me? I looked at Lucy, holding my hands palms up in bewilderment. She mirrored my gestures.

Laugher subsiding, Art said, "I had to endure that goddamn Evan my whole life. Evan this, Evan that —"

"Arthur, watch your language!"

"Arthur" ignored his mother and carried on with his diatribe against Evan. "Evan summed up my childhood. The guy's duller than dirt, but Mom thinks he's the best thing since — I don't know — sliced bread?"

I couldn't disagree with Art. Why had it taken me so long to notice Evan's dullness? Had my standards improved that much over the years? But his personality, or lack thereof, wasn't relevant at the moment. I noticed that the gun now rested at Helen's side and that she'd pulled her sweater around her like she was cold. Figuring her tears would divert her attention from me, I went for my pocket.

No such luck. "What are you doing now, Hazel?" A teary-eyed and sniffling Helen lifted the gun and aimed it at me. "What's in your pocket?"

"Just tissues." I pulled out several, taking care not to dislodge my phone in the process, and tossed them in her direction. "I thought you could use some."

She cast a wary eye on the pile, perhaps suspecting — what? — an explosive? After gingerly selecting a tissue, she blew her nose with her free hand.

The incongruity of Helen's gun and tears made an already bizarre situation more so. It was hard enough dealing with a woman who'd killed once and may kill again — a distraught killer added another level of danger. I needed to keep alert not only for an opportunity to contact Vince but to catch our two captors off guard.

Lucy, with a gentle voice, began, "So, Helen, you were fifteen when Evan was born?" When Helen nodded, Lucy prompted, "And you gave him up for adoption?"

Helen handed the gun to Art. "You tell the story, Art. I'm much too upset."

"Okay, okay, I'll tell it."

"And don't take your eyes off these two, especially this one." She hooked a thumb at me, aka "this one."

"Yes, Mother." Art rolled his eyes like a long-suffering adolescent, but quickly warmed to the subject, a classic tale of the fifties: when teenage Helen got pregnant, her parents sent her to a home for unwed mothers in upstate New York where she was sequestered until her baby was born. Then, strong-armed by parents and social workers, she gave the child up for adoption.

"She went back to Syracuse but didn't get along with her parents. She was seething from resentment at being forced to give up her baby. And she definitely didn't want to go back to the same high school. So she moved to Rochester to live with her grandmother. The old lady doted on her only granddaughter, never denying her a thing. Mom finished high school in Rochester and enrolled in secretarial school. She'd cut off ties with everyone in Syracuse except for Carol Mobley, the one she mentioned earlier. That was only because Carol had relatives in Rochester, so she visited often. And Carol's a persistent type; it's hard to say no to her.

"Mom didn't like being a secretary, so she drifted around a bit, doing this and that, until she wound up being a magician's assistant. It wasn't long before she married the magician, who turned out to be an abusive alcoholic. That marriage lasted less than a year.

"So she went back to Grandma, who sent her to art school. She still moonlighted as a magician's assistant, just with a different magician."

That explained the pictures with the rabbit and the man with the top hat. And now that I knew Helen's age, her being the young woman sporting a fifties-style hairdo made sense. "The magician's assistant job sounds familiar. Did I know about that?"

Art said, "I told you at the lunch. You asked what jobs Mom had when I was growing up. One was doing magic shows for kids. And someone talked her into doing gigs as a clown."

The first time Art had told me about Helen being a clown, I couldn't fathom the idea because I'd thought Helen too refined and dignified. Now, despite the tears streaming down her face, I considered her too evil to be entertaining children. Lucy looked startled — I guess I'd neglected to share that tidbit of information with her.

Art said, "Anyway, Mom stayed single for a few years. She held down various jobs and painted in her spare time. She didn't have to work, Grandma didn't mind supporting her, but Mom was always restless. Then she met and married Gordon Woods and they had me."

When Art paused, Lucy asked Helen, "Did either of your husbands know about Evan?"

"Not from me." Helen blotted her face with one of my tissues. Again, she had her cardigan wrapped tightly around her and I saw that she was shivering.

Art snorted. "You sure talked about Evan to me." Turning to us, he said, "Mom was obsessed with the guy. As for Dad, he was very bossy and controlling, but not abusive. Their marriage wasn't a model of open communication. But he provided well for us and that was all she cared about. When he died he left her pretty well set. Not that you could tell from the way she lives, but Mom's a born miser." Art swept his arm in an arc to indicate the unappealing apartment, illustrating his mother's tightfisted ways.

"If I didn't have to support you half the time I could do better. You can't even keep your dead-end jobs . . ." Helen trailed off.

Art opened his mouth to speak, then closed it. He looked mutinous but also helpless. Interesting that Helen supported Art. But it made sense — he couldn't be making much of a living wage at Walmart and he was frequently out of work. The book group never met at his place because he said it was too small. I pictured a mini version of his mother's apartment with books stacked to the ceiling.

I didn't want to digress into Art and Helen's far-from-ideal relationship, so I kept to the matter at hand. I asked Helen, "So did you do a search for Evan?"

But Art maintained his role as his mother's spokesperson. "She did. When Dad died in the early nineties, Mom started the search. She found out what she had to do and eventually, *much* to her surprise and delight, found him right there in Rochester."

"That was quite a coincidence," Lucy noted.

"Not really. She had Evan in Syracuse, which isn't that far from Rochester. Anyway, she contacted Evan and they talked for a bit. But Evan was more interested in medical history than in chatting. Mom wanted them to meet, but he put her off. She called him a few times but he wouldn't agree to meet. Finally he changed his number. She was devastated." I couldn't help but feel a pang of sympathy . . . a very small pang.

Art carried on with the sorry saga. "She consoled herself by remarrying, but she still pined for Evan. He hadn't told her anything about where he lived, worked, whether he was married — in short, nothing. She even considered hiring an investigator. As it turned out, she didn't have to go the PI route. In a serendipitous moment she saw Evan's name mentioned in an article about insurance fraud, the insurance company being Acer. The serendipity continued when she got a job there.

"As you can imagine she was in seventh heaven, getting to admire the object of her affection from a distance. They were in different departments, so never really met, just passed in the halls or cafeteria, greeting each other in the distant, polite way of strangers." This more or less squared with what Donna McCarthy had told me. "This went on for three years until Evan took early retirement and moved down here to teach.

"In three months, Mom sold her house in Rochester and headed south, with me tagging along. Once here in Richmond she found out where Evan lived and got an apartment in the same complex. She called all area colleges and found him at Tanson Community College and promptly enrolled. She didn't want to be *too* obvious and have Evan as a teacher, so she passed up the business courses and opted for computer ones. Down the road that would prove to be a good choice for her — but I'm getting ahead of myself."

I help up my hand. "Wait a minute. What about her husband?"

Art looked puzzled, like he couldn't remember his stepfather. "Oh, him — they got divorced." He continued, "Like in so many apartment complexes, especially an anonymous one like this one, the only way to meet people is in the laundry room. So she staked out that area for days until Evan finally showed up. She was no longer willing to admire him from afar; she wanted to establish a relationship, tell him they were mother and son. Problem was that she went about it all wrong. She started having him over for dinner on a regular basis. That went on for quite some time."

Lucy asked, looking skeptical. "Wait a minute. You said that Helen had talked to Evan on the phone in Rochester. And worked at the same company. Didn't he realize that he was now having regular dinners with the same woman?"

"Nope. When they met up down here, Mom told him she was from Rochester and had worked at Acer." Art, unfazed by Helen's tears, gave her an amused look. "She didn't care if he recognized her from Acer, but that was unlikely — when we got here she transformed herself into the hot chick you see now. She used to look like a frumpy housewife." Again, Art's tale paralleled Donna's.

"What she didn't want was for Evan to find out that she was his mother, at least for a while. Since she went through a couple of name changes, that wasn't a problem."

When we looked blank, Art amplified. "When she first contacted Evan she was Helen Woods. By the time she went to work at Acer, she had remarried. After she divorced Mr. Riley she circled back to her maiden name of Adams." Art gave an uneasy laugh. "And it helped that Evan wasn't exactly, uh, sharp. At least not in my opinion." When he slanted his eyes at me I spread both hands in a dismissive gesture.

Lucy asked, "So, Helen, did you ever tell Evan he was your son?"

She shook her head and remained silent. Try as we would to engage Helen in telling her own story, she just sat there, mopping up her tears and offering no more than a nod of assent here and there. But I detected a hyperalertness about her, a readiness to pounce if I stepped out of line. So Art continued to field our questions.

"One time when Evan was over for dinner she approached the subject in a hypothetical fashion. Like 'how about if a mother had to give up her child for adoption and years later found him and wanted to be reunited?' Evan said why not let things be — the mother gave the child up, so why the sudden interest?"

I said, "How devastating. And hardly the time to spring the news that she was a *very* interested mother . . . to him."

"Yeah, she'd trapped herself and knew it. After that, she was really skittish and didn't want to let him know. She resigned herself to being a mom-in-secret." Art twisted his mouth. Helen's weeping continued, unabated.

A tragic story, I thought, *on so many levels.* I felt acute frustration just thinking of it.

Surely if Helen had told Evan the truth he'd have reconsidered his position. He was responding to a hypothetical scenario. When I asked if Evan had ever told Helen he was adopted, Art said, "Not to my knowledge," and Helen moved her head from side to side. That figured. God forbid Evan should volunteer personal information. He and Carlene had been compatible in that department.

I asked, without even bothering to address Helen, "So, back to the dinners . . . How did they go? Did Evan think she" — here I glanced at Helen — "was interested in him, um, romantically?"

"Oh, no." Art looked at Helen. "She didn't want Evan to get that idea — she definitely wanted him as a son. In fact, one time she had a woman join us, someone from the building. She thought they'd be a good match."

"And were they?"

Art rolled his eyes. "No. Neither seemed interested in the other. The woman dominated the conversation, mostly complaining about her boss.

"That's when things backfired on Mom. Evan started to make excuses. More travel, more faculty meetings, more this, more that. And more obsession on her part. When he started seeing Kat she just about lost her mind." I had a vision of Kat being invited for dinner and having a poisonous substance added to her plate. I shivered just thinking about the vengeance she could exact on Helen and Art.

"Then Evan suddenly moved. Here one day, gone the next. Mom was in quite a state and it was Easter or spring break or something, so she couldn't just 'happen' to run into him at school. When she finally did he said he'd married a wonderful woman named Carlene and had moved into her house. Mom cajoled him into giving her the address so she could send a wedding gift. She invited both of them to dinner and he accepted. I guess he felt that marriage shielded him from her matchmaking efforts."

Art continued. "They only came to dinner once. Mom kept on inviting them to dinner, but they turned her down every time. We did get invited to the turkey dinners and she lived from one dinner to the next so she could talk to her darling Evan. She crossed paths with him at Tanson but he was usually in a rush and just said hi. Probably trying to avoid her." Art's bitter look made me wonder if he'd spent his entire life longing for just a moment of the adulation his mother bestowed on his half brother. "She still wanted to reveal that they were mother and son but couldn't work out how to do it.

"Somewhere along the line Carlene mentioned a mystery book group she'd started and asked Mom to join it. Naturally Mom jumped at the chance, dragging me along with her. Not that I had a problem with that. I'd always liked mysteries, but they were new to Mom. She figured that ingratiating herself with Carlene would keep her in the loop about Evan. It didn't work. You know how unforthcoming Carlene could be."

So that was why Helen belonged to a group that didn't share her values — she hoped to keep tabs on Evan through Carlene.

"When she found out about Carlene's plans to write a mystery, she enrolled in a Web design course at Tanson and talked Carlene into letting her design a site for her as a class project. She thought collaborating with Carlene would create opportunities to visit at the house. But again her plans were thwarted — Carlene wanted to review Mom's work online and communicate by e-mail."

I pointed toward the bedroom. "How did

she collect all those photos of Evan in there?"

"Did you ever see the ones on the bookcase in their family room?"

When I nodded, Art explained. "She took them with her digital camera one time when Carlene was hosting book group. Since Carlene always had the group upstairs in her living room, it was pretty safe. Essentially, they're photos of photos. And she cropped Carlene out of the wedding photos." A notion of cropping being symbolic of killing occurred to me. I felt chilled.

From her stricken look, I guessed that Lucy had a similar idea. After a pause, she addressed Helen. "Helen, I have a question and I hope you answer it yourself. How did you . . . do . . . ?"

"I put cyanide in her tea." Helen's blasé response contrasted starkly with Lucy's difficulty in even questioning Helen about how she killed Carlene.

Art quipped, "Straight out of the pages of Agatha Christie."

I said, "Yes, but *how* — how did you manage it? How did you get the cyanide in the tea? Did you go in the kitchen while the tea was unattended? Remember, Carlene left the tea for a while to look for towels."

"Mom didn't do it in the kitchen." I

wished we could muzzle Art and get Helen to say more than the occasional word.

When Art didn't elaborate, Lucy tried another tack. "Okay. Did she —" Now Lucy turned to Helen. "*You* go to the house earlier in the day and do, whatever it was you did, then?"

"Nope. She did it right in the dining room when the tea was on the table."

"But how could that be?" I wailed. "We were all there, listening to Carlene, our eyes on her, and the tea was on the table in front of her. You must be awfully clever, Helen, because I didn't see a thing."

Helen smiled through her tears. "It was magic."

CHAPTER 26

"Magic?"

"Magic." Helen's dreamy smile made me wonder if her grip on sanity was slipping away. If it hadn't already.

Art disclaimed, "Let me tell you this right now — *I* didn't want any part of it."

"Hah!" Helen retorted.

"So, you used magic," I prompted Helen.

"Yes, but —" Helen's smile faded. "Art, you're supposed to be telling the story." I was surprised she didn't want to do her own bragging.

"Remember her stint as a magician's assistant?" When we nodded, Art asked, "Ever hear of sleight of hand?"

Lucy said, "Tricking the eye?"

"Yes, tricking the eye with your hands. Hazel, remember when Mom pointed toward the living room and asked me to get a review that she'd brought? It was supposedly on the floor by her purse?"

"I do." I didn't add that I also remembered Helen calling him an idiot for bringing an AARP magazine.

Art shook his head. "There was no review. While you all looked toward the living room she used the diversion to pour the cyanide in Carlene's tea."

"Right in front of Carlene?" In my amazement, I found myself sputtering. "But — but — it all happened so fast."

"Mom's good at sleight of hand. And misdirection. She's quick. The hand is quicker than the eye."

Lucy and I both stared first at Art, then at Helen, stunned at the cold-bloodedness of what we were hearing. And apparently the "idiot" comment was part of the act. The fact that Helen had branded her son an idiot on other occasions lulled us into thinking that this was just more of the same abusive behavior. Lucy asked, "So, Art, you said you didn't want any part of it, but it sounds like you did have a part. What was it?"

"Let me start by saying that I liked Carlene and didn't want to do her any harm. At first I said no to Mom. 'You're on your own,' I told her. But," he spread his hands out, looking helpless. "I caved at the last minute." I guessed the reason for the caving: he didn't want to risk his mother's cutting off his financial support. He'd even help her kill. His wanting to hold on to Helen's purse strings also likely explained why he allowed her to dress him down in public the way she did. And there was his need for approval — I always thought Art was an obedient son, perhaps to get some of the love his mother bestowed on Evan. On the other hand, he wasn't a respectful son. I chalked the whole thing up to inexplicable and dysfunctional mother-son dynamics. At least I now understood his role in this sorry situation.

"Anyway, I knew about the bogus review. And I asked Carlene to tell us about her new book." Art's laugh came out like a strangled bark. "Mom knew that none of you liked her much and tried to avoid her, so she figured that once she started ranting about politics everyone would be itching for a change of subject."

"Liberals," Helen spat.

I thought to clarify my political position as being more moderate than liberal, but drawing fine lines in the political sand was off point.

Art said, "She also knew that everyone loved hearing about Carlene's writing. And she knew Carlene liked nothing better than to talk about her writing. So Mom started on stem cell research, even though she'd already gone on and on about it earlier, but it *is* her hot topic these days — and that was my cue to interrupt and ask Carlene about her book."

So Helen knew how annoying she was. Being obnoxious and irritating as all get-out as a way of getting away with murder had never occurred to me. I recalled my own intention to stop Helen's rant by asking Carlene about her book, not realizing that Art's beating me to it was part of a premeditated plan.

Lucy folded her arms and asked, "And you — she — wasn't the least bit afraid of being caught?"

"Not a bit. Like I said, she's good. And she had those long, fluttery sleeves that covered her fingers."

So I was right about the insight I'd had in the bedroom. The periwinkle georgette blouse with the ruffled bell sleeves provided a perfect cover for sleight of hand. It was too lovely an item to be put to such nefarious use.

But Lucy wasn't satisfied. "Oh, come on, Art. I can't believe she didn't have a contingency plan just in case she slipped up. And what if there hadn't been a window? What if, say, Carlene decided not to have tea that night? What if someone had phoned her earlier and she wasn't there in the dining room?"

Helen spoke up. "Well, it didn't have to happen that night."

"But you were raring to go, Mom. You knew it would be easier to make it look like suicide at Carlene's house."

I asked, "So, um, who wrote the suicide note?"

Helen looked proud and defiant. "Why, I did."

"When? And where did you put it?"

"I left it on the table next to her chair in the family room. The police and EMTs were all over the place. In all the commotion no one noticed." A vague picture of people milling around took shape in my mind, Helen likely one of the millers. Amplifying her response, she said, "After all, I'm an artist as well as a magician. The two talents go very well together. I had a sample of Carlene's handwriting and forged the note. Easy as pie." Helen gave me a coy look. "When I called you the next day I wanted to play up the suicide idea, so I told you about Carlene being with that man in her car. But you seemed cagey and I wasn't sure if you bought it."

Thinking back on that conversation, I

could see that Helen was trying to manipulate me into thinking that Carlene's guilt had driven her to kill herself.

My mind lit on Sarah. "Sarah wasn't in on this, was she?"

"Oh, God, no. She and Mom spar about politics but I think they enjoy that. I bet you're asking because of the towel thing. That was serendipitous for Mom because with Carlene out of the kitchen for a few minutes, anyone who was in there when the tea was unattended would fall under suspicion. If the suicide verdict was questioned and we needed to divert attention from ourselves we could say 'well, so and so was in the kitchen' or 'Annabel got a phone call and walked through the kitchen to take it.' 'Hazel and Sarah were standing by the fridge, talking.' That sort of thing. I got Kat to show me some exercises so that we — especially Kat — would be going through the kitchen. You know how she likes to show off her body."

Again, I envisioned Kat using her powerful body to exact revenge on Helen and Art. They'd better hope they landed in prison. The thought cheered me, or as much as I could be cheered under capture.

Art continued outlining his grim tale. "I tried to get the woman with the striped hair to join us in the family room but she was too busy stuffing her face with pumpkin brownies." I felt a pang of guilt thinking about how I'd suspected Linda. And Annabel. At the worst they were unpleasant, but not killers. At least not of Carlene.

Lucy looked at Helen. "Weren't you afraid of getting some of the cyanide on yourself?"

"I sprayed an adhesive bandage on my hands."

The arrogance and sheer audacity of this plan was beyond anything in my experience. I felt grudging admiration for this mother-son duo who had figured all the angles — although Helen was the obvious mastermind and Art just followed instructions. Of course, much predictability had worked in their favor — the tea, Carlene's willingness to talk about her book and the eagerness of the rest of us to hear about it. No one wanting to listen to Helen. And some unexpected events, like the towel outage. I shook my head in amazement when I realized how we'd all been unwitting participants in a play of sorts, part improvised, part scripted.

I asked, "Why did you decide to use cyanide?"

Helen said, "Oh . . . I did a lot of research — read everything I could get my hands on — and it seemed like a good choice." Yes,

Helen was a library hound. I recalled our car-side conversation after the memorial service when she'd lauded the public library. She'd even mentioned not wanting to see the printed word fall into oblivion. It made sense that she'd use the library for nefarious purposes. I thought of the Stella Nickell book I'd seen earlier in Helen's room. If Helen read everything she could get her hands on . . . then she left fingerprints. Just like Stella Nickell. And, allegedly, Annabel.

"Mom knew that Carlene was researching cyanide, reading a lot about it. Her dying from it would be the ultimate irony. She also banked on Carlene having her odious tea, thinking the tea would mask the taste of the cyanide — whatever cyanide tastes like."

"Yes, and cyanide figured so prominently in our earlier conversation that night."

"Yeah. Funny. Not planned on our part."

Lucy commented, "And I guess your research told you how to administer it, how much to use, all those pesky details." Like how potent cyanide from World War II would be in the present day — I felt sure Helen researched those details.

I asked. "Okay, so how did you get cyanide? Didn't you say something about it going back to World War II?"

"From Sam." Helen looked at me like I

was an idiot for not knowing Sam was the go-to person for cyanide.

"Sam?"

"Yes, Sam. Sam Smith."

"Oh, yes, we've met him. But why would he . . ." Lucy looked puzzled. "Are you and Sam in cahoots?"

Helen looked affronted. "Heavens, no. The man's a dimwit. And a liberal." Apparently in Helen's world liberal and dimwit were synonyms.

"He sure was smitten with Mom." Art started pacing back and forth behind Helen and she warned him to keep the gun pointed at us. He gave his mother a withering look and continued. "He seemed like one of those chumps, easy to manipulate." Art had no business sounding so derisive about the chumps of the world. I thought of those shadowy film noirs of the forties. Typically they featured a femme fatale who hooked up with a man whose brains were in his, um, nether regions, and she had no trouble getting him to do her bidding. And her bidding usually involved killing one or more persons. Barbara Stanwyck and Fred Mac-Murray in *Double Indemnity* was my favorite case in point. But this was real life, not the silver screen, and Helen as femme fatale with Sam as her lapdog didn't have the same appeal. Equally evil was her manipulation of her son to achieve her ends.

"But how did she get the cyanide from Sam?"

"Okay, you know Sam's a military historian?"

"Yes. In fact, much of his photography is military oriented. He gave me his card yesterday and I looked at his Tripod site. Lots of military stuff."

"Like Annabel said earlier, Sam Smith's uncle was a midlevel Nazi officer. Like many of those guys, he carried a vial of cyanide in case he got captured. He never did. When he died, Sam got all his Nazi paraphernalia . . . including the vial."

Art looked at his mother and offered her the floor, but she demurred. "No, Art, you're the historian."

He rolled his eyes and went on. "You see, Annabel introduced us to Sam at Carlene's signing. Annabel tried to get Mom interested in doing a website to showcase Sam's photography. He had a Tripod site — the one you saw — but Annabel wanted him to ditch that, get something professional. In the meantime, Sam and I discovered our mutual love of history, Sam being a military historian and retired professor whose specialty was World War II. He invited us to visit his farm in Scottsville anytime to look at his historical collection. He gave each of us a card with the Tripod site."

Art pressed on. "When Mom and I looked at Sam's photographs on the site I saw this metal item that could be mistaken for a bullet — but I'd seen it before and recognized it for what it was — a container for a glass vial of, get this, *cyanide.*

"Mom didn't like Sam's pictures, thought them amateurish, so she told him she was too busy to do a site for him."

But after the parking lot episode she thought about the cyanide container and Sam became quite attractive. She didn't know if the container even *had* cyanide, but it was worth a try. She called Sam and reminded him of the invitation to visit his farm and see his historical collection. They could talk about the website as well. She said that I was especially interested in the Nazi collection of pins and such and asked if he actually owned those items as part of his collection. Sam admitted that his uncle had been a Nazi officer and that he'd inherited the collection as his uncle knew of his interest in historical artifacts. Not that Sam approved of his uncle's activities; he just had the historical interest. They set up a time and Mom embarked on a flurry of research about cyanide. I found a brass cyanide container online and had it sent express delivery.

"We showed up at the farm at the planned time, with me feigning a sore foot, and viewed the collection. Mom put on quite a show of enthusiasm. First she wanted a tour of the farm and then they could discuss business matters. I stayed behind to peruse Sam's extensive library — the sore foot let me skip the tour. It took me no time at all to switch the containers. Then I sat in the library with a book in my lap and my foot propped up, waiting for them to return.

"When they did, I noticed that his ardor had cooled quite a bit. Apparently they'd had a series of arguments during the tour: politics, social issues, you name it." Art snickered. "Of course I had the cyanide in my possession by that point, so it didn't matter. I gave Mom the high sign, meaning that I had the goods. Having no more use for Sam, she quoted him a ridiculous price for the site. They argued some more, and he said he'd think about it. And so we left."

I remembered talking to Sam the day before at Annabel's, how he sounded so off on Helen. It looked like this time poor Annabel had escaped being thrown over for another woman.

"The police searched our purses and pockets. How did you conceal the vial from them?" I hoped she wouldn't say she hid it in a bodily orifice.

Art looked smug as he answered my question. "I slipped out the side door while we were waiting for the paramedics and put the vial in Mom's trunk. I didn't think anyone would miss me." He was right, we didn't notice. At least I didn't.

Helen sprang up and, brimming over with hospitality, proclaimed, "Time for refreshments! I for one need comfort food. Sarah brought some scrumptious-looking éclairs. I'll add a dollop of whipped cream. And don't worry, the coffee's decaf. Wouldn't want to keep you ladies up."

Did that mean we could go? After, of course, partaking of so-called comfort food.

As Helen moved toward the kitchen, she told Art to keep the gun on us. "Don't let them move." The woman put a unique spin on hospitality.

Suddenly it hit me. Helen told the truth earlier when she said she wouldn't shoot us — because she meant to kill us via poisoned éclairs. She'd probably doctor up the whipped cream. Or the decaf that wouldn't keep us up — ever. Then she'd force us at gunpoint to eat and drink. And she'd pin the whole thing on poor Sarah.

Lucy and I exchanged uneasy looks. Then I realized that Art wasn't watching us because he was watching his mother. I quickly took advantage of his inattention and found my speed-dial button, firmly pressing on it. I glanced over the counter that divided the dinette from the kitchen and saw Helen bustling around the kitchen. When she opened the refrigerator door and reached inside, Art tossed the gun down the hall. Judging from the clunk it stopped at Helen's bedroom door.

Art opened the front door that he'd been guarding. "Run," he ordered.

We ran.

Once outside we didn't waste time planning strategy or bemoaning the loss of our purses. I had my phone and recorder and it turned out that Lucy had her keys in her pocket, so we were better off than we might have been. Most important, we were out of that apartment. Helen wasn't happy, evidenced by her shrieking, "You idiot! You moron!"

To get to Lucy's car we needed to walk directly away from Helen's apartment, making us targets in case she came charging out, determined to gun us down. In tacit agreement, we ran to the left of the apartment, cutting through lawns, running past windows and bushes.

That's when we saw Vince, climbing a grassy knoll from the parking lot that served the next grouping of apartment units. Our silver-haired guardian angel had never looked so good.

I wanted to ask him if he had backup and if he had a gun, but when a shot rang out I put my questions on hold. Lucy and I dived under a large bush. Vince kept low to the ground as he moved toward Helen's apartment. The walkway to her door was well lit and we had no trouble seeing what was going on. The woman herself appeared, brandishing her gun, looking frantic as she looked in all directions, no doubt hoping to spot our fleeing figures.

"Put the gun down, Helen."

Who was that? Vince? I didn't recognize the commanding tone of a voice used to stop criminals in their tracks. It brought me up short.

"Put the gun *down*," the voice repeated. "Now!"

Maybe Vince startled Helen into dropping the gun, or maybe it was the years she spent holding male authority figures in awe. At any rate, we heard a satisfying clunk on the grass. Helen fell to the ground in a heap and started wailing, keening, and generally making god-awful sounds.

Vince and the backup team, moving slowly and carefully toward Helen, grabbed the gun.

Then the work started.

CHAPTER 27

It was 2 a.m. by the time the police let us go. They agreed to give us time to let Evan know about the breaking events of the last few hours before going public with the news. We had no trouble retrieving our purses and Lucy's knitting bag as the police found the items under a large bush by Helen's door. Whether Helen or Art had tossed them outside before or after our confrontation was anyone's guess.

The two of them were taken into custody. Art, unhurt, was found standing in the doorway watching his mother like she was performing on stage. The shot we heard had wounded the fish with the evil eye. The bullet was likely embedded in the brick wall behind the painting.

Exhausted, the three of us piled into Vince's car, figuring Lucy's would be safe until later. We pulled up in front of Evan's house and, in a replay of our earlier visit,

Lucy and I pressed on the bell and pounded on the door. Evan answered the door wearing the same scowl and ratty robe as before. I held up a hand like a traffic cop, but that didn't stop his "What *now*?"

"Evan, we have something important to tell you. Let us in." His frown deepened but he obeyed and ushered us down to the family room.

Trying for gentleness, I told him about discovering that the Helen he knew in Richmond was the same Helen who had called him long ago in Rochester with the news that she was his birth mother.

When I mentioned that I'd never known about his adoption, he shrugged. "Didn't know myself until Helen called one day, out of the blue, claiming to be my mother. Mom and Dad were gone by then, so I couldn't ask them. But I found the papers."

Speechless, I stared. What horrible parents, birth and adopted. How traumatic it must have been to hear such news at middle age, and from a stranger professing to be your mother — a murderous stranger, to boot.

"So, is this why you're all here in the middle of the night" — Evan looked angry and bewildered at the same time — "to tell me that Helen's my mother?"

"No, um, there's more." No more procrastination. When I told Evan that his mother, assisted by his half brother, had poisoned his wife, Evan took it all in with unnerving calm. I spared the details and he didn't ask for any. Nor did he ask how I came by that information. Likely he assumed that Vince had a hand in tracking down Carlene's killer.

Had Evan been so stoic during our long-ago marriage? I decided that he hadn't been called upon to show stoicism, or lack of it, during our brief union. Although I could be mistaking stoicism for shock. I didn't want to leave him, but didn't want to stay either. Lucy and I had been through a harrowing experience — probably were in shock ourselves — and would just as soon not prolong our visit.

Lucy went up to the kitchen and started opening and closing cabinets. I figured she was scouring the place for shock remedies.

"Anyone want brandy? Or tea?"

"Not for me," I called back, thinking of Carlene's teas. In fact I may swear off tea forever. Evan and Vince said nothing.

"It's my fault."

I stared at Evan, wondering how I should respond to this declarative statement. Or if I should respond at all.

"It's my fault," he repeated. "If only I'd been nice to Helen and Art, this wouldn't have happened."

In my view the parking lot sex was Helen's tipping point. But I didn't share that with Evan. Instead I softened my voice and, keeping my remarks simple, said, "There's no way of knowing that, Evan."

He leaned forward in his chair, elbows on his knees and head in his hands. Lucy handed him a juice glass. "Brandy," she explained. "Good for shock."

He sipped the fiery spirit and grimaced.

"Excuse me," I said. "Be right back."

Vince and Lucy stayed downstairs with Evan while I sprinted up to the bedroom, which I guessed was behind the closed door at the end of the hall. Time for Evan's lover to take over.

As I expected, Janet responded to my knock, tying a belt around a black satin kimono that I suspected came from Carlene's closet. She listened wide eyed as I updated her on recent events. Back downstairs, Evan insisted on telling Kat the news himself. I didn't think it a good idea but, as I was reminded yet again, he and Kat were family. The reminder no longer rankled — in fact, I counted my lucky stars I wasn't part of that family — I just doubted that

459

Evan had the finesse to tell her. I suggested that he call right away so she didn't first hear the news via the media. Kat could get hold of Hal and I'd take care of calling Georgia. Thankfully, Evan offered no argument and we left him in Janet's care.

Georgia cried and cried when I woke her at 3:30 a.m. I heard Gary in the background, so I didn't have to worry about her being alone. We agreed to talk later and I fell into an exhausted sleep.

The only call I returned later that day was Kat's. At her request, I detailed the events of the previous night. When I finished, Kat was speechless for a moment. "Too bad I wasn't there. They wouldn't have lived to tell it." She choked back sobs. "Gotta go. Talk to you later."

Over the course of the next few days Lucy and I, either singly or together, told and retold the all-over-the-place story of how Carlene's supposed suicide turned out to be murder. We started with her death and ended with the showdown with Helen and Art. We covered the man in the car; the love fugitive; Hal's rundown of the pool incident; conversations with Susie and Jeanette and the photos that Jeanette sent; my confrontation with the nude Linda — gales of laughter met that description — as well as the one with a clothed B.J.; the conversation with Sam; the dramatic visits from Annabel; finding that Helen and Evan had once been coworkers and then neighbors; how I wound up in Helen's bedroom, sneaking photos with my cell phone, finding the brass container, and that unforgettable experience of having a gun pointed at me. Art and Helen's confession, including the adoption bombshell. We tried for a chronological account, but found ourselves hard-pressed to keep on track. Something got left out with each telling.

Helen and Art fully confessed to their various crimes. According to Vince, they offered no resistance — in fact, their attitudes could only be described as fatalistic. My recording, which had lasted to the end, helped. As did the cyanide stash in Helen's lingerie drawer. I didn't think Art would fare well in prison, but I didn't dwell on his prospects. At their arraignment their combined charges included first-degree murder, aiding and abetting, assault, kidnapping, and forgery. The trial date was set for sometime in January.

Each person listened to our story with rapt attention, interrupting only with an occasional clarifying question and exclamations like "Amazing!" "Whew!" "Wow!"

461

"You're kidding!"

When I went to the Richmond Women's Resource Center and saw Georgia she cried and hugged me many times. Little work got done that day.

Georgia, looking rueful, said, "Funny, after all that, it wasn't over a man. Well, it was, but not in the romantic sense."

"Some women are just obsessed with their sons." I considered my own mother's attachment to my brother, her only son. I thought of Rachel, my unmarried niece who had two sons. In Helen's day, Rachel would have waited out her confinement in a maternity home and been pressured to sign away her child. What most people didn't know was the lifelong suffering those young mothers endured. And in Helen's case, the suffering morphed into killing.

When I told Sarah she shook her head and said, "I can't believe Helen put the cyanide in Carlene's tea right there in the dining room . . . in front of our eyes. We really knew nothing about the woman. And Carlene — who knew she was such a wild one?" Sarah was as pleased as Kat and Lucy had been upon learning of Carlene's wild ways. Middle-aged women admiring their sexually adventurous contemporaries boded well for the future of my series.

"But I'm enraged at Helen for claiming that I'd supplied the éclairs meant to be your last food on earth."

Sarah and Den were sitting in our living room, drinking coffee. In addition to admiring Lucy and me because we were women, Den now had a second reason — our recent adventures qualified us as *super*-women. Sarah noted his appreciative looks, shot daggers at him, made hasty good-byes, and wheeled him off, reminding me of their previous visit that had prompted my suspecting her of killing Carlene. Why the woman just didn't leave her flirtatious husband at home was beyond me.

Annabel's italicized exclamations dripped with insincerity. "Hazel, *what* an experience! I'm *so* sorry you had to go *through* that." From the way she pumped me for the details I suspected she was gathering material for her next best-seller.

She went on. "By the way, I saw Trudy Zimmerman the other day. The wedding didn't come off. No surprise there — the woman looks like she's *a hundred.* If anyone needs a good plastic surgeon, it's Trudy. Her face sags so much that one good hot flash could result in a meltdown not seen since the Wicked Witch of the West met her fate in the *Wizard of Oz.*"

Trudy had those pesky furrows that extended from the mouth to the chin, affectionately called marionette lines. Those of us afflicted with Howdy Doody syndrome didn't feel especially affectionate about it, but we smiled a lot to counter the effects of gravity. One of the great paradoxes of middle age was a woman who, while cranky as all get-out, maintained a huge smile. Rest assured, a bargain face-lift was the likely motivation.

I forced back a laugh. Annabel's take on Trudy's aging face was funny, but unkind. I didn't want to encourage her. "She's not vain, not concerned with stuff like that."

"I'll say."

Then Annabel more or less ordered me to remove her from the book group e-mail list, saying she was no longer interested. As there were precious few left in the group, the matter was a moot point. But I shrugged and said, "No problem."

"So, Hazel . . . I guess Helen was once your mother-in-law."

"She was."

"That means . . . it could have been . . ." Annabel trailed off.

I finished her sentence. "It could have been me with the cyanide cocktail." I didn't like to entertain the possibilities, but they loomed large these days. And I'd thought Evan's adoptive mother had been a pill. At least she hadn't tried to poison me. Probably considered it, though. If I'd stayed married to Evan . . . then what?

Even Linda called, wanting the lowdown. "I deserve to know since you were so sure I killed Carlene." I didn't know about the deserving part. True, I felt guilty about suspecting Linda — but still and all she was a would-be blackmailer. An obnoxious one to boot. But I told her anyway. Later I wondered how she got my number.

When Trudy called, she suggested meeting for lunch at Panera. We settled on the next day. "Trudy." I smiled as I greeted her. "When did you get back?" I didn't want to let on that I knew about the nonmarriage.

"Last week. The marriage didn't happen."

When I murmured, "I'm sorry," she waved a hand in dismissal. "Jerk fell for someone else on the ship. A New Yorker."

"Oh." I struggled for the right words, but could only manage another, "I'm sorry."

Trudy shrugged. "Don't be. I managed a nice tour on my own." She tucked her hair behind her ears, revealing a large tattoo of a flower on her neck. I cringed — the neck was too vulnerable an area for such artwork. I said, "I didn't know you had a tattoo. Is it new?"

"No, I've had it for years. My hair usually covers it." Trudy's hair fell like drapes around her face. "The library director doesn't approve of tats."

I remembered Georgia saying that Carlene had a toucan inked on her ankle. Maybe I'd follow suit — maybe being the operative word.

Over soup and salad I filled Trudy in on the details of Carlene's murder — an account I could by then recite in my sleep.

Once I wound down, Trudy shook her head. "Wow! You've just been through a bona fide murder mystery, beginning to end." Then she asked, "But . . . wouldn't cyanide lose its potency after, what, sixty years?"

I shook my head. "Vince says that cyanide is very stable and can remain potent for years. Helen claimed she didn't know that, but I'm sure she did her research and knew exactly what she was doing."

I drained my lemon water and asked, "Did I tell you about the book group?"

"Oh, I'm glad you mentioned that. I may be interested in coming back. Not to speak ill of the dead, but the group holds more appeal with my ex's lover out of the picture."

I didn't even try to feign ignorance as to

what she was talking about. "So you knew about Carlene's affair with him? After all, her name was different."

"I did. Eileen told me. She's friends with Annabel." Trudy explained that Eileen was one of her coworkers at the library.

When I told Trudy the group was down to me, Sarah, and maybe Lucy, and that at present we were skittish about murder mysteries, Trudy surprised me by suggesting a film group. I told her I liked the idea and asked her to organize it.

We fell to speculating about Annabel and her late and murdered husband. Still up in the air was the question of whether or not she had killed him and gotten away with it. Would Ronnie renew her efforts to implicate Annabel? Did her threat to expose Annabel via the alleged fingerprints have substance? Or did she only hope to profit financially by rattling Annabel? According to Vince, Ronnie would have to convince the Charlottesville police to reopen the cold case. Would the fingerprints even exist after all this time? Wouldn't someone have looked at the books in the past ten years and overlaid Annabel's prints? There had to be someone planning to murder someone who stood in her or his way. Or a mystery author doing research. Perhaps both — I wouldn't be surprised if

Annabel channeled her craziness, and perhaps her guilt, through her books.

Trudy had nothing to contribute on Ronnie's role in the Annabel mystery. "I don't know what she's up to. And I don't want to know. I'm keeping my distance from her." Of course, nothing was stopping me from visiting the odious Ronnie at UVA and making discreet inquiries. Nothing but my good sense, which I hoped would prevail.

Kat called on Monday evening. "I don't know how I can ever thank you for all you've done . . . but I'll try." Kat's appreciation took the form of an annual gym membership for me, Lucy, and Vince. "Starting with your renewal date." We talked for a while and she said she was doing okay. She was through with Mick. "I can't deal with all that BS. He isn't worth it."

Not five minutes later, Georgia was on the phone, offering me the tickets for the Costa Rica trip, saying she didn't have the heart to go through with it and besides, I'd certainly earned a nice trip. I accepted without hesitation. She said that Evan had the tickets and I could pick them up from him. "Just give him a call and arrange a time."

Needless to say, I picked Vince, my prover-

bial knight in shining armor, for my travel-
ing companion.

CHAPTER 28

The next morning Vince and I again found ourselves on Evan's doorstep, this time expected, so we didn't need to break down the door. And this time Evan answered dressed in the business casual attire he wore for his class: slacks, button-down shirt, polished loafers. No disreputable robe. He shook hands with Vince, but he and I only managed uncertain smiles, making no move to hug. It was as if a force field surrounded our bodies and prevented contact. This strain had its beginnings at Target . . . No, it went further back — to his marriage to Carlene. His wife's death at the hands of his biological mother had accelerated the process. Our relationship was beyond repair. I felt a mixture of regret and relief, mostly the latter.

I wasted no time. "The tickets?"

"Oh, right." Evan started up the stairs. He stopped and asked, "Do you want to take a look at Carlene's clothes, see if there's anything you want? Oh, wait, Kat and Georgia came over the other night and packed up everything and took them someplace, don't remember where. But there's still jewelry — and a lot of books."

I was about to say another time, but then I thought how I'd love more than anything never to see Evan again. I considered Carlene's jewelry, my mind lighting on those pesky silver bangle bracelets. Even her less annoying jewelry was silver. Being a gold person I passed on the jewelry. "I'd love to look at the books."

"Great." Evan came back down the steps and pointed toward the family room. "There are tons of books down there and in Carlene's den upstairs."

I asked, "When do you need to leave for your class?"

"Not till noon." That gave us two hours. Not that I wanted to take that long — the house stunk of stale cigarettes, so the sooner we got out the better.

"Speaking of books, what's going to happen with the one that's with Carlene's agent?"

"Don't know. That woman came to the memorial service — Dodie, Dorie, something like that — but I haven't been able to deal with all that stuff."

"Understandable," I said, allowing myself a modicum of compassion. "And what about the one she, meaning Carlene, was working on? The third book." I'd decided not to complete that one. I wanted to write about live bodies, having sex. And I did *not* feel inclined to deal with Evan over the inevitable legal issues involved in finishing his wife's book. Still, I asked.

"She really hadn't done anything with it; it was just an outline. Anyway," Evan rushed on, clearly wanting to leave the subject, "just help yourselves to the books. I'll grab some boxes. Coffee?"

"Oh. Not for me. Vince?" He shook his head.

While Vince made for the sofa and picked up a coffee table book, I stood in front of the oh-so-familiar bookcase in the family room. The gallery of photographs was gone, including the ones of Evan that had found a second home in Helen's bedroom. Maybe Kat or Georgia took them. I stacked a selection of glossy-paged Italian cookbooks and coffee table art volumes in one of the boxes that Evan left by the steps. When I ran up to Carlene's den with two more boxes, Vince remained in the family room, engrossed in a study of Picasso's blue period.

Upstairs, I heard Evan tapping computer keys in a nearby room that I guessed was his den. I shook off an uneasy feeling that came over me when I flashed to the last time I'd been in Carlene's den, being interviewed by Detective Garcia, and focused my attention on the bookcase. While the family room was devoted to reference material and oversized art books, Carlene had allocated her own den to mysteries, contemporary fiction, classics, and writing manuals, alphabetizing by author. I picked up a Marcia Muller book, *The Broken Promise Land.* The author had signed the hardback novel in 1996 at Book'em Mysteries in South Pasadena. Small world — I had been at the same signing. The year 1996 — it must have been shortly before Carlene fled California. It gave me a funny feeling to have been in the same space with her, especially during a time of such upheaval for her. I took the book along with a collection of Agatha Christies, Dorothy L. Sayers, and new-to-me authors.

I looked for the two family photos that had intrigued me when Carlene and I had stood in this room, having our last discussion. I considered the bewildering part of our talk when Carlene broached the subject of huge mistakes. With all the possibilities for mistakes in Carlene's life, I'd given up trying to pinpoint the one, or ones, that must have been on her mind, but likely they involved Linda and B.J. As for the photos, they were gone — had Kat and Georgia taken them along with the ones downstairs? Was Evan trying to erase Carlene from his memory? Or was he moving, hence the boxes? The laptop was gone as well.

I heard the familiar voices of CNN anchors. Apparently Vince had tired of the art books and was now catching up with the news. When I pushed the boxes into the hall and called to Evan that I was finished, he emerged from his den. "How about some tapes, DVDs?"

"All right," I said, thinking about Trudy's idea for a film group.

"They're in the family room and in the master bedroom. Bedroom's here." He waved a hand toward the room across from him. "Come on, I'll show you where they are."

I'd never been in Carlene and Evan's master suite. When I'd enlisted Janet's help with Evan the week before I hadn't entered the darkened room and so was unprepared for the dramatic effects. The bed was stripped of its black satin sheets and tiger print bedspread — they spilled out of a couple of large trash bags. A small rolled-up rug with a leopard design leaned against the wall. The headboard was padded with zebra fur. The wall border showed groups of jungle animals repeating around the room. A virtual safari. I guessed that Evan was sleeping next door these days, probably in a pink and white bedroom.

"Redecorating?" I asked.

"Eventually. Kat's coming back for this stuff." He grinned and pointed at the border. "But I'll keep the copulating animals."

"Huh?" I took a closer look and laughed. The animals were indeed mating.

Evan opened the doors of an armoire positioned diagonally across a corner of the room. The shelves overflowed with DVDs and VHS tapes. "Feel free to take them all."

He turned and looked like he wanted to say something but couldn't form the words. When he reached for me, mouth seeking mine, I screeched as I stepped back and crashed into the louver door of the closet. He grabbed my arm to steady me and tried for another kiss. I crab-stepped away and knocked over the rolled-up carpet. Thankfully Vince had the TV volume cranked up and couldn't hear the commotion.

Evan picked up the now unrolled rug and

tossed it on the bed. He looked at me and heaved a sigh. As for me, I tried to collect myself and my dignity.

"Evan, what was that all about?"

"I'm sorry, Hazel. I thought . . ." He trailed off.

"Thought what?" Did I really want to know?

"I thought you were interested in getting back together."

Trying to be gentle, I said, "I was at one time."

"Back when you were moving to Richmond, right?"

"Right," I whispered.

His smile was grim. "But then I met Carlene and she cast a spell on me."

Casting spells sounded dramatic, but Carlene had made a career out of bewitching men. It was satisfying to learn that Evan wasn't totally oblivious and that maybe we'd shared the same hopes of getting back together before Witchy Woman came on the scene. Refrains of the Eagles song by the same name sounded in my head.

"Right," I repeated. "But that was a long time ago. Now Vince and Janet are in our lives."

"Janet?" Evan knit his brow. "Janet and I are just friends. And I thought you and

Vince were just friends."

"More than that. We're getting married." That made the second time I'd used the marriage gambit to get out of a sticky situation, recalling the unwelcome specter of Helen's beige living room and her gun. But I liked the sound of it: "getting married."

"Married? You and Vince?" He shook his head. Why did the idea of me and Vince being married amaze Evan? "Oh. Well. Congratulations." Not exactly heartfelt congratulations, but the best I could expect. With a smile, he said, "Sorry for — before. And for that day at Target."

I started to say it was okay. But I stopped — because it wasn't okay. I wasn't without compassion — Evan was understandably riddled with issues, but a reunion with me wasn't the way to deal with them. Neither was his friends-with-benefits arrangement with Janet. I hoped he sought counseling.

As if reading my mind, he said, "I'm seeing a counselor. Great guy."

"That's good, Evan. I'm sure he'll help."

"So . . . no hard feelings?"

"No hard feelings."

After a friends-without-benefits-type hug, I said, "Maybe Vince and I will look at those DVDs now. We'll start downstairs." I wanted to get out of the bedroom and not come back without Vince. I still felt leery of the unstable Evan.

"Sure, like I said, take them all. I'm out of boxes, but I think I have some trash bags. Go ahead and start looking."

Vince turned off CNN and we started looting the entertainment unit that housed an enviable collection of 1940s and '50s noir, British mystery series, foreign titles, and unheard-of titles with interesting covers. Titles like *Mildred Pierce, The Postman Always Rings Twice, Jagged Edge, Poirot,* and *Kavanagh Q.C.* flew off the shelves. Taking Evan at his word, we loaded the lot into the trash bags he produced. A bonanza for the budding film group . . . They'd be thrilled. Like Carlene's spirit stayed on with us. We piled the bags by the front door and headed upstairs.

We found an impressive porn collection in the oak armoire. Impressive in quantity — I felt unqualified to judge the content, given my anathema to the subject matter. There had to be at least a hundred DVDs, including titles like *A Sex Odyssey, American Booty,* and the like.

The sound of a door opening downstairs sent Evan tearing down the steps. Soon voices wafted upstairs. "Janet," I muttered to Vince, recognizing her cigarette-laced tones.

A number of VHS tapes caught my eye, labeled C&B#1, C&B#2, C&R#1, C&R#2, C&E#1 . . . There were seven more in the C&E series. I surmised that the C&E ones featured Carlene and Evan. My curiosity got the better of me and I stuffed the initialed tapes into one of the trash bags.

"You're taking them?" Vince sounded surprised. I steadfastly refused to watch blue movies.

Even though Evan was downstairs, I lowered my voice. "I want to see if these are the tapes that Linda was planning to use to blackmail Carlene. Evan said to take them all — let him come looking for them if he misses them."

"Hazel, have you ever watched movies like these?"

"Yes. There was this professor . . ." To my astonishment, and probably Vince's, I found myself explaining my porn ban. I told of my years-ago relationship with a UCLA professor who could only get, um, *interested* while watching an X-rated movie. That experience forever turned me off to them. I added, "Not that I was ever big on the stuff. Pure sexploitation."

I didn't normally share intimate details of

past relationships with present-day lovers. Could this be a step forward for Vince and me? Or backward?

Vince took me in his arms, indicating a forward direction. "I understand. You know I'd never pressure you to do anything you didn't want to do. Just as I'm sure you know that I don't need movies to get interested."

I smiled and kissed him. "Yes, I *know.*" Too bad we weren't alone.

We found the lovebirds in the kitchen, embracing. They looked up when Vince and I appeared, seeming inexplicably surprised to see us. Evan gave me a sheepish look. Did Janet know she was "just a friend"?

Janet's sweater matched the lipstick smeared on her chin as well as on Evan's. And on the wineglass from my previous visit. Bubble-gum pink.

"Hi, you two." She grinned. Then she proclaimed, apropos of nothing, "I'm a widow you know." Her matter-of-fact delivery indicated her widowhood wasn't recent or that her marriage had been a loveless one. I looked from Janet to Evan . . . two widowed neighbors offering each other solace. Comfort sex. I wondered if their relationship preceded or followed Carlene's death. I'd probably never know.

"Yes, you said that at the memorial service." I kept my voice sweet and light. "I'm a widow as well." Funny, I never thought of myself that way, being so used to being a divorcée. But technically I qualified as a widow in good standing. Widow sounds dramatic, Victorian, while divorcée had a sophisticated ring. My mind segued to the *The Gay Divorcee,* one of those luscious Fred Astaire and Ginger Rogers movie pairings from the thirties. Maybe I could persuade the film group to indulge in a dance musical.

"Um," I started. "We're ready to leave."

"Did you get all the books you wanted?" When I nodded, he asked about the movies. "Oh, yes," I assured him, holding up the aptly named trash bag containing the tapes.

"Do you two want to join us for lunch next door?" Janet asked, with a nearly imperceptible head shake. I'd recently read an article on nonverbal communication. Out of politeness, someone asks if you'd like something. If they want you to say no, they give a little head shake.

"No, perhaps another time," I answered for Vince and myself. "We'll just take the tickets and leave you to . . ." I felt myself blushing. Janet smiled. I wondered if she knew that Evan and I were onetime spouses — who knew what Evan shared with her beyond his body. I still smarted about not knowing about the adoption. At least we hadn't had kids — with Helen as Evan's mother, the gene pool was flawed. And heaven only knew who Evan's father was — I envisioned a high school jock in a letter sweater and crew cut. Helen's pregnancy had likely propelled both sets of parents into a tizzy, with Helen being whisked off for confinement with other unwed mothers while letter sweater got off scot-free. No youthful indiscretion would ruin his career. Boys will be boys, after all.

"Here are the tickets." Evan handed me an envelope. "Need some help with those boxes?"

"Sure." While Janet stayed behind in the kitchen, the three of us carted the boxes and bags out to Vince's car.

I asked, "So, do all these boxes mean you're moving?"

"Not for now. I just got them to help out with Carlene's stuff."

Once we loaded up his trunk and backseat, Evan said, "I hope we can all remain friends."

I thought of my hopes of never seeing him again. But I could afford to be generous — I'd fared far better than he had. And so for the second time that day I found myself hugging him, saying, "Absolutely. We'll always be friends."

And I meant it.

When Lucy came home later and I filled her in on my conversation with Evan, she asked, "Were you tempted? Even a little?" She sounded like she hoped for a "no" answer.

I didn't disappoint her. "No. Like I told him, too much has changed. It could never work. I feel really bad for him — he's a mess. Anyone would be in his situation. Hopefully his counselor will help. But it was nice to hear that at one time we were both thinking about reuniting."

"So Vince is looking pretty good, isn't he?"

I pretended to think about that before agreeing. "Yeah, he's looking pretty good."

"You did say you were going to marry him . . . Remember, that night at Helen's."

"Yes, you've mentioned that several times since. And thank you for reminding me of that night."

"So what about the marriage?"

"We'll see how the trip goes." I smiled. "Want to watch these tapes?"

Lucy gave me a long and amused look before saying, "Yes, let's."

We spent the next thirty minutes watching

Carlene, by turns dominant and submissive, engaged in all manner of, let's say, *alternative* sexual activity. As I'd guessed, the C&B tapes featured Carlene and B.J., while Randy was the "R" in C&R. I passed on C&E — I didn't have the heart, or stomach, to watch Evan showing his stuff on tape.

"Well, that was icky," Lucy proclaimed. "When you were over there, did you see any S and M getups and paraphernalia?"

"No. But Evan said that Georgia and Kat took stuff somewhere, probably a thrift store. I wonder what lucky place got that largesse?" I laughed when I pictured a staff person or volunteer unpacking the boxes.

"I bet that one of those C&B tapes was the one Linda sent to Carlene. I wonder what Linda would say if she knew we were viewing it right now. Her little blackmail scheme wouldn't have worked." Lucy petted Daisy as she curled up on her lap.

I agreed and added, "So now it looks like Carlene wasn't worried about the tapes — probably what she feared was Linda killing her. As for Evan — my guess is that he got off seeing Carlene with other men."

"Well, let's make some popcorn and watch something nice. What else do you have in those bags — *Little Women, Pride and Prejudice*?"

The next evening Vince and I sat in front of the fire, bookended by cats. As we reviewed our trip itinerary, I composed a list of travel items. Vince was in favor of throwing a random assortment of warm weather items into his luggage. My reminders of bug spray and rain gear met with eye rolling. I put the list on the coffee table and sighed, but it was a contented sigh.

I thought of our trip. I envisioned us marrying in the Costa Rica rain forest, accompanied by monkeys and exotic birds. Then my practical side took over, fussing about pesky details like marriage licenses. And of course we needed to actually discuss the matter.

I put my head on Vince's shoulder. We sat like that for a while. We kissed. The cats up and left, leaving us unchaperoned.

I pulled away and sat up straight, turning to face Vince. I stared into his blue eyes. My heart sped up a beat or three. I took a deep breath.

"Vince . . . Let's get married."

BOOK GROUP PICKS

In happier days, the Murder on Tour book group enjoyed a holiday tea at the Jefferson Hotel in historic Richmond and compiled a list of our favorite mystery titles. The results pretty much match up with the member.

Annabel favors J. A. Jance, whose hard-hitting police procedurals are so like the ones she herself pens; Art is in heaven with Civil War–era tales, and *Chickahominy Fever*'s setting is our own Richmond, Virginia; Carlene is the original Christie-phile and devours everything turned out by the renowned "Queen of Crime."

I've never been to the Lone Star State where Susan Wittig Albert places the China Bayles herbal mysteries, but I enjoyed the authentic Texas barbecue that Kat, sporting a leopard cowgirl hat and boots, hosted. Annabel accessorized her power suit with stunning silver boots.

Detectives with a religious worldview appealed to Helen, so she selected a Father Dowling tale. Kat enjoyed seeing a good-looking man on the cover of her book and Robert Crais is, in her words, a handsome devil. Katherine Hall Page provides readers with recipes in her culinary-themed New England series featuring caterer Faith Fairchild. When we toured the region, Lucy treated us to the same muffins and cookies that Faith bakes. Sarah finds John Dunning's Denver-based tales combining book lore and suspense riveting, and erudite British tales such as the ones by the late Sarah Caudwell draw Trudy like a magnet.

Annabel: *Birds of Prey,* J. A. Jance
Art: *Chickahominy Fever,* Ann McMillan
Carlene: *The Mirror Crack'd,* Agatha Christie
Hazel: *A Dilly of Death,* Susan Wittig Albert
Helen: *Triple Pursuit,* Ralph M. McInerny
Kat: *L.A. Requiem,* Robert Crais
Lucy: *The Body in the Moonlight,* Katherine Hall Page
Sarah: *The Sign of the Book,* John Dunning
Trudy: *The Sirens Sang of Murder,* Sarah Caudwell

ACKNOWLEDGMENTS

Many thanks to my wise and wonderful agent, Mel Berger, and to my equally wise and wonderful editor, Natasha Simons.

D. P. Lyle, M.D., answered my many questions about poison, both personally and in his valuable resources, *Forensics for Dummies* and *Murder and Mayhem.*

Vince O'Neill, Retired Firearms Training Coordinator at Oklahoma Council on Law Enforcement Education & Training (and my high school classmate) generously shared his vast knowledge of guns.

The late Rev. Fred Spivey of the West End Assembly of God in Richmond, Virginia, graciously allowed me to interview him about the practices and beliefs of his church.

My readers, Alyson Radcliffe Ross, Lelia Taylor, Jan Freeman, Marcia Phillips, and Glen King made many helpful suggestions along the way.

The Richmond Police Department Ride-

Along program was an eye-opener; John Lamb, mystery author and former homicide detective, gave me sound advice on realistically depicting police interaction with amateur detectives.

James Pendleton, author and professor emeritus of creative writing at Virginia Commonwealth University, told me never to let anyone discourage me.

My interesting family and friends have gifted me with story ideas for years to come.

I've met many great people at book groups through the years. The AAUW mystery group of Santa Clarita, California, served as a model for the Murder on Tour group described in these pages.

I thank the great cats who have "owned" me: Marie, Shammy, Daisy, Morris, and Olive. Special thanks go to Shammy and Daisy who performed well in their supporting roles in this story.

Last but not least, I thank Glen for his love, support, companionship, and undying faith in me.

ABOUT THE AUTHOR

Maggie King grew up in North Plainfield, New Jersey, graduated from Rochester Institute of Technology, and worked as a software developer in Los Angeles for many years. She is a founding member of the Sisters in Crime Central Virginia Chapter. Her short story "A Not So Genteel Murder" was published in the *Virginia Is for Mysteries* anthology. Maggie lives in Richmond, Virginia, with her husband, Glen, and two cats. Visit her at MaggieKing.com.